CHRISTOPHER HINZ

BINARY STORM

A Paratwa Novel

ANGRY
ROBOT

ANGRY ROBOT
An imprint of Watkins Media Ltd

Lace Market House,
54-56 High Pavement,
Nottingham,
NG1 1HW
UK

angryrobotbooks.com
twitter.com/angryrobotbooks
Double jeopardy

An Angry Robot paperback original 2016
1

A catalogue record for this book is available from the British Library.

ISBN 978 0 85766 620 8
EBook ISBN 978 0 85766 622 2

Set in Meridien and Swisz by Epub Services.
Printed in the UK by 4edge Ltd.

For Melissa, Jacob, April, Seth, Brandi, Levi and
bright futures near.

For Esme, Avery, Jasper, Oliver, Emery and bright futures far.

For Etan who always believed.

For the BNWB gang who keep it real.

All is lost
in rage and fear
The world is doomed

Take flight tomorrow
today is sorrow
The end is near

– from THE OPTIMISM TUTOR PLUNDERS CHAOS

PART 1

THE BINARIES

ONE

A hundred years ago this month, Nicholas Guerra had been nearly stabbed to death. He was pretty sure the three knife-wielding men ambling toward him weren't here to toast his centennial.

Philadelphia was enjoying rare atmospheric conditions this evening. Its normal smog layers had been swept out into Delaware Bay and there was a deep chill in the air, uncharacteristic of late summer. The moon was nearly full. Pristine lunar light glimmered off the knives as the trio closed on Nick in the dead-end alley.

Six long blades, one in each hand. Seersucker hoodies embellished with human bone fragments. Camo pants stained with the blood of victims.

If those things weren't enough to ID their gang affiliation, the flextubes running from belt pouches to nostrils clinched it.

Mokkers.

The pouches would contain mok-1, the sweet-smelling addictive vapor they inhaled with alarming regularity. Nick had snorted, swallowed and vaped more than a few illicit pharmaceuticals in his teen years a century ago. But he'd never understood the attraction of a drug that could transform even the most serene yogi master into a psycho with issues.

The mokkers moved slowly, deliberately, knowing he was trapped. The scenario had been similar a hundred years ago, back in 1995, the last time Nick had been bladed.

He glanced around. The alley lacked doors and first-floor windows. He could try clambering onto the ancient dumpster that pissed foul liquid from rusted cracks. But even if he found footholds in the brick wall, the upper windows were barred.

"Howdy," he drawled, softening the word with a friendly smile as the mokkers closed to within two paces. They halted, eyed Nick like a pack of hungry megalions. The slashing, stabbing and screaming were imminent.

He'd known this was a cul-de-sac, having checked satellite scans of the area. Still, he hadn't figured on a total lack of escape routes. It didn't help that the sat scans had been made decades ago, well before clandestine jammers and AV scramblers thwarted nearly all forms of surveillance here in Philly-unsec. Even passive technologies like sat imaging weren't immune to such electronic countermeasures.

The mokker in the middle stepped forward, signifying he was leader of the pack. A hairy giant, he had a diecast face molded from slaps, neglect and a hundred other catastrophes of poverty and abuse.

"Howdy," Nick tried again. "Nice night, huh."

"Suck twig, ya fuckin' midget."

"Technically, I'm a proportionate dwarf," he said. "And not to brag, but I'm at the upper end of the range for the definition. If I'd been taller by only a few more centimeters, I would have avoided the label entirely. And consequently, you gentlemen wouldn't be here *sizing* me up."

He grinned with the pun. The leader glared and unleashed a wad of spit that splatted against Nick's jacket.

It was a bit ironic that this South Philadelphia alley was just across the Delaware River from his old stomping grounds, site of his first stabbing. Back then he'd been asking for it, or at least taunting the gods to smack him down. An eighteen year-old punk, he'd been running with some Jersey gangbangers out of Camden, having proved to them that despite his diminutive size and white-boy sheen he could kick ass with the best of them, not to mention reprogram *Duke Nukem 3D* and other popular videogames of the era to make them faster and cooler – the real source of his street cred. But then a small-time dope deal in an alley not unlike this one had gone to hell and he'd been stabbed nine times by a raging meth freak.

He wiped the mokker's dripping commentary from his chest with a sleeve and continued his spiel.

"I'm not averse to the term 'midget'. Sure, some folks object to it, insist it's not PC. But I feel there's *little* to be gained by being *small* about the *tiny* things in our *short* lives."

The leader's face remained ironclad but the wingmen laughed. That was Nick's intent. His humor had gotten him out of scrapes in the past. Putting at least two of the mokkers at ease gave him a shot.

His chances were slim. His neck implant was an encrypted attaboy, the most advanced com link available. But with this level of jamscram, calling for help was out of the question. He had some fight skills but he was forty-two years old, no spring chicken anymore. His only real weapon was his Swiss army first-aid knife. But the safak's longest extension was no match for the mokker's twenty-centimeter serrated blades.

He'd been forced to leave his handgun at the transit station where he'd exited the secure section of Philadelphia to venture into the "zoo", the street name for Philly-unsec's urban wilderness. Like all of the world's gated cities, Philly-sec sought to keep projectile and energy weapons out of the hands of the zoo's impoverished millions, who outnumbered them twenty to one. *No guns across the border* policies maintained an uneasy coexistence between sec and unsec realms, preventing those at the bottom of the economic pyramid from gaining access to technologies that might flip the status quo.

"What the fuck you doin' here?" the leader growled, ejecting fresh spittle with every word. "You some kind of sec spy?"

Nick had dressed down for tonight's excursion. But his tattered pants and jacket weren't enough to fool the zoo's more hardcore residents, who had a knack for spotting outsiders.

"Actually, I'm here on official business. I'm with ODOR, the Office of Dumpster Operations and Retrieval." Nick gestured to the leaking receptacle behind him. "This one doesn't meet code."

One of the wingmen laughed hysterically. The other leaned forward and barfed a stream of bloody puke. Mokkers tended to throw up a lot, an unavoidable side effect of the constant vaping. The ones who survived gang life on the streets tended to die young of respiratory problems.

"Ya think you're funny?" the leader challenged.

"Well, not comedy club, Jim Carrey kind of funny."

"What the fuck's a gym carry?"

The mokkers would take whatever cash Nick had on him and, either postmortem or premortem, cut off his fingers and slice out his eyes. His body parts would be put on ice until they could be sold to a poacher who would mule them across the border into the secured area of the city. There, some associate with a clean record would try using Nick's digits and orbs at a terminal in the hopes that he had financial accounts worth emptying. He saw no upside to informing the mokkers that such efforts would be a waste of time, that his accounts were protected by far more advanced technologies.

The leader's face twisted into an ugly sneer. Time was running out. Nick had to make his move.

"Prior to you gentlemen displaying your prowess with edged weaponry," he began, "there is something of great value I'd like to willingly hand over. Consider it a token of peace and friendship." He gestured toward his inside coat pocket. "May I?"

"Real fuckin' careful."

Nick undid his overcoat's flap, eased his hand inside and withdrew the small jewelry box. It was covered with bioluminescent weep fabric, an ever-changing array of dripping hues that resembled tears. Weep fabric looked exotic and expensive but was neither, at least not for someone with ready access to high-tech products.

But the way the mokkers' eyes widened indicated they'd never seen such an item before, having probably lived their entire lives in the zoo. Enough clarity remained in their drug-addled minds to conclude that the box contained something of great value.

Nick took a step closer and extended the offering. "If you could just see it in your hearts to allow me to leave here in peace, I'm sure that this gift will more than compensate you for any troubles. Remember, it takes a big man to spare a little one."

The wingmen laughed again. This time the leader joined in, although with a caustic brutality that made it clear what he really thought of Nick's proposal.

Had he ventured into the zoo to meet any of his other confidential informants, he could have hired some off-duty Earth Patrol Forces soldiers to serve as bodyguards. But no one could know about tonight's rendezvous with his most secretive and extraordinary CI, Ektor Fang, who'd set the time and location. If Nick had brought EPF into the zoo as muscle, Ektor Fang would have found out and wouldn't have come within ten klicks of this alley.

Then again, he's not here anyway. That was disappointing on a number of levels.

The leader eyed Nick suspiciously for a long moment. Finally he took the bait. Holstering his knives, he snatched the box. As he did, Nick eased sideways, slowly enough not to alarm the mokkers. He was now positioned in front of the shorter of the wingmen, the one with the maniacal laugh.

The man didn't appear to be wearing body armor and it was doubtful he had access to a crescent web or other energy shielding. Better yet for Nick's purposes, his tight camo pants revealed only a natural male bulge and no hint of a groin protector.

The leader opened the box. The mokkers were instantly entranced. The one standing farthest from Nick was so taken by what he was seeing that he vaped a triple snort of mok-1 up his nostrils and shuddered with delight.

The box contained a large silver ring with a massive diamond setting. Its perimeter was studded with what appeared to be emeralds, rubies and sapphires.

Nick tensed, ready to spring into action as the leader reached a hand toward the box. But the mokker hesitated at the last instant, suspecting a trick of some sort.

He has to touch it.

"Here, let me show you some of its beautiful features," Nick said, lunging forward and making a grab for the ring.

The leader reacted as expected. He yanked the box away with a possessive growl that would have done an angry mutt proud.

Good boy. Now pick up the damn thing.

The leader gripped the prize between his thumb and forefinger and held it aloft. The diamond's polished facets gleamed under the lunar light, suggesting the ring was extraordinarily valuable. In reality, it was a clever fake. Nick had bought it for nineteen dollars from one of the licensed beggars who plied their trade in Philly-sec's Rittenhouse Square bazaar.

Body heat from the leader's fingertips activated the thermal switch. The tiny flashbang hidden inside the ring triggered.

Blinding white light.

Earsplitting noise.

A flashbang this small couldn't produce the severe disorienting effects common to its larger brethren. But the sudden eruption of light and sound was enough to startle the mokkers and buy Nick a few precious seconds.

He stepped forward and swept his right leg upward. The toe of his reinforced boot caught the short mokker in the crotch. The man grunted, grabbed his junk and crumbled to his knees. Nick dashed past him and ran for all he was worth toward the alley's exit. His ride, an '89 Chevy Destello, was right around the corner, optically camouflaged in the recessed doorway of an abandoned factory building.

The leader and the other wingman recovered from the flashbang's effects quicker than anticipated. Nick could hear their loud footsteps. There was no need to glance back to realize they were closing fast.

I'm not going to make it.

The physics of human locomotion were against him. Short legs couldn't compete with long ones. The two mokkers were seconds away from tackling him. At that point, extremely bad things would happen.

He was five meters from where the alley funneled into the street when two more men stepped around the corner. Their faces were silhouetted by a dim streetlamp at their backs. His first thought was that they were more mokkers.

His only chance was to crash through the pair. He lowered his head and mentally steeled himself to be an unstoppable battering ram.

The newcomers whipped up their arms in tandem. From the left hand of one and the right hand of the other, beams of twisting black light erupted. The luminous streaks flashed past Nick's head on opposite sides, passing so close that the heat of the burning energy warmed his earlobes.

Startled gasps emanated from behind him. Nick stopped, whirled around. The two mokkers had been hit. Smoldering fabric and flesh over their hearts marked the beams' entry points.

The mokkers collapsed face down in the alley. Their backs revealed the exit wounds of the hot particle streams. They

writhed for a few moments as the thermal energy spread
through their chest cavities, baking internal organs. In
seconds they segued to a motionless limbo from which there
would be no return.

Back at the cul-de-sac, the surviving mokker had
recovered from Nick's crotch kick. Having seen the fate of
his companions, he was huddled at the side of the dumpster,
frantically vaping. But inhaling all the mok-1 in the known
universe wouldn't make him fearless enough to confront a
Paratwa assassin.

TWO

Nick hunched over to catch his breath before turning to his savior.

"You're late," he grumbled.

Ektor Fang answered in stereo, seamlessly alternating the words between his two mouths.

"My"

"tardiness"

"could"

"not"

"be"

"helped."

The ricocheting speech from the pair sounded as if it was coming from a single person, as well it should. Ektor Fang was not two people, he was one: a Paratwa, a solitary consciousness simultaneously occupying two bodies. The ability to alternate words or syllables back and forth between the tways was a well-known characteristic of the binary interlink phenomenon, although not nearly as disturbing as the fierce combat skills of binaries like Ektor Fang, who'd been trained as assassins.

"Not exactly the safest place for a meet," Nick said.

"Perhaps. Then again"

"you're"

"alive."

"Yeah, barely."

Ektor Fang broke into a pair of identical smiles. "Had I not a-"

"rrived in time"

"I'm sure"

"your ex-"

"ceptional skills"

"would have"

"ensured"

"victory."

Paratwa were usually composed of dissimilar tways. Other than the necessity of being roughly the same age, the halves of a binary could be wholly unlike. Short and tall, skinny and plump, sable-skinned and pale as mountain snow. In rare cases the tways could even be mélanges – male and female.

Ektor Fang was an exception to the dissimilarity rule. His tways were twenty-five year-old identical twins, genetically engineered products of a Korean breeding lab owned by the Seoul-based Bhang Che conglomerate. The breed's street name was *Du Pal*, which to Nick's ears always sounded like "toupee."

This Du Pal had no need of hairpieces. The tways were buzzcut blonds with intense blue eyes. They were garbed the same too, in knee-length gray jackets and loose trousers. Nick had never been able to tell them apart, not that it mattered.

They were, after all, the same person.

Ektor Fang put away his Cohe wands, inserting each into a slip-wrist holster hidden beneath the loose sleeves of his jackets. Unless you had the pleasure or pain of seeing a Cohe in action, it was hard to imagine that such an innocuous device, the size and shape of an egg with a tiny sliver of metal projecting from one end, was the deadliest hand weapon ever devised.

"Let's walk," Ektor Fang suggested. This time the words came solely from the tway on Nick's left.

"You sure that's a good idea?" The alley offered a level of privacy, the surviving mokker notwithstanding. That supposedly was why Ektor Fang had chosen it for tonight's rendezvous.

"We're not going far," the other tway assured him.

Nick fell into step between his host. They headed onto the pavement of the narrow street, which was flanked by row homes that had been old when Nick was a child. More than half of them appeared decrepit and abandoned. The buildings now housed squatters of every race, creed, addiction and perversion.

A dozen cars were scattered curbside, mostly small electrics made by the surviving major automakers from Nick's original era. Hondas, Buicks and Nu-Teslas seemed to dominate. All were battered and dented, and a few were speckled with bullet holes. It was a rite of passage for urban teens in unsecured regions to stone, shoot, or in any way possible damage moving vehicles.

They walked two blocks in silence. Nick wasn't surprised they encountered no pedestrians. At night, with mokkers, necros and other nefarious types slinking about, the majority of the zoo's populace tended to huddle indoors.

Still, for reasons that puzzled urban sociologists, the habits of Philly-unsec's denizens were wildly disparate. Most neighborhoods were nearly deserted after dark. Yet a few became choked with humanity, although "humanity" was somewhat of a misnomer, considering the violence zoo residents often visited upon one another.

The tways steered Nick left onto a similar street. They encountered their first pedestrians, a ragged quintet of men and women at the far end of the block. The group was huddled around a bonfire, roasting an animal skewered on a stick. From this distance, it looked like one of those meter-long mutant foxrats increasingly rampant in the zoo. Occasionally the animals were caught and served with crème de menthe as a delicacy in Philly-sec's finer restaurants. But here the dining was more basic. Five pairs of hands greedily ripped into the foxrat's edible parts.

"Bon appetit," Nick muttered.

Ektor Fang made a final turn toward the third house from the corner. It appeared to be one of the abandoned ones. Nick followed the tways up the crumbling steps and through a splintered portal where a door had once stood. They trooped single file through a trash-littered hallway, past a bedroom splayed with mattresses. The squatter's nest was deserted but the foul odor of urine and feces indicated recent occupation.

The tways entered an empty closet, knelt in tandem and dislodged a floorboard. Mounted within the cavity was a Paratwa unity lock. Ektor Fang pressed his two left palms onto the ID plate of the double-handprint modem. There was a hiss of air and the closet's rear panel slid open. Nick trailed his host into a darkened space.

One of the tways uttered "lights." Bioluminescent gases erupted from ceiling pockets, transmuting the command into a soft overhead glow. The door whisked shut behind Nick.

He'd heard of binary safe rooms but had never been in one. The space was small but comfy: sofa, two chairs, kitchenette. A pair of cots were aligned headboard to headboard, the favored sleeping arrangement for a Paratwa.

An open door revealed a bathroom built for two with a wide shower stall. Twin sinks faced one another. There were no mirrors. Tways often attended to personal grooming by gazing at one another. The toilet was the real oddity, a tortured clump of faux-porcelain splitting into side-by-side seats. Bladders and bowels, like all of a Paratwa's internal organs, were metabolically interlinked, parts of a single autonomic nervous system. When nature called, a binary's unique form of homeostasis could prompt the tways to urinate or defecate in unison.

"Would you"

"care for"

"re-"

"fresh-"

"ment?"

Nick shook his head. "I'm good."

One of the tways removed two water bottles from the small fridge. He pitched one bottle to his other half, whose back was turned. The second tway reached an arm behind his head and caught the bottle without looking.

But of course he *was* looking. A Paratwa constantly perceived its environment through two sets of eyes. If positioned back to back, Ektor Fang's field of view encompassed three hundred sixty degrees.

Nick suddenly realized that a safe room for assassins wasn't the safest place for a non-binary like himself to be. Since he now knew the location of this one, the night could only end with two scenarios. Either the safe room would not be used again after this evening or Ektor Fang would make sure that Nick couldn't tell anyone of its existence. He took solace in the fact that after going to the trouble of setting up their meet, it wouldn't make sense for the Du Pal to kill him. Then again, the actions of Paratwa assassins didn't always follow rational paths.

Ektor Fang popped open his water bottles, alternated sips between his two mouths. An arm motioned toward the sofa. Nick flopped down onto a stiff cushion.

One tway sat in the chair facing him while the other lay down on a cot and closed his eyes. The ability to take a nap while remaining wide awake seemed an enviable trick. According to Ektor Fang, it was a trick that didn't come naturally to Paratwa and could only be accomplished through years of practice.

Binaries were a different species, or at least a hybrid version of *Homo sapiens*, depending on which school of taxonomists was generating definitions. An artificially grown cellular mass called the McQuade Unity accounted for the tways' interlaced neural systems. When split in two, the halves of a McQuade Unity had the amazing ability to remain in telepathic contact with one another. By injecting the halves into two human fetuses, whether carried in the womb of a single mother or different mothers, the fledgling brain patterns of the fetuses interlaced. From that point on, they grew and developed as one mental-emotional consciousness.

The tway who remained awake stared intently at Nick. He sensed Ektor Fang's reluctance to get started, a trait he'd noticed before in his CI. He'd always assumed the hesitant attitude was prompted by a sense of guilt. In Paratwa circles, providing information to a human would be considered traitorous.

"So, what do you have for me?" Nick prodded.

Ektor Fang took another sip of water and finally unburdened himself.

"Your E-Tech Board of Regents has a ruling counterpart among my people. It calls itself the Royal Caste. For more than a decade they've been working in secret to unite all the binary breeds. The goal of the Royal Caste is to bring into being a world lorded over by the Paratwa. We would become the master race. Humans would be reduced to our servants or slaves."

Nick hunched forward, feigning interest. In truth, E-Tech, Nick's employer, knew all that. But in the clandestine realm in which he often operated, the goal was one-way information flow, eliciting knowledge from a source while providing no feedback about whether or not the information was of any importance.

"The Royal Caste consists of five Paratwa," the tway continued. "Codrus, Aristotle, Sappho, Theophrastus and Empedocles. The Royals are not like the rest of us. They are from a very special breed known as the Ash Ock."

Nick gave a noncommittal nod. E-Tech knew those facts as

well with one exception, the name of the breed. *Ash Ock*. That was new. The name had an unpleasant ring to it.

Ektor Fang smiled. "I suspect you already have some knowledge of these things."

"I guess my poker face isn't what it used to be."

Nick didn't believe he'd given anything away. He'd trained himself against making inadvertent revelations with body language. Even if the safe room was outfitted with hidden analyzers to measure micro expressions and other subtle bio indicators, he'd attained good control of his tells. He'd augmented that control by spraying his face with a neuro relaxant.

Then again, there was still much humanity didn't know about the Paratwa phenomenon. Although they originated from the same DNA as humans and were blessed with the same basic forms of mental-emotional perception and cognition, it was possible they were naturally shrewd at reading people. Or perhaps they possessed unknown technologies that enabled them to function as high-order lie detectors.

"The Ash Ock are believed to have murdered their own creators, the genetic engineers who gave them life. And they're different from other binaries in a number of ways. They have incredibly keen senses, particularly taste and smell, far surpassing those of the average human. They also have extended lifespans, beyond a century, although I don't know the full range." Ektor Fang paused. "But their greatest advantage is their ability to unlink, function as two individual beings instead of just two halves of a single entity. An Ash Ock Paratwa can choose to be one person or two."

Nick contained his surprise. If Ektor Fang was being truthful – and thus far all his information had stood up to verification – that last revelation was indeed major news.

A Paratwa was defined by its singularity, by the fact that its tways were essentially the halves of a single consciousness that existed contemporaneously in two locations. The idea that one of the breeds was capable of truly separating into a pair of distinct individuals went well beyond Ektor Fang's trick of having one of his tways remain awake while the other slept.

Paratwa spies had infiltrated human society over the years. Although there was no absolute way to tell if an individual was a binary, short of the most detailed autopsy, in many cases the infiltrating tway had been exposed.

The fact that the spy was not a single person but only half of one gave rise to certain behavioral quirks. Nick had been the primary architect of an E-Tech computer program that analyzed such quirks and assigned statistical probability to the likelihood that a suspect was not an entire person, only half of one. The program had been used to expose Paratwa infiltrators holding down top positions in various governments, organizations and corporations.

But the existence of binaries able to unlink into separate individuals raised a disturbing possibility. In theory, the tway of an Ash Ock could insinuate itself into human society without providing such tells. Nick's program likely wouldn't be able to ID such infiltrators.

"Any idea of the whereabouts of these Ash Ock?" Nick asked. "What country or countries they operate out of?"

"No tactical information. I've told you that from the beginning. Too easy to be traced back to me."

He shrugged. "Can't blame a guy for trying."

The tway shifted in his chair and gazed up at the bioluminescent glow hovering beneath the ceiling. The gases occasionally swirled, rendering certain areas momentarily brighter. Nick had a feeling that the Paratwa was getting close to the heart of the matter, the real purpose of their meet. What he'd revealed thus far were only appetizers.

"I need your assurance that what I'm about to tell you doesn't leave this room," the tway said. "It is not actionable intelligence but for your background edification only. You are not to pass it on to anyone, not even in a clandestine manner. Not to your immediate superiors, not to friends, and certainly not into the E-Tech archives in any way, shape or form."

"You know I can't promise that."

"Then we have nothing further to discuss."

Nick met the Du Pal's sharp gaze. Whatever Ektor Fang had for him, it clearly was more sensitive than the information he'd provided in the past. Besides what he'd revealed tonight about the Royal Caste, much of the previous intel related to the skill sets and quirks of the various Paratwa breeds, as well as traits common to all binaries: how their dual-location brains functioned in real time; their deep-seated urges to periodically erupt into madness, a behavior known as flexing; their early training with the deadly Cohes; their sometimes demented sexual proclivities.

He divided most of the information learned from those meets into seemingly inconsequential tidbits before feeding them into the archives, E-Tech's massive database. In that way, the organization received a more complete picture of binaries in a way that lessened the chances that the info could be traced back to either Nick or his source.

He'd always sensed that the Du Pal possessed far more sensitive intel, however, and that he was slowly building up to providing it. Perhaps he'd needed time to feel he could trust Nick, confirm that what he'd revealed in previous meets wasn't coming back to bite him.

Nick proposed a compromise. "What if I keep what you tell me sequestered at E-Tech's highest levels?"

"Not good enough. I suspect there could be one or more sleeper agents within your organization."

"Wouldn't surprise me." Such deeply embedded spies, most likely humans loyal to the Paratwa cause, could remain hidden for years before their masters ordered them activated.

"Even if it isn't actionable intelligence," Nick continued, "I'd at least need to bounce it off someone at E-Tech, if for no other reason than to evaluate its validity. How about I limit it solely to the Executive Director?"

The tway seemed to consider the idea. "You have access to him?"

"I do," Nick lied. If the information was as important as Ektor Fang was intimating, he'd find a way to get it into the hands of Director Witherstone, E-Tech's top official.

The tway stood. He began pacing back and forth in front of the chair. In their five previous meets, Nick had never seen him acting so nervous.

"Your director also would have to swear to keep the information secret. Under no circumstances could he reveal it to your Board of Regents." Ektor Fang scowled. "That illustrious group leaks like a sieve."

"No argument there." Private deliberations of the regents, E-Tech's fifteen-member governing body, too often found their way into the media. "I'm sure I can convince Director Witherstone of the need for the utmost secrecy."

Nick had never met the man, who operated out of the executive level eight floors above Nick's modest workstation in Intelligence. But he liked him. The director had no-nonsense views about the growing danger represented by the Paratwa. Like a majority of the world's sec populaces, he felt binaries needed to be corralled before it was too late.

Nick secretly shared those beliefs, a viewpoint that present company would be less than thrilled to learn. Then again, Ektor Fang wasn't naive. He undoubtedly had a good idea of Nick's true feelings.

Could Director Witherstone be held to Ektor Fang's mandate? That was questionable. Still, he sensed that whatever the Du Pal wanted to pass on tonight was worth taking the risk, even if it meant the director might betray Nick's trust, and thus the trust of a confidential informant.

Ektor Fang continued to hesitate. "Perhaps I should meet personally with your director to convey this intel."

Nick contained his surprise. The request was unprecedented, not to mention outlandish.

"No way is Director Witherstone coming into the zoo. In fact, unless you're willing to have a sitdown with him on the executive floor of E-Tech headquarters, I don't think that's a workable idea."

"Probably not," Ektor Fang said with a nod.

On the cot, his slumbering tway also nodded, as if in agreement. Either asleep-awake or awake-awake, a Paratwa displayed fascinating eccentricities. In another life, Nick might have enjoyed being a researcher studying and documenting the binary interlink phenomenon. Of course, in that other life, an undeclared state of war would not have existed between humans and Paratwa.

"This may at first seem rather illogical," Ektor Fang began. "But I assure you it's true..."

As Nick absorbed the Du Pal's big secret, he realized his hunch about the impact of this revelation was correct. He didn't even try to play mind games and hide his surprise. There was no need. Certainly, no such information supported by such a wealth of details had ever been passed along to humans before tonight. All he could do was sit there and nod dumbly.

He was still trying to process the ramifications of Ektor Fang's disclosure when the tway abruptly stood. At the same instant, the other tway swiveled his legs off the side of the bed and rose to a standing position. The second tway's eyes remained shut. Some portion of the Paratwa's bizarre dyadic consciousness must still be resting.

The meet was over. The tways walked swiftly toward the door, the awakened one in the lead. Nick followed a pace behind. The manner in which the binary's quartet of legs moved in tandem reminded him of the gait of a trotting horse.

Ektor Fang waved a hand at the portal. Sensors read the motion and the door whisked open. They reentered the closet. The leading tway again dislodged the floorboard but this time lifted the entire unity lock out of its cavity. He folded the double-handprint modem into quarters and slipped the compacted device into a jacket pocket.

From another pocket he withdrew a brown sphere the size of a golf ball. He chucked the sphere into the safe room. It rolled to a stop against the back of the sofa and began to emit a translucent cloud of vapor.

Nick had heard of eliminators but had never seen one in action. The technology was rumored to be exclusive to the Paratwa, yet another of their scarily advanced tech toys.

The eliminator's vapor expanded to fill the entire space, including the bathroom. Before Ektor Fang closed the door, the vapor activated with a quivering hiss. In short order, the eliminator would prove worthy of its name and dissolve everything it touched. Furniture, kitchenette, sink and twin-seated toilet would decompose into fluttering ashes as the vapor interacted with the special plastics of which everything in the safe room would have been constructed.

"You really didn't have to do that," Nick offered as he trailed the tways down the hallway. "I'd have never revealed this location."

"The safe room has been overused. I was tasked to clear it before it could be compromised."

It had been apparent to Nick from their first meet that Ektor Fang was part of the Paratwa hierarchy, that he served the Royal Caste. The Du Pal had admitted as much but refused to make clear just how high up he was and who he answered to. Prior to this meet, Nick had concluded that probably one of the Ash Ock's top lieutenants was his immediate supervisor. But now, with the evening's stunning revelation, Nick realized he must be even more highly placed. He likely had direct contact with one or more of the Royals.

Exiting the house, the second tway opened his eyes. The pair resumed side-by-side walking, again flanking Nick. To the men and women huddled around the bonfire at the end of the block, their foxrat feast consumed, nothing would indicate the presence of a Paratwa. Just three regular men, albeit one of them unusually diminutive and the other two either twins or clones.

"I'll accompany you back to the border," one of the tways said.

"No need. I'm sure you put the fear of God into every mokker in this part of the zoo, at least for tonight."

"Mokkers aren't the only dangerous humans roaming these streets."

"Just get me as far as the alley. I'm good from there."

They walked in silence, encountering only a few people. The sole potential threat came from a gang of teen boys. Perched on a crumbling stoop, they were well-inebriated, judging by the empty bottles of PlusPlus. The concentrated beer amplified with a modified oyster sperm derivative was said to be a powerful aphrodisiac.

Several of the teens rose to block their path, eyes flashing with that peculiar blend of malice and lust inherent to PlusPlus drinkers. But something in Ektor Fang's double glare convinced them not to make trouble. They quietly backed off.

Nick couldn't get the Du Pal's revelation out of his head. If indeed true – and he'd been given no reason to doubt Ektor Fang thus far – it had monumental consequences for the world.

They reached the alley. The mokkers were gone. The surviving one, no doubt nursing a sore crotch, likely had scrambled out of there as soon as Nick and Ektor Fang had left. No evidence remained to indicate what had happened to the bodies of his two mates. As was the case throughout the globe's unsec areas, corpses contained value. Not only could they be stripped of attire and weapons, but their organs could be sold or traded, their flesh abused or consumed.

Nick pressed the fob implanted beneath his wrist, pointed

it toward the doorway of the abandoned building next to the alley. There was a ripple of light as the optical camo deactivated to reveal his old Chevy Destello. The vehicle resembled an early twenty-first century Segway but with space for two riders, one behind the other, and with a pair of rubber spheres instead of tires. It boasted all-weather shielding to protect against precipitation, thrown rocks and low-end projectile weapons.

He hopped on the Destello. The vehicle confirmed his identity and hummed to life. It extended a back cushion for him to lean against and take some of the weight off his legs.

"Till next time," he said.

"There may"

"not be"

"a next time."

Nick didn't take the words seriously. Ektor Fang had said pretty much the same thing after every one of their previous meets. Sooner or later, he'd secretly contact Nick to institute another rendezvous. These clandestine get-togethers were more than just an opportunity to pass along intel. He suspected that they provided the Du Pal with a kind of emotional fuel, that they met some deep inner need that Nick had so far been unable to fathom.

"Remember your promise," one of the tways warned. "For the ears of your director only. And he must promise to keep the intel in the strictest confidence."

"You have my word."

Nick extended his right hand. The Paratwa sandwiched the palm between his own right hands.

Ektor Fang broke the three-palmed grip and stepped back. Nick pressed the accelerator. The Destello rolled down the street, picking up speed until it hit forty-five mph, its maximum speed. By the time he glanced at the rearview cam display, the Du Pal was gone.

THREE

Nick's twentieth-century stabbing had been one of the best things that ever happened to him. Weeks in the hospital had altered his perspective. Being a gangbanger lost its macho coolness. After being released from medical care and doing a short stint of five-oh-rehab – three months in Camden County Jail – he'd migrated to the other side of the country. First stop had been Seattle, where he'd wormed his way into a programming gig at one of Bill Gates' secret development groups. His computer skills had served him well in that era, as they did in 2095.

His mind returned to those enjoyable couple of years at legendary Microsoft as he drove the Destello back to Philly-sec. It had been a relatively carefree period in his life. Although technology had changed immensely over the past century, no one had yet invented a time machine capable of transporting a person back to the days of his youth. Too bad.

The ride back took twelve minutes. There was little vehicular traffic this time of night, not that there was all that much in the daytime either. Foot-power ruled. The zoo had its own generating plants but they were old and suffered frequent breakdowns, and electricity was often apportioned. Keeping streetlamps bright and cars fully charged was a challenge, as it was in most unsecured regions.

Nick zigzagged the Destello from one shadowy street to the next, avoiding the same route he'd come by to lessen the chance of muggers who might have tracked him on the ride out and set up slip chains to ambush his return.

He raced past several groups of dicey individuals, including a gang of juvenile urchins who slingshotted paint bombs at him. The Destello's translucent shielding repelled the colorful bombardment. It also kept a pack of wild basbucks who chased him two blocks from biting his legs.

The ungainly mahogany-furred animals, crosses between basset hounds and buckeye chickens, were surprisingly fast. Native to Philadelphia, their ancestors had been crafted by a South Street arts collective back in the 2050s, that decade of unfettered and often crazed genetic experimentation. In addition to basbucks, the Fifties had produced such aberrations as megalions, winged tortoises and saber-toothed cockroaches the size of puppies. On a more ominous note, it was the era that had given rise to the first binaries.

He reached the transit station. The one-story round building squatted like a pancake in the midst of an expanse of land denuded of foliage and structures: the DMZ. The narrow demilitarized zone was flanked by a six meter high wall that extended in both directions as far as the eye could see. Not even landlines connected the two realms, although there were frequent attempts to hijack power and telecom from Philly-sec via burrow drones threading cables deep underground.

Razor wire topped the wall but was mainly for show. A formidable appearance was meant to discourage zoo citizens without permits from attempting to cross over. The real deterrents were drone patrols, detection grids and sat surveillance, all linked to lethal geo cannons that would be used in the event of a worst-case scenario – Philly-sec's greatest fear: a mass invasion by those occupying the lower rungs of the pyramid.

Beyond the wall, moonlight illuminated the towers of center city. The cluster of glass and steel skyscrapers, some linked by aerial walkways, resembled Disney's Tomorrowland on steroids. Tonight's rare atmospheric conditions were already starting to wither. The farthest towers took on a murky appearance as the omnipotent smog mass crept back up Delaware Bay.

The tallest buildings, temples of the global corporate and governmental infrastructure, topped out at one hundred and forty stories. Even with the smog, their heights could provide an impressive view of the region. Nick rarely had the pleasure of such views, however. He worked in E-Tech's more modest fifty-seven story building. And although technically his workstation was in Intelligence on the forty-ninth floor, which had a few windows with decent views, he spent the majority of his days underground, in the tombs on Sublevel 3 with the other hardcore programmers.

The E-Tech skyscraper on Filbert Street had been the organization's international headquarters for the past seven years, following destruction of its original offices, along with most of Washington DC, by a nuke smuggled into the city by a still unidentified terrorist group. Fortunately, the former US capital had received advance warning that a detonation was imminent and most of the citizens had been able to evacuate. There had been less than twenty thousand casualties, far less than the mega losses suffered by Bogota, Karachi, Pittsburgh and other cities that had suffered nuclear attacks.

Philly was the new US capital, a bit ironic considering that it was the original one back in the era of the American Revolution. Today, the city had far better protection against the threat of nukes than DC and those other unfortunate metropolises. Still, Nick knew that no defensive measures were perfect.

The transit station parted a door as he approached, its scanners having done a preliminary read that he matched the description of personnel authorized to enter Philly-sec. Nick parked at the entry lot. The Destello would be scanned and processed separately and be waiting for him on the other side.

He entered the massive anteroom, which was crammed with two thousand utilitarian chairs. During morning and evening rush hours, it would be packed with commuters waiting to be processed.

Most would have permits for entering the secured part of the city for daily work in the low-paying manufacturing industries just inside the perimeter walls. Some of the commuters would be licensed beggars, hoping to score enough empathy handouts to feed their families back in the zoo. A smaller percentage would have access to the homes of wealthy residents who employed human servants rather than mechs, either for compassion's sake or, more frequently, snobbish bragging rights.

Oh, my dear, in our home we only *use humans to wait on us,* Nick had overheard a society woman recently boast. *Mechs are so... well, you know,* mechanical.

At this hour the anteroom was nearly deserted. Only a handful of people were waiting to go through customs, all bunched at the far end near the sole active ingress portal. Nick ambled over to join them, aware that hidden sensors were tracking and reconfirming the initial ID scan.

He sat beside a gangly teen boy whose skin was decorated with subcutaneous gold swirls, an expensive dye job favored by contemporary gays. If Nick were to guess, the kid was returning from a clandestine rendezvous with some zoo-bred bad boy his rich parents didn't approve of.

The teen was popping lime-green crackers in his mouth as if they were food. The inorganic digestibles were baws – blast ad wafers – marketing freebies distributed by corporations. Each baw contained a dozen or more advertisements that the consumer would experience as subliminal brain flashes. The teen was literally ingesting more than a hundred ads per minute, most of which he wouldn't be able to consciously recall.

"I'm shopping for a new fridge," Nick said to pass the time. "Any suggestions?"

"The Pyrochill Five-X-Five is one of a kind!" The baw warped the teen's face into a salesman's smile as he uttered the product's promotional slogan. "All-temperature freezing and heating will ice your budget even as it warms your heart!"

Subliminal advertising had certainly existed when Nick was a teen in the 1990s. But the crowd he'd hung with back then wouldn't have volunteered to become full-bore commercial memes, at least not without financial compensation. Many people today seemed willing to accept levels of emotional manipulation by corporations, governments and individuals that citizens of a century ago would have found appalling.

Then again, he was probably being a bit hypocritical. He practiced his own variety of devious, behind-the-scenes influencing.

It took three minutes for customs to process several of the others before Nick's chair beeped. The system's nonlinear selection system had chosen him ahead of the teen. As he stood, he gave the boy a pat on the shoulder.

"Kid, here's some free advice. Only put things in your mouth you're willing to swallow."

Not waiting for a reaction, Nick made his way through the portal to face the battle android in the next room. The BA was a hulk, two and a half meters high, and designed to look as threatening as possible. Its hunter green metallic body had sensory nodes in lieu of a face. Chest panels revealed compartments for confiscating contraband or carrying weapons and supplies when in the field. Hips were studded with the retracted barrels of energy and projectile weapons.

A builder plate on the left upper torso identified the BA as a product of the bio-robotics division of Moscow-based Voshkof. Nick didn't like that it was built by a company that also supplied one of the deadliest Paratwa breeds, the Voshkof Rabbits. But history was rife with corporations arming both sides of a conflict.

The BA ran a remote DNA scan while checking his permit, which authorized a single back-and-forth crossing to visit an aunt and uncle. His real ones were long dead, the permit a clever fake.

He stood immobile with arms and legs outstretched while the android scanned him. It reached a three-fingered claw into his overcoat and withdrew his safak and the other mini flashbang, that one hidden in a vial of lip balm.

"Purpose of these devices?" the BA demanded, its deep-throated male voice programmed for menace.

Nick was tempted to reply that the safak's tool assortment was meant for disassembling battle androids. But he held his tongue. Should the BA's capacity for registering sarcasm be less than hoped for, he didn't relish being locked up for making terroristic threats to machinery.

"The safak and flashbang are for self-defense and urgent medical care," he said.

"Proceed." The android backed up against a wall and went into freeze mode until the next victim arrived for intimidation.

A wall compartment slid open. Nick retrieved his handgun, a slimline Glock 36 that he'd picked up in a vintage weaponry store a few years back. He tucked it into a shoulder holster sewn into his overcoat.

The station's inner door parted, emptying him into a street flanked by row homes. Style-wise, they were similar to those found in many parts of the zoo. But most had legal occupants and were better maintained.

He sensed his implanted attaboy becoming active again as he entered Philly-sec. It was always unsettling to be off the grid during his treks to the other side. But there was nothing to be done about that. Sewers, caverns, subway tunnels and basements throughout the zoo were so packed with hidden jamscram devices that it would take a monumental effort to eliminate them.

There was little incentive for anyone to do so. The zoo's impoverished masses were rife with smugglers, gangbangers, revolutionaries and a host of other screw-the-status-quo types, most of whom preferred conducting business in the electromagnetic shadows. As for the denizens of Philly-sec and other secured cities, comfortably segregated from the rabble, they saw no upside to spending their wealth on such projects.

His Destello was waiting for him in the parking lot. He hopped on and drove the several kilometers to his apartment. It was in a vintage three-story row home with a dormer window protruding from the top floor. Its strip siding was less than a year old but was so weathered and stained that it appeared to have been installed centuries ago. Like the owners of many private dwellings, Nick's landlord wouldn't spring for weekly steam cleaning, one of the few methods for countering the corrosive effects of the world's increasingly acidic and polluted atmosphere.

He parked the Destello out front. There was no need to turn on the camo. Vehicular thievery wasn't unknown in Philly-sec but when it did happen, the thieves would likely use camo-busting hardware. In any case, the chances of anyone wanting to swipe such an old ride were slim.

He headed up the stoop into the entry hallway. A sensor array ID'd him as a resident and the inner door clicked open. He proceeded up the staircase to the top floor, where more sophisticated sensors of his own design handled access to the compact two-room apartment. Even after several years here, he continued renting on a week-to-week basis. In the unstable waning years of the twenty-first century, with secured cities fearful of being overrun, vaporized or beset by a dozen other calamities, he figured it was best not to put down roots.

The door confirmed his identity and swung inward. An old

LED floor lamp turned on as he entered, spilling amber light into the living room.

He threw his overcoat across a chair. "Hey Sosoome, where ya hiding?"

"Lemme alone," an abrasive male voice replied from under the sofa.

"Any messages while I was out?"

"Whaddya think, Mister 'Oh, I'm so goddamned special.'"

"Wow, we're in a mood tonight, aren't we? Anything important?"

"Only if you're looking to purchase bionuke shelters in the Australian Outback or discount K&R insurance."

The marketing of shelters in isolated regions against what many perceived as a coming global apocalypse was, at best, chum to lure preppers, and at worst a total scam. And Nick already had a standard kidnap and ransom policy through E-Tech.

Sosoome wormed his way out from under the sofa. He'd been crafted to resemble a domestic calico cat, with a mottled coat of fake fur in tortoiseshell and white. His head was slightly larger than a real cat's in order to contain a hodgepodge of sensors. Only in the shadows could he be mistaken for an authentic feline.

The little mech glared up at Nick. "Wanna tell me where the hell you've been?"

"Late night business meeting. Worried?"

Sosoome erupted into a caustic laugh that sounded like sandpaper being rubbed together. He dashed into the kitchen. Bounding onto the countertop, he extruded a set of wiry fingers from within his paws and stood on his hind legs to open the liquor cabinet.

"Dude, you want a vodka and tonic?"

He nodded. Sosoome's 360-degree sensor array read the signal without turning. Fixing the drink, the mech trotted back to the recliner Nick had settled into and hopped up on the armrest.

"Thanks," Nick said, taking the proffered glass.

"That's what I'm here for," Sosoome grumbled. "You know how much I just *love* being an indentured servant, Master Nick."

Off-the-shelf serving mechs were programmed for attentiveness, grace and civility, which to Nick's way of thinking meant they had about as much character as a twentieth century vacuum cleaner. He preferred interacting with an edgier personality to keep him mentally sharp. He'd recalibrated Sosoome's biocircuits to enable the mech to respond with mild contempt and inventive sarcasm.

But this evening had provided more than a fair share of edginess. He needed to wind down.

"Go to sleep," he ordered. "Butterscotch pencil."

The final words were a command phrase for overriding Sosoome's standard responses. The mech leaped off the armrest, belly-flopped on the carpet and squeezed back under the sofa.

Nick sipped his drink and reviewed Ektor Fang's information, in particular that last disclosure. Because it wasn't actionable intelligence, there was no pressing need to pass it along to Director Witherstone. Yet he acknowledged a strong urge to do so, to swap ideas with the man about the intel's ramifications.

Still, that was easier said than done. He couldn't exactly put the information in a memo or risk making a call that could be overheard, or worse, that the line was tapped. And although he was well known on the forty-ninth floor and among the sublevel nerds, getting serious face time with executive level personnel, let alone the E-Tech director himself, could be a challenge.

He tapped the side of his neck, activating his attaboy. He thunked E-Tech's directory; it appeared as a cerebral readout in his mind's eye. Locating the number for the director's office, he thunk-dialed.

The husky female voice that answered through his implanted earpiece identified itself as an AI. "Sir, you've reached Director Witherstone's office. How may I help you?"

"Nicholas Guerra," he said aloud, adding his security code for verification. "I have urgent business that requires a meeting with the director."

"Sir, I can schedule you for a five minute presentation with one of the director's assistants on the twenty-third at 4:50 pm."

An assistant wouldn't do. Not to mention the date was two weeks away.

"My urgent business requires an immediate face-to-face meeting with the director," he clarified.

"May I inquire as to the nature of your urgent business?"

"It's for the director's ears only. I require a private meeting."

"The director does not schedule private meetings with non-executive personnel. Representatives from Legal and Operations would have to be present."

Nick sighed, knowing it was a lost cause but pushing on through sheer inertia. "And when could that happen?"

"The next available slot for a private meeting with the director under the conditions outlined would be October the eleventh at 11:15 am."

"That's months from now. Does the word *urgent* ring any bells?"

"Urgent is a relative term, sir. The director receives many such requests."

Nick hung up. The bot was clearly under orders not to deviate from an established protocol. There were probably code phrases known by the director's friends and associates for penetrating the protocol and reaching a more useful level of the bot's awareness. He considered calling back and slamming the little pencil pusher with a program he'd created for ferreting out such codes but quickly decided against it.

There was a chance that E-Tech Security would be alerted, infinitely complicating matters.

It was disheartening that the nonprofit Ecostatic Technospheric Alliance, an organization less than half a century old, had grown increasingly hierarchal in the nine years he'd been involved with it. Dedicated to the idea that putting the brakes on unfettered science and technology would produce a more rational world and a saner populace, E-Tech should have been a guiding light for transcending traditional, hidebound organizational structures. For one thing, it should have tasked humans to field calls, even late night ones.

But that was nitpicking. The real problem with E-Tech, the way it seemed to have fallen into the same trap that dominated the majority of corporations and agencies that ruled the urban sanctuaries of 2095's bisected civilization, was adherence to a bureaucratic mindset. In E-Tech's case, an ever-growing list of arcane rules as to what technological devices were permitted and which ones outlawed seemed the height of irrationality.

Nick wasn't allowed to bring his mech to work or use his attaboy. He could step onto a shoeplate and have smart footwear fit itself to his lower extremities, but only if the shoeplate was manufactured prior to 2088, and by companies that followed certain tech-limitation guidelines. Unfortunately, such nonsense went hand in hand with having to pole vault over a series of hierarchical fences just to have a private meeting with the boss.

He sighed. *Bureaucracies.* Everywhere they seemed increasingly pervasive.

They had certainly existed during the three-plus decades encompassing Nick's first earthly stint, from 1977, the year of his birth, to 2010, the year he'd volunteered for an early, experimental form of stasis. But when he'd been awakened in 2086, the world had grown complex to the point that such bureaucracies often interfered with what should have been a natural flow of communications within an organization. The more strident media doomsayers touted that fact as yet more evidence of an imminent apocalypse.

He didn't entirely disagree with those appraisals. The world did seem to be heading for some sort of Armageddon, especially in light of what he'd learned tonight from Ektor Fang. Still, by nature he was a glass-half-full kind of guy, incapable of looking at things solely through a lens of doom and gloom.

He concentrated on the problem at hand, came to a decision. There were ways to circumvent even the most rigid bureaucracy. In the morning when he got to the office, he'd make a personal appearance on the executive level, try a more direct approach to gain face time with the director.

He was about to take the last sip of vodka and tonic when Sosoome squeezed out from beneath the sofa. His collar pulsed red, which meant that somewhere in the world, there was big trouble. The mech scanned and monitored the net 24/7.

"Quezon City in the Philippines," Sosoome announced. "The newsphere is reporting a biological attack, toxin or toxins unknown. Early reports indicate a minimum of ninety thousand dead. You want video?"

"No. Have the perpetrators been identified?"

"Paratwa assassins representing the Awasta breed have claimed responsibility. According to a statement released to the media moments before the attack, it was meant to punish the city for the recent effort by the Philippine National Police to arrest and deport all binaries, even noncombatant ones engaged in law-abiding activities."

Nick recalled the incident. It had happened last week. A peaceful group of Paratwa musicians and performance artists in Quezon City had been caught in a police dragnet. Accidentally swept up in the arrests and subsequently killed in a long and costly battle with the authorities was an Awasta assassin.

The French-Arab breed was known for hiring out as mercenaries and for being generally apolitical. As a rule, the Awasta steered clear of taking formal positions in the unofficial war between humans and binaries. But now it appeared that their neutral stance had ended.

He suspected that many of the breed, like all too many others, had fallen under the Ash Ock's spell. This level of mass murder wouldn't have been carried out without at least the tacit approval of the Royal Caste. And, he realized grimly, it also happened to fit perfectly with Ektor Fang's news.

Ninety thousand dead. He sighed. It wasn't just bureaucracies that had changed for the worse. However warlike the late twentieth and early twenty-first centuries had been, the Earth of 2095 had left it in the dust. Similar mass-casualty events seemed to occur across the globe on a weekly, if not daily, basis.

He swallowed the rest of his drink and asked Sosoome for tomorrow's ToFo. If the Toxicity Forecast was seven or above he'd have to take his meds.

"Gonna be a bitch," the mech answered. "Eight-point-five minimum. Bio pollutants will be exceptionally high with infectious bacteria leading the way. Carbon monoxide and particulate matter will also be pushing the envelope."

The planet's atmosphere was worsening by the year. But a number of decades-long geoengineering projects to eliminate the pollution were scheduled to come online over the next twelve to sixteen months. Nick still nursed some optimism that the global degradation could be reversed.

"Glad I don't have to breathe that shit," Sosoome added. "You ought to move us to a respirazone."

"I have a job here, remember?"

"Oh right, like you need the money."

"Go to sleep. Barium rainbow."

The mech again returned to its hiding place and shut down. Nick headed for the bathroom. It was after two in the morning and he was due at work by eight.

Sosoome's comment about moving to a respirazone was tempting. There were a dozen of them scattered across the planet, relatively small areas of fifty thousand square kilometers or less ringed by obscenely expensive atmospheric detoxers that on most days kept the pollution to a minimum. But E-Tech Philly was where he needed to be. Clean air was a secondary concern.

He stripped, showered and dialed his ToFo bottle to the eight-point-five setting. The container mixed and dispensed the proper amount of meds to enable him to safely breathe for the next twenty-four hours without having to wear an air mask. He downed the sour liquid with a glass of water.

He trooped into the bedroom and set the inducer on his bureau for a five-hour slumber. Chime-like tones filled the air as he climbed into bed. The inducer's subliminal rhythms and sedatives collapsed Nick's cerebral functions. In less than a minute, he achieved temporary respite from a world that seemed madder by the day.

FOUR

Annabel Bakana wondered who the little man was. This was the second time this morning she'd come across him in the outer hallways of the executive level. The first time he'd been chatting with some staffers from Operations. And now as she headed to the break room to grab a slice of birthday cake someone had brought in, he'd worked his way up to cornering Rory Connors, the chief assistant to Director Witherstone.

"Who is he?" Bel asked Rory as she watched the little man amble off in the other direction.

Rory, a thirty-something with spike-teased blond hair and an engaging demeanor, shrugged. "Didn't catch a name. But he's up here lobbying for a one-on-one with the director."

"Not likely, I imagine."

"Not in this lifetime," Rory said with an impish grin.

Bel continued on to the break room and retrieved a small piece of chocolate cake. Returning to her office, she ran into the little man again. This time he was leaning against the wall outside her office module, presumably waiting for her.

She guessed he was older than her by five years or so, which put him in his early forties. His blond hair was slicked back and he wore a cobalt-blue suit that looked a size too large and hung loosely on his frame. An aesthetic choice, she concluded, not sloppiness. He had a handsome face with intense blue eyes suggestive of either a man filled with deep inner pleasure or a slick hustler.

"Howdy," he offered, stepping forward and blocking her path to the door.

"Good morning." She smiled pleasantly and moved to step around him. "Excuse me, please."

"Nicholas Guerra," he countered, reaching out to shake her hand. "My friends call me Nick. I'm told you just might be the person I should see to solve my little problem."

His drawl hinted at the American Southwest, maybe Texas. Yet there was something false about the accent. Bel had a good ear for languages and his words sounded cultivated, as if he'd been born elsewhere.

"Nice dress, by the way," he said. "Is that a restoration of an original Oscar de la Renta?"

"A reproduction," Bel said, impressed. Only the most exclusive style circles would know that the famed twentieth century fashionista was making a comeback.

"Love those old A-line brocades. More women today should wear them. And that shade of green not only matches your eyes but contrasts nicely with the way your hair drapes across your shoulders."

A hustler *and* a charmer, Bel thought.

She considered giving him the brush-off. She had a busy morning: three meetings before lunch and a host of fresh reports to analyze, including new details on the carnage in Quezon City. The casualty total had already climbed past a hundred thousand and likely would go higher. As Associate Director, Media Relations, it was her job to coordinate and issue E-Tech's official response to the attack.

"I won't take much of your time," he promised. "I know you're busy. Meetings galore, reports to analyze, coordinating our PR statements about that tragedy in the Philippines."

She didn't believe in mindreaders, which meant he was reasonably well informed about the nature of her job. She glanced at the visitor's pass hanging from his lanyard. It was only a D authorization, which allowed him access to one of the executive floors for a maximum of one hour. Considering she'd first spotted him at least forty-five minutes ago, it wouldn't be long before his pass expired. At that time, Security would be automatically notified and escort him to the nearest elevator. She supposed she could spare a few minutes. Besides, there was something oddly intriguing about him.

Bel ushered him through her outer office and past the half-dozen desks occupied by her youthful staff. Their median age was twenty-four, young enough not to have had all their enthusiasm and positivity trampled on. They were dedicated to E-Tech's mission and fiercely passionate about making a difference. Still, in her less upbeat moments, she wondered how long it would take for the stark realities of the world to rub away their idealism.

She motioned Nick toward her private offices.

"Why don't you go in and make yourself comfortable. I'll be right there."

Bel waited until he was out of sight before turning to her chief assistant, Maria Jose. Dark complexioned with generous hips and a pretty face, she was the oldest member of her staff at thirty-three. Today she'd done her nails in chroma gloss and every time she moved her hands, her nails changed hues and released whiffs of cheap perfume. Bel knew that Maria Jose didn't have the means to dress haute couture but she wished the woman would try taking a step up from such tacky street styles.

"Do me a favor, Maria Jose. Run a check on where he's from."

Bel provided the little man's name. Her assistant typed it into her laptop.

"Nicholas Guerra works out of Intelligence. His profile says he's a Tier One programmer assigned to the E-Tech archives.

One of those brainiacs who spends more time on the sublevels with the hardcore data nerds than at his workstation on forty-nine."

"How'd he get authorization to be up here?" It was rare for someone who frequented the tombs to be allowed access to the fifty-seventh floor unless they had an appointment. The way he'd been freely wandering around suggested that such was not the case.

"His D pass is unusual. Doesn't list a purpose-of-visit or who authorized it. But it expires in fifteen minutes."

"A fake?"

Maria Jose shrugged. "If anyone can fake passes, it's someone from that department. Want me to contact Mr Dominguez's office?"

Pablo Dominguez was Associate Director, Intelligence – Nick's boss. Bel shook her head. She didn't need a full rundown for what was likely to be a quick and inconsequential meeting.

Bel entered her private office suite. Nick stood in the main room by the window wall, his gaze directed downward and to the southeast. The smog was thin enough to make out an array of Philly-sec skyscrapers.

"This nation isn't the first cradle of liberty," he began. "But considering it's had a run of three-hundred-plus years, it's definitely been one of the spryer ones."

She didn't need to see the object of his attention to realize he was looking down upon Independence Hall a few blocks away. The US Declaration of Independence and Constitution had been signed within the reconstructed walls of that modest brick building. It had also been the original home to the Liberty Bell, whose fate remained unknown following its brazen theft by a heavy-lift drone three years ago. Because there'd never been a ransom demand, authorities believed it had been stolen by a wealthy collector.

"The Hall is one of my favorite sights too," she said, closing the door with a wave of the hand. "Reminds me of what humanity at its best is capable of."

Motioning him to a plush chair across from her desk, she was surprised when he hopped onto the armrest and balanced himself by crossing his legs beneath him. Bel was petite but still had ten or twelve centimeters on him. The armrest's added height put them at eye level.

She settled in behind her desk, took a long sip from her coffee mug. "Now, what can I do for you, Mr Guerra?"

"Please, just plain Nick. May I call you Bel?"

"Feel free," she offered, surprised he knew her nickname, which she never used in public. Everyone at E-Tech who knew her well enough to dispense with a surname called her Annabel. However, she was no longer surprised by his presumptuousness. She wondered if it came from a lifetime of overcompensating for his size.

"I need an immediate private meeting with Director Witherstone. His assistant Rory couldn't help me but said you had the man's ear and are the go-to gal."

Bel took another sip of coffee to hide a grimace at the "go-to gal" remark. It sounded archaic and vaguely sexist, although in a naive rather than mean-spirited way. And he was definitely lying. Rory Connors was too savvy to dump a potential problem into the lap of an associate director, someone technically above him in the chain of command.

"I don't believe Rory would have done that," she said firmly. "Who exactly authorized your visit to this floor?"

He held her gaze for a long moment. Then his face melted into an "aw shucks, you got me" look. He slid off the armrest, *walked* across the seat cushion and balanced himself on the opposite armrest.

"Let's start over," he said, still wearing that uber-confident smile. "No more bullshit. I did a little fudging on the D pass. And you're right, Rory Connors was no help at all. I picked you because you seem to have the right qualifications."

"Which are?"

"Exec-level personnel whom I might be able to charm into doing my bidding," he said, beaming from ear to ear.

"I have very little to do with Director Witherstone's scheduling."

"This is important, Bel. I'm not here for some half-assed reason. I don't want to lobby the man for a budget hike or persuade him to donate to the save-the-spotted-Wookie foundation."

The latter reference was mystifying. In any case, he was practically admitting that he was some kind of hustler. And faking a pass was a serious matter, possibly even a fireable offense.

She saw nothing positive coming out of continuing the meeting. She was about to get up and escort him toward the door when his smile fell away, replaced by a pleading expression.

"Please, Bel, listen to me for a moment. I have vital information. The director needs to hear it."

Her take on him took an even steeper plunge. She now suspected he had serious psychological issues. Maybe he was one of those delusional misfits who made outlandish claims in order to make themselves feel special.

She didn't get the impression he was dangerous. Still, it might be best to humor him to avoid any unpleasant confrontations. His D pass would expire in a few minutes and then he'd be out of time and out of her hair, either leaving voluntarily or being dragged away by Security.

"Nick, why don't you put this vital information in a memo? Leave it with me and I'll pass it on to the appropriate department."

As she spoke she unrolled her thinpad until it stiffened. She pressed a palm against its back surface for biometric authorization but the pad was old and glitchy. She had to palm it three times before it unlocked.

The pad wasn't the latest technology, not even close. She would have loved to be using modern gear such as an implanted attagirl or a personal mech with synthetic bio enhancements. Even a data mitten would have been a step up the tech ladder. But those devices ran counter to E-Tech's espoused goal of reining in scientific development and regulating unchecked technological growth.

At least when it came to E-Tech's top executives and administrators, such tech was discouraged if not outright forbidden. Less stringent limitations extended to the building's staffers, who nonetheless were mandated to use primitive non-quantum computers with keyboards when at work. It wouldn't look right in the public sphere if E-Tech officials and their staff, dedicated to such a noble cause, were employing state-of-the-art technology.

Nick shook his head. "Memos won't do in this situation. This information is incredibly sensitive. For reasons I'm not free to divulge, it must go straight to the director."

"And how did you come by this information?" She was barely paying attention to him now as she scanned this morning's PDB, the private daily briefing limited to associate directors or higher.

"One of my confidential informants gave it to me last night."

Bel hid her skepticism. E-Tech personnel were certainly known to use informants and CIs were the province of the Intelligence department. But it seemed unlikely that a programmer, a relatively low level position, would be gathering intel in the field.

In fact, Nick's entire spiel was ludicrous. She figured he was lying about having CIs. Maybe it was another aspect of a pathological and possibly delusional personality. Perhaps he had a substance-abuse problem.

She took another sip of coffee while highlighting key sections of the PDB for later review. "Even if your information is as important as you say, it would first need to go through Mr Dominguez's office."

"Not a good idea. First of all, it would have to pass through too many hands before it even reached my boss. That's a prescription for unwanted disclosure."

"Uh huh. Well, perhaps in that case you should try voicing your concerns directly to someone in Security."

"I don't like to speak out of turn but Security is dysfunctional. They're not keeping their eye on the ball in terms of their fundamental responsibility of safeguarding E-Tech personnel." He waved his lanyard at her. "Visitor's passes in this day and age? Really? I understand our goal is to limit technology, but Security shouldn't be relying on methods that were low-tech a century ago. If ever there was an E-Tech department that could benefit from a complete overhaul, they're it."

What arrogance, Bel thought, not even bothering to respond to his outrageous statements. Besides, an item on the PDB had caught her eye, concerning an attempted coup in Oslo. Norway was one of the many midsized nations fully supportive of E-Tech's goals. She sent a note to Maria Jose to keep abreast of the breaking story and start generating bullet points for E-Tech's formal response.

Nick must have realized that she was now paying scant attention to him. He hopped off the armrest.

"Bel, listen, thanks for your time. Really, I do appreciate it."

"Sorry I couldn't be more helpful."

She offered a sympathetic smile and walked Nick out into the staff office. She'd certainly have to make some calls about him, let his supervisors in Intelligence know about his behavior and inform Security he was faking passes.

Still, she didn't want to see him get fired. Tier One programmers were exceedingly rare and valuable. E-Tech needed more of them, not less. Besides, there were far too many lost souls in the world. Better to try salvaging a person than dumping them out with the trash.

Perhaps her complaints about him could be phrased in terms of a psych issue. E-Tech had good counseling programs for employees suffering from a range of maladies, from pharma abuse to chronic pessimism disease and everything in between. Maybe with some therapy and vacation time, Nick could return to his job and continue with the organization as a productive worker.

As Bel guided him past Maria Jose's desk, the emergency alarm blared. Every office computer automatically switched to the Security channel.

"Oh, dear God in heaven," Maria Jose whispered. "I think we're being attacked."

FIVE

Bel stood with Nick, riveted to Maria Jose's laptop. The pulsating image of a red alert klaxon filled the screen, blinking in sync with sirens wailing here and throughout the building. What scant information was available appeared as a repeating crawl across the bottom.

TWO INDIVIDUALS HAVE DISCHARGED WEAPONS IN THE MAIN LOBBY. SECURITY IS DEALING WITH THE INCIDENT. THE BUILDING IS IN LOCKDOWN. ALL PERSONNEL MUST REMAIN AT THEIR STATIONS.

Bel tabbed an icon on her pad, muting the sirens in her office module. They could still be heard from other parts of the floor. Nick leaned over Maria Jose's shoulder. "Switch to Security Channel One. We need to see the surveillance cameras."

Maria Jose shook her head. "I don't think I can access any of the Security channels from–"

She got no further. Nick shoved her wheeled chair off to the side and hunched over her computer. His fingers moved with blinding speed across the keyboard, in seconds accessing a root directory. More rapid-fire typing brought up SEC 1.

The screen was segmented to show the views from a dozen key surveillance cams. Nick enlarged the one displaying a wide-angled overhead view of the lobby. Dozens of people were running in all directions. Although there was no audio, the level of pandemonium was obvious.

Bel's heart raced. Three guards, two males and a female, lay face down on the floor. Nick zoomed the camera down on one of the men. In the middle of his back, his uniform betrayed a smoldering hole.

"Cohe wand," Nick said. "The attacker is likely a Paratwa assassin."

The rest of Bel's staff had left their desks and gathered around her computer. Several of the assistants let out frightened gasps.

"Must be a Pa, not a Ma," Nick mumbled, scanning through additional cameras scattered throughout the building, searching for other signs of trouble.

"Pa and Ma?" Bel asked. "What are you talking about?"

"Pinpoint assassination, not mass annihilation. If it was the latter, the Paratwa would have tried taking out the entire headquarters with a bomb or missile, or injecting lethal poison into the air handlers – something of that sort."

Bel's youngest assistant, Renee, shook her head in confusion. "But why assassinate guards?"

Nick threw a sharp glance at Bel. She grasped his meaning.

"The guards weren't the target," she whispered. More than likely, the target or targets were high-ranking officials, E-Tech directors like herself.

Nick continued rapidly scanning through the hundreds of surveillance cams throughout the building. Everywhere, people were moving fast, some panicked, others milling about in confusion. But there didn't appear to be additional incidents or fatalities other than the three lobby guards. Updated info crawled across the screen.

SECURITY CONFIRMS THE TWO ATTACKERS HAVE LEFT THE BUILDING. LOCKDOWN STATUS CONTINUES. ALL PERSONNEL MUST REMAIN AT THEIR STATIONS.

"Thank God," a male staffer whispered. "It's over."

Nick shook his head. "What happened in the lobby was a diversion. That Paratwa acted as a decoy to send Security people scrambling to the wrong location. The main event's yet to come. The real assassin is elsewhere."

Renee let out a frightened squeal and popped a lime-green cracker in her mouth. Bel forbade the ingestion of baws at work. But considering the circumstances, she wasn't going to stop a staffer from distracting herself by chewing on subliminal ads.

Nick switched SEC 1 to display the cameras covering the elevators. Most of the compartments were empty. The handful that were occupied showed small groups of nervous passengers. Many were probably wondering why the elevators had stopped, trapping them between floors.

"Elevators automatically go into lockdown," Bel said. "Standard Security protocol."

"Yeah, I know, but there's one I can't access. What's today's entry code for the Exec?"

Bel hesitated. She wasn't supposed to reveal the code.

"What is it? Quickly!"

"Delorean Eighty-Five."

Nick typed in the words, followed by an additional jumble of letters and numerals that came too fast for Bel to make sense of. An overhead view from inside a plush elevator filled the screen. The walls were covered in weep fabric that cycled through a pleasing array of greens and blues. Exec was an express elevator reserved for the director, associate directors and the Board of Regents. It normally accessed only three floors: the lobby and the executive levels, fifty-six and fifty-seven.

The compartment had stopped between floors thirty-eight and thirty-nine. There were two occupants, men in dark gray business suits. One was tall and skinny with a side ponytail, his coal-black hair wrenched to the left and attached to a gold ringlet hanging from his earlobe. His companion was shorter and had the shaved head and unnaturally pale skin of an albino dye job. The pair stood motionless, arms hanging at their sides. Bel didn't recognize them but the building housed thousands of employees. Most were strangers to her.

Nick zoomed in. She noted that both men were tapping the index and middle fingers of their left hands against their pants legs, as if impatient for the lockdown to end.

He panned the camera to the elevator's small control panel. An odd device with the shape and patterns of one of those old Rubik's cubes appeared to be magnetically attached. The small squares of the pocket-sized device were cycling through what appeared to be a random array of colors.

"What is that thing?" a staffer whispered.

"QKI," Nick said. "Quantum keystone interloper, a powerful override device. He used it to access the elevator. And he's now using it to bypass the lockdown."

"I didn't think that was possible," Bel said.

"Pretty much anything's possible for a Paratwa assassin with access to the most advanced technologies."

Renee let out another squeal. "An assassin? It's coming up here?"

"Nothing much down on fifty-six but conference rooms and exec support services. So yeah, I'd say this floor is his target."

Renee burst into tears. Several of the others, both female and male, looked ready to join in. Bel knew that despite the wonderful qualities and dedication of her staff, all hailed from comfortable upper-class backgrounds. As far as she'd been able to ascertain, none of them had ever set foot outside the borders of secured cities to witness firsthand life's grittier and more dangerous aspects. Deadly threats were something they only read about or viewed online via their newsphere and entertainment platforms, or experienced as safe adventures via full-immersion VR.

Nick hopped up onto a chair next to Bel and Renee so that

he towered over them. "All right, everybody, eyes on me. Listen up. We have a bit of time to prepare. The assassin who hit the lobby must have mistimed the attack. The elevator went into lockdown a few seconds earlier than planned, before it could reach our floor."

"How long?" Bel asked, trying to quell her anxiety and keep her voice from shaking.

"A minute or two at the most. The QKI will be scanning trillions of codes for the sequence to bypass the lockdown and that takes a bit of time. But as soon as it hits paydirt, the elevator will start up again."

"I don't want to die," Renee sobbed. Her face suddenly brightened. "At least not without enjoying the opportunity to buy the new 2096 Swiftlane Cruiser, the very latest in automated vehicular–"

Nick smacked Renee across the face. Other staffers gasped, shocked by Nick's act. But Bel realized the slap had served its purpose, neutralizing the recently ingested blast ad and forcing the young woman's attention back where it belonged, in the frightening here and now.

"You won't die," Nick assured her. "Not if you listen to what I'm telling you and do exactly as I say."

He leaned down and gently squeezed her shoulders to take the sting out of his actions. Bel marveled at how composed he was, one of those rare individuals who grew calmer the more desperate the situation became. Even though she'd faced a few dire threats in the past, her chest was pounding madly. She figured she was doing only a bit better than her staffers from freaking out completely.

"I doubt if the assassin is here for any of you," Nick said. "It's a Shonto Prong, a breed specializing in taking out high-value targets."

He threw another glance at Bel. Fear lanced through her as she realized the meaning of his look. An E-Tech associate director certainly met such criteria.

"A Paratwa in assault mode is hyper-offensive. It operates at an elevated state of awareness, primarily keying off movement and sound. Anyone or anything in motion or making a lot of noise will be presumed to be an enemy. It will instantly attack them."

Paranoid thoughts ripped through Bel's mind. How could he know all these things about binaries, even the name of the breed? Could Nick be involved somehow? Was he a traitor, secretly working for the Paratwa, his presence here this morning part of some complex plan?

But even as the notions churned through her, common sense dictated they had no basis. She wasn't sure why but she trusted this strange little man.

"When it gets here," Nick continued, "all of you need to be in nonthreatening positions. That means face down on the floor, arms outstretched, palms open. Make as little noise as possible and avoid looking at the tways. Above all, no swift movements."

He focused on Renee who had started crying again. "Listen, you're going to be OK. Just do as I tell you. Got it?"

She managed to wag her head and bring her tears under control.

"Remember, keep still and no sounds. Even if you hear screams, gunfire or explosions from other parts of the floor, do not react. Do as I say and you *will* survive this."

Nick whipped his attention to Bel.

"The Shonto Prong is almost certainly on a tight schedule. It will have gauged exactly how long it can stay up here before the nearest authorities arrive, at least those authorities it views as a potential threat."

Bel nodded. She figured that local cops were already onsite. But they would be of no help. In Philadelphia, as in most large municipalities, the labor agreement between the police union and city hall prohibited cops from attempting to fight Paratwa assassins. The cops didn't want to die en masse in no-win situations, and municipalities didn't want to lose a significant chunk of their police force in a single battle. They would set up a perimeter and handle crowd control but little else.

"Your best shot is hiding," Nick said. "Unless you're the primary target, it won't spend excess minutes searching for you."

For Bel, five words from his speech resonated. *Unless you're the primary target.* If she was, any actions she took likely wouldn't make the slightest difference.

"The elevator's moving," Maria Jose hissed.

"All right, everybody down," Nick ordered.

He grabbed Bel's hand and practically dragged her toward her offices, pausing in the doorway to make sure the staff had followed his directions. Satisfied, he yanked Bel inside with him and slammed the door behind them.

"OK, where are you going to hide?"

The question caught her by surprise. From the moment the crisis began, Nick had been barking orders, on top of the situation. And now he was asking *her* for advice?

"You know your suite better than anyone. Didn't you ever play hide and seek as a kid?"

She nodded, focused her thoughts. "There's a small storage closet in the bathroom. The door is flush, has invisible hinges. Unless you know it's there, you can't tell from outside. I believe I can just squeeze in."

"Go for it."

She raced into the spacious bathroom, palmed a section of wall and slid it back. The closet was half-filled with clean towels. Nick pulled out the pile, stacked them beside the sink.

Bel had to squat down and bring her knees up against her chest. Her dress rode up, providing Nick with an unflattering view. Making matters even more embarrassing, today she'd elected to wear a pair of fashionable Upeeps, the latest style in diaphanous panties. The closet was such a tight fit that she couldn't do anything about it. She was mildly surprised that at a time like this she was worried about flashing him.

"Nice shoes," Nick said, judiciously pinning his gaze to her feet. "I've always liked that slingback heel style. And the olive green really completes your ensemble."

"Thanks," she muttered, realizing he was trying to put her at ease. Unfortunately, it wasn't working. "What if the assassin's using scanners?"

"Then it'll find you fast. But don't think about that. Concentrate on being silent. Even if you get a muscle cramp, swallow the pain and remain perfectly still."

"What are you going to do?"

"I'll play possum out there with your staff. If the Paratwa asks where you went, I'll make up some crap, tell it you went into a safe room when the alarm went off."

"The building has no safe rooms."

"Yeah. Remember that deficiency when this is over."

He started to close the door.

"Wait!" she blurted out. "I'm scared."

"I know. And that's entirely normal." He smiled. "The human who doesn't fear is the human who's lost her boundaries."

Somehow, the words proved calming, took the edge off her terror. She wanted to ask him more questions, but a distant scream short-circuited the urge.

"Good luck," Nick said, sliding the door shut and sealing her in the cramped darkness.

SIH

Nick exited Bel's office, leaving that door wide open to suggest that someone had left in a hurry. He positioned himself face down among the staffers, choosing a spot closest to the main aisle and next to the woman who'd been crying. She was obviously trying hard, but she couldn't control her fear, couldn't keep still. Muscle tics were causing her legs and arms to spasm. At times her whole body quivered as if ready to explode.

One of the male staffers also noticed. "Goddammit, Renee, stop moving! You're going to get us all killed!"

"I can't help it," Renee whimpered, on the verge of fresh tears.

From somewhere on the floor came the bark of an automatic pistol. The Shonto Prong had reached their floor.

Nick identified the gunfire as coming from a ninety-round Smith & Wesson with laseguide bullets. It was Security's favorite and a formidable weapon. But it was no match for tways protected by crescent webs and skilled in the deadly arts of the Cohe wand.

The gunfire ended, replaced by overlapping screams – probably civilian staffers in panic mode. By making such noise and no doubt running, they were likely signing their own death warrants.

Nick silently cursed the poor preparations of E-Tech Security, which long ago should have instituted emergency drills for just such a scenario. Instead, the department issued periodic and often contradictory memos advising staffers what they should do in a crisis. Some of the protocols favored by Bull Idwicki, Security's director, had been out of date when Nick was a kid.

Renee began weeping hysterically. "Oh God, please! Please make it stop!"

"Shut up!" another woman hissed.

"I don't want to die!"

Nick realized that Renee wasn't going to get through what was coming. Fortunately he had a Plan B. He dug the safak out of his pocket and withdrew the detachable hypodermic needle from between the scissors and hacksaw. Flipping open the med griddle, he located the fast-acting tranquilizer from the row of emergency drugs. He stabbed the hypodermic into the tiny dot, instantly withdrawing the medicine.

"Ouch!" Renee cried out, as Nick plunged the tranq needle into her neck.

Her eyes opened wide, and tear-stained cheeks went oddly pale.

"I feel funny," she said.

"Everything's good," Nick whispered. "Sleep tight and don't let the bed bugs bite."

The drug took effect before she could respond to the childhood ditty Nick's mother used to say as she tucked him in. Renee's eyes fell shut and her head lightly smacked the floor. Depending on her metabolism, she'd be out between fifteen and twenty minutes. By then, the assassin would be gone.

More screams erupted. Fresh rounds of gunfire from Security personnel followed, this time sounding much closer. There came a long moment of unsettling silence. Nick had a moment to consider whether the attack had something to do with his meeting with Ektor Fang last night, but his gut told him that the proximity of the two events was likely coincidence, nothing more. Something else was behind the assault.

He planted his ear to the floor, heard the vibrations of footsteps carried through the sheet carpeting that extended out into the hallway. Four legs were approaching in swift tandem, a synchronized gallop.

The outer office door whipped open. Nick had positioned himself facing that direction. Through slitted eyes, he watched the Paratwa rush in. It moved in primary attack posture, back to back. The head that faced him, the albino tway, panned across the frozen bodies, scanning for threats. The taller ponytailed one gazed backward, covering its rear.

Each tway gripped a Cohe wand in one hand and a thruster pistol in the other. Although Paratwa choice of weaponry beyond the omnipresent Cohes varied from breed to breed, many preferred the wand-gun combo. The tways had also donned thin-profile slant goggles to bounce invisible photon streams off surrounding walls, enabling the Paratwa to see around corners.

A soft hum filled the office, the telltale sound of two active crescent webs. The defensive energy shields protected the fronts and backs of the tways and were invisible except for occasional crimson sparks when the tways brushed against one another or some other object. A web could not only repel bullets and deflect energy blasts from thrusters and Cohes, but could protect the wearer from gases, poisons and a wide range of high and low temperatures.

Weak spots existed at the sides of the webs between the front and rear vertical crescents. Some types of weaponry could penetrate there. But even if Nick had managed to smuggle his Glock into the building, no way would he have made the attempt. Paratwa assassins had genetically modified neuromuscular systems that gave them scary fast reaction times. He could think of better ways to commit suicide.

The Shonto Prong addressed them in alternating tway-speak.

"Where"

"is"

"Anna-"

"bel"

"Ba-"

"kana?"

"She was called away suddenly," Nick said, injecting a flutter of fear into his voice for authenticity. "She ran out just before the alert sounded."

He felt rather than saw the albino tway glaring down at him. He kept his face on the floor, avoiding looking directly at the creature. In its heightened state of combat awareness, eye contact could be perceived as a challenge.

A Security man lunged through the door. Before he could even think to fire his thruster, a Cohe beam lashed into his side just below the right shoulder. The fiery energy severed his gun arm and sliced halfway through his torso. He crumpled to the floor. The hand and arm, still clutching the thruster, bounced off a desk and landed centimeters from the face of a male staffer. The man let out a panicked shriek.

Fortunately for the staffer, the Paratwa ignored his outburst. The tways trotted past Nick into Bel's office suite. He was surprised when they emerged a moment later. It had been a cursory check at best. The assassin hadn't even bothered looking in her conference room or bathroom.

The Cohe wands flashed, this time in tandem. Albino flicked his wrist, causing his beam to perform a hairpin turn and align itself with Ponytail's. The two beams, in parallel centimeters apart, made a ninety degree turn around the corner of the open hallway door.

Sharp grunts sounded from outside. An instant later, two Security men collapsed face down just beyond the door, victims of the Paratwa's slant-goggle technology. The beams had pierced their chests. Whiffs of smoke rose from smoldering spots in their backs. The energy strikes had gone clean through their standard body armor with the ease of knives through gelatin.

They should have been wearing crescent webs. Without the energy shields, anyone going up against an assassin was hopelessly outmatched. It was yet another failure on the part of E-Tech Security to prepare for a worst-case scenario.

Still, even crescent webs probably wouldn't have saved the Security men. Most Paratwa assassins had incredible mastery of the tricky Cohe wands, could whip or curl the beams to hit unprotected areas. And the Shonto Prong, originally created by an offshoot tribe of the Navajo Nation but later sold to a French-German armaments firm, were among the more dangerous of the breeds.

The Paratwa reversed locomotion. With Ponytail now facing front, it galloped back out into the hallway. Nick waited until he could no longer hear its quartet of retreating footsteps before glancing around and whispering to the staff.

"OK, good job everyone. But let's keep pretending we're koalas on quaaludes."

Faces gazed at him in confusion. Nick realized the analogy was too twentieth century and rephrased.

"Stay in position and stay quiet. Don't want to give it any reason to come back this way, right?"

Maria Jose and a couple of others responded with fearful nods.

New sirens wailed in the distance, these emanating from outside the building. It signaled the arrival of troops, probably a battalion of US Marine commandos from the nearest local base on Philly-sec's north side. Nick would have preferred EPF as first responders, who had more experience fighting Paratwa. But the nearest EPF station was in Berks County, about a hundred klicks to the northwest. He figured it would take them at least another ten or fifteen minutes to be onsite.

Nick froze. The Shonto Prong's footsteps were again approaching, this time at full gallop.

"Freeze!" he hissed. "It's back!"

He got the warning out just in time. The back-to-back Paratwa rushed past them, its four boot heels pounding the floor, Albino again on point. The assassin headed straight through the open door of Bel's office.

Nick risked craning his head to watch. Ponytail had spun around so that the tways faced the same direction. Now side by side, they fired their thrusters in unison at the window wall they were approaching at breakneck speed.

The glass fissured into hundreds of tiny cracks. An instant later, their twin Cohe beams etched a pair of man-sized circles in the weakened section.

Without slowing down, the tways crashed through the glass and plummeted downward.

"Stay here!" Nick ordered.

He dashed into Bel's office and eased close to the shattered windows. His caution was unnecessary. The Paratwa was already more than a block away and some ten stories below the executive floor. The seemingly crazed leap from hundreds of meters above Filbert Street was the finale of a well-executed escape.

The tways had landed face down, one atop the other on the narrow surface of a skyboard drone. The unmanned aerial vehicle, shaped like its simpler cousin, the surfboard, had probably been put in flight prior to the attack and exquisitely timed to be in position at the moment of their leap. Nick watched with a mix of anger and frustration at the creature's getaway.

The Paratwa headed southeast at high speed. The skyboard flew over Independence Hall. It took a sharp dive between a pair of towering office buildings and vanished from view.

SEVEN

The timed tranquilizer Bel had ingested after midnight awakened her at 6:30 am as planned. She gazed out the window of her office bedroom. This morning's smog layers had dulled the dawn into a typical brooding miasma, bleak and gray. She wanted to roll over and go back to sleep.

It was the fourth day since the vicious attack and Bel had managed little natural slumber. She'd resorted to tranqs every night, which she normally opposed on philosophical grounds. E-Tech called for reducing human dependence on most pharma as part of its overall mindset for reining in runaway technology, and she tried adhering to those sanctions. She took only her nightly ToFo drink and tried to avoid most other nanomeds. She stayed away from recreational drugs and limited alcohol consumption to an occasional glass of wine.

But every rule had exceptions and she'd needed the sleep, most of which she'd gotten here in the office. She'd ventured to her city-center condo a few times for changes of clothes but hadn't stayed there since the attack. There was too much to get done, too many official reports to be parsed and issued, too many coworkers with whom to commiserate.

Too many funerals to attend.

Forty-one E-Tech employees had died in the assault,

including Director Witherstone. He was believed to have been the primary target. The media was speculating that he'd been killed for his unvarnished and often publicly stated views that the Paratwa assassins were the single greatest menace to human civilization since the Nazis of the mid-twentieth century, and that their rampant spread needed to be contained. Bel had heard through the grapevine that the Board of Regents had been urging him to tone down his rhetoric. In retrospect, it was advice he probably should have followed.

The rest of the fatalities, with one exception, had been office staffers who hadn't had the benefit of Nick's advice, or Security people who'd bravely tried to stop the killings. The exception, an elderly woman who'd been about to exit the building when the first Paratwa stormed the lobby, had suffered a stroke and died a day later in University of Penn Hospital.

Bel's shock and grief over the massacre had been augmented by a seething anger. The Paratwa could just as easily have assassinated Director Witherstone at home or while he was flying around the world drumming up support for E-Tech's mission. Instead, the monster had elected to carry out the attack in bold fashion at global headquarters, and with callous disregard for bystanders. The newsphere was speculating that the assassin was sending a message to everyone in the organization that no E-Tech employee was safe.

Bel did her morning stretch under the covers, swiveled her legs onto the floor and stripped off her pajamas. Behind her, the muted whirr of autosheets made the bed. The sheets were one of her few guilty pleasures, something she'd grown up with and loathed surrendering. E-Tech's internal policies were flexible enough to permit its employees a handful of tech luxuries as long as ostentatious displays were avoided. The E-Tech official who last year had been found to secretly own fourteen automobiles had rightly been fired.

Bel's pad chimed as she sauntered toward the bathroom. She unrolled it and palmed its back surface for authorization, but the pad was glitchier than ever this morning. She gave up after five tries and reminded herself to have someone from the Tech-Apps department retrieve it for repairs or get her a new one. There were frustrating disadvantages in having to utilize older technologies.

She headed into the main room to answer the call on her secure landline. She couldn't help glancing at the replacement sheets of glass in the window wall where the assassin had escaped. The metallic borders were a tad shinier than the surrounding panes.

"Annabel Bakana," she answered.

The male caller identified itself as a bot and uttered the A-prime code sequence. In turn, she recited the authentication, an equally convoluted string of letters and numerals; a new one requiring memorization at the beginning of each week.

Her identity confirmed, the bot instructed her to be at an address on Philly-sec's west side in twenty minutes. She didn't know what the summons was about or which individual had issued it, but there was no disputing the urgency of an A-prime directive. E-Tech's highest echelon required her presence.

She dashed back into the bedroom to dress, hoping she'd make it in time.

EIGHT

Nineteen minutes and forty seconds later, the driverless limo deposited Bel in front of a two-century-old Queen Anne house with wraparound porch, overhanging eaves and fancy trim work atop its steep roofs. The front lawn, like most in this modest neighborhood, was withered and patchy. Although strains of genetically modified grasses able to withstand the relentless air pollution were available, over the years Bel had noticed fewer and fewer people making efforts to keep their lawns and exteriors in topnotch condition. The doomsayers claimed it was yet another sign that people had stopped caring about the world and that an apocalypse was imminent.

Bel didn't believe that. There could be no doubt that the world was in serious trouble. But she was convinced it would ultimately come to its senses and pull through.

She rushed up the stairs and knocked on the door. An elderly man opened it. For a moment, Bel was too astonished to utter a word.

He had a wild thatch of white curly hair, a matching beard and old-fashioned spectacles. He was hunched forward, a bit precariously she thought, his hands folded on the knob of a twisted cane formed from a gnarled tree root.

The man smiled warmly and motioned her to enter.

"Annabel Bakana, I'm pleased to make your acquaintance.

It's a delight that we can finally meet."

He extended an arm and she shook his hand. For a ninety-five year-old, his grip was surprisingly robust.

"Sir, the pleasure is all mine. I have dreamed of meeting you since I was a little girl. I carried an autographed photo of you in my wallet all through middle school. I used to show it to my friends. It bored them silly, but I did it anyway."

Bel knew she was fan-gushing but couldn't help herself. Standing a meter away from her lifelong hero, the man who'd inspired her to join E-Tech, was the last thing she'd expected upon coming here. She'd seen him once across a crowded room at an E-Tech function years ago. But face to face, the experience was extraordinary.

"I used to brag about you all the time," she said. "I'd tell everyone that you were one of the greatest minds of the twenty-first century."

"Just *one* of the greatest?"

His eyes twinkled and he gave a self-effacing laugh. She wouldn't have expected anything less from Doctor Weldon Emanuel, a trailblazing neurosurgeon and expert in subliminal mnemonics who'd achieved even greater fame for his passionate mid-century writings on the long-term negative impacts of unrestricted science and technology.

Those writings had inspired a diverse international group to chart a saner and more peaceful path for humanity. That group had gone on to become the founders of the Ecostatic Technospheric Alliance. But throughout the organization, as well as in the public imagination, Doctor Emanuel remained E-Tech's spiritual patriarch.

"Please come with me," he said.

Walking with effort, he hobbled down a short hallway with faded wallpaper. Leg implants or a snap-on exoskeleton would no doubt have made locomotion easier, Bel realized. E-Tech rarely opposed medical tech that alleviated human suffering so it wasn't a matter of him hewing to idealism.

Perhaps he declined such gear out of a sense of pride, of not wanting to be perceived as old and handicapped.

He motioned her into a large windowless conference room that looked to have been created by removing the original downstairs interior walls. Nine individuals were scattered around the long table. Amid the empty spaces, six more were represented by shimmering holos generated by virtual amplifiers mounted within the chairs.

She recognized every face. Gathered in this room, either in person or via transmitted image, was the entire Board of Regents, the fifteen men and women who oversaw E-Tech. They were an esteemed group that represented the most influential of global power players: famed politicians, corporate titans, brilliant scientists, academics and engineers. Nowhere else in the world did there exist such a diverse and multipotent group united in such a just cause. Bel was proud to serve them.

Three of them were part of the organization's original group of founders, contemporaries of Doctor Emanuel. She noted that two of the trio wore exoskeletal braces and the third had a mech replacement arm. Their assistive technology made Doctor Emanuel's lack of such devices more pronounced, made him seem even more exceptional.

He motioned her to assume the open seat at the far end of the table. She'd met with the regents once before, when they'd confirmed Director Witherstone's appointment of her last year as associate director, Media Relations. But that meeting had taken place at E-Tech headquarters and had been a lighthearted affair. Today, the board members looked appropriately somber.

"Welcome, Ms Bakana."

The voice came from the chair facing her at the opposite end, from a dark-skinned woman with probing hazel eyes. Suzanna Al-Harthi was an environmentalist with the EuroAfrican League and a leading authority on global atmospheric degradation. She'd been elected to the rotating biennial term of E-Tech board president three months ago.

"We're in a safe house," Al-Harthi said, anticipating Bel's first question. "For now, the Security people felt it prudent to stay low-key and avoid gathering at headquarters. And I apologize for the hasty summons. Again, Security's prompting. Although we're aware of no impending threats, accelerated scheduling is believed to be a safeguard against the possibility of further assassinations."

Bel didn't disagree with Security's precautions. Still, since the attack she'd been dwelling on Nick's blistering critique of that department, that it was dysfunctional and in need of an overhaul.

She had a pretty good idea why the board had summoned her. They would be interviewing every E-Tech associate director to get firsthand details about the attack. Also on the agenda would be the beginning of what likely would be an extensive interview process for selecting Director Witherstone's replacement.

For Bel, that latter agenda item would be little more than a formality. Media Relations had never been a springboard to the top leadership position. Traditionally, the Executive Director was chosen from either Operations or Intelligence. Bel's money was on the well-liked guru of the latter department, Pablo Dominguez.

Besides, she had no desire to head the organization. In addition to being laser-painted as a target for Paratwa assassins or other fanatics, she'd have to bear the major brunt of anti-E-Tech sentiments. In person and on the newsphere, Director Witherstone had often been branded a naive egalitarian and misguided Luddite. And those had been some of the nicer things said about him.

"Before we get started, would you like some refreshments?" Al-Harthi asked.

"Coffee would be great." Bel had been in such a hurry to

get here under the wire that she hadn't even slapped on a caffeine patch, her go-to stimulant when there wasn't time for fresh-brewed.

She assumed Al-Harthi would summon a serving mech to the room. Instead, Doctor Emanuel stood up and limped toward an end table clustered with drinks and snacks.

"I can get that," she offered, starting to rise from her seat.

"Nonsense, young lady," Doctor Emanuel said with a smile. "You're our guest."

He transfused a mug with fresh brew from a suspended starbuckian. She fought an urge to ignore his command and rush over to help him.

His hands trembled slightly as he handed her the coffee, another infirmity of aging. She'd read that he'd suffered two heart attacks in recent years, on both occasions refusing hospitalization, preferring the selfmed route and treating himself at home. His whole career had been marked by that sort of stubborn independence.

He took a seat in the corner behind Al-Harthi. She'd heard that the great man often served as a special adviser to the board, although there were rumors that it was a token position, intended mainly to honor his special place in E-Tech history. She hoped they didn't have him here just to serve refreshments.

"Let's begin, shall we?" Al-Harthi said. "First off, Annabel, how are you doing? We've all read the Security report on the attack. It must have been terrifying hiding in that closet."

"It was," she admitted, while privately acknowledging a sense of guilt over her actions. While she'd huddled in a dark space, according to witnesses, Director Witherstone's final moments had been spent glaring defiantly at the assassin as it stabbed a pair of Cohe beams through his eyes.

"But I'm OK now," she added, twisting the mug's flavor ring to inject a shot of cocoa cream into her coffee.

"Your survival instincts are obviously excellent. Are you

aware that yours is the only department the Paratwa entered that did not suffer any casualties other than those Security people? Elsewhere, panic overwhelmed all too many staffers, and with tragic results."

Bel started to tell them that Nick had been the one responsible for saving their lives, but Al-Harthi cut her off with a wave of the hand.

"Yes, we're aware of the contribution of this programmer. But we also know that it was your strength and stamina in the face of life-threatening danger that spared the lives of your staff."

Looking at the surrounding faces, it was obvious they wanted her to take the credit. She didn't like the idea but knew all too well how large organizations functioned, how they sought to reward and glorify the highest officials. She might not be able to dodge the focus of their praise here in this room. But she intended to push E-Tech into issuing a proclamation that formally acknowledged Nick for his heroic actions.

Besides that, it would give her a valid excuse to see him again. She had found herself thinking increasingly about Nick since the attack.

"What's important now," Al-Harthi continued, "is for E-Tech to recover its poise as quickly as possible. We need to reassure the world that the attack has not deterred us from our mission."

"I couldn't agree more."

"Excellent. That's one of the reasons why we're in agreement. We want you to be E-Tech's new Executive Director."

Bel was taking her first sip of coffee when Al-Harthi's words hit her like a shockwave. She quickly lowered the mug lest a suddenly nervous hand caused an embarrassing spill.

"I realize our choice must seem somewhat odd."

That doesn't even begin to describe it, she wanted to shout, but held her tongue.

"We think you're qualified in a number of ways to lead

the organization. First, you possess excellent political savvy and the ability to navigate friendly and hostile waters with equal skill in this increasingly challenging era. Second, although you've suppressed your personal beliefs in support of organizational goals, your writings and speeches prior to assuming your current position suggest that the establishment of the Colonies should be E-Tech's primary focus."

The massive space cylinders, under construction for decades at a pair of gravitationally stable regions located hundreds of thousands of kilometers from Earth, were seen as humanity's best hope for survival if an apocalyptic catastrophe ever did come to pass. Some of them were nearing completion and accepting immigrants.

"The Colonies are of the greatest importance," the holo of a middle-aged Taiwanese man said. His name was Vok Shen and he controlled an array of manufacturing industries throughout Asia and Africa. A translation bot rendered his native Mandarin into English with a scarcely noticeable time lag. "Can we assume, Ms Bakana, that you still adhere to the belief that we need to establish a strong E-Tech presence there?"

"More than ever," Bel assured him, recovering her poise enough to take a desperately needed sip of coffee. "If a worst-case scenario should occur and survival on Earth becomes impossible – and for the record I don't believe that will happen – the Colonies will serve as a safe haven for millions. They represent the best chance for humanity's continuation. E-Tech must play a major part in that."

She wondered if they would raise the topic of the world's second great survival initiative. Star-Edge, the construction of twenty-six massive starships in Earth orbit, was meant to enable hundreds of thousands in stasis sleep to reach distant colonizable planets.

The Colonies were a public-spirited venture, largely funded by men and women like the ones present in this room, along with an international consortium of governments and thousands of wealthy patrons. It was intended that the Colonies be as egalitarian as possible. Star-Edge, although ostensibly controlled by a consortium of respected scientists, was largely underwritten by private monies. Berths on the vessels were sold for exorbitant fees and at least some of them had been purchased by criminal enterprises. The more cynical voices, including the majority of the E-Tech faithful, saw Star-Edge as lifeboats for super-rich crooks.

"I'm pleased our thinking is aligned," Al-Harthi said. "Is there anything you would do differently in terms of our stated initiatives?"

Bel hesitated, aware that several of the regents were focused intensely on her. Better that she had some time to consider such a weighty and open-ended question.

"E-Tech is involved in a great number of projects. At the moment, I could only talk about those I've had direct knowledge of. What I'd like to do first is better familiarize myself with them all from the perspective of my new role."

Several of the regents nodded, pleased by her prudent and diplomatic response.

Vok Shen jumped in. "Not to speak ill of the dead, but Director Witherstone's relentless and increasingly confrontational stance toward the Paratwa at the expense of the Colonies and other vital efforts has alarmed us for some time. Frankly, many on this board were considering the need to replace him. In light of events, it is most unfortunate that we didn't act on those considerations." He paused, gazed around the table at the assemblage. "Our reticence was caused by too lengthy a debate, a problem plaguing all too many of our discussions these days."

Vok Shen didn't look at any particular board members when he uttered that last sentence. Al-Harthi nodded, clearly in agreement with him. But several other regents frowned.

One of the male dissenters rose to his feet and turned to

the industrialist's holo. His voice was calm but his words stern, yet oddly delivered with a faint smile.

"Those lengthy debates are the key to effective governance, Vok Shen. Reckless decision-making characterizes all too many organizations these days. E-Tech must pave the way to better governance while also not straying too far from public sentiments." The man paused. "It's obvious that our late director was firmly in touch with the feelings of a vast majority of our citizenry. The Paratwa *are* a grave threat and should be treated as such."

Bel didn't know much about R Jobs Headly, the youngest and most recent addition to the Board of Regents. The sandy haired thirty-three year-old, a financier of some renown, came from old money. He'd inherited a family fortune built on the development of twentieth century computer software.

"And do we wish to align ourselves with the humanity's lowest common denominator, your so-called vast majority?" Vok Shen countered. "Do we lead E-Tech down the path of war and violence? Is that the only solution to the schism between humans and Paratwa?"

"Better that than to awaken one day to find ourselves enslaved by a world ruled by binaries. History offers numerous lessons about the dangers of constant appeasement."

As well as their obvious disagreement, the subtext of the heated exchange between Vok Shen and R Jobs Headly was clear to Bel. The regents might display a united front in public but, behind the scenes, factions existed. As director, she would have to learn about those factions and develop ways to maneuver among them.

And she'd have to be careful not to go out on a limb by giving overly strong support to any initiatives that were fiercely debated in this chamber. Most, if not all, of the regents knew the value of a well-timed media leak and were prone to using such methods to bat public support in one direction or another. If Bel wasn't careful, she might find herself functioning as the batted ball, perpetually up in the air and swatted back and forth.

Al-Harthi regarded her with a piercing gaze. "Both prior to and since the attack, your public statements regarding the Paratwa have been free of antagonistic assertions. You have adhered to a position of neutrality, which aligns well with the majority of this board. Although it doesn't impact your appointment one way or the other, I am curious about your real take on this issue. Have your feelings about the Paratwa changed in any way since the attack?"

Bel again chose her words carefully. "I believe it's important for E-Tech to attempt to unite all groups under a common umbrella of understanding. Scientific and technological restraint is a worthy goal for one and all, whether human or Paratwa."

"Thank you," Al-Harthi said, no doubt aware that Bel had sidestepped the meat of the question. "We're certain you'll work diligently to orchestrate those goals."

Bel stood up. "I want to say to all of you how honored I am to have been chosen. I look forward to continuing to receive input from all the regents, either individually or as a group. It'll be a steep learning curve but rest assured I'll give this job my all."

"That's appreciated. And with regard to that learning curve, you won't be entirely on your own. Doctor Emanuel has offered to act as your mentor to help bring you up to speed. If you're willing to have him, of course."

"Absolutely." Bel could hardly contain her pleasure. "I'm thrilled at the idea."

Doctor Emanuel gave a gracious nod from his corner seat. Bel smiled back at him, genuinely excited by everything that was happening. Yet doubt flickered at the edge of her mind – not over whether she could do the job she'd just been handed, but over the unstated reason that they likely had chosen her.

They want someone who won't rock the boat.

She would be that person for them, at least in public. But privately, especially when it came to the Paratwa, her true beliefs would continue to guide her, beliefs she'd held from well before the murderous Shonto Prong had extinguished the lives of her coworkers. Unlike Director Witherstone, she'd been careful never to reveal those beliefs in public forums. Had she done so, and had the regents learned of it while vetting her, it was unlikely she would ever have been offered the job.

The core of her personal beliefs was simple. She agreed with R Jobs Headly that the assassins were the gravest threat humanity had ever faced. But her answer to that threat was more radical than her predecessor's, who'd only called for controlling their numbers and limiting their influence.

If our species is to survive, we need to wipe out the Paratwa.

NINE

Nick sat in his cubicle on the forty-ninth floor, reviewing the latest information he'd surreptitiously retrieved from the workstation of a midlevel Security administrator, a man who remained oblivious to how easily he could be hacked. Attempting to persuade Security Chief Bull Idwicki, whose ignorance was equaled only by his obstinacy, to fortify his porous data systems was an issue for another day. Right now, the information and what it indicated was all that concerned him.

The administrator had learned through a contact in the EPF that the decoy assassin, the one who had initiated the attack by killing those guards in the lobby, had been discovered late last night. An EPF patrol had found the male tways, or what was left of them, in the zoo, along a deserted section of Delaware River waterfront. The ten-square-block region was generally avoided by even the most desperate street people because of lingering radiation from a terrorist dirty bomb set off back in the 2080s.

The dead tways had been identified as a *Machismo Energía*. It was one of the newer breeds, the product of a Venezuelan fossil fuels company that sought to diversify its portfolio by expanding into genetic engineering projects, including binaries.

In the Paratwa scheme of things, the Energía were low-end creations, barely adequate as assassins. Given growth hormones to accelerate physical maturation and developmental programs to do the same intellectually, most were under the age of ten in real years even though they had the physiques of young adults. With their training expedited as well, their usefulness was limited. They were hired mainly as cheap grunts by a thousand mercenary armies fighting a thousand lost causes.

Nick studied the images captured by the EPF squad. The Energía had been chopped apart by Cohe wands, its heads, arms, legs and torso segments gruesomely divided into neat little piles. No doubt the assassin had been slain by Royal decree as the ultimate punishment for sloppiness.

The Energía had mistimed the assault in the lobby and its failure to achieve split-second accuracy had resulted in the Shonto Prong being trapped in that elevator for a short period. Not only had the murder of Director Witherstone been jeopardized but unnecessary risk had been added to the Shonto Prong's mission. If the marine commandos had arrived at E-Tech headquarters minutes earlier, they would have had an opportunity to confront the Paratwa. On a good day, with the heavens aligned in their favor, they might even have killed it.

There was something odd about the Energía's inclusion in the attack, however. Nick wondered why the Royals had paired such a low-end assassin with the far superior Shonto Prong. Human killings ordered by the Ash Ock were exquisitely planned. A mission of such critical importance – the assassination of an E-Tech director – should have called for a more skilled decoy.

In any case, this wasn't the first time the Royal Caste had ordered the murder of one of their own, and in such a way that it served as a message to binaries everywhere that the Ash Ock did not take kindly to failure. And this wasn't the first time Nick had seen the perverse body-chopping signature of the assassin who he was certain had slain the Energía. He didn't know its name, only its breed and moniker. It was a Jeek Elemental, one of the deadliest of the breeds. It was known as the liege-killer.

Said to possess legendary combat skills, the liege-killer was the Ash Ock's special errand boy, dispatched to terminate assassins who refused to be united under their banner or failed to carry out their orders. Had the liege-killer preyed only on its own kind, Nick might have almost supported its effort – any way you looked at it, one less Paratwa in the world was a good thing. But the liege-killer was also responsible for human casualties believed to number in the tens of thousands through a series of mass annihilations.

Nick spotted something on the Energía's severed torso pieces and zoomed in on the images. The chests and backs of the tways revealed crisscrossing lash marks, indicating a flogging with Cohe wands, undoubtedly done premortem. The liege-killer had not considered death to be enough of a punishment for the Energía's failure.

On several occasions, Nick had tried to learn more from Ektor Fang about this assassin who dispensed the Ash Ock's most brutal justice. However, the CI always clammed up when he broached the subject. He sensed it was more than just another topic that the Du Pal considered off-limits. Ektor Fang didn't spook easily but Nick had a hunch that even he was afraid of the liege-killer.

The landline beeped. It was Maria Jose. She'd ascended in the E-Tech hierarchy following yesterday's announcement of her boss's promotion and was now chief assistant to E-Tech's new director. Rory Connors, who had served Director Witherstone in that role, also benefited from the changeover. He'd been transferred and bumped up into Bel's former position. Rory was the new Associate Director of Media Relations.

"Director Bakana would like to see you at your earliest convenience," Maria Jose informed him.

"I'll be right up."

There was no need to fudge a pass this time. A Security terminal in the hallway outside his floor's cafeteria issued a B authorization, which had no time limit for his stay on the executive level. He hopped the next elevator.

Bel's new position came with a full Security detail, beefed up since the attack. Nick counted half a dozen Security men and women patrolling the floor between the elevator and the director's suite, all armed with thruster rifles. A battle android, which had supplemented Director Witherstone's human bodyguards when he was in public, stood guard at the suite's main entrance. During the attack, the BA had been summoned from its normal station in the garage, but it had arrived on the fifty-seventh floor too late to join the fight.

The precautions looked impressive. But Nick knew that in reality they were meaningless. The rifles offered no tactical advantages over handguns within the tight corridors of an office building. In fact, had such weaponry been used during the attack there would likely have been even more casualties, victims of friendly fire. As for the android, its single greatest advantage, autotargeting firepower, would be rendered ineffective against most assassins, who were outfitted with personal jamscram devices.

Still, Nick supposed that the Security presence did have one benefit. It made workers feel more secure.

The android noted Nick's B pass as he approached and didn't challenge him. He entered the suite's outer office. It was more spacious than Bel's previous area, with three times as many workstations.

Several of the staffers who had been with Bel in Media Relations and had been there during the attack stared at him as he walked by. One of them stood up and started clapping. Others joined in. He wanted to tell them that he really wasn't their savior but settled for smiling and nodding. One of the core group was missing: the terrified young assistant, Renee. He'd heard that she'd quit E-Tech the day after the attack.

Maria Jose, who now had her own office adjacent to Director Bakana, greeted Nick with a beaming look that seemed on the verge of dissolving into tears. Before he could utter a word, she gushed out a heartfelt "thank you" and threw her arms around him. Nick wasn't fond of sentimental displays but there wasn't much to be done about this one.

"I know what the official line is," Maria Jose said, unwilling to release him from a crushing bear hug. "But we all know what you did for us. You saved our lives."

"Hey, we all did what we needed to do. It was a team effort."

"It was God's will."

He broke away from her as soon as he could without giving offense.

"May God be with you always and look out for you," she whispered.

Wiping her tears away with a hankie, she opened the inner door and ushered him into Bel's office.

TEN

Annabel Bakana, the fourth director in the organization's history and its first female, came out from behind an impressive oak desk. In her case, Nick wouldn't have minded a soul-swallowing hug. But Bel limited her greeting to a formal handshake.

"Thank you for coming," she said. "I hope I'm not taking you away from any important work."

"It's cool. Just the normal day-to-day stuff."

He gazed out the two intersecting window walls of her spacious corner office. On a clear morning, he would have been able to look across the Delaware River into Camden, his old 'hood. Today was more typical, however, offering only a gloomy view of poisonous gray smog.

Most office buildings used smartglass that could be altered from translucency to any imaginable scenic view. But part of E-Tech's mission was facing the world as it was, not hiding the outside environment behind visions of the Roman Colosseum or zebras dashing across an African savanna.

He drew his gaze back into her office, nodded his approval at the elegant furnishings. "Nice crib."

She stared blankly. Nick sometimes reverted to 1980s street lingo learned as a child, forgetting how out of date it was. And although technically this wasn't a residence, "crib" did seem the proper term. He had a fair hunch that Bel would be spending more time here than at her apartment.

"Nice office," he corrected, gesturing to an impressionist landscape painting, green and gold foliage against cloudy skies. "That's an original Renoir, isn't it?"

"I'm told it is."

The painting hung from a short partition that served as a view block for a well-stocked bar. Director Witherstone was known to have had a passion for drinking, especially straight-up WeBoys. The cinnamon-infused and obscenely expensive vodka was fermented from corntatoes, a GMO mashup of corn and potatoes. Its high price was due to a sophisticated snob-appeal marketing campaign by the owners of the WeBoys distillery.

Passion for a rare drink was hardly unique to the murdered director. It was common for elected officials and the heads of nonprofits to have a private liquor or vaping bar in their office. Back in the era in which Nick had grown up, that would have been frowned upon, the individual likely fired or at least forced into rehab.

"I'm not much of a drinker," Bel said, gesturing to the bar. "I'll probably do an office makeover and have it removed. But for now, there's quite a selection available. If you'd like, feel free to fix yourself something."

"Thanks, I'm good. And I wouldn't be too hasty in ditching readily available alcoholic beverages. A couple months into this job and you might find yourself needing the occasional jolt."

She motioned him to an L-shaped sofa. It had no armrests for him to perch on. He stacked two cushions and sat atop them to equalize their height differential.

Bel sat down on the other leg of the L. The seating arrangements suggested this was an informal meeting although her manner and poise came across as stiff. He chalked it up to the newness of her job, of not yet having settled in. After all, she'd officially been director for less than twenty-four hours.

"Sometime in the next week or so," she began, "I'm planning to present you with a formal proclamation. It will be given in conjunction with a modest celebration honoring your brave actions during the attack."

"Don't take this wrong, Bel. I appreciate the thought. But if you really want to do right by me, forget about all that stuff."

She raised an eyebrow. "Care to tell me why?"

"I'm more of a behind-the-scenes kind of guy. Publicity is something I'd prefer to avoid."

She seemed to relax a bit, settling back into the cushions. "I read that about you. In fact, I read your E-Tech bio. I was surprised to learn that you slept through most of this century."

"Yeah, missed out on a few dozen wars, not to mention the fourth season of *Breaking Bad*."

She gave him another blank stare before continuing. "Your bio is rather incomplete, particularly from the era you were born into. Frankly, I couldn't find any useful information on you."

"I like to fly under the radar. Always shied away from social media."

That was only part of the reason for the scarcity of an infotrail. Prior to going into stasis, he'd hacked every Internet database he could find, everything from the hospital records where he'd been born to his tax files with the Internal Revenue Service. And what personal information he hadn't been able to eliminate had been wiped off the net fortuitously in one of the great viral scourges of the 2050s.

Bel went on. "Your bio doesn't even say why you volunteered for an underground stasis program, only that you did so in 2010. Those were primitive days for preservation techniques. The chances of your body surviving long enough for advancements in technology to enable your revival were considered close to zero."

"Guess I thought it was worth the risk to awaken in a better place." That wasn't the truth, just the reason he gave when asked about his unusual past. He added a bitter chuckle. "Talk about a serious miscalculation."

She smiled coolly and made an odd gesture, running her palms down across the hips of her dress, a dark blue A-line. The garment was a bit more conservative than the Oscar de la Renta repro she'd worn during their first meeting. But Nick still found both her attire and the gesture strangely alluring.

Who am I kidding? Alluring didn't begin to describe what he felt when he looked at Annabel Bakana. The truth was, he found her incredibly sexy and desirable. It had been a long time since he'd felt such an immediate attraction to a woman. But that's exactly what had occurred when he'd first encountered her in the hallway minutes before the attack.

Since that day he'd tried to force such thoughts out of his mind. An intimate relationship wasn't likely to spring up between them even though he sensed that the attraction was mutual, that on some level she had or could have feelings for him. But he hadn't allowed himself such distractions since being brought from stasis nine years ago. His earlier life, and all the pain and guilt that had swirled around it, had taught him the value of staying focused.

Stick to the plan, he told himself. He'd formulated the broad outlines of what needed to be done since that last fateful meeting with Ektor Fang. Her predecessor's assassination had altered his focus to a new director, but the overall goal hadn't changed. He'd known that Bel would summon him for this discussion and he knew what he needed to accomplish during the meeting. That was all that was important.

"Jumping into the future isn't all it's cracked up to be," he said. "You've heard about some of the side effects of being under for a long time?"

She gave the textbook answer. "Diluted senses of taste and smell, a mildly escalated need for sleep, desensitization of memories bearing a strong emotional component."

He'd never found that last one particularly relevant. Some of his emotions were as powerful or even more powerful post-stasis.

"Even the stasis physiologists don't know exactly why those things occur," he said. "Anyway, I wouldn't recommend the experience."

"I could never do something like that. For better or worse, this is my time."

Nick wondered if she'd at least considered the possibility. Many people did these days. A growing percentage actually went through with it, choosing stasis to escape a troubling world or personal demons. But something in Bel's utterance indicated that she was serious about her beliefs, that she'd never evade life in the present by leaping into a distant and unknown future.

He admired her for that. And whether it was that admiration or his attraction to her or some combination of the two, he decided to detour from his game plan and reveal some of his inspiration for choosing stasis.

"My life back in 2010 had become too hard. I'd lost my sister and my parents within the space of a few years." There was another reason, a more important one that had driven him into stasis. But it wasn't something he was willing to talk about.

"I tried the standard escapes to obliterate my troubles. Moved around a lot – Europe, Asia, throughout the US – all the while existing on massive amounts of alcohol and casual sex. When those things were no longer enough to keep the pain tamped down, I switched over to heroin and abstinence."

He hesitated, surprised by the turbulent feelings his confession was bringing up. *Why am I revealing such things to a woman who's nearly a total stranger?*

"One night, I ended up in a hotel room in some Texas border town. That's where I bottomed out. I stole a .45 caliber handgun, set my ass down in front of the TV and put the barrel in my mouth."

Nick grimaced with the memories. Even though the events had occurred more than eighty-five years ago, in real-time they'd happened less than a decade ago. The torments remained close to the surface.

He pushed on. "Just when I'm about to eat a bullet, this preview comes on for a documentary about cryonics, about people who arrange to have themselves placed in subzero storage after they die. And suddenly I'm pulling the gun out of my mouth and thinking, why the hell not?

"I start doing some research into cryonics. I had a good chunk of money from a settlement involving my parents' deaths – they were killed in a terrorist attack in Europe – and within a few weeks, I'd invested a bit of it with this underground group. They helped me commit suicide but in a much gentler way, with drugs. They froze my body the instant my heart stopped beating."

Bel looked amazed and saddened by his story. "It's truly a miracle you're here today."

"Yeah, tell me about it."

"Must have been an incredible shock to wake up in our era."

"Not so much shock as disappointment. After I got acclimated, I realized I'd jumped from the frying pan onto the burner." He laughed bitterly. "The world of 2086 was even crazier and more disjointed than when I went under.

"Back in 2010, it looked like humans were at least starting to address the major problems threatening life on Earth. Global warming, chemical and organic pollution, shrinking resources, extinction of species, religious crazies lusting for nukes. A whole shitload of troubles, all exacerbated by an endlessly increasing population.

"But when I woke up, things were way worse. Self-interest seemed to have totally triumphed over the common good. The twin gods of profit and progress were rampant back in my time as well, but there's no comparison to today's vast inequality between the rich and poor. It's so extreme now that we sequester the haves from the have-nots, force most of the poor to live behind walls.

"Back then the planet had nasty wars and genocides as well. But the 2090s have upped the ante in terms of the sheer numbers and the degree of brutality. And if all those things aren't enough, science goes and creates a quirky little organism called the McQuade Unity, whose cells can remain in telepathic contact with one another even when physically separated."

Bel finished his thought. "Which paves the way for genetic engineers to breed binaries."

"Yeah. But do you want to know the worst thing of all about this era, even worse than the Paratwa assassins? It's the hopelessness that people feel. The average person seems to have given up. They believe that there's no future, that the Earth is doomed. Not everyone, of course, but billions of them, and not just those living in the unsecured areas. And that sense of despair robs people of their best qualities, their compassion, their concern for the welfare of others. They become incapable of looking beyond the narrow borders of their immediate lives."

He sighed. "I understand part of the reason people become this way. The world can be a hard and tough place for anyone. But when you combine personal pain with a civilization that seems to be crumbling all around us, even the brightest optimist can begin to feel lost and coldhearted."

Bel went quiet for a time, staring at him with an expression he couldn't read. Nick hopped off the sofa and walked to the bar. If there was ever a time for a drink, this was it.

He was tempted to go for Witherstone's favorite vodka, but the bottle of WeBoys rumored to be kept in his office was nowhere in sight so he settled for a modest brandy. Pouring a shot, he downed it in a single gulp.

Bel broke the silence. "When they awakened you from stasis, E-Tech must have seemed like a breath of fresh air."

"A place where people truly believe in a better future, where they work to keep hope alive? Hell yes. That's the main reason I joined up."

He had an urge for a second shot of brandy, and possibly a third and fourth one after that. Resisting, he sat back down. This time he'd didn't use the pillows to come up to her level. He felt smaller but it had nothing to do with their size differential. Talking about his past, at least the parts he felt he could talk about, always took something out of him. It sapped his strength, somehow made him feel smaller, less significant.

"I'm sorry for what happened to you," Bel offered.

"Don't be. And I wasn't trawling for sympathy. I just wanted you to know the truth about my earlier life." *Or as much of it as I can reveal.*

She seemed to be looking for a way to move the conversation to more fruitful topics. Nick was eager to oblige.

"Anyway, Bel, getting back to that proclamation you want to give me. It wouldn't be a good thing."

She frowned. "I guess being in the spotlight would jeopardize your relationships with your confidential informants."

"Yeah, that's definitely a consideration."

"Of course I'll honor your request. No proclamation, no celebration. But there are some things I'd like to know regarding the attack."

"Specifically?"

"How did you realize that those two men in the elevator were a Paratwa? And how'd you so quickly identify the breed? Security was only able to confirm that after several days based on analysis of similar attacks."

Nick was tempted to get in another lick at Security's incompetence but decided it wouldn't be fair. He'd learned details about assassins from Ektor Fang that few humans were privy to.

"Most breeds have giveaways. For the Shonto Prong, the telltale is a kind of nervous tapping, two fingers of corresponding hands. Plus, they're known for using a decoy assassin." He assumed she'd already seen the report on the Energía's grisly demise.

"What about that terminology you used? Pa and Ma, pinpoint assassination and mass annihilation. Intelligence isn't familiar with it."

"Some of the assassins use those terms." It was another tidbit he'd picked up from Ektor Fang. Like the Shonto Prong's telltale, it was information he hadn't passed on to E-Tech. Leaking too many details, even seemingly inconsequential ones of that sort, might enable the Royals to uncover the identity of his CI.

Bel raised an eyebrow. "And you gleaned all this knowledge from your informants?"

"Most of it."

"Then some of them must have direct access to binaries."

He shrugged in lieu of an answer.

"How long have you been using these CIs?"

"Some of them have been my sources for a few years. Others are more recent."

"And why don't you share what you learn from them with the rest of E-Tech?"

"I do." He explained how he secretly fed much of the intel gathered from Ektor Fang and his other CIs into E-Tech's database in a way that precluded the data from being traced back to its sources.

Bel seemed to mull that over for a moment. When she spoke again, it was to bring up the one subject he'd hoped they could avoid.

"I'm going to need the names of these informants and their background profiles."

"I can't. We're talking here about serious deep throats. Besides, I gave my word that their identities wouldn't be compromised."

"Naturally, I'd keep whatever you tell me in the strictest confidence."

He believed her. Still, he wasn't ready to open up about his CIs, especially Ektor Fang. The mere hint that a human had a working relationship with a Paratwa assassin would be seen by many as an act of treason.

He had a hunch that Bel might perceive things differently, that she shared his feelings about the extreme danger to human survival that the Paratwa represented, that she would support the idea that one of his sources was an assassin. But he needed to be absolutely certain of her beliefs before he risked talking about the Du Pal.

"I'm sorry. I can't reveal anything about my informants."

"That's not good enough. I need to know more."

She seemed adamant. He needed to buy some time. "Let me think about your request for a few days."

"And let me be frank, Nick. Programmers in the Intelligence department do not run CIs, not under any circumstances. I double-checked the matter with Pablo Dominguez and others, and they confirmed it." She paused. "I didn't bring up your name, at least for now. I felt that you were owed an opportunity to discuss the issue before I considered the need to take formal action."

The threat was clear. If Nick didn't come clean she might report him.

"My CIs aren't officially authorized. I meet with them on my own time."

"Nevertheless, you're an E-Tech employee. You signed an oath prohibiting you from engaging in such activities."

Nick realized they were on a collision course. The last thing he needed to have happen was for this meeting to end in an ugly stalemate.

Her face hardened. "I need those names as well as the full range of intel you've been receiving from them."

She was fixated on the wrong issue. He needed to switch

the conversation to the right one before it was too late.

"The Royal Caste was behind the attack," he said. "They gave the order."

Having the liege-killer murder the Energía in such a symbolic and public way had been the final proof Nick needed. The Ash Ock had arranged for Director Witherstone's assassination. And the public manner of his execution and that of the Energía suggested that either they wanted the whole world to know or didn't care if it did.

"The evidence does indicate that possibility," Bel admitted.

"And there's something else. Have you wondered why the Royals wanted you to become E-Tech's new Executive Director?"

"What are you talking about?"

"I believe that the assassination of your predecessor had very little to do with the fact that he was making anti-Paratwa statements. They wanted him dead for some other reason. The Royal Caste might not have liked his views but they wouldn't have gotten so worked up over his words alone. I mean, hey, it's not like Director Witherstone was out on a limb with his beliefs. The latest polls show that nearly eighty-five percent of humans have strong anti-Paratwa sentiments."

"But he wasn't just anyone. He was a well-regarded public figure."

"Nevertheless, the important thing to recognize here is that the Royals specialize in the most intricate forms of manipulation. They thrive on it. You're part of a puzzle, one piece in a carefully designed plan."

"That's ridiculous."

"Media Relations was the only department to suffer zero casualties. You'd like to give me the credit for that. But now I realize it wouldn't have made any difference whether I was there or not to instruct your people. None of them would have been harmed.

"In several other departments on the executive floor –

namely, Intelligence and Operations – the staff also knew enough about the nature of Paratwa attacks to adopt the same unaggressive postures for survival. Despite that, nearly a dozen of them died. I reviewed the Security footage of how it happened. It's very subtle but the evidence is apparent to someone who knows what they're looking for. The Shonto Prong deliberately provoked some of those staffers into reacting. It then used their reactions as an excuse to kill them."

Bel frowned. "Why would it do that?"

"To set the stage for your ascendance. In any kind of tragedy there's a common dynamic that occurs. After the tragedy, people seek to amplify perceived heroics and glorify the heroes. Those who died bravely – in this instance, Director Witherstone, Security personnel, staffers – are elevated to near-mythical status. But they're not as useful as living heroes. The assassin went out of its way to make you into one."

"That's absurd. I ended up hiding in a closet."

"I've been monitoring the newsphere about you since the attack. Sympathy and support for Annabel Bakana is through the roof. You have a global Q-pop score usually reserved for the sainted."

She grimaced. "And most of that is nonsense. I didn't do a damned thing."

"Doesn't matter. C'mon, Bel, you're a media professional. You know better than most that perception is everything, that it beats the truth nine times out of ten. The Board of Regents praised you for keeping a cool head, for making sure that your staff was given instructions for surviving the attack before worrying about your own safety."

"But I didn't do any of that, it was all you. And anyone interviewing my staff will quickly learn the truth." Her gaze turned suspicious. "How do you know what they said to me?"

"Educated guess."

It wasn't a guess. He had a source among the regents. He'd known about Bel's promotion before she'd even learned of it.

"Your staff will line up to support the invented story," he continued. "Maria Jose practically said as much to me before I walked in here. They're loyal to you and dedicated to E-Tech. Besides that, they all moved up in the world with your promotion, so it's to their benefit to go with the flow and not make waves. And I'll bet a month's pay that every single one of them has been directly contacted by a regent or their proxy and encouraged to toe the line.

"E-Tech needed a hero, a living one. Your department was the only one spared casualties. And the assassin passed through your suite twice. It was no accident that the Shonto Prong returned to your office, that it engineered its escape from there. It was just another part of a well-conceived plan to make you the focus of attention.

"And once that focus was established, the regents picked up the ball and ran with it. They buried the lead – that I was the one really responsible for instructing your staff. Then they used their vast resources to embed the idea of 'Annabel Bakana, E-Tech Hero' in the public mind."

Nick could tell she was considering his deductions. Still, she wasn't yet ready to buy in.

"I don't believe the regents 'buried the lead', as you say. They simply chose a path that was politically expedient."

He piled on more evidence. "First thing this morning, my boss comes to my office. I'd never so much as had a casual conversation with Pablo Dominguez and the next thing I know, we're BFFs. He gives me this heart-to-heart spiel about the importance of downplaying what I did on the day of the attack, which of course is fine by me." He paused. "He got the message from the regents, just like your staff did."

Bel nodded. "All right, let's say I believe what you're saying, that all this manipulation is happening to put me in the director's chair. Why? For what purpose?"

"Certainly not for the reason everyone thinks, that the Royals want someone running E-Tech who expresses a more even-tempered philosophy toward the Paratwa. That's just fodder, something to feed the masses.

"The main reason for the attack was the elimination of Director Witherstone. Secondarily, they wanted you as his replacement. I just don't yet know the reasons behind those actions."

In truth, he had an idea why Bel had been chosen. But he saw no upside in revealing it to her, at least not with her so new in the job.

She stood up. Nick found himself admiring the gentle sway of her hips as she strolled over to the corner that joined the window walls.

Don't get distracted, he told himself. *Stick to the plan.*

So far that plan had worked. He'd gotten his main points across to her: that the attack had a hidden purpose, that she was part of the real reason behind it and that the Royals were far more manipulative than E-Tech generally gave them credit for. From his perspective, there was really no good reason to remain in her office, at least none that flowed from his calculated scheming.

Bel gazed upward, as if seeking answers from the bleak skies. Protocol dictated that she be the one to end the meeting. Not that Nick minded staying longer. Simply being in her company invoked a certain pleasure.

She turned back to him. "For the time being, I'll ignore the issue of you running confidential informants in violation of E-Tech policy. But I need your assurances that you'll refrain from recruiting any new CIs, as well as engaging in any additional actions that violate your E-Tech employment contract."

"I'll do my best."

"Also, I'll revisit the issue of your CIs at a later date. And when that time comes, I'll expect straight answers."

"Fair enough."

"Moving on. On the day of the attack, you said that you had sensitive information that needed to go straight to the director." She allowed a faint smile. "Here I am."

Nick hesitated. He saw no reason to hit Bel with Ektor Fang's revelations when she'd officially been director for less than twenty-four hours. Because the intel wasn't time-sensitive or actionable – he could perceive no logical strategy to counter it – a delay would make no difference. His urge to share it with Director Witherstone had been based solely upon a desire to bounce ideas back and forth about its ramifications.

He wanted to do that with Bel as well. But he could afford to hold off for a little while, give her a chance to get her feet wet in the new job. Still, even as he made the call he wondered about his rationale.

If someone else was the director, someone I wasn't attracted to, would I still have such concerns? Would I be trying to cushion that person from information overload?

He wasn't sure.

Bel was staring at him with an expectant look. Nick needed to tell her something.

He revealed what the Du Pal had said about the Royal Caste, that they called themselves the Ash Ock. He told her their tways had the ability to unlink, function as two distinct individuals. Her expression told him that the disclosure was suitably impactful.

"Let me be the one to pass this info along to our relevant departments," he concluded. "I'll filter it, make sure there's no blowback on my CIs."

"All right. There's something else I'd like from you."

A tantalizing image flashed through his mind, of the two of them lying on this sofa, making love.

"Shoot," he said.

"How familiar are you with La Gloria de la Ciencia?"

"I know a bit about them."

The pro-science organization had come into being not long after E-Tech's formation several decades ago. Their goal was the exact opposite of E-Tech's: remove all checks and balances on scientific research, allow unfettered growth and no restrictions on the introduction of new and improved products and applications. They seemed oblivious to societal realities, believing that humanity's problems could always be solved by ever greater applications of technology.

"La Gloria de la Ciencia has been actively thwarting our efforts on a number of fronts," Bel explained. "They've been twisting our message, accusing us of being Luddites, of being against sci-tech growth in general rather than just putting some rational limits on it."

"No argument. They're mostly a bunch of whack jobs who don't know what they're talking about."

"Yes, but well-funded whack jobs. According to their published history, they were a grassroots movement that spontaneously developed in reaction to E-Tech's rise to prominence. But La Gloria de la Ciencia had no such accidental beginnings. It was secretly created and funded by a consortium of big tech corporations concerned about losing revenue and market share.

"Frankly, they're becoming dangerous. La Gloria de la Ciencia used to limit themselves to organizing protests and lobbying politicians. But they've upped their game. I just received intel indicating they were secretly behind that attempted coup in Norway. Fortunately it failed and a pro-E-Tech government remains in power in Oslo. Any information that might help us declaw La Gloria would be invaluable."

"You want me to check with my CIs, see if any of them can provide any evidence of the coup?" Nick asked.

Bel hesitated. He could tell that, despite her prohibition against him using informants, she was tempted by what they might bring to the table. Finally, she shook her head.

"If you already have information gleaned from a source,

fine. But no new contacts with them. Limit your search to legal means."

Nick had little hope of learning anything useful with one of his best methods hobbled. But he forced a smile.

"I'll see what I can find out."

ELEVEN

The new limo Annabel Bakana rode in as E-Tech's chief was similar to the one she'd had access to as an associate director. But there was one notable difference.

It came with bodyguards.

Two beefy men shared the front seat. Even more impressive was that one of them was actually driving the car through Philly-sec's dense midday traffic.

Bel had been seven or eight years old the last time she'd been in a vehicle that wasn't self-directing. Her two grandfathers had taken her for a high speed ride in an antique, gasoline-powered Ford pickup. She remembered being terrified sitting on Grandpa Austin's lap as he wrenched the steering wheel and stomped the pedals, manhandling the big loud machine along a winding country road while Grandpa Rudolph bellowed from the passenger seat for them to go faster.

Such childhood terrors had been overcome long ago, replaced by the more abiding fears of adulthood. Besides, she'd been assured by E-Tech Security that the driver was highly skilled. Nick's skepticism of Security notwithstanding, he and his companion came across as professionally competent.

The bodyguards monitored police and EMS channels through their attaboys. Frosted I-glasses fed them real-time data from the vehicle's sensors and high-altitude drones that scanned the route ahead for potential threats. They carried projectile and energy weapons. In the words of Bull Idwicki, the blustery Security Chief, "The men trained to protect you are highly skilled professionals ready to address any operational crisis."

But Bel had learned from some of her contacts in Security that "operational crisis" was a code phrase used by the department for situations that *excluded* the presence of Paratwa assassins. Translated, it meant that in the event the Royal Caste gave the order to have her killed, the bodyguards would be as useless as everyone else in stopping it.

We have to do something about that. She wasn't thinking specifically about the attack on headquarters. Realistically, she knew that if the Royal Caste wanted her dead, little could be done to prevent it. Assassinations, "Pa" killings in Nick's parlance, as well as "Ma" attacks, such as the biotoxin that had devastated Quezon City, were nearly impossible to prevent.

Still, Pa and Ma attacks represented a minority of Paratwa-related incidents. Most of the conflicts involved some form of open battle, often with a company or battalion of soldiers pitted against a single assassin. Such firefights inevitably resulted in a terrible loss of human life, and even then, the Paratwa usually escaped. That led to the demoralizing perception among the citizenry that the assassins were invulnerable. Now that she was the director, she vowed to surreptitiously steer some of E-Tech's vast resources toward the goal of finding a way to change that perception.

"ETA is ten minutes, ma'am," the driver announced.

"Thank you."

She was heading to the Imperius, the new convention center south of downtown. The E-Tech fundraiser, aimed at soliciting new patrons, had been planned months before Director Witherstone's assassination. Bel would give opening remarks before introducing Doctor Emanuel as the main speaker.

She should be using the ride to fine-tune those remarks. Yet she found her thoughts again turning to this morning's encounter with Nick.

What he'd revealed had extraordinary ramifications. She still found it difficult to accept that the Royals wanted her running E-Tech. If true, she couldn't fathom their reasoning. Even more disturbing was that the Ash Ock apparently could function as two individuals rather than just halves of a single person.

But most surprising of all were the annoying notions churning through her since seeing Nick, notions that had nothing whatsoever to do with her advancement or Paratwa assassins.

He didn't compliment me on my attire.

In preparation for their meeting she'd worn the only other A-line brocade dress she owned. She'd also donned a pair of slingback high heels. They were the same type of shoes she'd worn the day of the attack and which had earned his praise as she huddled in the closet.

But he didn't utter a single compliment, not a word.

That she was dwelling on such things was absurd. She was acting like some preteen girl hyperventilating over a first crush.

She forced herself to view the situation logically. Why on earth would she expect praise from Nick? And why would she want it? He wasn't her type. He came from a different time, a different world. He had a street savvy that was almost unheard of within E-Tech. The two of them had little in common.

She couldn't deny that Nick's combination of keen intelligence and shadowy skills was enticing. She'd always been attracted to such men. But he wasn't exactly in the same financial sphere as Bel, as well as her family and friends, most of whom were quite well-off. Despite her egalitarian beliefs, she knew that romantic entanglements between those who came from wealth and those who didn't rarely worked out.

What would her coworkers and the people close to her think if she and Nick began an intimate relationship? Her parents, who ran Lookati, an image and reputation management company franchised in hundreds of cities, would be mortified. They'd given her a rough time over her last boyfriend, Upton DeJesus, whom she'd broken up with less than a month ago. They'd never thought he was a good fit for her and although she hated to admit it, they'd been right. Still, Upton enjoyed a degree of fame for being on the vanguard of SATSI – Synaptic Alteration Through Surgical Induction – a radical and controversial technique for excising bad memories. Nick, by contrast, was a mere programmer.

And then there was the reality of Nick's size to consider. She had no problem with it but knew that her parents and others would consider his proportionate dwarfism a negative. Even the fact that it was a growth hormone deficiency and not genetically rooted – any future child of theirs wouldn't be impacted – still would leave them dead set against a wedding.

She shook her head, perplexed at where her thoughts had so quickly spiraled. *Marriage and children? Am I that smitten?*

A commotion outside the limo caught her eye. Two cops were pinning a man to the pavement. His grungy clothes suggested he was an unsec beggar. He'd probably been caught beyond the confines of one of the authorized mendicant zones. If so, he'd likely be stripped of his panhandling permit and deported back to the zoo.

She acknowledged a moment of sympathy for the man. The bifurcated world they lived in, with a functional high-tech civilization walled off from billions of unsec citizens like the beggar, was a grotesque mockery of her core beliefs. Bel saw an egalitarian society as the ideal. People shouldn't have to live in such radically different worlds.

But they do.

The notion flashed her thoughts back to Nick.

We're not going to have an intimate relationship. The idea is crazy.

Bel had never allowed herself to be guided by hormones and emotions. Even as a teen she'd prided herself on a high degree of self-control.

Then why do I keep having these fantasies of him being attracted to me and the two of us making love?

Had Nick done something to engage her libido? He was certainly one of the more emotionally manipulative men she'd ever encountered. If he had slipped lusties or some other illicit pharma into her food or drink to trigger immediate sexual desire, she would have recognized the signs and quickly taken one of the commonly available antidotes. But he could have used one of the more subtle and harder-to-detect drugs that incited long-term emotional desire. "Pitstop" was the latest and most devious, having reached near-epidemic usage on campuses.

She shook her head, trying to gainsay such paranoid thoughts. Nick wasn't like that, not deep down. She sensed an inherent goodness in him. He'd never pitstop a woman, slip her pheromone induction tranqs to force her to obsess over him.

Get a grip, Bel.

She needed to short-circuit these ridiculous thoughts by concentrating on the here and now. She unrolled the shiny new pad Tech-Apps had provided to replace her glitchy one and began a final review of her opening remarks at the fundraiser. After some heartfelt words and a moment of silence for Director Witherstone and the other victims, she would launch into her main points.

Supporting the Ecostatic Technospheric Alliance is one of the most important contributions you can make to the future of our civilization.

E-Tech was created to put the brakes on the profit-progress cycle that drives relentless technological advancement. Contrary to what you may have heard, we are not opposed to every new technology.

Sci-tech growth and advancement are as important to us as they are to you.

But advancements must be made for the right reasons, and with a sense that the outcome will benefit society in general. Accelerating technological development merely to create and sustain small pockets of massive wealth in a bifurcated world of haves and have-nots is no longer a tenable path for humanity.

Unfettered sci-tech has enabled us to ascend from our animal roots to the most extraordinary accomplishments. But we've climbed too far, too fast. Human evolution changes us slowly but technology does so at breakneck speed. That dichotomy creates friction, and that friction morphs into a dangerous energy that violently disrupts the social order – a social order already pushed to the edge by overpopulation.

The profit and progress cycle has accelerated to runaway levels. Product obsolescence once measured in years is now often charted in months or even weeks. Few of us can keep up.

And as we fall behind, as the twin gods of profit and progress achieve ever more formidable velocities, our vital cultural links break down. This leads to callous feelings, to hopeless feelings, to the idea that there is no future, that the complex social fabric that should unite us has been immutably damaged.

Most of us were taught in school that democratic capitalist societies are self-correcting, that they ultimately bring their worst binges under control. But that has not happened for a long time. Today, historians of all political stripes are convinced that too many years of unrestrained free-market capitalism on the part of the most advanced nations was a primary cause of unchecked sci-tech development, ultimately leading to the sec-unsec divide.

The bottom line, ladies and gentlemen, is that we've placed too few limits on our worst excesses, thus allowing them to get out of control. This Earth that we all share has been brought to the edge of destruction.

But there is hope. Our destiny is not preordained. By working together we can-

The limo screeched to a stop. Bel was thrown forward,

almost dropping her pad.

The bodyguards came alert, drew their pistols.

A few meters ahead, a crowd had surged into the middle of the street between a pair of hulking skyscrapers. Traffic in both directions had been forced to halt. Bel estimated there were at least a hundred people. But she couldn't see beyond the first few rows. It could be two or three times that.

"Flash mob," the driver announced. "Police are on their way to break it up."

"Who are they?" she asked. The mob carried no signs and shouted no messages. She couldn't ascertain a common denominator. They were male and female, old and young and everything in between. Styles of garb ranged from business chic to party funk. Several appeared to be families with young children.

One young woman arrived late and dashed toward the crowd. Wheeling close behind her was a translucent mech stroller containing a sleeping baby, a girl judging by the pink canopy. Bel guessed the baby was about a year old and the woman her mother.

Whatever the mob's rationale for forming, it didn't seem to involve Bel or E-Tech. None of them were paying the slightest attention to the limo. It was apparently a coincidence that they'd chosen this moment to occupy the street.

"We locked onto their frequency," the driver said. "There's attaboy traffic coming from a man in the center of the mob. He's broadcasting a countdown."

"A countdown to what?"

"Don't know. But it just hit twenty seconds."

Bel had an uneasy feeling. If the crowd had been demographically similar, such as all young people, she would have assumed it was one of the frequent pranks or protests staged daily by flash mobs across the globe. But the faces that she could make out looked too intense, even for a serious protest.

"Can you get us out of here?" she asked.

"Sorry, ma'am. We'll have to wait it out. We're penned in. Traffic is snarled on the far side too."

"Ten seconds," the other bodyguard said.

The crowd turned in unison to face outward. In that instant, Bel knew what was happening.

"They're doomers," she whispered.

Every natural instinct warned her not to bear witness to the horror about to unfold. But primordial human curiosity got the best of her. She couldn't turn away.

"Five seconds."

She'd seen doomers before. Everyone had. But she'd viewed those incidents through the distancing effect of video, as newsphere items after the fact. This one was happening right now in front of her.

In unison, the crowd lifted its gaze to the heavens. Bel saw expressions ranging from resignation to rapture.

"Three... two... one..."

The end of the countdown would transmit a go signal to every attaboy, attagirl, pad or other com device in the mob. Each doomer would be wearing a form-fitting leotard dipped in military-grade incendiary. In theory, each would have the final decision as to whether they activated their fuses.

A man at the edge of the mob was the first to immolate. One instant he was alive, the next a shadow writhing inside a pillar of blue-white flame.

Several more columns of fire erupted from deeper in the crowd. And then it seemed as though the rest of the mob ignited in unison. The fiery pillars touched one another and accelerated the conflagration. Flames from the mass suicide erupted twenty meters into the sky.

The limo had strong shielding, quandonium plates sandwiching a flow-through energy web. Bel knew it could withstand the high temperatures.

Not everyone had triggered their fuses. The young mother

was dashing away from the inferno. For a hopeful moment, Bel thought she'd come to her senses.

Then she realized the mother was chasing the mech stroller. It had overridden her programming and was racing along the sidewalk to escape the flames. The stroller's AI might be relatively primitive but it was smart enough to try sparing the baby from harm.

The mother clearly had other ideas. She was yelling at the top of her lungs for the stroller to stop and enraged it wasn't obeying. Whoever had programmed the mech must have given it a strong independent streak when it came to preserving itself and its cargo.

"You're coming with me!" the mother screeched. "We're going to a better place!"

Bel didn't pause to think about what to do. She simply reacted. Hopping from the limo, she ran toward the stroller, ignoring the bodyguards hollering for her to return.

Waves of heat blasted her. Although there was little smoke at street level, the air was thick with invisible gases from the incendiaries. She struggled to breathe while trying not to be overwhelmed by the vile odor of burning flesh.

The mother caught up to the stroller in front of a luxury emporium. The show window displayed holos of the latest in controllable housepets, black panthers and snow leopards with implanted microregulators.

The mother grabbed the stroller's handle, pressed the manual override. The mech wheeled to a halt. Snarling, she reached down to retrieve the baby. The glint of translucent VR lenses covered her eyes, ready to be activated, ready to transport consciousness to some heavenly vista at the moment of corporeal ignition. Even through the lenses, Bel could see the madness in those eyes.

She lowered her shoulder and bodyslammed the mother in the guts. The woman went down hard, her head smashing into the pavement. Stunned, she tried to get up but only made it to her knees.

Bel picked up the baby from the stroller. Amazingly, the little girl wasn't crying or in any noticeable way upset by events. She stared up at Bel with an expression of intense curiosity.

"She's mine!" the woman screamed. "She goes where I go, to a better place!"

"Not today," Bel warned, protectively cradling the infant.

With surprising speed, the woman roared to her feet and lunged at Bel. Her right hand dipped into her jacket pocket. Bel knew she was reaching for whatever device triggered her incendiary fuse.

We're too close! The fire would consume all three of them. Bel turned away to shield the baby as best she could.

The woman ignited. But just as she disappeared into an upright stream of roaring flame, the bodyguards arrived.

They fired their thrusters. The mother flew backward under the weapons' invisible energies. She crashed through the window of the emporium and disappeared into its depths, a twisting burning mass leaving a fiery debris trail. The display holos disintegrated, reforming seconds later into another set of big cats, cheetahs and jaguars.

Bel checked on the baby, sighed with relief when she realized the girl was OK.

The store inferno was escalating. The heat was becoming more intense. The driver was hollering for them to get back in the limo. The other bodyguard grabbed Bel's shoulders and propelled her in that direction.

They reached the safety of the vehicle. She checked on the baby again, by this time expecting tears of confusion. But the tiny elfin face wore a smile.

The baby's expression brought to mind Bel's final words from those opening remarks she'd been rehearsing.

But there is hope. Our destiny is not preordained. By working together we can restore the Earth and again make it into a livable home.

Yet despite the baby's expression and those uplifting words, she was stricken by doubt. Doomers were the ultimate expression of surrendering hope, but the feelings they espoused were increasingly embedded in all walks of society. Everywhere she turned, a global pessimism had taken root.

The words of her speech now seemed more like a taunt, as if some godlike jester had composed them in order to mock Bel's naivete, to stain such human dreams, to destroy the idea that what was good and hopeful could triumph. Billions of citizens were convinced that the world was heading for an apocalypse. For the first time in her life, Bel found herself believing they could be right.

TWELVE

With op names like Slag, Basher and Stone Face, Nick half-expected the three men to be dressed in loincloths and smell like day-old road kill. But the trio sauntering toward his booth in the rear of the Zilch tavern were garbed in biz casual, their dark jackets and turtleneck tees exuding a quiet professionalism. Their scents weren't bad either, an amalgam of modest colognes and deodorants.

They slipped into his booth. Slag and Basher sat opposite him, Stone Face at his side. They registered no discernible reaction at his smallness, a good sign. People who exhibited surprise wouldn't be suitable. He needed men who took the world as it came, who weren't susceptible to amazement and its concurrent neurological impact of slowed reaction times.

"Thanks for coming," Nick began.

"You told us you'd be alone," Slag said. His accent was British and his index finger was pointing up at Sosoome. The fake feline was perched above the booth on a shelf, sharing it with a vintage wine bottle emblazoned with skull and crossbones.

"That's just my mech. He doesn't count."

"Screw you," Sosoome muttered.

"He's got an active AV scrambler," Nick said. "He'll make sure no one listens in on our conversation."

"AVs can be overridden," Basher said. He was the tallest of the trio, with deep sable skin and a bionic left ear replacing the original, lost in a firefight. Even relaxed, his face looked threatening.

"This ain't no cheap-ass home AV scrambler," Sosoome snarled, tail rising defiantly. "It sure as hell can handle eavesdroppers in a shithole like this."

"He's right," Nick said. "It'll distort close surveillance, active or passive. Trust me, even a lip-reader won't be able to monitor us."

Slag gave a noncommittal shrug. He had a wiry build and unnatural red irises, either a genetic modification or an injection job. He was only about fifteen centimeters taller than Nick, atypical for his profession. Soldiers that short were rarely recruited for the EPF, let alone its deadliest spec-ops unit, Delta-A.

But Nick had done extensive research on the trio, running them through his own psych profiling program to gauge individual expertise and compatibility. On paper they were the kind of individuals he sought, a perfect blend of independence and group-think, of the teachable and the lethal.

"I assume you've received your funds."

"Wouldn't be here if we hadn't," Slag said.

Nick had paid them appearance money, two thousand apiece. As EPF soldiers, even elite Delta-As, they only made about eight grand a month. They were getting a week's pay just to listen to his pitch.

"What are you drinking?" he asked, waving his hand to summon one of the women behind the bar.

The Zilch was old school. It used only live waiters, no mechs. That had pissed off Sosoome. Nick had bought the mech with the finest available synthetic bio enhancements, including a pair of retractable penises and a pleasure center programmed for max titillation. He figured even robots deserved to get laid now and then. Normally when they went out, Sosoome tried seducing the mech help. He was left high and dry in a place like the Zilch.

But Nick liked the bar. It was near the northern edge of the city, a stone's throw from the DMZ and the wall. Although safely within the confines of Philly-sec, the crowd could have made the grade in one of the zoo's raunchy subterranean taverns. There were no poseurs here, no one likely to go all weak-kneed and call the cops if a kick-ass fight broke out.

The waitress arrived with bowls of pretzels and booze-soaked microplums, a house specialty. Her curly sable hair was pulled back in a bun. Maori tattooing covered her face, a complex pattern of black lines and swirls.

"Whaddya want?"

Her tone verged on disdain. That was fine by Nick. He preferred authentic reactions to the corporate-inflicted phony smiles of downtown servers, human or mech.

Nick, Slag and Basher ordered half-liter pumps of the house beer. Stone Face, a bruiser of a man with a forehead that looked capable of repelling blows from a tire iron, selected a more upscale brew.

"Down to business?" Nick asked as the waitress departed.

"Your bucks, your agenda," Slag said, crunching on a pretzel.

"I want to recruit you. The gig is one-year minimum. The pay is twenty-five thousand dollars a month per man."

Nick let them absorb that for a moment. His profiling had revealed that none of them were exclusively money-driven. He couldn't have used them if they were. Still, a tripled salary was not an incentive to be quickly dismissed.

"We're still here, mate," Slag said.

"You'll train in secret at various locations. Your training will be intense, even more than what you're used to. The focus will be on developing a complex and sophisticated level of teamwork. A fourth individual will be added to the team at a later date. Naturally, if you feel the training regimen is too tough, you can quit at any time."

Nick knew that if they signed on, they wouldn't take advantage of that option. Men like this didn't quit.

"At the end of your training, you'll be sent into the field. Your assignments will be of a clandestine nature." He paused, steeling himself for the hard part. If they were going to walk out on him, this next revelation would be the impetus.

The waitress returned with their drinks. He paid her in cash and left a generous tip. She mumbled a bored "thanks" as she walked off.

Slag and Basher dialed their translucent beer pumps to medium chill and broke the seals. They took big gulps. Stone Face set his pump to lukewarm and sipped his brew as if it was a rare cabernet.

Before Nick could continue, Slag discerned the nature of his pitch and beat him to the punch.

"A small squad, special training, complex teamwork. You want us to go up against Paratwa assassins."

Lesser men would have been heading for the door about now. Nick was pleased that the threesome stayed put.

"I like how you guys think," he said.

Slag and Basher traded skeptical looks.

"Look, pal, this kind of shit's been tried before," Basher said. "It's the wet dream of Delta-A and every spec ops unit in the world."

"Nobody's come close," Slag added. "Best anyone's ever done going full frontal against a hardcore twofer is fifty, sixty casualties. And three quarters of the time the assassin got away."

"We've fought these fuckers, seen what they can do. They're as nasty as it comes. Two-headed super-predators, trained from birth to hunt and kill."

"A full company against an assassin is SOP." Slag paused. "Personally I'd prefer battalion-sized."

Basher drew another sip of beer. "If it were up to me, I'd

never use soldiers to fight them. Just saturation bomb the whole area and to hell with collateral damage."

The idea wasn't as unrealistic as it sounded. Appallingly, some nations, particularly those with little or no history of civil rights, had adopted such methods. Basher was right, it was effective, at least if you didn't mind the horrific numbers of civilian casualties.

Nick dialed his beer to max chill and watched ice crystals form through the pump's window. Best to keep quiet for a moment, let them make the next move.

Three sets of eyes were locked onto him. Intimidating stares, trying to read his tells, trying to determine whether he was a deluded dreamer, a psycho or someone with a viable plan. Nick met their gazes, revealing nothing.

Slag ended the standoff. "Even if we thought you were the lone genius who's figured out a way to fight them that no one else in the world has come up with, we couldn't help you."

"We're hitched to EPF for another two-plus years," Basher said. "And they don't take kindly to deserters."

"Not a problem," Nick said. "I can make certain arrangements that will legally free you from your military obligations."

Slag and Basher didn't look impressed. He sensed they believed him, at least on that point. But they weren't ready to hop on board, not without further probing.

"So what's your hot-shit plan?" Basher demanded.

"We all agree a Paratwa assassin is the deadliest creature on the face of the Earth. But it has a weakness. I've found a way for a small team with the right attributes to beat it in straight-up combat."

"Need more than that, mate. Need some proof."

"I've developed simulations that–"

Slag cut him off. "Forget it. We've seen every kind of sim there is. No training holo is worth shit compared to live combat."

"In most cases that's true. But my sim is different. It will translate into real time."

Slag narrowed his eyes. The red irises seemed to brighten, giving him a devilish appearance.

"You're talking shit," the Brit concluded. "I think you're trying to scam us. I think this is some kind of con."

Basher picked up on the theme, ran with it. "He's an arrogant little prick, ain't he? Thinks he can feed us this crap and we're gonna lap it up like it's genuine filet mignon."

Nick's first inclination was to respond to the filet mignon remark with a pun, tell them that he'd *stake* his reputation on the success of the sim he'd developed. But he sensed that lightening the mood wasn't going to work with this bunch.

"This isn't a con," he insisted. "I know what I'm talking about."

They didn't believe him. The conversation went from insulting to downright menacing.

"You think we're gonna listen to some dwarf-child asshole," Basher growled. "Shit, man, you ain't even tall enough to suck my cock."

"Maybe he would be if you got him a highchair to stand on," Slag proposed.

"I say we just take him out back, get the truth out of him. Let Stone Face use his head for soccer practice."

Stone Face took another delicate sip of beer, gave no indication that he'd heard the threat.

Nick wasn't intimidated. He knew routines like these well from his gangbanger days. It was time to throw some trash back in their faces.

"First off," he began, "I don't like threats. Secondly, if your big dummy friend here ever tries kicking my head, I'll break his goddamn foot."

"That so?" Basher challenged.

"Yeah. It's so. And if you ever happen to get your cock stuck in my mouth, it'll be the last time you'll ever use it. I'll bite that little pencil clean off and ram it through the limey's eye."

Basher's arm lunged across the table, grabbed Nick by the throat, and yanked him half out of his seat. Their faces were a mere twenty centimeters apart. His assailant didn't look angry. His expression was closer to someone about to swat a pesky fly.

Nick was impressed by his lightning speed. Like many Delta-A soldiers, the three of them had enhanced neuromuscular systems. Their modifications weren't prenatal like Paratwa assassins; they'd never reach that epitome of quickness. Still, with the right training and coordination, they could be highly effective.

At the moment, however, Nick couldn't express his admiration. He had a more important concern, namely trying to breathe. He didn't even attempt to break Basher's iron grip on his neck. The effort would have been futile.

Sosoome came alert, ready to spring to his aid. The mech was waiting for his SOS signal – in this situation, a specific pattern of blinks, left-right-left. But Nick knew he had to get out of the dilemma on his own.

The only option was to show no fear and dis them back. Despite Basher's choking hand, he managed to work up a good ball of spit.

He unleashed the hocker. At such close range he couldn't miss. It splattered on Basher's left cheek.

Fingers tightened around his neck. Nick glared, unyielding. For good measure he managed to hiss, "Fuck you."

Slag gave a subtle nod. Basher let go. Nick flopped back into his seat, sucking down deep breaths and massaging his sore neck.

Basher carefully wiped the spit from his face with a napkin. He and Slag appeared satisfied. Nick wasn't someone who was going to lead them down the rabbit hole and then wimp out when the going got tough.

"No hard feelings?" Basher offered.

"It's cool," Nick said hoarsely. "Not the first time I've been choked."

"I'm guessing it happens a lot," Slag said, looking amused.

"Oh, it does," Sosoome chimed in. "Remind me to tell you about the time he called that kickboxer a clumsy kangaroo. She really kicked his ass."

"So who's running this little show of yours?" Slag asked.

"I am. For now, that's all you need to know. I'll explain more once you've signed up. I need a commitment first."

Slag and Basher exchanged looks. But it was Stone Face who spoke first, in a deep drawl that sounded exactly like Sam Elliott, an actor who'd come to prominence when Nick was a boy. These days, cloned voices of twentieth century celebrities were all the rage.

"Where do I sign?"

"Hallelujah," Sosoome said. "Now, can we get out of this shithole? The night's still young and I've got the urge to find me some accommodating receptacles."

THIRTEEN

Bel stood to greet their guest. Doctor Emanuel did likewise, rising from his seat on her office sofa and using his gnarled cane as a third leg to maintain balance.

The man swept into Bel's domain with the flourish of someone accustomed to being treated in a lordly fashion. His blue-green robes swirled behind him. Imperious eyes in an angular face scanned the room, taking in everything.

Bel had been told he was in his early fifties. His thick gray pompadour, streaked with white, seemed to bear that out. Yet encountering him in person for the first time, she had the odd impression that he might be either younger or older. There was a timelessness about him, an immeasurable physical quality that seemed to disguise his true age.

She forced a smile and stepped forward to shake his hand. "Bishop Rikov. I'm pleased to make your acquaintance. I believe you already know Doctor Emanuel."

"Of course. Weldon, it is *wonderful* to see you again. How *are* you doing?"

Bishop Rikov rushed across the room to clasp the older man's palms atop the cane.

"I am well, bishop. At least as well as can be expected given the infirmities of aging."

"Your years serve to complement your *gifted* brilliance.

They give praise to a life *well* lived. May the Spirit of Gaia forever encompass your destiny."

Bel hid a grimace. His affectation, placing extreme emphasis on certain words, was as annoying in person as it was during his grandiose speeches as head of the London-based Church of the Trust.

She gestured to the sofas. Everyone sat down.

"Refreshments?" she offered. She'd taken Nick's advice and decided to keep the bar, at least for the time being.

"I'm a teetotaler."

"Another beverage?"

"Thank you, I'm fine. And thank you for taking this meeting on such *short* notice. This is my first visit in years to your beautiful city. I was *truly* hoping we might speak."

"The pleasure is ours."

"First, let me offer my *deepest* condolences for the recent tragedy suffered by your organization. And for you personally, Ms Bakana, I hope that the healing process is well underway."

"It is."

"A number of the survivors of the massacre are church parishioners. We have strived to offer what support we can in their time of need. Should you or anyone else within E-Tech require counseling, our doors are *forever* open."

"Very generous."

Bel considered herself a spiritual person although she wasn't aligned with any organized religion. However, if she'd been forced to choose a faith, Bishop Rikov's would have been at the bottom of her list. It seemed to be a mashup of the world's classic denominations, cherrypicking the most popular aspects of each one.

Worse, there was no sense that the Church of the Trust had grown naturally from the spiritual urges of its founders. Instead, she had the impression it had been deliberately and cynically crafted to function as a revenue generator. Judging by the latest confidential figures she'd seen, the church was wildly successful in that regard, achieving the most unholy profit ratios. It had practically cornered the market on orbital vaporization, the expensive but popular funeral ceremony. Many of its parishioners were being convinced to turn a sizable portion of their estates over to the church in order to be cremated in low-Earth orbit.

Bishop Rikov favored her with a sympathetic smile. "I was also *deeply* moved by your selfless actions in saving that baby from the doomers. How *is* the child doing?"

"A kindly aunt and uncle have taken her in. They've begun the adoption process."

"*Most* pleasing. A tragedy with a silver lining, indeed a rarity."

Weeks had passed since those tumultuous events – the attack on headquarters, her surprise appointment to director, the mass suicide of the doomers. Bel wished people would stop bringing those things up. She'd moved on and wished everyone else would as well.

That last part wasn't quite true, particularly in regard to saving the baby from the doomers. Since that day, Bel found herself dwelling more and more on the idea of becoming a mother. She'd always assumed she'd have children someday, although not for a long time. Given that she had access to the best medical care, she could safely become pregnant into her sixties. Yet cradling that little girl amid the conflagration had somehow served to activate her biological clock.

The bishop went on, "I realize how *very* busy both of you are so allow me to come straight to the point. The church's council of priests has voted to grant full and *unequivocal* support to E-Tech's primary mission of putting limits on science and technology."

Bel hid her surprise. None of the world's other major churches had taken such a stance. All preferred to maintain neutrality so as not to risk offending members on either side of the issue.

"That's a generous offer," she said. "Naturally, we're pleased."

E-Tech needed all the support it could get. But Bel was suspicious of the bishop's motives. Certainly the Church of the Trust's position would offend many of its own parishioners and negatively impact its revenue stream. She wondered if the church wanted something from her or E-Tech in return.

"No strings attached," Bishop Rikov said, sensing the direction of her thoughts. "We would in *no* way attempt to influence E-Tech policy. You have my *solemn* word as a servant of the Spirit of Gaia."

Bel's doubts weren't appeased. Still, there was no practical choice open to her.

"Of course we accept, pending final approval from the Board of Regents. But I'm sure that they will be equally supportive of your church's proposal."

"Excellent. I'll have my people contact your offices to finalize the details. Perhaps a joint announcement?"

"That would be workable."

Bishop Rikov rose from the sofa. "I'll take up no more of your time."

"Would you care to dine with us this evening?" Bel asked.

She had a selfish reason for extending the invitation. In a relaxing atmosphere she might better probe what was behind the bishop's unexpected support.

"Alas, I must fly back to London." He produced a weary smile. "The Church of the Trust can be a stern master. So *little* time for culinary delights, sightseeing and other pleasures of the flesh. May I be granted a rain check?"

"Of course."

They said their goodbyes. Bel walked the bishop out and returned to her office, eager for Doctor Emanuel's input.

"What do you think?"

E-Tech's spiritual patriarch rose to his feet, rested his full weight upon the cane.

"Beware of bishops bearing gifts."

FOURTEEN

Bishop Rikov stepped from the elevator into E-Tech's lobby, pleased at how the meeting had gone. He'd expected more questions and probing before the church's offer had been accepted, not so much from Annabel Bakana as from that shrewd old fossil. Doctor Emanuel continued to have a great deal of behind-the-scenes input into E-Tech policy decisions, far more than the organization publicly admitted.

But Sappho had been right. She'd predicted they would quickly recognize that they had no real choice but to accept the church's offer. Any suspicions they might have about the motives behind it would have to be sublimated for the greater good.

It was a cunning plan, as were most plans that bore the Ash Ock imprimatur. By throwing the church's full support behind E-Tech, human sci-tech development would be hindered. The Paratwa, however, would continue to have no such encumbrances; they would be free to pursue, in secret, unlimited technological growth. As a bonus, E-Tech would be forced to publicly acknowledge the expanding influence of the church, which in turn would help the church grow even more formidable.

Sappho, of course, had been the prime architect of the plan, as she was in all such things. Bishop Rikov and his tway, either individually or when united into the singular consciousness of their powerful monarch, Codrus, certainly were contributors. But there could be no doubt that they followed the will of Sappho.

When interlinked, the bishop could sense a good deal of Codrus's thoughts, especially those with a strong emotional component. He was aware that his monarch on occasion acknowledged a certain bitterness over the extent of Sappho's influence. Power was supposed to be shared equally among the five members of the Royal Caste – or at least among four of them for now. Empedocles, youngest of their breed, remained in the late stages of his training.

In any case, sharing wasn't a reality. Still, Codrus accepted the way things were, as did the bishop and his tway. Besides, they had no real choice in the matter. As brilliant as Codrus was, the monarch recognized that he couldn't match the subtlety of Sappho's machinations. Her scheming was legendary. She crafted plans within plans, buried true intentions beneath layers of deception and fabrication. She was as different from the other Royals as a binary was from a human. Who truly knew what went on in that ethereal and impenetrable mind?

But Codrus had his area of expertise, a financial wizardry that was making a real contribution to the Ash Ock's covert rise to power. The bishop had arranged for much of the church's profits to be siphoned into the Royals' treasury. And his tway had brought even greater riches to the table, having managed to infiltrate and gain access to a pool of existing wealth.

The bishop exited the building and headed for his driverless limo waiting curbside. At that moment, a shaft of sunlight pierced the smog cover, bringing a sudden brightness to the busy street. He stopped and looked up, as did many of the pedestrians, pleased to feel the rare warmth from above.

It brought back a memory of his childhood in Thi Maloca,

the secret Ash Ock stronghold in the depths of the Brazilian rainforest where he and the other Royals had been bred and trained.

Back then, sunshine had still been plentiful in many parts of the globe. He and his tway would lie on the riverbank, basking under that burning orb while engaged in unity/duality games, gauging how fast they could go back and forth between existing as two individuals or the singular consciousness of their monarch.

He sighed. Those had been such pleasant carefree times. He supposed that many humans, as different as they were from binaries, were also capable of such nostalgic longing for youthful days. The way in which they were fixated upon the light from above suggested that such was the case.

But humans lacked the discipline to tear themselves away from the pleasurable warmth. The bishop did not. Turning away from the sky, he got into the limo and ordered it to head for Philly spaceport.

Tonight, back in the UK after a brief suborbital jaunt, he would give his first sermon from the church's new cathedral in the heart of London. Church of the Trust facilities now existed in nearly every major city. The disintegrating state of the planet was fueling religious fervor, with every major denomination experiencing a sharp uptick in true believers. The church's new cathedral, replacing that small original building on a narrow inconsequential street, was a lavish structure worthy of the other classic religions.

His words would be streamed live across the planet, celebrating the opening of the new facility while reinforcing the church's messages among its true believers. But the real bonus would be the millions of new converts.

It was a potent religion, carefully designed with specific rituals yet flexible enough to adapt to changing conditions. The wily Aristotle had come up with the basic format, and the brilliant scientific mind of Theophrastus had linked its various components into a systemic whole. Codrus had added his input, particularly the notion of the *Spirit of Gaia* through which believers could gain access to a wondrous afterlife, the key part of any lasting religion. And of course Sappho had added a series of mystical elements, fine-tuning the religion and bringing it to life.

But for the bishop, it was still all about profits. Those new converts from tonight's sermon alone were projected to translate, over the space of a decade, into more than a billion additional dollars funneled to the Royals.

As the limo pulled out, the shaft of sunlight vanished, overcome by the omnipresent smog. These brief sunbursts were all that most areas enjoyed these days, although there were still places where the sun could shine through for hours at a time. The bishop was aware of a cult, the Sol Surfers, which tracked meteorological forecasts and whose members jetted around the world to partake of those brief solar pleasures.

The unusual nature of an Ash Ock – three individual minds, two of which could interlace to form the third, a powerful binary – also enabled the bishop and his tway to keep certain things hidden from their monarch. Codrus would never learn – *must* never learn – that the bishop entertained thoughts of giving up his prescribed life, which required him to jet constantly around the globe to grow the religion and expand the church's treasury. Codrus would never approve of some of the bishop's more arcane fantasies, such as surrendering to nostalgia and becoming a Sol Surfer in pursuit of the sun's last earthly light.

PART 2

HUMANITY S AVENGER

FIFTEEN

Bel had avoided meeting or speaking with Nick since that morning of the doomers' mass suicide. He'd tried to make several appointments over the intervening weeks but she'd instructed Maria Jose to inform him that she was too busy. She'd made it clear that she expected him to pass any information he gained through the appropriate channels, rather than directly to her. He hadn't pushed the issue, hadn't tried to wangle another illicit pass to the executive level. She assumed he'd gotten the message that she didn't want any contact.

On the surface, her rationale was simple. Her days had grown increasingly busy: analyzing endless departmental reports, conferencing with supporters and politicians across the globe, mediating contrary opinions among the Board of Regents to maintain a united front for E-Tech. As important as Nick's concerns might be, she just didn't have time to deal with them. If the Royal Caste did want Bel in charge of E-Tech as Nick claimed, so be it. At the moment she was too busy to puzzle over their reasons.

Her professional concerns for avoiding Nick were clear. On a personal level, things were even simpler.

I don't need the distraction. She'd been fantasizing about him less and less, and that was a good thing. *Out of sight, out of mind.*

But now, after what she'd learned from Intelligence only hours ago, it was necessary that they talk. She'd ordered Nick to meet her at Philly spaceport when her flight landed.

She was returning by plane from Boston-sec with Rory Connors and several of his Media Relations staff. There, they'd led a cheer-the-troops rally. It was yet another drain on her time but a necessary one to boost sagging morale.

Nineteen employees of that city's E-Tech office had been among seven hundred or so Bostonians who'd died from Koheemi disease, one of the genetically engineered plagues springing up across the planet, deliberately unleashed for political or personal reasons. The only apparent connection among them was they were all highly contagious and lethal in the majority of cases.

A disgruntled biolab employee angry about his lack of promotion had spread this latest infection. Boston, like many cities, had reinstituted primitive corporal punishments in what Bel regarded as a misguided attempt to stem the escalation of terrorist acts. The city known as "The Cradle of Liberty," having fast-tracked the man's conviction under the new federal no-appeals statute, planned to tar and feather the perpetrator. He would be paraded through Beacon Hill inside a translucent mech wagon before being consigned to life in prison.

Bel had urged the surviving E-Tech employees to oppose the tar and feather portion of the punishment on humanitarian grounds. But their hurt and anger remained too close to the surface, and she and Rory had been shouted down. A part of her couldn't blame the employees. In twilight moments on the edge of sleep or sometimes in her dreams, she'd experienced nasty vengeance fantasies against the assassin responsible for the slaughter at headquarters.

Her private jet vertical-landed a stone's throw from the waiting spaceliner, a VG 947. Her next flight would cover a far greater distance, a three-hour suborbital journey to convene with top government officials in Canberra. She hoped that a face to face would serve to convince the Australians to support a new E-Tech initiative aimed at stopping the overheating of their territorial waters. Several corporations with poor environmental records had been tapping deepwater thermal vents for electrical generation, resulting in the massive extermination of sea life.

Her bodyguards hustled her from the jet to the spaceliner, made sure she was safely ensconced in her first-class cabin before heading for their seats on the lower deck. She checked the manifest, saw that Nick was already aboard. He was just one of half a dozen men and women she planned to meet with in person while waiting for the liner's scheduled liftoff in an hour.

Not allowing even sixty minutes to be wasted was a necessity in her new role. Multitasking, she'd quickly learned, was her only hope of not being overwhelmed by the demands of the director's job.

She called an assistant and told him to show Nick to her cabin. She would grant Nick the same amount of time as each of the others: ten minutes. Yet even as she issued the order, an irritating thought occurred.

I don't need to see him in person. I could have done this by holo.

She refused to dwell on any hidden psychological reasons behind her decision. There were sensible advantages to live encounters, she told herself. Besides, E-Tech employment policies discouraged holocommuting, which was felt to diminish organizational goals and lead to employees feeling isolated. Of course, the Board of Regents exempted themselves from such policies. Power did have its perks.

Still, Bel believed strongly that physical meetings were best. You could get a stronger sense of a person's state of mind, read body language indicators that didn't always come across in a holo. She was flying halfway around the world to speak with the Australian government for just that reason.

She decided to change before Nick arrived. Securing her dress and shoes in a drawer, she slipped into a standard amenity of VG-947 travel: a loose-fitting flight suit with attached boots. Many women preferred wearing the garments, especially during the microgravity portion of the journey when the liner was cruising in low-Earth orbit, and where attire such as a dress could drift and reveal.

She checked herself in the mirror, pleased at how the frumpy flight suit disguised her natural curves. There weren't too many other items of attire a woman could wear that made her look so totally unsexy.

No distractions.

There was a knock on her door. She set her solitary implant, an old-fashioned wrist fob, to signal when ten minutes was up and called for him to enter.

Nick wore the same loose-fitting blue suit he'd worn on the day they'd first met, the day of the attack. Bel politely shook his hand but quickly broke away. She was determined to keep the meeting strictly formal.

"Mr Guerra, how have you been?"

"OK, Ms Bakana. And you?"

"Fine. This won't take long. I'm sure you have plenty to keep you busy back at headquarters. Thank you for coming out here to meet me."

He grinned. "When the boss says jump, I ask, 'How high?'"

Bel motioned him to a chair and sat across from him. There were no detachable cushions with which to elevate his stature and he didn't attempt any armrest stunts. She liked being able to look down upon him from a slightly higher elevation. The power dynamic was more appropriate to their professional relationship, boss to employee. Too often in their previous encounters the situation felt reversed, his knowledge and insights serving to place him in a superior position.

"Let me come right to the point. Intelligence has informed me that you've arranged to have three elite soldiers released from their obligations by offering the EPF a bribe. Is this true?"

"I wouldn't describe it as a bribe. More like a mutually beneficial business transaction. I got what I needed and EPF received a cash infusion to purchase some major goodies that were trimmed from their latest budget."

"You promised me that you'd refrain from further actions that violate your E-Tech employment contract, which this clearly does."

"Actually, what I promised is that I'd do my best."

Her anger rose. "I'm not going to mince words with you, Nick. You're perilously close to being dismissed from E-Tech and possibly facing criminal charges."

"And you're focused on the wrong issue. You should be asking *why* I needed those soldiers."

"That doesn't concern me. All that's important here is your relentless disregard for the rules."

"I'm going to train them to hunt down and kill Paratwa assassins."

His answer was so surprising that Bel was momentarily at a loss for how to respond. Nick jumped into the void, bombarded her with details about how he'd developed a simulation that would enable a four-person team to successfully defeat an assassin in a straight-up fight.

She heard him out before shaking her head in disbelief. As at their previous meetings, he seemed to make the most preposterous statements, which somehow put her at an instant disadvantage. Most annoying was that he always seemed to know what he was talking about.

"The Paratwa have a weakness," he continued. "And I've found a way to exploit it."

"A way that not even the most skilled combat experts on Earth have discovered? What makes you such an expert?"

"Bel, that's a question I honestly can't answer. I don't know why I am the way I am. I've always seen the world differently. I see patterns where others see randomness. I see structure amid chaos."

He paused, stared hard at her. "And sometimes, if I'm really lucky and the stars align and the Force is with me, I can even see people's real emotions, see past the shields they put up to hide what's really going on inside them."

And what do you see right now? Bel wanted to ask. *A woman who is desirable?*

Her self-discipline was already starting to crumble. She stiffened her resolve, forced herself to stay focused. She would not let herself be distracted by the intense feelings that surfaced whenever she was in the company of this confounding little man.

Not for the first time, her thoughts turned to the possibility that her attraction to him wasn't natural, that she was being manipulated in some fashion. A standard self-test for unknown drugs in her system had come up negative. But pitstopping was far more difficult to detect and required a series of exams by a specialist. She didn't have the time, or at least that's what she'd been telling herself.

She forced herself to return to the issue at hand. "Putting aside for a moment that bribing EPF officers is unethical, where did you come by the money? It must have been a significant amount."

"Several million dollars."

She contained her astonishment, pressed on.

"Which means you must not be working alone in this endeavor. Who exactly is funding your little escapade?"

"I am."

"On a programmer's salary? Where would you get that kind of money?"

"Back in 2010, even after paying for stasis, I had a lot left over from my parents' settlement. I arranged a series of clandestine investments in a number of product categories that I judged had the potential for spectacular growth. I was extremely fortunate. Most of those investments paid off handsomely. And nearly a century of compound interest helped as well."

"You're telling me that you're rich."

"As are you. Your parents own the Lookati franchise and are one of the wealthiest families in Philly. Neither of us would ever have to work, and certainly not for a relatively low paying nonprofit like E-Tech. We're both here because we believe in the organization and have more important concerns than accumulating cash."

Bel should be used to being shocked by Nick's revelations. Yet each time she thought she was getting a handle on him, he spouted a fresh surprise.

"And you've managed to keep this fortune hidden?"

"A challenge, but not impossible."

"OK, but with all this wealth, why a low-level job as a programmer? Why not seek a more influential position?"

"I told you, I like to fly under the radar. Being in the spotlight puts a person under more scrutiny, limits their freedom of movement. Besides, I enjoy being a programmer. And as long as I accomplish my quota of tasks, the hours are somewhat flexible."

"Which gives you time to train elite soldiers."

"Among other things."

Something he'd said earlier finally penetrated. "You're training three soldiers. But you mentioned that a four-person team would go up against the assassins. Are you that fourth person?"

Nick erupted into hearty laughter. "Seriously?"

"Why not? You seem to have an endless range of impressive capabilities."

And why on earth am I complimenting him? I should be nailing him to the wall for the illicit bribe.

"Bel, trust me, I do know my limitations. I definitely wasn't built for combat. Besides, I consider myself more of a lover than a fighter."

If that last sentence was meant to arouse her, it succeeded. Fantasies she'd been trying to repress for weeks slipped into consciousness.

Concentrate, Bel. Concentrate.

"So who is this fourth team member?"

"I haven't found the person yet."

Her wrist fob pulsed. Nick's ten minute session was up. As fascinating and disturbing as a meeting with him was, she needed time to process what he'd said. Besides, she had five more people to attend to before the liner lifted off.

She stood up. He did the same.

"I'm really hoping we can talk again soon," he said.

"Count on it." She tried to make the words sound vaguely threatening but wasn't sure if she'd succeeded.

He again extended his arm to shake hands. This time when she grasped his palm, his grip was tight, unyielding. Slowly, inexorably, he pulled her toward him.

"What are you doing?" she demanded.

"I want to kiss you."

"Don't be ridiculous."

Her own voice lacked conviction. She put more effort into it.

"Nick, you need to go. This is improper."

Her second objection proved even less effective, the words emerging as barely a murmur. She felt her chest heaving and her skin becoming flushed.

"What are you doing to me?" she whispered. Paranoid thoughts again ramped into consciousness, that he was pitstopping her or employing some equally nefarious means to instill an attraction.

"You're a beautiful woman, Annabel Bakana. I want to kiss you. It's really as simple as that."

"Nothing is ever simple," she said, leaning down and planting her lips on his.

They kissed. He wrapped his arms around her and she did

the same. Their embrace was strong, vibrant, freeing in a way that Bel hadn't felt in a very long time. She didn't want the kiss to end.

They pulled apart, both sensing that this was as far as things could go at the moment. Nick backed toward the door, beaming with pleasure.

"There's more we need to discuss," he said. "A lot more."

"Yes."

"Why don't you call me as soon as you're back from Australia. We can get together. Maybe in a more private location where we can discuss certain important matters without any interruptions."

"Yes."

He left the cabin. Bel called her assistant to send in the next appointment. She tried to compose herself but it was a futile effort. She could steer neither her mind nor her body away from the intense pleasure of kissing Nicholas Guerra.

SIHTEEN

"I've come to a decision," Nick announced to Sosoome. "I'm going to do it."

When Bel arrived at his apartment, he would tell her about the momentous "buried lead" from Ektor Fang's revelations as well as the fact that his source for the information was a Paratwa assassin.

"I'm going to come clean to her. I'm going to tell her everything."

"Horse crap," Sosoome said. The mech was lying on the sofa, belly up with legs spread, exposing an undercarriage bristling with probes and receptors. Even for a machine it was an unflattering pose. "You enjoy your little emotionally manipulative games too much to go all 'I cannot tell a lie' on her."

He wanted to argue but Sosoome knew him too well. "OK, so maybe I'll keep a few secrets."

"Like the fact that you have an equally important source among the regents."

"Yeah, that."

"And the fact that you were married once, and that you opted for stasis, leaving your wife and–"

"Why don't you vacuum the rug and refilter the air?"

"I vacuumed yesterday," Sosoome replied smoothly. "And

the air is max oxygenated and ninety-nine point eight percent free of inhalable contaminants."

"Shoot for ninety-nine point nine percent."

Nick turned to the wide oak bookcase, ostensibly to make sure his twentieth century paperback collection was aligned in neat rows but more to hide the fact that the mech had touched a sore spot.

He replaced a couple of stray paperbacks in their slots and scanned the other titles, paying particular attention to the ones that might prove as offensive today as they had when he'd trotted them out in various PC enclaves more than a century ago. His youthful intention back then had been to shock. But that was the last reaction he wanted from Bel.

He debated removing and hiding *Boys Are Mucho More Smarter Than Girls* written by the pseudonymous "Fearless Juan," as well as several other tomes, including *The Big Book of Dwarf Juggling* and *Rectal Probing for Dummies*. But he figured that if Bel did notice those books or others of their ilk, she was sophisticated enough to realize they were satires, even if in some cases that might not have been the author's intent. And if she did take offense, he could treat it as a teachable moment, ideally leading them to mutual laughter and perhaps the opportunity to slip under the covers for a deeper education.

The eclectic book assortment, a mix of the offbeat, genre novels and serious nonfiction, had been in one of the few storage modules that had survived his long stasis nap. Even in Nick's first life in the early twenty-first century, there'd been growing digital access to books, making these paper editions silly mementos. He wasn't sure why he'd gone to such great lengths to save them, even having them treated with deacidification sprays and arranging for temperature and humidity-controlled storage.

"I don't think ninety-nine point nine percent is achievable," Sosoome said.

"Why are you still arguing with me?"

The mech emitted an annoyed sigh, rolled onto his feet and extended his air-filter array. He raced back and forth across the rug in silent vacuum mode.

Sosoome knew pretty much everything about Nick's past. He wouldn't have been very useful as a challenging foil if he wasn't privy to Nick's deepest personal secrets. Still, sometimes Nick regretted having told the pseudo-feline about his wife, Marta. She remained an open wound, one unlikely ever to fully heal.

Since yesterday's impromptu decision to reveal his feelings to Bel aboard the spaceliner, he'd been mentally previewing how this evening might unfold. Their kiss had proved the attraction was mutual. He'd been pretty confident of her reaction, would have been surprised if she'd outright rejected him. Still, now that she was coming here, and knowing that events potentially could spill into the bedroom, he found himself nearly as apprehensive as the first time he'd made love to his long-departed wife.

He needed to keep busy. He rearranged the paperbacks into alphabetical order by author, then decided it made more sense to separate fiction and nonfiction as well.

Sosoome took notice. "Being a bit anal, are we?"

"I want things to be perfect."

"Too late, dude. Your girlfriend's on the stoop." Sosoome finished cleaning and leaped onto the kitchen counter. "Let her in?"

"No, make her stand outside."

"I hope she appreciates your sarcasm as much as I do."

Sosoome remote-triggered the entryway door. Nick positioned himself at the apartment door and swung it open when he heard her footsteps reach the third floor landing.

"Welcome to my crib," he said with a smile.

A hooded scarf cloaked her head, hiding most of her face. It made sense for an E-Tech director to disguise herself before an evening rendezvous at the apartment of an employee.

She wore loose gray pants and a plain jacket. He'd been hoping for sexier attire, something that made it clear upfront where the evening might be headed.

"You look great," he said.

"Thank you."

He peered down the stairs. "Bodyguards?"

"They're close if I need them." She pointed to her wrist fob, which no doubt contained a panic button.

Bel removed the scarf, handed it to him as she entered. He hung it in the closet and gestured for her to have a seat on either chairs or sofa. Instead, she ambled around the room's perimeter, pausing to examine the framed prints in his small collection. Most were by Frederic Remington and depicted scenes of the nineteenth century American West.

"I like this one," she said.

A man with a pipe in his mouth on horseback was positioned at the edge of a cliff, gazing into the distance. Nick was pleased. It was his favorite too.

"It's called 'The Lookout,'" he said. "I checked a couple years ago to see if I could buy the original."

"Too much money?"

"It went missing from a museum in the American Southwest some thirty years ago during one of those urban water riots."

She ended her wandering in front of the bookcase. A smile crept onto her face as she scanned the paperbacks. He wished he could tell which title or titles had conjured the expression.

"You kids want me to fix you a snack?" Sosoome asked, his tone all bright and cheery. He'd configured his head sensors into a mocking imitation of a human smile.

"I'm fine," Bel said. "Maybe later."

"How about a drink? Got some forty-proof, fresh from Master Nick's backyard still."

He glared at the mech. "Sosoome, why don't you head out for a while, get some air?"

"But the air is spick-and-span in here, Master Nick. Ninety-nine point nine percent."

Bel looked surprised by the robot's challenging tone. Nick felt obligated to make introductions.

"Bel, meet Sosoome. He's one of a kind."

"He says that to all the women he brings up here."

"Be cool."

"Just kidding, Bel. Cross my heart, you're the first female to make the grade. I'm really impressed, although kind of curious about what you see in him."

Nick grimaced. "You really need to go."

Sosoome hopped off the counter, squeezed into a narrow aisle beside the fridge. At the far end of it was a cat door. Modified to be airtight and unbreachable, it accessed a ledge to the rear fire escape. Just before they heard the door snap shut, Sosoome yelled back a final retort. "You kids behave. Don't do anything I wouldn't do."

"He's different," Bel offered. "But somehow he fits you."

Nick hopped onto a pair of waiting cushions on the sofa, left ample room for her to sit beside him. Bel chose to resume her wandering.

"I'm really glad you came," he offered.

"You did say you wanted to discuss important matters without any interruptions."

"Yeah, I said that, didn't I? Why don't you sit down, relax a bit?"

"First off, I'd like us to be clear about yesterday, about that… moment. It wasn't something I intended to happen."

"I didn't plan for it either."

"This job, being director. It puts me under a lot of pressure to maintain a strict schedule and avoid spontaneity."

"No fun in that."

"I don't do well with relationships, Nick. My last boyfriend…" She trailed off.

"The SATSI quack?"

"Upton DeJesus and I had our issues but he's no quack. I believe that in due time, Synaptic Alteration Through Surgical Induction will be seen as a legitimate medical technique."

She ventured closer but instead of sitting went into a tight orbit around the sofa. Each time she passed in front of him she met his gaze for a moment, then swiftly looked away before strolling behind his back and reaching apogee.

"Upton and I were together for nearly two years when out of the blue he tells me that he wants to go on a gender vacation, switch sexes. Last I heard he had the conversion done and planned on living as a biological female for a while. I guess I'm a bit of a traditionalist. I just never had any interest in transforming into a man, even for a holiday."

"Completely understandable."

"I realize that none of that is probably news to you. With your access and your sources, I'm guessing you already know plenty of details about my personal life. Besides, the thing with Upton has been plastered across the net since I became director, although it was a reasonably amicable parting and not the huge fight reported in the sleazier areas of the newsphere. I'm sure you know as well as anybody that half the stories you come across are outright lies. Tabloid journalism run amok."

She was talking fast, on the edge of babbling. He debated an intervention, concluded it was best to keep quiet and let her vent.

She carried on for three more sofa orbits, telling him all sorts of things: that her parents never approved of the men she dated; that in the back of her mind she feared they were right since she always ended up having her heart broken; that her dedication to E-Tech was one of the few things that kept her on an even keel; that she'd once planned a medical career and had studied to be a doctor; and that she increasingly felt the urge to have a baby yet remained wary of bringing a child into such a crazy world.

She stopped circling, stood in front of him with her arms

crossed tightly across her chest. The posture struck him as somehow both vulnerable and defiant.

"I don't know what this is, Nick, what we're doing here."

He patted the cushions beside him. "Why don't you sit down?"

"Whatever happens, I need it to be real. But I don't know if it can be."

"Please, Bel. Just sit down."

She slipped in beside him, close but not too close. He reached over, took hold of her hand.

"I want things to be real between us too. Will it turn out that way? Who the hell knows? Life is messy. Shit happens."

He realized he was coming across like one of those demented advice bots that recommended embracing chaos to deal with the world's instability and craziness. He shifted gears.

"I'll do everything I can to make things work between us."

She gave a slow nod. "Before this goes any farther, I need to know something."

"Shoot."

"Have you been manipulating me subliminally? Pitstopping or something along those lines?"

"Bel, absolutely not. I'd never do anything like that, trick a woman into an emotional relationship or into bed."

She sighed. "The thing is, I don't even know who you are, Nick. Not really."

He suddenly found himself blurting out things he hadn't revealed to a living soul since emerging from stasis.

"I was married back in my first life. Her name was Marta. When I bottomed out in that Texas border town, when I was ready to put out the lights for good, my final thoughts were about her."

The pain and the guilt came flooding back. He forced himself to push on.

"Marta and I had divorced a couple months earlier.

Irreconcilable differences. The truth is, looking back on it, I was pretty much the problem. I was a real asshole."

She was looking intently at him. He looked away, trying to avoid getting lost in that dreamy gaze. Now that he'd started down this path, and before anything else that might happen this evening, he needed to get these things off his chest.

"Marta and I had married fairly young. We didn't know what we were doing. We ended up arguing a lot. Somehow we managed to stay together for a decade. The truth was, not until after we split did I realize how much I needed her, that she was my stability.

"I tried to reconcile but she was too angry and wanted to move on. She was already seeing someone else, a divinity professor of all things." He gave a bitter laugh. "Hell of a change from a punk with attitude and a weird-ass skill set."

Bel took hold of his other hand, squeezed his palms. He gazed into her eyes, saw the willingness. It was time to stop talking. But he'd come this far with his story. There was one more part, the most difficult and guilt-inducing part, that he needed to reveal.

Too late.

Bel pulled him to her. Their lips met. The rest of his story and the pain that went with it were lost beneath a tidal wave of repressed need.

Hands groped. Fingers explored. They pulled apart for a moment, looked at one another, saw no doubts, slammed back together, clawing at fabric, undoing snaps and zippers.

Nick had prepped the bedroom, bought new autosheets, even fallen for the pitch by the sales bot that three hundred thread count, animatronic cotton resulted in a twenty-two percent increase in sexual pleasure as measured on the Diggins all-position, homohetero scale.

They didn't make it to the bedroom. He drove into her. She bucked with pleasure. The sofa was comfortable enough. It was all good.

SEVENTEEN

Nick awoke naked in bed. Bel was cuddled beside him in a similar state of undress. He checked his attaboy. It was almost 5:30 am.

They'd made love three times since the start of the evening. There'd been that frantic first time on the sofa. Then twice in the bedroom in the throes of a gentler and more sustainable passion, with a short break between locations to reheat a couple of slices of Sosoome's homemade pizza. The mech had returned during that intermission and, thankfully without uttering a word, had immediately exited again. Presumably, his sensors had detected biological cues suggesting more sex was in the offing.

Nick carefully moved an arm that was cradling Bel's shoulder and in danger of falling asleep. He felt her waking up.

"Sorry," he whispered. "Go back to sleep."

"Too late." She smiled and tapped her wrist fob for the time, checked the subcutaneous readout. "Damn. Almost morning."

"Need to be anywhere?"

"Uh huh. Some early appointments. But I guess I can lie here for another ten minutes."

"We couldn't do as much in ten minutes as I'd like," he

said, putting on a sad face.

"Probably not as good as the way we did it last night."

"Yeah." He kissed her cheek. "Want some breakfast?"

"No, let's just stay here. In fact, let's blow off the day, the month, the whole year. Stay in this bed forever."

"I wish."

She stared at him, silent for a time.

"There's something troubling you," she said.

Marta used to be like that too, acutely attuned to his thoughts and feelings, especially after sex. It was one of the things he'd loved about her.

"There's always something troubling me," he said with a grin, hoping to prevent serious matters from pillaging the mood. "I could provide you with a detailed list but it would take you years to go through it."

"Be serious."

She wasn't going to be diverted. He sighed. "OK. I told Sosoome before you got here last night that I was going to tell you some things. Really important things."

"I suppose you'd better get to it then."

"That intel I got from my CI, the stuff about the Ash Ock, about their tways being able to link and unlink?"

"Uh huh."

"I left something out. Something big. Actually, a couple big things. You might say I buried the leads."

She rolled onto her side, propped her head up with her arm. "Am I going to be angry with you?"

"There's a fair chance of that."

"I guess you'd better plunge forward and hope for the best."

"Yeah."

Why am I doing this, now of all times? I just had my greatest night since coming out of stasis. And now I might be taking a wrecking ball to it?

But he knew the answer even as he posed the question. It was important, both personally and professionally. From here on out, he needed to be as straight as possible with this incredible woman.

"My number one confidential informant isn't human, he's binary. An assassin."

Bel sat up and pulled the sheet up toward her neck. The smart fabric sensed her need, coiled the cloth around her.

"You're telling me that one of them is your source?"

"His name's Ektor Fang. He's a Du Pal. And he's in the service of the Royals. Although he hasn't actually confirmed this, I suspect he's a high-ranking lieutenant with direct access to the Ash Ock."

Her eyes widened. "How? I mean, how is something like that even possible? Our field agents have been trying to get a source among the assassins for years. The closest we've ever come is some low-level intel from servitors."

Nick scowled at the name. He hated servitors, humans who, for various reasons – admiration, misanthropy, money – voluntarily served the cause of the assassins. He saw them as traitors to humanity, which in some ways made them even worse than the Paratwa.

"Trust me, it's possible," he said. "The problem with E-Tech agents is that they don't look in the right places for intel. I'm not saying Pablo Dominguez isn't a smart guy and that he doesn't do a good job running Intelligence. But his field agents, they just don't go where they need to go to make the right sort of connections. No offense, but too much of E-Tech is filled with well-bred, well-meaning people who have little or no street smarts. The social circles they move in aren't where you find the richer pools of intel."

"I know what you're saying. Pablo's aware of the deficiency. He's been trying to recruit savvier agents, men and women from unsec areas." Bel frowned. "But if this Paratwa of yours is really under the sway of the Royal Caste, how can you be sure you're not being played?"

"A disinformation campaign? Believe me, I've given a lot of

thought to the possibility that Ektor Fang is feeding me false intel. The thing is, I've come to trust him. The information I've gotten from him has always checked out. I admit I'm not a hundred percent sure of his motives. If I had to hazard a guess, though, I'd say that he secretly despises the Royals."

"And what if Ektor Fang's being played? How do you know the Royals aren't using him without his knowledge to muddy the waters?"

"I don't think so. But I suppose it is possible."

"Your source doesn't know about this Paratwa team you're putting together, does he?"

"Hell no."

Bel gave a slow nod, absorbing his revelations.

"Angry yet?" he asked.

"No. I mean, I understand why having a Paratwa as a CI would make someone extraordinarily cautious. You said there were a couple big things. What's the other one?"

There was no going back now. If she was going to be pissed, the fact that he'd held back from telling her about the CI's final revelation would do it.

"Ektor Fang made me swear that this is for the director's ears only, that it go no further. It could get my informant killed. You can't trust any of your own people with this intel, not even the regents."

"Understood."

"I wanted to tell you earlier. But you were so new on the job and with everything else going on, I didn't want you to feel overwhelmed."

"OK."

"But looking back, it was probably foolish of me not to have told you–"

"Nick! Just say it, all right?"

"The Royal Caste *want* an apocalypse to occur. Their overall goal is for life on Earth to be wiped out and for the planet to be abandoned."

Bel's face registered the same astonishment Nick had experienced when Ektor Fang made the revelation in that binary safe room more than a month ago. She shook her head, unwilling to believe.

"Why would they desire something so horrible? It's their planet too. They'd be destroying their own home."

"Ektor Fang doesn't know why, only that it's definitely what they want. Among other things, they've been secretly promoting environmental degradation, overuse of natural resources and the extinction of species. Plus, encouraging human overpopulation in order to exacerbate all those problems.

"He claims that the Ash Ock are responsible for many of the miniwars racking the planet. Remember that tourist a couple years ago who inadvertently crossed the Angola-Zambia border and triggered a ninety-day conflict with hundreds of thousands of casualties? That was one of theirs. Behind the scenes, they worked to accentuate tensions between the two countries, made sure that only a spark was needed to ignite hostilities. They've arranged for dozens of such sparks.

"They're also responsible for many of the urban nukings and the releases of plagues, maybe even that one in Boston that the lab worker took the heat for. And the biotoxin attack in Quezon City, although officially blamed on the Awasta breed, more than likely can be traced to them."

Bel remained skeptical. "Your source can't be right. They must have fed this Ektor Fang false intel."

"For what reason? You think the Royals would go out of their way to invent a fake story that would give humanity even more reason to hate them, to want to see them wiped out?"

"But it makes no sense. Unless..."

He finished her thought. "Unless they have an escape plan."

"The Colonies? I suppose it's possible. But E-Tech already has a testing procedure in place for immigrants to prevent that very thing, to stop binaries from entering the cylinders."

"I know. I wrote some of the programs myself that are being used to ID infiltrators. The colonial customs system isn't perfect, however."

"True. And from what you've told me about these Ash Ock, their ability to exist as separate individuals, they might be able to sneak in." She shook her head, doubtful of the notion even as she uttered it. "But it wouldn't make sense that they'd only want to save themselves."

"Definitely not. They see the other breeds as their ultimate strength. They wouldn't put themselves in the position of being leaders without followers. It's hard to imagine an entire army of Paratwa making it through Colonial customs."

"Do you think they could be planning to engineer some sort of mass escape through Star-Edge?"

"That makes even less sense. Sending giant spaceships on a voyage to the stars with no guarantee of finding habitable planets is a risky proposition to begin with. Besides, it doesn't fit with what we know about them. It would signify a retreat. The Royals wouldn't do that. They're conquerors. I can't think of a single rational reason why they'd want to run off into deep space."

"So what then?" she wondered.

"There is a third possibility. Going underground. Literally. We already suspect that the Ash Ock have been building secret facilities around the world. What if their plan is to go into stasis and ride out the apocalypse? Awaken in some future era when they might have the whole planet to themselves?"

"That's one giant leap of faith. Most estimates are that if an apocalypse does occur, presumably biological, ecological or nuclear, or some combination thereof, it would take hundreds of years for the planet to be made livable again. And if all goes well for the Colonies, the Paratwa would still have a powerful human civilization to deal with when they came out of stasis."

"Good points," Nick admitted. "But two things we already know about the Royals. They're not afraid of bold initiatives and they're partial to long-term planning."

"We need more intel from your source. If this Ektor Fang doesn't have the answers, he must be in a position to uncover them."

"I have no way of contacting him. It's one-way com only. He's more than a bit paranoid about security. He transmits a message when he wants to set up a meeting but the message takes a convoluted path to protect it from being traced. It's sent to a coded net address, rendered into a physical note, then delivered to a private mailbox. Sosoome picks up the mail and brings it to me." Nick paused. "Anyway, next time we meet I'll try to dig more out of him."

Bel went silent for a time. When she finally spoke it was to ask the question that had been challenging Nick since Ektor Fang had made the revelation.

"So what do we do with this information?"

"I don't think there's anything we can do."

"It doesn't seem right just sitting on it."

"Yeah. But here's the thing. We have no way to prove that the Ash Ock are trying to bring on Armageddon. I'm convinced Ektor Fang is right, but without persuasive evidence, releasing it would only cause a lot of public turmoil. And even if there was a way of doing it that wouldn't potentially boomerang on my CI, putting it out there might actually serve to accelerate the Ash Ock's plans."

She nodded. "People would be even more outraged, more hateful of the Paratwa."

"Which could translate into escalated violence and increased conflicts in the world, the exact conditions the Royals seek. Under that scenario, an apocalypse could occur even faster. I think Ektor Fang realized all this when he said that it wasn't actionable intelligence. 'For your background edification only' were his exact words."

Bel seemed to consider his conclusion for a moment. "OK, so I guess we keep it between us, at least for now."

She hopped from the bed and headed for the bathroom. He admired the sway of her naked buttocks in retreat.

"So, girl," he called after her. "You mad I didn't tell you all this stuff sooner?"

She vanished into the bathroom but peeked around the door frame. "No, Nick, I'm not mad. I will say, however, that this isn't the sort of pillow talk to which I'm accustomed."

She closed the door. He smiled and looked forward to seeing her again.

EIGHTEEN

Anyone could make a Cohe wand work. In theory, it was a simple device to operate. Squeezing the egg-shaped weapon sent the deadly black beam coursing from its needle. The amount of hand pressure dictated intensity and distance. The beam's direction was controlled by flicking the wrist.

In practice, however, the Cohe was the most notoriously challenging weapon ever created, which was why the deadlier Paratwa breeds were given toy wands to play with even before they learned to crawl.

By the age of five, a budding assassin was upgraded to a stinger, an operating Cohe that, although nonlethal, could nevertheless give a painful bite. By age ten, most trainees had gained enough respect for the weapon's potential to be given the real thing. And by their teen years, most tways could use their Cohes to devastating effect, either singularly or in tandem.

Humans, by contrast, weren't trained with such ruthless efficiency and were rarely allowed access to weapons at such early ages. It was unusual to find a human who'd even handled a Cohe prior to the typical military service years. And by then, many weapons experts believed it was too late to develop the subtle motor coordination and muscle memory of the assassins.

Possession of a wand by civilians was illegal in most countries, although the enforcement of such laws was generally lax. And because it required such a long and complex training period, most of the world's policing authorities and armies, including special forces, considered the Cohe more trouble than it was worth.

Another negative factor was production cost. Due to a complex manufacturing process, Cohes cost on average fifteen times as much as a conventional projectile or energy sidearm, primarily due to the intricate wetware batteries needed to power them. Consequently, the weapon, originally made by Nagasaki-based Coherence-Kushiro Corp, remained almost exclusively the province of the assassins.

Almost.

Nick stood in the control room, a hastily constructed steel and concrete bunker in the corner of the abandoned warehouse, his attention on an array of video screens and test monitors. Basher and Stone Face stood behind him. Sosoome was sprawled atop an old filing cabinet in the corner. The building wasn't far from the Zilch where Nick had recruited the EPF men. He'd bought it months ago in preparation for converting it into a training facility.

He tabbed the mic switch. "Slag, send him in."

"On his way," the Brit replied on speaker from the adjacent anteroom.

Nick's camera array showed a door opening and a man entering the largest area of the partitioned warehouse, a makeshift gymnasium twenty meters long and half that in width. The walls and ceiling had been reinforced and were further protected with overlapping, high-powered energy shields.

The monthly electric bill could have bankrupted a small nation but the alternative was worse. Although the population in this region of Philly-sec was fairly light, a stray Cohe beam piercing the walls might hit a passing vehicle or pedestrian or, equally bad, result in someone sighting the beam and reporting it to the authorities. Marine or EPF battalions descending on the warehouse in search of a Paratwa assassin were not part of Nick's game plan.

The candidate took his place on the marked spot in the center of the gym. He was of medium height with a slim build. His bio indicated he'd seen action with the US 168th Airborne, which had fought in the bloody Alaska-Yukon border wars.

Nick had begun the process of recruiting the fourth and pivotal member of his Paratwa-fighting team by placing discreet ads on GAN, the Global Arms Net. Concealing his intentions so as not to alarm the authorities or risk attracting a real Paratwa, he'd passed himself off as a scientist needing paid volunteers for a research study. Ostensibly, the study was meant to test the physiological side effects of handheld energy weapons, including the Cohe wand.

Nearly eight hundred men and women had answered the ads. Ninety percent of them had no experience with the Cohe and were eliminated immediately. Almost a quarter of the remainder turned out to be biwannabes, the most extreme version of servitors.

Biwannabes were disturbed individuals who claimed to have been born into the wrong species and glorified all things binary. They believed that by pledging loyalty to the Paratwa, some mystical metamorphosis would occur after they died. *Rebirth comes, two not one!* was their motto and rallying cry. They were convinced that they would be reborn into two bodies, become genuine twofers.

Further computerized psych profiling had reduced the list of potential candidates to seventeen. A deeper set of evaluations and a complex vetting process had whittled that group down to five.

Three of the finalists had been tested yesterday. All had proved unsuitable. One had been a total bust, with reaction times far too slow for combat. The others had been reasonably fast but wildly inaccurate. The final pair of candidates was being tested today.

"Are you ready?" Nick asked.

The man nodded and launched the Cohe into his hand from the slip-wrist holster. Nick triggered the targeting program and carefully observed his monitors.

Three animated training holos shaped like soldiers erupted into existence, two in front of the man and the third behind him. The man nailed the front pair of moving figures with straight Cohe shots to the heart, then whirled to take out the third. His speed and accuracy were impressive.

"Not bad," Basher offered.

Nick shook his head. "You or I could make those kind of head-on shots with a little training. Let's see what he can do with a curved beam."

He gave the instructions for the second phase of the test. The man waved, signaling he was ready. Nick activated a new set of holos, this time limiting the test to two opponents but increasing their speed.

The man fired at the swift-moving figures, flicking his wrist to bend the beam. He tried to hit the one on the right but missed by a meter and nailed the far wall. The beam splattered against the energy shielding in a burst of fireworks.

Nick gave him another chance, then a third. There was no improvement.

"I'm better with head-on shooting," the man explained.

"Yeah, we can see that. But our research schemata are designed to measure the more refined levels of neurological grasp control."

The words were pure gobbledygook. The man nodded as if he understood.

"Thanks for coming in," Nick said.

"I still get my money, right?"

"See Slag on your way out."

Half an hour later, the final candidate arrived. He was tall and fashion-model handsome, with blond hair cascading to his shoulders. Put a cape on him and give him an oversized hammer and Nick figured he could pass for Thor, the old Marvel Comics character.

"Ready?" Nick asked.

Thor twisted his wrists and sent *two* Cohes shooting into his waiting palms from hidden holsters.

"Double your pleasure, double your fun," Sosoome chimed in.

Nick gave him the same test as the first candidate, starting with three holo targets. Thor was even faster. Using only the Cohe in his right hand, he nailed the figures with perfect head shots.

"So far so good," Basher said.

Nick advanced him to the two-target test. This time, using the wand in his left hand, Thor took down both figures with solid chest strikes. Better yet, he curved the beams into gentle arcs.

Nick was starting to get his hopes up. Reaction time, speed and accuracy were all well within the ballpark. Thor had no military background but had spent years as a stunt performer with a Swedish circus. His main act involved firing his twin Cohes and just missing a series of live targets, presumably volunteers.

"Mind if I show you what I can *really* do?" Thor asked.

"Be my guest," Nick said.

"Give me four moving holos, two in front and two behind. Double their speed."

Nick made the proper adjustments. The quartet of figures took shape and raced across the gym floor in different directions.

Thor fell into a crouch, followed their movements for a few seconds. Then he suddenly rose into a pirouette and fired both Cohes simultaneously, using short controlled bursts.

For a moment, the twin beams seemed to be everywhere at once, circling the room in a frenzy. He hit all four targets. Smiling brightly, he took a bow.

"Could be our boy," Basher said.

"If he was a mech, I wouldn't kick him out of bed," Sosoome added.

"Good work," Nick said over the mic. He wasn't yet ready to reveal the true purpose of the testing. But it was time to drop a few hints, determine whether Thor might be willing to put his life on the line.

"Why don't you head back to the anteroom?" he suggested. "Before we proceed further, there are some things I'd like to discuss."

"Of course," Thor said. "But before we do that, allow me to show you my pièce de résistance."

"That's really not necessary."

"Please. It's something I developed only weeks ago. I would be honored to have you bear witness to its very first public performance."

Nick was getting the feeling that no matter how skilled with the wands, Thor lacked certain other qualities necessary for taking on Paratwa assassins. He seemed too applause-driven. Still, with the right kind of training and positive reinforcement, such a flaw might be correctable.

"OK, go ahead, do your thing."

"Same settings, please. Only this time, I will be in full motion as well as the targets."

Nick reactivated the holos. Thor lunged forward in an erratic series of steps while again firing in short bursts. Cohe beams whipped wildly through the room as he dashed amid the curling streams of deadly light. Some of the beams appeared to miss him by centimeters.

"Man's crazy," Basher muttered.

"There's good crazy and bad crazy," Nick said, uncertain which type he was witnessing.

Thor nailed the first two targets dead center, whirled to attack the other pair coming up behind him. But the combination of turning fast and firing at the same instant caused an ever-so-slight miscalculation.

One of the beams boomeranged on him. He seemed to dash right into the black streak. It pierced his chest. A surprised look crossed his face as he crumpled to the floor.

"Not quite performance level," Sosoome said drily.

Slag raced out of the anteroom, checked for a pulse. He shook his head. Thor had done his final act.

"Well, that's fucked," Basher said.

The accident was a crippling blow to Nick's plans. Not only was the man dead but he'd been the best candidate by far. Placing a new series of ads was unlikely to attract a better crop.

A dismal thought took shape. It had taken more than a year to develop the sim built around a four-person Paratwa-assault team fronted by an expert with the Cohe. Yet now he might have to abandon the entire concept and return to the drawing board.

Slag ambled into the bunker. "What now, mate?"

"How did our candidate get here?" Nick asked.

"Taxi. Came alone."

Sosoome broached the obvious question. "Any of you gentlemen have experience disposing of bodies?"

Stone Face stepped forward, gave a deep-throated drawl worthy of his vocal prototype.

"I'll take care of it."

NINETEEN

Very little about her new boyfriend surprised Bel anymore. After two weeks together, she supposed she was getting accustomed to Nick's capacity for making astonishing claims and taking unexpected actions. Still, when he sauntered into her apartment and realized just who her other guest was, she'd secretly hoped it was her turn to surprise him.

No such luck.

She didn't even get the chance to make introductions. Doctor Emanuel rose on his cane from his seat by the window, his face brightening. Nick rushed toward him with a delighted smile.

"Weldon! Great seeing you again in the flesh. Been too long this time."

"It has indeed, my boy. It has indeed."

They embraced warmly, patting each other on the back. Her boyfriend and her personal hero not only knew one another but apparently were old and intimate friends. Bel acknowledged a stab of jealousy but instantly rebuked herself for feeling that way. Doctor Emanuel had outlived his entire family. If he'd found in Nick a warm friend, who was she to resent it?

"How'd the two of you meet?" she asked.

"The doc would probably call it fate," Nick said. "But it was more me learning all about him when I came out of stasis and being thoroughly impressed. I desperately wanted us to get together. I tracked him down and hounded him for a while. He finally concluded I wasn't a stalker."

"A rocky start," Doctor Emanuel admitted. "But we worked at it, helped it grow into a most worthwhile relationship. Nick is a remarkable individual as I'm sure you're already aware."

"He's OK," Bel said with a bored tone and straight face. Although she and Nick had agreed to keep their affair confidential, she'd felt comfortable confiding in Doctor Emanuel.

It was early Sunday evening, a rare occasion when she wasn't at the office. She'd invited them both for dinner.

Her condo was on the hundred and first floor, with a window wall facing west. The smog had been particularly brutal of late, a smothering envelope of browns and grays constricting the vista in the fading daylight. An apartment in the skyscraper down the street at her level had a balcony greenhouse full of orchids and roses, dazzlingly colorful and exquisitely cared for. But over the past few weeks, the greenhouse might as well have been located within one of the lunar or Martian research bases. She hadn't glimpsed so much as a single flower.

The ToFo had climbed to nine-point-seven, one of the worst air toxicity days Philly had ever experienced. Even with the proper meds, air masks were being recommended for more than a few hours of outside exposure.

Back when Bel was in her early twenties, she'd campaigned vigorously – albeit naively – for local voters to pass a resolution authorizing Philadelphia to become a respirazone. The measure had been soundly defeated. The huge cost of ringing the area in atmospheric detoxers would have required a serious tax increase. It had been an early lesson for her in the truism that people voted with their wallets.

Still, she sometimes found it amazing that the majority

of the world's masses didn't try moving into the existing respirazones. Despite their relatively clean air, many of the zones were actually sparsely populated.

Human beings can adapt to anything, even air unfit for breathing. Such adaptability was the species' greatest blessing, as well as its curse.

Bel hadn't ventured past the walls of her sealed condo since yesterday. She'd popped her meds an hour ago and inhaled a monthly lung restorative prescribed by her ecospheric physician. She usually tried to avoid the restorative as she was prone to its side effects. The complex drug cocktail left her feeling intoxicated.

Doctor Emanuel was nursing a goblet of cabernet sauvignon. Nick poured himself a glass and extended the bottle toward Bel. She shook her head. More alcohol would certainly worsen her condition.

"Hope you're hungry," she offered, waving them toward the dining area, part of a single large space that constituted the majority of her center city home. The condo featured sleek metallic furniture. She'd offset its chrome chill with a bevy of earth-toned cushions and abstract wall hangings rich in ambers, greens and maroons.

Earlier in the week she'd broken down and purchased a drudge to handle cheffing, serving and cleaning. She'd run the decision by the regents first to make sure they didn't feel it was too ostentatious and violated the spirit of E-Tech's limitations on excessive technology. They'd dismissed her concerns. Any device that could save time and effort on the home front was worthwhile, they'd assured her. It would allow her more hours for important work.

A simple drudge was far down the ladder from the sort of multifunctional personal mech that Nick owned. However, having experienced Sosoome's mouth in action one too many times, she'd ordered the drudge without a speech module.

She signaled through her fob, instructing the drudge to

bring out the first course. Nick and Doctor Emanuel took their seats. Elevator legs on Nick's chair automatically raised him to table height.

The drudge emerged from the kitchen balancing a large serving platter on an upraised hand. The mech was humanoid, slightly shorter than Nick, and had come equipped with a wardrobe. Although she found it rather silly, today the drudge had elected to don the black suit and bowtie of a traditional maître d. The outfit was apparently meant to give the impression that they were dining at a four-star restaurant.

Bel moved toward the table to join her guests. But in her inebriated state she tripped over a chair leg and came perilously close to taking a tumble.

"You OK?" Nick asked, rising from his chair.

"Absolutely. No problem whatsoever."

She ought to come right out and tell them about the side effect from the lung restorative. But she felt oddly embarrassed to make the admission.

"How come no Sosoome this evening?" she asked Nick, watching the drudge carefully as it spooned seasoned broccoli soup into their bowls. Even though mechs had been ubiquitous in her household growing up, she hadn't used one in years. Tonight was something of a trial run. She hoped the drudge would perform to spec.

"I had some chores for him this evening," Nick said. "Besides, he'd probably try hitting on your new friend." Nick gestured to the drudge as it leaned over the table to ladle their soup.

"It's an asexual model."

"Sosoome's not that fussy."

The three of them traded small talk through the main course of orange-braised tilapia, one of the few ocean-raised fishes still abundant enough not to be on the endangered species list. Bel found it delicious. Her guests' expressions indicated agreement.

As the drudge cleared the table in preparation for dessert, Doctor Emanuel asked if there'd been any progress on recruiting a fourth team member. Nick had kept Bel abreast of the issue and, obviously, had confided in the doctor.

"No luck," Nick said, shaking his head. "I've run a host of new ads, widened the search. We reviewed dozens of fresh candidates. But none have come close to having the skills that my sim indicates are required."

Doctor Emanuel turned to Bel. "What do you think of Nick's plan?"

"I think it's important to consider all options for combatting the assassins."

"A very reasonable answer, yet one that I suspect hinges on the necessity of navigating political waters. Clearly, this is not something that falls within the jurisdiction of E-Tech bylaws. A secret team of soldier-hunters whose purpose is destroying Paratwa would be construed by many, including a fair number of the regents, as lowering ourselves to the level of the assassins. Killers going after killers."

"Such people are likely in the minority," Nick pointed out.

"Indeed. But frankly, I'd like to hear Bel's genuine feelings on the matter." He smiled to take the sting out of his next words. "The carefully filtered responses of 'Director Bakana' have no place among the three of us at this table."

He was putting her on the spot. Yet even alone with the two men she'd come to trust more than anyone else in the world, Bel remained hesitant. She'd guarded against broaching her real feelings about the Paratwa for a long time.

They were watching her intently. She had a sudden thought that the two of them had conspired to push her into a disclosure. Normally that might have bothered her but at the moment she couldn't care less. If past experience with the lung restorative's side effects were any measure, her drunkenness was rapidly approaching its peak.

"All right, gentlemen. Since you have my back against the

wall and insist on pushing, I'll say here and now what I will never utter publicly. Naturally, this is to go no further than this room."

She rose to her feet but immediately felt woozy. She gripped the table edge for support, hoping they wouldn't notice.

"Even before Nick told me about the Royals' desire to bring on an apocalypse, even before the attack on headquarters, I've believed this: we should end the threat of the Paratwa permanently." She decided her remarks required more venom. "We need to wipe out those suckers! And do it before it's too damn late!"

Cursing wasn't her strong suit. From an early age, her parents had encouraged her not to swear. It was one of the aspects of their childrearing that betrayed an old-fashioned upper-class snobbery – persons of refinement could always find dignified words to express their feelings.

"It's not just blind hatred," she clarified, feeling flushed as she sat back down. "I admit to sometimes experiencing that, though. After the attack, I fantasized about ways to hurt the assassin who attacked us, cause him extreme pain. I even had a dream that he'd been captured and I was watching him being tortured."

Such an event was likely to occur only in a dream. As far as anyone knew, no Paratwa assassin had ever been captured. They fought to the death. Always. And if one tway died in combat, its surviving half quickly descended into incurable madness and committed suicide.

A solemn feeling came over her. "Does it make me a bad person to want to do something like that? Does it lower me to the level of an Alvis Qwee?"

Doctor Emanuel grimaced at the name. Even among other Paratwa assassins, Alvis Qwee was said to invoke disgust. A Du Pal, the same breed as Ektor Fang, Alvis Qwee had been terrorizing the west coast from San Francisco to Vancouver, British Columbia, for the past eighteen months.

Alvis Qwee kidnapped families, apparently at random. He tortured and ultimately murdered the family members in front of one another, but always selected one of them to be spared from any harm. The survivor was set free at the end of the ordeal. Not surprisingly, the survivors were left with terrible psychological scars. Many of them later took their own lives.

"You're nothing like that freak," Nick assured her. "Alvis Qwee is an outright sadist."

Doctor Emanuel reached across the table, laid his hand on hers. "Nick's right. And your desire to see the creature that attacked headquarters suffer is based on the anger and revulsion you feel at the slaughter of your fellow workers. It's a natural response, wanting to hurt those who've hurt us. It doesn't lessen your humanity."

Bel wasn't so sure about that. She found herself staring at the far wall, consumed by silence. An immense sadness came over her. Despite Doctor Emanuel's reassuring words, she was sure that such violent feelings of revenge and her abiding hatred of the assassins were far from normal. There must be a better way for people to live.

A distant horizon seemed to beckon, a place untouched by the everyday horrors of the late twenty-first century, a realm swaddled in the grander and nobler qualities of human beings. A realm of peace and comradeship. A realm where sadistic Paratwa didn't torture families and human mothers didn't try immolating their own babies.

The idea of babies again brought to mind her growing urge to become a mother. She wasn't about to let herself get pregnant, not now, not with the immense responsibilities inherent in the director's job. Still, the notion seemed to trickle into consciousness at least once a day.

She noticed Nick and Doctor Emanuel trading puzzled looks at her distracted state.

Get it together, Bel. She forced concentration back to Doctor

Emanuel's original question.

"The truth is, I don't believe we have any choice but to wipe out the Paratwa," she told them. "They're superior to us in so many ways. Worse, they know it. If we allow the binary threat to continue to grow, I believe they'll eventually supplant humans."

"Evolution 101," Nick agreed. "They're the dominant species in this ecosystem. It's analogous to *Homo sapiens* versus *Homo neanderthalensis*. Except this time we're on the losing end, the ones threatened with eventual extinction."

An idea occurred to Bel, something she hadn't considered. In light of her diminished capacity, she was surprised she could still process such cogent thoughts.

"Anything that might escalate the conflict between humans and Paratwa serves the Royal Caste's needs, correct?"

The two men nodded.

"So, about their desire to bring on an apocalypse. I wonder if they somehow could have learned of my real feelings about them, what I just expressed here. Could that have something to do with the reason they wanted me to become the next E-Tech Director?"

"An interesting idea," Nick said, after a few moments' thought. "In theory, the more dedicated their enemies, the faster their desired apocalypse occurs. Still, I tend to doubt it. Besides, you said you've never revealed these feelings to anyone. Frankly, if you had, it would be plastered all over the net by now."

"The purpose behind their manipulation lies elsewhere," Doctor Emanuel said. "I've studied the Royals for many years. They constitute a level of behind-the-scenes social engineering that far surpasses history's typical dictators. They've elevated such manipulation to an art." He paused. "Think of them as painting a picture of how they want the world to be. However, the broad brush strokes are not where we should look for their rationales. Their true motivations lie in the subtlety of the colors."

Bel was still mulling that over when the drudge returned to the table with coffee and dessert, a lemon-lime mousse. They interrupted their discussion long enough to sample the delicate pudding. Finishing first, she resisted the temptation to order a second cup.

Doctor Emanuel ended the interlude. "On the issue of Nick's team of soldier-hunters, it appears the three of us are in agreement. It would be to humanity's benefit to utterly destroy the Paratwa."

Bel nodded, hiding her surprise at Doctor Emanuel's strong opinion on the matter. Having admired him from a distance for so long and having always perceived him as a beacon for peaceful conflict resolution, it was strange hearing him talk this way. In truth, his views seemed to mirror Nick's. Under the surface, the two of them were more alike than she had initially thought.

The older man continued, "However, the idea of eliminating the binaries is likely an impossible task. There are tens of thousands of them, with those trained as assassins estimated to comprise at least six or seven thousand of that total. One small team, no matter how successful, would not make a substantial dent in those numbers."

"The benefit of the team would be primarily psychological," Nick said.

"Exactly. Its successes would inspire hope among the populace, promote a sense of optimism that Paratwa assassins can be defeated by methods that don't result in overwhelming losses of troops and civilians. A positive outcome for the team would spill over into other aspects of people's lives. It could serve to instill a renewed sense of pride in our species."

"Humans aren't helpless," Bel said. "We can fight back and win against an enemy perceived to be superior."

Doctor Emanuel nodded. "Yet the very nature of this team carries with it a serious drawback. It would need to operate in total secrecy. In no way could it have any direct connection with E-Tech or any other public organization."

"Absolutely not," Bel said, mortified at the idea.

"Paratwa retribution against anyone openly sponsoring such a team would be immediate and devastating."

"For a different reason, it also shouldn't be linked to or run by any military units or intelligence agencies," Nick added. "EPF, the CIA and others have the skills and savvy to run black ops, but they'd end up involving too many people. There'd be a heightened possibility of the missions being compromised by leaks."

"A small operation," Doctor Emanuel continued, "overseen solely by the three of us. Great care and effort will need to be taken in publicizing the team's successes. Not only to protect the team from exposure but to endow it with a kind of superhero mythos."

"Humanity's Avenger," Bel murmured, "striking from the shadows."

"I like the metaphor," Nick said. "And we could use the notion to publicize the team. Careful leaks to certain underground organizations, whispered rumors spread throughout sec and unsec regions. If we do it right, knowledge of the team's successes will migrate up from the street and disseminate to all corners. People will vicariously adopt this Paratwa slayer as one of their own. They'll share in the knowledge that Earth has a secret champion. Humanity's Avenger."

Doctor Emanuel turned to Bel. "Your media relations skills could come in handy in this regard."

She nodded, aware of several avenues of exploitation that wouldn't carry any risk of blowback on E-Tech. "But aren't we all forgetting something?"

Nick gave a wry grin. "Yeah. A fly in the ointment, as they used to say."

Doctor Emanuel raised an eyebrow. "Might you be referring

to the fact that you do not yet have a fourth member to make your team viable?"

"Kind of a buzz kill, isn't it, doc? But without someone skilled with the Cohe, all of my team simulations break down. The next best possible outcome, one that doesn't require someone to be wielding a Cohe wand, is a sim that would require a minimum of twenty-seven soldiers."

"Four versus twenty-seven?" Bel wondered. "Why such a big gap?"

"The formidable power of the Cohe. Plus, once you go above four, the soldiers start getting in one another's way. They become a liability during combat instead of an asset. The sims become increasingly chaotic until you reach that higher number, at which point there's an entropic crossover that reintroduces stability."

"I'll take your word for it."

"Twenty-seven does constitute somewhat better numbers than the current success rate enjoyed by traditional companies or battalions," Doctor Emanuel offered.

"Yeah," Nick said. "Still, not exactly the sort of odds to inspire hero worship."

"Indeed."

"So where do we go from here?" Bel asked, rubbing her temples. She was starting to get a headache. It was generally the final aspect of the inhalant's inebriation effect.

Doctor Emanuel scooped the last of his mousse from the cup. He took a long sip of coffee before favoring them with a cryptic smile.

"I believe, my young friends, that I have a potential solution. Where we need to go from here is deep into the unknown, into uncharted realms."

TWENTY

Within days of the after-dinner conspiracy hatched by Bel, Nick and Doctor Emanuel, the first phase had been achieved.

Nick had tapped his own funds to offer another bribe to the Earth Patrol Forces. This time, the amount contributed to EPF's ever needy treasury as well as enriching the personal accounts of the officers and hundreds of grunts who would take part in the assault.

Bel had done her part. With her director's access to the highest level intel from E-Tech Intelligence, data that even Nick had trouble hacking, she'd forwarded the appropriate information to him. That had helped nail down the identity of a number of possibilities. Nick had combined Bel's intel with some facts he'd dug up on his own to make the selection.

Doctor Emanuel naturally had final say. He approved Nick's choice. The assassin in question was deemed a suitable candidate.

Although they hadn't been able to identify the breed of their target, they had established its locality. This assassin lived and killed within a limited geographic region, a densely populated area of Upper Bavaria, Germany.

Most Paratwa, particularly those not under the sway of the Ash Ock, were territorial, doing their killing within relatively small areas generally encompassing no more than twenty-five thousand square kilometers. Nick had designed a series of computer programs for tracking down the assassins based on probability analysis. His programs analyzed subtle movement patterns and assigned probabilities to a Paratwa's whereabouts at any given moment.

The EPF battalion had been given the greenlight. Three hundred and fifty seasoned soldiers, including two Delta-A squads, had surrounded and stormed an auto parts store that the Paratwa owned and operated when it wasn't earning its primary income murdering humans. The creature lived onsite, having converted a section of the store into a modest home complete with an impressive wine cellar. Within the stone walls of that cool and dank subterranean vault, it made its final stand.

The assault was successful – a single tway was terminated. As expected, the victory came at a severe cost. Seventy-nine soldiers died and scores of others were injured. The assassin's lair had been heavily booby-trapped. Casualties not resulting from Cohe wand strikes and thruster blasts had been caused by frag grenades, heat-seeking firedarts and a dirt floor mined with acid twisters that had sprayed the assault team with skin-melting fluids.

The surviving troops, aware they would receive hefty bonuses should the mission be carried out to the letter, rose to the occasion. Encouraged by Slag, who had accompanied the attackers as Nick's liaison, the soldiers restrained their lust to avenge their fallen comrades and succeeded in capturing the other tway alive. Slag had administered a powerful soporific to keep the creature in a deep state of unconsciousness lest it succumb to bisectional hemiosis, the technical term for the screaming madness of a Paratwa quite literally torn in half, and which if left unchecked quickly led to its suicide.

After the attack, the troops had vaporized the auto parts store with a micronuke to eliminate any evidence of a survivor. The tway had been placed in a stasis coffin and whisked off the continent aboard an EPF suborbital flight.

Slag and the colonel in charge of the assault had delivered the tway and its Cohe wand to Nick's clandestine warehouse, where a first-class mobile surgical theater had been set up. The colonel hadn't been told the reason they needed a living tway for surgery and remained furious about the loss of his troops. He'd expressed his profound hope that Nick would subject the tway to the most horrific of surgical procedures, all without benefit of anesthesia. Escorting the man out, Nick promised they'd do their best.

The EPF troops had garnered intel from the assassin's lair before vaporizing it. They'd nailed down the slain Paratwa's origins. It was a Fifteen-Forty, a moderately dangerous breed. Initially created and trained in the genetic labs of virulent, anti-Rome Jesuits, the priests had been forced to sell their entire operation in a bankruptcy proceeding to a Canadian intermodal transportation firm whose owners were eager to expand into more profitable arenas.

Fifteen-Forties, like many breeds, were sold as mercs. But once an assassin's period of indentured servitude was fulfilled and its owner fully compensated, most were set free to pursue their own futures. A small percentage retired, but the majority, like this Fifteen-Forty, went into business for themselves as independent contract killers.

Although a Fifteen-Forty wasn't considered as outright nasty as a Voshkof Rabbit or a Jeek Elemental, it possessed a midlevel skill set on par with breeds like the Du Pal. And as Nick could attest, Ektor Fang was no slouch when it came to wielding a Cohe wand.

"A perfect candidate, huh?" Nick said as he scrubbed for the operation beside Doctor Emanuel. The doc would perform the neurosurgery remotely using a tentacled med robot. Nick would be available in case any routine assistance was required.

"Far less than perfect," Doctor Emanuel complained as

they finished scrubbing and entered the OR. "The candidate suffered a moderate head injury prior to being subdued. That could negatively impact the implantation process."

"Couldn't be helped," Slag said over the intercom speaker. He was observing with Basher and Stone Face from beyond a glass partition. "The prick needed some persuading to go down. A couple of the soldiers love-tapped him with their sandrams."

"These aren't love taps," Doctor Emanuel replied.

Nick had to agree. The left side of the tway's head was bloodstained and partially caved in from multiple blows with the hammerlike weapon. Still, none of the brain scans showed signs of permanent damage. Neurologically, this surviving half remained intact, or at least intact enough for the surgery to have an eighty percent survival rate according to standard World Health Organization guidelines, at least if it was performed on a normal person. However, considering that the procedure was never known to have been done on a tway, such percentages probably weren't applicable. As the doc had stated at Bel's dinner table that night, he was going to take them into uncharted realms.

Doctor Emanuel finished programming the med robot. It descended slowly from the ceiling on stiff cables, reminding Nick of the facehugger from a monster movie he'd seen as a kid. As he recalled, the movie had scared the crap out of him.

Three of the robot's tentacled hands clamped the tway's head to keep it stable. A fourth pierced the front of the skull with an interlocked set of microdrills. Hands five and six descended with the implants.

Doctor Emanuel monitored the procedure from his control panel, making slight programming corrections as the drills withdrew. He inserted the first set of tiny mnemonic cursors deep into the ancient reptilian part of the brain that controlled the body's most vital functions, then added distribution connections to the later evolved limbic system and neocortex.

Together, that trio of neurological components roughly corresponded to the physical, emotional and intellectual functions of consciousness.

It was a lengthy procedure. Judging by the doc's frequent nods and occasional soft muttering, it seemed to Nick that things were going well.

"The seventh and final insertion," Doctor Emanuel said at last.

Almost two hours had passed since the surgery had begun. Like the six earlier sets of mnemonic cursors, the final one sparked to life on one of the monitor screens. It had successfully begun the process of interfacing with a wealth of synaptic junctions throughout the tway's triune consciousness.

"We good?" Nick asked.

"At this stage, yes."

"Congrats, doc. Looks like you haven't lost your touch."

Doctor Emanuel unleashed an uncharacteristic grunt as he leaned back in his chair. "These days, *touch* for a neurosurgeon is quite the misnomer. The only thing I touch now is a control panel. Back when I was a young man and a neurosurgical intern, we were still doing a fair portion of such operations the old-fashioned way."

"Sounds bloody," Nick said, noting that the doc was gripping the chair's armrests to stop the occasional trembling of his hands, an effect of old age that even the best meds couldn't control.

"How long before he's ready?" Basher asked over the speaker.

"Twenty-four hours for post-op recovery," Doctor Emanuel replied. "Another day or two of submnemonic probing to ascertain whether full synaptic reconfiguration has taken place. If he's doing well at that time, we'll move forward into the final stages, hypnotic trancing followed by facial reconstruction."

"And then he'll be ready to pick up his Cohe?"

"If his spirit is willing."

Nick knew the real test would come after those milestones were reached. Would synaptic reconfiguration, performed successfully on humans, work with a tway? Would the false memories they'd implanted by way of the mnemonic cursors be potent enough to overcome bisectional hemiosis?

When he awakened, would this remnant of a binary accept as normal the set of artificial thoughts and feelings that Nick and Bel had crafted for him, reinforced by the brand new face he'd be receiving? Would he be able to totally forget his real heritage? Would he believe he was actually a human named Jannik Mutter, a man whose beloved brother had been slain by a Paratwa assassin?

And, most critically of all, would Jannik Mutter possess the right combination of rage and willpower to motivate him to seek vengeance against the Paratwa assassins for the death of an imaginary sibling?

TWENTY-ONE

Bishop Rikov was too stunned to fully process the news. For ten minutes he just sat there in his private quarters three stories below the Church of the Trust's new London cathedral, staring at the special transceiver. The dyap resembled an upended corkscrew mounted on a dinner plate. It was one of only ten in existence.

Invented by the brilliant Theophrastus, the dyap violated Einsteinian physics to allow the widely scattered tways of the Ash Ock to send faster-than-lightspeed messages to one another with no possibility of interception. It was the prototype for an even grander FTL transmitter, one that Theophrastus believed would enable communication over truly monumental distances.

But from this moment on, a pair of those ten dyaps would be silent. A member of the Royal Caste, a member of the most powerful and exclusive group of creatures to ever grace planet Earth, had perished.

Bishop Rikov found himself unwilling to believe the report, but it had come directly from Sappho. There could be little doubt of its veracity.

Aristotle was gone.

His tways, one the mogul of a Venezuelan energy corporation, the other the prime minister of Free Brazil, had perished when a fire-fall nuke was detonated above Cape

Town, South Africa, where the monarch had been staying. Thus far, no terrorist organization was claiming credit for the nuking, which was believed to have resulted in over a million civilian deaths.

The bishop felt nothing for those casualties. After all, most if not all were mere humans. But the untimely loss of Aristotle, who through bad luck just happened to be in the city...

That was worthy of being mourned.

A powerful desire came over the bishop to do just that, to bring on the interlace, to unite into his monarch, Codrus. He could sense the faint presence of his tway, who had just received the identical news through his own dyap. Although his tway was thousands of kilometers away, an interlink could be accomplished irrespective of distance.

But he also knew his tway's schedule and now was not a good time. The E-Tech Board of Regents was about to begin their afternoon meeting in Philadelphia. As his tway was a member of that esteemed group, any sudden alteration of consciousness – two tways linking into monarchy – might be noticed by one of the other regents. And then there was Doctor Emanuel, whose keenness of mind was greater than his advanced years might indicate.

Bishop Rikov sighed. True mourning would have to wait until he and his tway were simultaneously free of obligations. For now, he would have to settle for a dulling of the emotions.

He got on the intercom to one of his assistants, gave the woman explicit instructions that for the next hour he was not to be disturbed. Unlocking a private liquor cabinet, the bishop withdrew one of his finest bi-bottled wines. The double-necked glass container was partitioned to contain a '69 Argentine malbec and a '71 New Zealand sauvignon blanc. He preferred the red; his tway enjoyed the white. Ideally, they enjoyed their drinks together.

He uncorked the malbec neck, allowed the wine to breathe briefly before filling his glass. Sappho and Theophrastus had

never shown any interest in the joys of a fine wine. Aristotle
had been the only monarch to share Codrus's passion.

Turning his chair symbolically toward the south, the
direction of Cape Town, the bishop raised his glass. "A toast
to the departed. To Aristotle of the Ash Ock."

He took a long sip. The wine went down smoothly. A
fruity aftertaste lingered, a mix of mulberry, raspberry and
seventeen delicate spices, each readily identifiable. Aristotle
and his tways, fellow oenophiles and malbec connoisseurs,
would have given the wine a most favorable rating.

TWENTY-TWO

The Board of Regents had elected to emerge from secrecy and again gather in the spacious fifty-sixth floor conference room at E-Tech headquarters. It was felt that an E-Tech safe house would be of little deterrent to any future assassination attempts.

Bel was running a few minutes late. Considering how far she had to travel to get here – hop an elevator near her office and descend one floor – she had no excuse. Still, there was a reason for her tardiness. Just minutes ago, Intelligence Director Pablo Dominguez had made a startling revelation, one that she didn't dare to share with the board. She was still dwelling on the impact of what he'd divulged when she reached the corridor outside the conference room.

Security Chief Bull Idwicki had stationed a trio of armed guards at the door. They made Bel go through a scanner, show ID and repeat a code phrase before allowing her to pass. She'd gritted her teeth, annoyed that the procedure tacked extra moments onto her tardiness.

Recently, she'd called Idwicki to her office to voice her doubts about the effectiveness of his beefed-up security, particularly the bodyguards who accompanied her everywhere outside the building. He'd taken offense.

"The men and women I've assigned to protect your life

are seasoned veterans, each one of them an A-plus graduate of multiple training seminars," he'd boasted. "Their abilities cannot be questioned."

Everybody's abilities can be questioned, she'd wanted to counter, equally annoyed that he hadn't really responded to her criticism.

Idwicki was a compact man of large girth whose first name was eminently suitable. Nick said he was built like a brick shithouse and had a mind to match. It was a peculiar description but one that seemed fitting.

She'd learned to take Bull Idwicki's bold pronouncements with a modicum of skepticism. But as annoying as she found him, she knew that attempting to have him replaced would result in expending a great deal of political capital. Over the years, the Security Chief had managed to ingratiate himself with many of the regents. They'd held him blameless in the attack on headquarters, preferring to take the commonly held view that an encounter with a Paratwa assassin was comparable to an unpredictable onslaught of bad weather – in the parlance of the insurance industry, an act of god. Bull Idwicki's entire approach to his job seemed based on simply ignoring problems that were beyond the capabilities of his department to handle.

As Bel entered the conference room, she passed a young woman in the uniform of a private security service on her way out. That meant the meeting was starting late anyway.

The woman carried a multiphase scanner. Board president Suzanna Al-Harthi was obsessively concerned – some might say paranoid – about the possibility of electronic eavesdropping. Even though Bull Idwicki had his Security people sweep regularly for bugs, Al-Harthi insisted that their efforts be confirmed by her own independent contractor, and done so just moments before the start of every meeting.

As usual, all fifteen regents were present. Today, eight were here in person and seven were holocommuting. Doctor

Emanuel occupied his usual corner seat. Bel took her place at the head of the table.

"I apologize for running a bit late," she offered. "I have to remember to add a bit more time to allow our Security people to do their jobs."

Al-Harthi gave a curt nod and opened the meeting by deferring to one of the virtual regents, Lois Perlman. A tall woman with fishnetted black hair, she was science adviser to the Mideast Coalition. She struck Bel as a woman who would appear graceful in any social setting.

Perlman began with a report on the latest E-Tech plan to secure the backing of some of the Mideast Coalition's less advanced nations and city-states. Understandably, those governments wanted to catch up to their more sophisticated brethren before having to limit their own sci-tech development. Perlman was proposing substantial grant monies to lessen their objections and smooth the waters.

Bel listened only half-heartedly. Instead, she kept scanning those fifteen faces as the words of Pablo Dominguez echoed in her mind.

We have a mole among the regents.

The Intelligence head had passed along the startling news during a hastily called private meeting. Dominguez was physically imposing, two meters in height with a chiseled face and long black hair. His lineage went back to a Spanish colonist who'd mated with a Native American woman of the Lenni Lenape tribe in the eighteenth century.

"One of the regents is secretly feeding information to the Royal Caste," he'd announced grimly. "We do not know his or her identity."

It was well known that delicate matters discussed at board meetings often found their way into the media. Various individuals or factions among the regents were savvy at the old political game of leaking information to gain support for pet projects or other initiatives. But Bel found it hard to believe the board had been infiltrated by a servitor and said so.

"Our intel does not necessarily point toward a servitor," Dominguez said. "Evidence supports the contention that the mole could actually be the tway of a Paratwa assassin."

She'd sent Nick a message immediately to tell him the news. He revealed rare surprise but also voiced suspicion about the validity of Dominguez's intel. Although the Intelligence head was proving to be a solid supporter of Bel's initiatives, Nick had the impression that he was a bit resentful of her promotion.

"Could be dirty tricks on his part," Nick proposed. "Feeding you false intel to poison your relationship with the regents."

The idea wasn't completely off the wall. Bel knew there was a certain amount of jealousy on the part of the associate directors. Many of them, as well as others throughout the organization, believed that Pablo Dominguez should have been promoted to Executive Director and were disappointed when the regents chose her. Still, she preferred to believe he wouldn't go so far as to lie in order to sabotage her.

Nick had said he hoped to learn more about the mole this evening. Whether it was coincidental or related to Dominguez's intel, Ektor Fang had just contacted him for another clandestine meeting across the border. The Du Pal would be in communication again shortly to provide details for their rendezvous.

"I want to meet him," Bel had messaged. "I'm coming with you."

"Not a good idea. He will object. We only meet alone."

"Not this time. Like it or not, tell him I'll be there."

"Director Bakana, any comments on Ms Perlman's report?"

Al-Harthi's question drew Bel's attention back to the conference room.

"Nothing at this time," she said, having reviewed the plan prior to the board meeting. "But I would like to have

Operations do a more detailed analysis before we commit resources in the form of grants."

"Agreed?" Al-Harthi asked, scanning the faces for dissenters and seeing none. "Moving on, I'd like to discuss the proposal for streamlining our colonial immigration program–"

"Important as that may be," Vok Shen's holo interrupted, "I would suggest that the attack on Cape Town receive our full and immediate attention. We should discuss a substantial aid package."

Bel suspected the Asian industrialist's concerns weren't strictly humanitarian. One of Vok Shen's corporations had a subsidiary based in Cape Town. A factory had been destroyed and an unknown number of his employees killed.

She automatically turned her attention to R Jobs Headly even before the younger man stood. Her experience with the board thus far had revealed a number of ongoing conflicts between members, none more intense than the constant and somewhat childish feuding between Shen and Headly. It had devolved to the point that if one man said yes, the other said no automatically, and vice versa.

"The Cape Town tragedy certainly deserves our attention," Headly said, offering up his trademark faint smile, which Bel suspected was mainly intended to annoy Shen. "But I would suggest we stick to Ms Al-Harthi's meeting agenda."

"A death toll of more than a million souls is certainly more important than streamlining a bureaucracy," Vok Shen snapped.

Al-Harthi, as ever thrust into the role of peacemaker between the two, held up her hand. "Gentlemen, please. Is this really worth an argument? Both issues will be addressed in due course."

Bel's wrist fob pulsed, indicating she had a message. She unrolled her pad, read the note. It was from Nick.

He says OK, you can come along. But you're not going to like where we're going or how we need to get there.

TWENTY-THREE

Nick was right. Bel didn't like the location of tonight's encounter with Ektor Fang. She'd almost changed her mind twice during the short interval between leaving Nick's apartment on the back of his Chevy Destello and reaching their initial destination.

He was also correct in that she didn't like how they needed to get there. The midnight incursion into Philly-unsec had to be done covertly and at an out of the way location far from the nearest transit station. With Nick's help, she'd arranged to sneak away from her bodyguards. There'd be hell to pay when Bull Idwicki confronted her about it in the morning, but that was the least of her concerns.

If she and Nick were caught attempting to enter unsecured territory illegally, that alone would create a firestorm within E-Tech, horrifying her staff, coworkers and regents. Bad enough that such a crossing in either direction was considered a felony. Even worse would be the political blowback. She could see the headlines plastered across the newsphere.

E-Tech Director snared in attempt to sneak into unsecured regions.

Mystery rendezvous entices head of E-Tech to risk the terrors of the zoo.

Annabel Bakana: Arrogant? Above the law? Undiagnosed mental health issues?

But as Nick had explained, a legal crossing through a transit station wasn't an option. E-Tech would surely be notified and there'd be too many questions she couldn't answer. Even if they used fake permits and she employed a physical disguise, it was unlikely she'd fool the DNA scanners and other sensors.

Still, no matter the risk, she was determined to meet Nick's source. Her reasons were complex and perhaps not altogether rational.

The idea of being up close and personal with a Paratwa, actually having a conversation with it, intrigued her. She'd spoken to them before but they'd always been from the entertainment field: standup comedy duets, selfboxers, antonymous acrobats, all swift and pleasantly diverting. Those binaries, once she'd gotten over the inherent oddness of their possessing dual bodies, seemed altogether human, capable of experiencing laughter and tears and every emotion in between. Yet they were said to be a far cry from the creature she would encounter tonight.

Twice in her life she'd had close calls with assassins. During the most recent one, the attack on headquarters, she'd hidden in a closet. But on the first occasion, that luxury hadn't been available. She'd come within a few meters of the Paratwa.

The incident had occurred at the tender age of eleven while vacationing with her parents in Abu Dhabi. Strife between religious factions led to an assassin being hired to slaughter worshippers on their way to a mosque.

Although Bel and her parents had been on the periphery of the attack, she could still recall the horror of seeing soldiers decapitated by the slashing Cohe beams wielded by the tways. Moments later the creature had run past them in back-to-back formation. She remembered being terrified at those four churning legs, at those two heads rhythmically jerking back and forth as they scanned for threats.

What happened in Abu Dhabi had shaped a lifetime attitude toward the Paratwa. It had propelled her toward the belief that every last one of them needed to be destroyed.

She knew that such savage emotions, amplified by the attack on headquarters, were irrational. Lately, a growing feeling had come upon her that she needed to walk a brighter path. She found herself increasingly imagining that distant horizon, where peace and comradeship reigned in place of the endless hatred and violence between those born as one and those born as two.

That feeling had led her to speculate whether there might be another side to the assassins. Did they possess qualities above and beyond their ferocious reputations, qualities that offered an opportunity for reconciliation, for a chance at harmonious coexistence with humans? Could Ektor Fang, whom Nick described as intelligent and well-educated, reveal a means to reaching that brighter path?

Bel wasn't overly optimistic. Still, she needed to explore the possibility, seek answers to those questions.

Nick made a sharp right turn off the main road onto a gravel shoulder. Her seat back adjusted to the sudden angling, keeping her upright. The Destello wove through a nest of pine trees, many dead or dying from exposure to the relentless smog.

A narrow bridge took them across winding Cobbs Creek, which roughly paralleled Philly-sec's western boundary. Instead of the typical flat denuded ground that constituted the DMZ separating the two realms, the terrain here was mainly rolling hills. A few hundred meters ahead, beyond one of the hills, the crest of the six meter high wall rose ominously into the bleak skies.

"This is it," Nick said, gliding the Destello to a stop behind a decrepit stone building shrouded in wild ivy.

She disembarked, lowered her night-vision visor and panned the area. It appeared to have once been grassland but was now overgrown with tangled shrubbery. Odd clumps, vaguely rectangular and evenly spaced, rose slightly higher than the surrounding foliage.

It took her a moment to realize that the clumps were tombstones, relics from an era before earthbound cremation and orbital vaporization became the obligatory methods. Back then, many people opted to have their decaying corpses buried in the ground. The cemetery, like numerous others, was slowly being reconquered by nature. Soon, even the scant visible evidence of the graves would be hidden.

Nick activated the optical camo. The Destello instantly blended into the stone and ivy backdrop.

"What is this building?" she whispered. She wasn't only concerned about audio sensors at the wall picking up her voice. The solemnity of the cemetery, being here among the dead, seemed to demand hushed tones.

"It's a mausoleum," Nick said, using his normal speaking voice. "Back in its day, one of the fancier ones."

He swept aside a nest of shrubbery at the entrance and located a door protected by an old digital lock. He punched in a twelve-digit code.

"Are you sure they can't hear us?" she asked, gesturing in the direction of the wall.

"Not a chance. I hit their security system with a short-term virus. Drones, sat surveillance, sensor grids – they've all been disabled in this sector."

As usual, she was amazed by the extent of Nick's capabilities. Still, doubts surfaced. "Won't that draw more attention to this sector, cause them to dispatch ground forces?"

"Trust me, we'll be gone well before they go to that extreme."

So far in their relationship, his cocky attitude and wide-ranging expertise hadn't disappointed. Still, there was always a first time...

The door groaned as he pulled it back. He activated his headlamp and stepped inside. Bel followed. The air within was dank and faintly sulfurous. According to inscriptions on the walls, the mausoleum harbored the sealed remains of a dozen individuals from a family named Carlucci.

Nick got down on his knees, scoured dirt away from a spot on the floor to reveal a circular hatch with a metal handle. He pulled hard on the handle but the hatch wouldn't budge.

"Give me a hand."

Together they managed to free the hatch. A shaft with a rickety plastic ladder descended into the darkness.

"Smugglers' tunnel," he said. "They use it to bring illegals into Philly-sec and move tech and weapons in the other direction. It's deep enough that the wall's detectors can't pick it up."

"How'd you learn it was here?"

"A million-dollar bribe."

Nick climbed down. Bel followed, pulling the hatch shut behind her.

They descended some thirty meters to a muddy floor. A narrow rectangular tunnel of reinforced concrete ran westward. It was high enough to walk upright. The vile sulfurous odor was stronger but didn't seem to bother her as much. Maybe she was getting accustomed to it.

"This isn't so bad," she said hopefully.

"Wait until we reach the water."

"The water?"

He grinned and scurried into the tunnel. Bel sighed and trailed after him.

"Why didn't you bring Sosoome along?" She wasn't crazy about Nick's caustic housemate but it did possess some defensive capabilities. "He might be helpful if we run into any smugglers who didn't share in your generosity."

"Trust me, this tunnel is ours tonight."

"Was that part of the bribe?"

"Actually, a separate trespass fee. Another million."

Not for the first time, she wondered just how wealthy Nick was. Bribes to smugglers, massive payments to EPF, that warehouse for the team to train – his resources seemed unlimited. Two days ago he'd given her a necklace of authentic Neptunian crystals. She didn't even want to guess what it cost.

"As for Sosoome," Nick continued, "Ektor Fang has strict rules about mechstalking. Air-breathers only at these meetings."

They walked in silence. The tunnel made a few sharp turns to avoid large chunks of bedrock that protruded into the concrete. Inevitably, the passage reverted back to a westerly course. The sulfurous odor grew stronger and the air felt increasingly damp.

They'd trekked for about ten minutes when Nick abruptly halted. He motioned her to move up beside him.

"Here comes the fun part," he said.

The tunnel ended. They stood on a narrow ledge a meter above a submerged canal, its flanks cradled in ancient bricks. The canal flowed parallel to the tunnel. She estimated it was ten meters across. Another opening on the far side marked the tunnel's continuation.

The water was clearly the source of the foul odor. Standing this close it was nearly unbearable. Her visor lamp played across chunks of unidentifiable debris floating past, bobbing in the gentle current.

She grimaced. "Is that fresh sewage?"

"Not sure how fresh it is. But yeah, this is part of one of the city's oldest disposal systems. It doesn't even show up on current maps. You ready?"

"You mean we have to swim across?"

"Of course not."

"Thank goodness."

"It's not that deep. We can wade."

With an impish grin, Nick hopped off the ledge and landed with a soft splash. The water was nearly up to his chest. Several brownish clumps stuck to his clothes. He batted them away. They circumnavigated his body and continued their journey downstream toward some unknown and foul destination.

"They couldn't have built a bridge or left a boat?"

"The stench is part of the smugglers' system to avoid detection. The wall is almost directly above us. Transit stations send down sniffer worms to search for the deeper tunnels. The smell plays havoc with their sensors."

"Wonder why," she muttered, taking a tentative step into the water. It was clammy and cold, and every bit as loathsome as she'd anticipated.

She pinched her nostrils shut and pushed through the muck as swiftly as possible, twisting from side to side in a futile effort to dodge the larger clumps of refuse. Had Ektor Fang been willing to meet virtually, this entire trek would have been unnecessary. They could have had the encounter in almost any secured area of the city, even at her condo, short-circuiting her desperate urge to take a lengthy perfumed shower. But as Nick had explained, the Du Pal was ultra-cautious and wary of holo transmissions being intercepted. He would only do face to face meetings in unsec territory.

They reached the far side and climbed over the lip into the second tunnel. It was identical except that it ran uphill on a slight gradient.

Ten minutes later they arrived at a wall with an ancient wooden door. Nick opened it to reveal an upward staircase. A two-story climb took them to another door. Reaching for the knob, he hesitated.

"Remember, try not to lie to him. He's got a pretty good bullshit detector. If he asks a question you don't want to answer, just be straight and tell him so."

She nodded. Nick had already given her a host of warnings about to how to behave at the meeting. He'd also sprayed their faces with a neuro relaxant to deter body language giveaways.

He opened the door. Bel was pleasantly surprised to discover a small modern locker room outfitted with premium air showers. If there was another way in or out of the room, it was well hidden.

She couldn't believe the stink emanating from her body and scurried into the nearest cubicle fully clothed. Setting the controls to maximum fragrance, she closed her eyes, spread her legs and raised her arms, allowing the demoisturizing suckers head-to-toe access. Twenty seconds later she exited, her skin, pants, blouse and shoes dry and reasonably fumigated.

"I never expected smugglers to have such a place," she said to Nick as he stepped out of the adjacent cubicle.

"Cleanliness is not just the province of the law-abiding."

The voice wasn't Nick's. It came from overhead. Bel whipped her gaze upward.

One of Ektor Fang's tways hung upside down from the ceiling, his legs wrapped around an exposed pipe. Bel recognized the buzz-cut blond from Nick's description.

The tway released from the pipe, back-flipped and landed on his feet in front of her. Startled, she jerked away from him. Her back slammed hard against a locker. She winced, rubbed a bruised shoulder. She had a hunch the tway had startled her on purpose, that it was some sort of test of her reactions.

Nick scowled at him. "Was that necessary?"

"Perhaps not. My apologies, Ms Bakana. I'm Ektor Fang. I'm pleased to make your acquaintance."

He extended his palm. Bel shook his hand. It felt weird, like such intimate contact with an assassin was some forbidden act. She was thankful when he released her.

Prior to the meeting, she'd decided she would treat her conversation with a Paratwa assassin with the same diplomatic sensitivity she might employ upon meeting a foreign dignitary for the first time. But the boldness of his entrance prompted her to reevaluate. There was a directness to him that suggested he would expect the same in return.

"Where's your better half?" Nick asked.

"Security duties. Without the smugglers using and guarding this building tonight, a breach is possible. The streets above are densely populated and rampant with starvation."

"People would break in here looking for food?" Bel asked.

"No. They would break in to hide from the necro packs. Several large ones are roaming the area."

"Necro packs?"

"Gangs of cannibals."

She repressed a shudder. At the tway's invitation, they sat down on opposite-facing benches, Nick and Bel on one side, Ektor Fang on the other. The tway gazed back and forth between them.

"Your meeting," Nick said. "Your agenda."

"I have two items. First, Aristotle's death."

Bel and Nick exchanged surprised looks.

"I gather you were not aware of it."

"We weren't," Bel said.

Ektor Fang fixed his gaze on her. His stare was so intense that it was making her uncomfortable. Presumably satisfied that she was being truthful, he provided what little was known about the Ash Ock's demise in Cape Town. Bel thought she detected sadness in his voice, but it was subtle and she couldn't be certain.

"Any idea who was responsible for the nuking?" Nick asked.

"No. I would ask you the same question."

The tway again locked his eyes on Bel, expecting her to answer. She'd discussed the South African tragedy earlier with Pablo Dominguez.

"We have no solid intel and very few leads," she admitted. It was an honest response.

She guarded against revealing a surge of excitement at the idea that one of the Ash Ock had been killed. Her thoughts reverted to her former role in Media Relations, and she speculated about how such information might be used against the assassins. She'd have to schedule an exploratory discussion with Rory Connors first thing tomorrow. Although she couldn't openly reveal to Rory what they'd just learned and would have to wait for Nick to employ his usual surreptitious methods for spreading the information about Aristotle's death, she could subtly prep Rory for the uproar bound to be generated when word of the Ash Ock's demise went public.

Rumors of the Royal Caste's existence had been spreading since the attack on headquarters, helped along by a series of clandestine E-Tech disclosures. Now that the public was aware that many of the assassins had united under a breed of Super Paratwa – the media phrase being used for the Ash Ock – revealing the death of a Royal was a great opportunity for launching a coordinated PR slam against the Paratwa's presumed invincibility.

"Sappho is understandably upset about the loss," Ektor Fang continued. "She has dispatched the liege-killer to find and terminate the perpetrators. But, like many such calamities in our world, those responsible may never be found."

"Will Aristotle's passing change any Ash Ock plans?" Nick asked.

"Doubtful. It certainly won't hinder their desire to bring about an apocalypse."

"How are they planning to survive the end of the world?" Bel wondered. "Secret stasis facilities deep underground?"

"Such facilities exist or are being constructed. I suspect they are indeed part of the Royals' survival plan. However, I cannot absolutely confirm that."

"What do you know about the attack on E-Tech headquarters?" Nick asked.

"Sappho and Theophrastus planned the assault. Codrus gave it his blessing but wasn't involved in the preparations.

Aristotle was against it, preferring a pinpoint assassination solely against Director Witherstone. But he submitted to the majority will."

This time Ektor Fang's sadness was readily apparent. Bel took a shot in the dark.

"You liked Aristotle."

"Yes. Liked and admired. He was always the most reasonable of the Ash Ock, a deep thinker capable of the most extraordinary insights and subtle reflections. Theophrastus is brilliant as well. But he possesses a cold intellect, riveted to the hard sciences, and with an open disdain for the weaknesses he perceives in humankind. He's the one most responsible for the Paratwa's advanced technologies.

"Codrus is a financial genius, yet too much the loyal foot soldier, rarely willing to challenge the status quo. I've gotten the impression that Sappho and Theophrastus often keep him in the dark about their more sophisticated schemes. I'm not even certain Codrus knows they're guiding the planet toward Armageddon. As for Sappho..." The tway hesitated. "There is a strangeness about her that defies comparison. She is truly a unique creature."

"What about the fifth one, Empedocles?" Bel asked.

"Youngest of the breed and still in training. We've never met."

She was fascinated by the revelations. In this one meeting, she felt she'd been given more insights into the personalities of the Royals than E-Tech Intelligence had uncovered in years.

Ektor Fang went on. "The Ash Ock's perception of E-Tech is complicated. On one hand, they see your organization as being aligned with their own purposes. By limiting human technology, binary technology can advance unrestricted. Yet they also perceive E-Tech as an entity capable of disrupting their long-range plans. This dichotomy, and how it impacts their decisions, is not something I fully grasp. Their methodologies, as always, can be elusive."

Bel was reminded of Doctor Emanuel's words at dinner the other evening about the Ash Ock's manipulations. *Look for their rationales not in the broad brush strokes but in the subtlety of the colors.*

"That said, it had been apparent to the Royals for some time that Director Witherstone was not the ideal E-Tech person to be in charge because of his relentless anti-Paratwa stance. They'd discussed impacting a change. But that wasn't the real reason Yiska was sent."

"Yiska?"

"The Shonto Prong the Royals ordered to attack your headquarters. Yiska is more than just a typical representative of his breed. He's as dangerous as many a Jeek Elemental or Voshkof Rabbit I could name. His skills are matched only by his ruthlessness."

Bel thought back to that endless string of funerals she'd attended after the headquarters attack, to the dozens of innocent staffers who'd been so callously murdered on that terrible day.

"Yiska's primary mission was killing Director Witherstone. Of secondary importance was elevating your status within the organization so that your Board of Regents would see you as the logical candidate to replace him." Again, the tway's gaze seemed to drill into her. "In his place, they wanted someone who not only lacked Witherstone's strong and well-publicized convictions, but who possessed far less political savvy and experience."

"Someone easier to manipulate," Bel concluded.

"Yes. Essentially, a weak director who could be counted on to follow the board's dictates and not upset the status quo."

I was chosen because the Royals saw me as the perfect patsy.

It was a sobering thought, one that Bel should have found demeaning. But she'd questioned her promotion from the beginning, suspecting it wasn't based solely on native talent or abilities.

Nick seemed to be avoiding her gaze. At that moment, she realized he'd known all along, or at least suspected, why the Ash Ock had manipulated the attack so that she would be elevated into Witherstone's job. She should be angry with him for holding back the truth from her. But she wasn't. She knew he'd done it for the right reasons, to spare her feelings.

I think Director Bakana will ultimately prove to be a surprise to the Royal Caste," Nick said. "She has rare qualities that are only now coming to the forefront."

The tway shrugged. "Perhaps. In any event, the real reason for the attack was to assassinate Director Witherstone. And it wasn't because of his public statements, although that story has played well in the media. The actual decision was made abruptly and the attack carried out with great urgency. They needed him dead in a hurry."

"Witherstone learned something about the Royals?" Nick speculated. "Something the Ash Ock couldn't afford to have made public?"

"Yes. Which brings us to the second item on my agenda. The Royals' most clandestine base is called Thi Maloca. It is where the Ash Ock were created and where Empedocles remains in training. No one other than the Royals' top lieutenants know of its location. But even among that rarified group, only Meridian has knowledge of what really goes on there."

This wasn't the first time Bel had heard that name. Meridian had surfaced in a number of Pablo Dominguez's classified Intelligence reports. A Jeek Elemental, he was believed to be the Ash Ock's most trusted adviser.

Ektor Fang continued. "Thi Maloca harbors many secrets. The most closely guarded one is an experimental lab designed for a solitary research project. I don't know the nature of the research. It's tightly controlled by the Ash Ock and Meridian. But by all estimations, if this project bears fruit, the balance of power between binaries and humans could be forever altered in favor of the Paratwa."

"Some new kind of weapon?" Nick wondered.

"That is one speculation among many. But whatever the nature of this game-changing research, I believe Director Witherstone learned of it through a source."

"You have evidence of this?"

"No, but a number of circumstantial trails point to this conclusion. As a security measure, the researchers were not permitted to leave the base. But recently, one of them managed to escape. I believe that this person may have communicated in some fashion with Director Witherstone shortly before the attack and passed on vital intel about Thi Maloca."

Bel was skeptical. If true, Witherstone would have told others in E-Tech or, at the very least, recorded the intel. Pablo Dominguez had personally reviewed all of the slain director's personal documents after the attack and hadn't found anything suspicious. And according to witnesses to his killing, the assassin hadn't accessed his pad or other private files with an eye toward erasing such incriminating information.

"If the director had such a source," she said, "we would have known about it by now. The intel would have been distributed, at least within E-Tech."

"Not necessarily," Ektor Fang argued. "The speed with which the attack was greenlit suggests Director Witherstone had just come upon the information, likely having had his encounter with the source that very morning. He may not have had time to engineer dispersal of the intel. And because of the extremely sensitive nature of the information, he would have been more concerned about leaks than usual and likely exercised exceptional caution." The tway paused. "Be very careful about who you trust within your own headquarters. The Paratwa have spies everywhere. There are rumors that one of them is a deeply embedded sleeper agent operating at your highest levels, perhaps even one of your associate directors."

Bel had heard such rumors over the years. Still, there were probably far fewer spies than there were rumors about them. Such suspicions had grown so rampant throughout society that psych professionals had even come up with a name for the syndrome: Social Infiltration Paranoia.

Then again, just because people were paranoid didn't necessarily make them wrong. Considering there was a mole among the regents, it wasn't that much of a stretch to imagine a highly placed sleeper agent operating within E-Tech headquarters. Just the other day, Pablo Dominguez's people had outed such a spy in a low-level Intelligence position, a woman secretly in the employ of La Gloria de la Ciencia.

The train of thought reminded Bel to prod Nick about getting intel they could use against the proscience fanatics. Thus far, he hadn't come up with anything of value. It suddenly occurred to her that Ektor Fang might be helpful in this regard.

She was about to broach the subject of La Gloria de la Ciencia when a muted banging came from behind her.

Startled, she jumped off the bench and spun around. A trio of locker doors had pivoted open as one, revealing the room's other entrance.

A woman stepped through the portal.

TWENTY-FOUR

She was tall and slim, and garbed in a sleek tan dress with a wide hemline that swished across the tops of high-heeled brown boots. Her skin was pale, her hair a color reminiscent of ripening peaches. Cut short, it was parted into bangs that framed a face dusted with dimples. Behind her, Bel glimpsed the lower landing of a dark staircase spiraling upward. It must access the basement of a building above them and serve as egress to the zoo.

She guessed the woman was in her late twenties. But with the popularity of cosmetic modification and the late-twenties look topping the fashion charts, she could be decades older.

The woman smiled and sat down beside Ektor Fang's tway. The two of them greeted one another with a kiss. Their lips pressed together long enough to suggest to Bel that they were more than just friends.

Ektor Fang made the introductions. "Nick Guerra and Annabel Bakana, I would like you to meet Olinda Shining."

"Hello," the woman offered, smiling and leaning forward to shake their hands. "I'm pleased to make your acquaintances."

"I asked Olinda to join us. No need to limit our conversation on her account." The tway paused. "My wife and I keep no secrets from one another."

"True, although sometimes I wish it wasn't so." Olinda

laughed lightly at some private joke and massaged the back of the tway's neck. The gesture was affectionate yet oddly reminded Bel of an owner stroking a favorite pet.

"Olinda possesses a rare wisdom. She is, in truth, my better half."

"Ektor exaggerates. But he does so from the heart and therefore can be forgiven."

Bel stared at the woman, trying to wrap her head around the idea of a Paratwa assassin being married to someone who projected such a warm and friendly attitude.

Olinda reached out and patted her hand as if they were old and dear friends. Bel resisted an urge to flinch.

"Don't be shy, Ms Bakana," Olinda said, her eyes sparkling with amusement as she sensed Bel's nervousness. "Ask me whatever you like. I promise I don't bite."

"Call me Bel." Even as she voiced the invitation, she wondered why she'd revealed her private nickname to someone she'd met only moments ago, and the wife of a deadly assassin no less. The woman possessed a disarming quality.

"Bel it is then," Olinda said, turning her attention to Nick. "Ektor speaks highly of you. He says you can be trusted."

"Glad to hear it," Nick said.

His tone remained neutral yet his face betrayed a hint of suspicion. He would be wondering, as Bel was, whether they were talking to a human or a binary.

Bel decided to ask. But before she could even get the words out, Olinda beat her to the punch.

"You wish to know whether you're speaking to all of me or merely a half, yes?"

She nodded.

"Which answer would most lessen your opinion of me and engender mistrust? If I told you I was a Paratwa or if I admitted to being a servitor?"

"That's not a very fair question."

"Nevertheless, I ask it."

Bel answered without guile. "If you're a binary, I'd be less inclined to trust you. If you're a servitor, I believe I might trust you a bit more even while regarding you as deeply misguided."

"I appreciate your honesty. I am what you refer to as a servitor, although I admit to finding the label somewhat disparaging."

Bel glanced at Nick, was glad to see he was hiding his displeasure. He disliked servitors intensely.

Olinda stared at him, seemingly aware of his true feelings. "I realize how our kind is all too often perceived. Yet to enjoy the company of both human and binary does not necessarily make us misanthropic or mercenary. I would humbly ask that you try to keep an open mind."

"Fair enough," Nick said, his expression neutral.

Another question popped into Bel's head. But it was of a more personal nature and definitely not the sort of thing you asked a woman with her husband sitting beside her.

Olinda seemed attuned to her reluctance. "No need for modesty, Bel. If I may risk another guess, I would say that you're curious about our sex life."

Bel felt like an open book. Nick's neuro relaxant seemed useless.

Olinda grinned. "Rest assured, I'm no mindreader. It's just that the subject of Paratwa lovemaking intrigues people no end. Did you know there are over two billion online sites that discuss human-binary sexual relations?"

"Many of them featuring the most exotic and fetishistic sex imaginable," Ektor Fang added with a grimace.

"And most of them ignorant of the true nature of love and eroticism. In truth, our sex is deeply gratifying, yet rather staid when measured against the gamut of such speculations. Suffice it to say, bringing pleasure to one tway brings pleasure to the whole man. Much of our lovemaking is no different from the common style of human couplings practiced since the Stone Age. That's not to say we don't experiment."

She patted her husband's thigh, her eyes twinkling. There was an openness and passion to the woman that Bel found strangely intriguing.

"All very interesting," Nick said, injecting boredom into his words. "But I assume you didn't join us just to talk about your sex life."

"Nick grows impatient, my dear," Olinda said. "Best we return the conversation to more appropriate subjects."

Ektor Fang kissed her lightly on the cheek and caressed her arm. Bel was fascinated by their intimacies, so alien to her preconceptions. The studies she'd read all indicated that assassins, whether in relationships with other Paratwa or with servitors, were ruthlessly efficient when it came to sex, unconcerned with anything beyond immediate physical gratification.

Studies done by humans, she reminded herself. Bias crept into all forms of social research, a problem exacerbated when the widely despised binaries were the subject of interest.

"Are you aware that one of your E-Tech regents is a mole?" Ektor asked.

Bel nodded. "I just learned this morning that we have a spy on our board. I'm told it's possibly a tway."

"It is indeed."

"You knew about this all along?" Nick quizzed the tway. "Why didn't you say something?"

"I had suspicions but only confirmed them a few days ago. This mole is not just any tway. It's one of the Royals. It's a tway of Codrus."

Nick hunched forward. "You're sure about that?"

"There can be no doubt."

"Do you know which regent?" Bel asked, stunned by the revelation.

"No. But I know that sapient supersedure was utilized to make the switch."

Bel figured as much. It didn't seem believable that one of the E-Tech board, all well known and highly respected within their various areas of expertise for many years, would suddenly turn traitor. But with sapient supersedure, the process of killing an individual and assuming his or her identity, the infiltration made sense.

The very idea was scary, not least because it was relatively easy to carry out. Numerous supersedures had been uncovered of late involving both humans and tways. Imaculada Merkhoffer, a Portuguese lawyer who'd worked in E-Tech's legal department before becoming a US Supreme Court Justice, had written the definitive text on the subject. She'd detailed the three steps needed for a successful supersedure.

First, the perpetrator had to gain thorough access to the victim's history and medical charts. Second, they had to use that information to alter themselves, through a combination of surgery, skin morphing, and genetic and biorhythmic camouflage, to match the appearance of their victim. Finally, when they were as physically indistinguishable as possible, they had to murder the prototype in such a way that the body would never be found.

"Any clues at all as to who this mole might be?" Nick asked. "When the switch might have been made?"

"No. I know only that the plan to infiltrate your board was Sappho's idea."

"No surprise that the witch was responsible," Olinda said, her tone darkening.

"Our intel says that Codrus is a mélange," Bel said.

Ektor Fang nodded. "Male and female tways. As with many mélanges, Codrus prefers to think of his monarch as masculine."

"Which reveals in him a certain level of male insecurity," Olinda added. "Whether Paratwa or human, testosterone can burn so white-hot that males are forced to reject or downplay their feminine aspects."

Bel silently agreed. She'd read a number of psychosocial theories, all backed up by convincing evidence, that the underlying cause of many of the planet's woes could be traced directly to an overabundance of that male hormone.

"Do you know which of Codrus's tways infiltrated the Board of Regents?" Nick asked.

Ektor Fang shook his head.

Bel realized that even if they somehow nailed down the perpetrator's sex, it likely wouldn't help. According to Merkhoffer, perps sometimes underwent a sex change to pull off a supersedure. Permanent reassignment surgery and gender vacationing were both popular and relatively easy to accomplish. Her former boyfriend Upton had done the latter as had millions of others.

Severe height differences for a substitution required a more serious level of commitment. But with bone expansion and skin stretching, they weren't out of the question.

"Any thoughts on how we might expose this mole?" Bel asked.

"With fifteen suspects, it will prove challenging," the tway said.

"Stick to the tried and true method for unveiling a spy," Olinda offered. "Track the leaks. Narrow down the potential suspects. Set a trap."

"One way or another, we'll out the bastard," Nick promised.

Bel wasn't so sure. Merkhoffer and other experts believed that the great majority of supersedures went undetected.

A series of tremors passed through Ektor Fang. His left hand twisted and jerked in rapid fashion as if wielding an invisible Cohe wand. Olinda raised a finger to her lips, urging them to remain silent.

The tremors passed. The hand relaxed. His wife gingerly touched his wrist. He flinched but then relaxed.

"Is it over?" she asked.

"Yes. A disturbance upstairs. A frightened little girl broke in. She was trying to get away from three necros."

A concerned look came over Olinda. Ektor Fang patted her hand reassuringly. "It's all right. The child is safe."

"And the necros?" Nick asked.

"They've hunted their last food."

"Do you need to be together?" Olinda asked.

"It's probably wise. I suspect the necros were advance scouts. When they don't return, their pack may come looking for them."

Ektor Fang stood and gave his wife a peck on the cheek. "Don't be long," he urged.

"I won't, dear. I'll join you shortly."

The tway opened the hidden locker portal and rushed up the flight of stairs. Olinda turned back to Bel and Nick.

"You should probably leave as well. The necros won't get past my husband. Yet the commotion could compromise the security of this building. If the tunnel should be found, the smugglers may blame you. They may refuse to grant you safe passage in the future."

Bel and Nick rose. But she had another question for Olinda and no longer felt reticent about being blunt.

"Why is your husband an informant? Why is he a traitor to his species?"

"I don't consider him a traitor. Yet I can see why he might be perceived as such." Olinda sighed. "That's not a question with a simple answer."

"Give it a try," Nick said, a bit sharply. Now that Ektor Fang was gone, he was making less of an attempt to hide his true feelings toward this woman, this *servitor*.

"You may believe that my husband hates the Royals but that is far from the truth. He has great respect for their abilities, for the style of their leadership, for how they've been able to unite the breeds. With the newsphere entirely controlled by humans, much of the violence and bigotry directed against binaries is often ignored or underreported. The Ash Ock, in many positive ways, provide an outlet for the frustrations of Paratwa everywhere."

"As well as giving the Royals an ample supply of recruits," Nick added.

"I'm not defending that. Their admirable traits, unfortunately, are too often mere abstract concepts when compared to the horrors they're inflicting upon the world. There is too much needless violence and destruction on both sides, and the Royals are making it worse." Sadness came over Olinda. "If the Ash Ock could turn their powerful minds away from notions of conquest, we would all reap great benefits."

"Not likely to happen," Nick said.

"No, it's not. But there will continue to be many of us, human and Paratwa alike, who oppose their will, and who work openly or in secret to countermand their impact. My husband and I count ourselves among those people. A better world is possible as long as such idealistic beliefs don't falter."

"Admirable sentiments," Nick said, not sounding like he meant it. "And what exactly have you been doing to oppose them?"

"I have my ways," she said cryptically, turning away from him to extend her palm to Bel. "I hope the two of us can meet again."

They shook hands. As before, Bel sensed a genuine warmth and compassion emanating from this strange woman.

Olinda exited through the portal, closing the lockers behind her. Nick and Bel headed into the door to the tunnel.

"A wealth of intel," Nick said as they walked down the steps to begin their trek back to Philly-sec. "Usually with Ektor Fang, these meetings are like pulling teeth. He was way more open than usual."

Because his wife was there, Bel wanted to add. *It made him feel more comfortable*. But she held her tongue, knowing what Nick thought of the woman.

"Worth wading through a sewer for, huh?"

She gave an absent nod, still trying to absorb Ektor Fang's incredible revelations, the death of Aristotle, the Codrus mole among the regents, the mysterious intel received by Director Witherstone that apparently had led to his murder. Yet perhaps the most surprising thing of all was Olinda Shining herself. Bel not only liked the woman but felt a kinship with her.

She too dreams of that distant horizon, a place of peace and comradeship. She too seeks a brighter path.

They reached the bottom of the stairs. As they were about to enter the tunnel, Nick turned to her, curious about her silence.

"Penny for your thoughts?"

For a moment, she didn't grasp the reference. Then she remembered that a penny was an extinct form of coinage.

"I'm just evaluating what we learned. Olinda was... quite unexpected."

He gazed at her intently. "Don't be fooled by her charm. Notice how she dodged my question about what she does."

"Other than that, she seemed quite forthcoming."

Nick's face darkened. "Never forget who and what they are. A Paratwa assassin and his servitor bitch. If it served their needs, they'd kill the two of us in a heartbeat."

Bel nodded, feigning agreement. But for the first time since meeting Nick, she had a hunch he was dead wrong about something.

TWENTY-FIVE

Nick was impressed as he watched the action in the gym from his control-room monitors. The team was performing better than he'd hoped and in a remarkably short time. With Jannik Mutter at the forefront guiding the attacks against two swift-moving holos representing an assassin, Slag, Basher and Stone Face rose to the occasion.

The quartet moved almost as one, their crescent webs humming and sparkling as they twisted to dodge hits from the harmless beams emanating from the holos. Jannik's slashes and stabs with the Cohe were augmented by well-timed thruster blasts from the three soldiers. Nick's analysis gear was recording strike after successful strike against the holos.

"All right, good job," he called out over the speaker as the last sim dissolved. "Let's take a break."

Despite his compliment, they hadn't yet reached a level where he felt secure turning them loose against an assassin. He felt certain the three soldiers could up their game, increase speed and coordination factors by several notches. As for Jannik, the main drawback was a recurring issue with the Cohe. He hesitated at odd times during the combat, often failing to carry through with a kill thrust when a weak side portal of his target's crescent web was within range. The hesitation was too subtle to be seen in real time but obvious during analysis of slo-mo playback.

Nick had pointed out the deficiency to him several times. Jannik halfheartedly acknowledged the problem yet dismissed it as inconsequential. During this latest sim it had happened twice. Nick realized it was time to be more forceful.

He left the control room and entered the gym. Slag, Basher and Stone Face were slumped against the wall, toweling off heavy perspiration and rehydrating with specially formulated drinks steeped in neuromuscular accelerants. Jannik, as usual during a break, was pacing back and forth, eager to plunge into the next round. His hyperkinetic activity was an additional concern. He didn't seem able to relax, even for a few minutes.

Nick called him over. He tucked his Cohe back in its slip-wrist holster and sprinted across the gym as if his life depended on it.

"Good work," Nick offered, reaching up to give his agitated team leader a hearty pat on the back. Doctor Emanuel suggested that positive reinforcement, both physical and verbal, would help Jannik's implanted memories become more deeply embedded.

On that front, there'd been no conspicuous glitches. This man who had once been the tway of an assassin now believed he was as human as the next person. He'd adapted well to his new face, surgically reconstructed to be longer and more angular, with protruding ears and a dark Mediterranean complexion. However, Nick had caught him gazing into a mirror a few times, either straining to recall some aspect of his original self or unconsciously wishing to see his lost tway staring back at him.

Still, such lapses shouldn't be an issue. The doc claimed that even a radically different countenance was no guarantee against occasional mnemonic leakage. As long as it didn't happen in the heat of battle, Jannik's mind would rationalize such moments and not attach undue importance to them. Everyone daydreamed and experienced random odd thoughts, not just those with falsified memories.

His backstory had him being born in Berlin-sec but immigrating to Algeria as a child along with his big brother, who'd raised him and who had been as close to a father and mother as Jannik had ever known. Following the brutal murder of his sibling by an assassin under the sway of the Royals, he'd needed a change of scenery. Moving to Philadelphia, the story went, he'd worked a series of odd jobs and become fluent in English. But always he'd dreamed of avenging his brother's death.

Because German was Jannik's native language, it was more deeply ingrained than most other aspects of his personality. That had led to the decision not to try concealing his Teutonic heritage and to give him another German name. Doc believed that would help him better deal with any prototype memories that seeped past the implanted filters.

His command of English was part of a standard language matrix embedded during the neurosurgery and assimilated via a high-speed diction program. He'd adapted well to his cloned dialect, displaying only a faint accent and the periodic use of a German word or phrase.

"We are more than good, Nick?" he uttered, alternately snapping his fingers. It was another oddity, possibly a habit from his binary life. "We are ready to kick *arsch!*"

"Yeah, you're almost there. Binaries, watch out! I can't wait to see you get some payback."

"Payback, *ja!*" He did a 360-three sixty degree pirouette on his back heel, came to a jarring halt and repeated the snapping routine. "We are whirlwind fast. Lightning in a bottle! A *donnerwetter* on the prowl!"

His speech was as frenetic as his movements. The doc had expressed some concern about that but Nick wasn't worried. Everyone had quirks. As long as they didn't impact his reactions under fire.

"Whirlwind fast, definitely," Nick said. "But there's one thing we should discuss, Jannik. That hesitation with the Cohe. My instruments are still picking up on it."

"Nothing to worry about."

"Yeah, maybe. But I'd feel a lot better if you'd work on a fix."

"A fix?" Jannik looked puzzled. "How can I fix something that's not broken?"

"Not broken. Just something that needs a bit of refinement."

"Unnecessary. Trust me, it's not a problem."

Nick tried another angle. "Remember what you quoted to me the other day. 'The man who seeks perfection is the man who seeks the ultimate truth.'"

"What are you talking about? I never heard that before." He grinned. "Did you just make that up, *kleiner mann*?"

Nick didn't care that Jannik called him "little man," which he'd been doing since the awakening. But he felt a tinge of worry about his reaction to the *seeking perfection* quote. It was another implant, meant to inspire Jannik to strive to achieve peak performance levels. But now he was claiming not to remember it.

Nick repeated the quote. Jannik snapped his fingers.

"Words are meaningless, it's all about action. And I say we are ready for some! So how about it, give us a greenlight. The team is ready to hunt twofer!"

He whirled to face the others. "Right?"

"Yeah, mate," Slag offered. "We're good."

Jannik spun back to Nick. "See? They know. All we need is our first target. Let's get out of this *scheifhaus*. Let's kill us some tways!"

"I hear what you're saying, Jannik. And it's going to happen soon. But the thing is, I believe you can still improve–"

"Let's kill us some tways!"

"Yeah, man, I know you're eager. But I still think–"

"Let's kill us some tways! Kill us some tways. Kill us some…"

He trailed off. Vacant eyes stared straight ahead as if he was in a trance. Nick reached out and touched his arm.

"Are you all right?"

Contorting with sudden fury, Jannik pulled away from him.

"*Dummkopf! Dummkopf! Dummkopf!*"

He screamed the word over and over at the top of his lungs. Slag and the others roared to their feet, hands reaching for holstered weapons.

Nick took a step back and slipped a hand into his left pocket, grasped the trigger for the hidden smartnet. He'd had the soldiers disguise the net in a light fixture and mount it to the gym ceiling prior to the first training session. Its software was keyed to one of Jannik's mnemonic cursors. All Nick had to do in an emergency was pull the trigger and the net would drop and enshroud its victim. The cords were coated in a fast-acting knockout drug activated on contact with skin or clothing. A full dose would put a man down in three seconds flat.

If this didn't qualify as an emergency, Nick didn't know what did. Yet he hesitated. Once that net came down, Jannik's trust in them would be shattered and everything they'd done thus far thrown out the window. They'd have to start from scratch, subject him to fresh neurosurgery and implants, and with the added worry that worse behavioral glitches would surface – a common problem when a second round of mnemonic falsification was required. Factoring in recovery time and having to start from scratch with the training sessions, the team would be set back weeks, perhaps months.

Jannik snapped his fingers madly and began pacing in wide circles. The circumference of the circles shrank, spiraling inward. He picked up speed, reached a full gallop. His head darted behind him as if looking for someone. Each time he realized no one was there his face crumpled into an agonized expression.

His actions were clear to Nick. Subconsciously, he was looking for his tway. Whatever mnemonic misfires were occurring, they were swiftly getting out of control.

Nick's remaining doubts were vanquished. He depressed the trigger.

The smartnet exploded from its ceiling pouch with a hissing *bang*. Blossoming into a three-meter wingspan, the net swept down upon its target.

But Jannik was quicker. He launched the Cohe into his waiting fingers. The black beam whipped upward, slashing wildly. He cut the net into three pieces before it could touch him.

The largest piece retained enough homing savvy to land on his left side. Its cords wiggled and thrashed, tightening as they entangled one of his arms and legs. Jannik twisted like a madman, frantically trying to break free.

"Nein! Nein! Nein!"

His protests morphed into a piercing scream as he flogged at the net with his Cohe. He cut through enough cords to sap the net of its remaining intelligence. It fell to the floor and writhed for a few seconds before expiring.

The knockout drug had oozed from the net the moment the cords touched him. He hadn't received a full dose but it was enough to render his movements sluggish.

His pain and rage had dissipated, replaced by a haunted look, like that of a child who'd just learned of some horrid parental betrayal. Nick was surprised to realize that Jannik's expression was tugging at his own emotions. A sense of guilt touched him over his role in creating such a false persona, a persona that was now crumbling.

Jannik pivoted slowly to face the team. Slag, Basher and Stone Face had spread into a triangular attack configuration and had their thrusters trained on him.

Even physically impaired by the drug, Jannik would still be dangerous in a firefight. He could maim or kill the team, making a bad situation far worse.

Silence gripped the gym. The only discernible sound was the faint hum of four crescent webs.

Nick had a second emergency device. But it was only intended to be used if all was lost, if no hope remained for salvaging and reconfiguring the tway's memories and endowing him with a fresh personality.

As much as Nick hated admitting it, they'd arrived at the point.

He tapped the side of his neck, activated his attaboy. A shiny scarlet button, recently installed, glowed ominously in his mind's eye.

Jannik turned his back on the team and faced Nick. Their eyes met. The haunted look was gone, replaced by an expression of a man resigned to his fate.

His fingers tightened around the Cohe. It was clear to Nick that he was preparing to attack. Enough of the drug had been absorbed to make his movements seem like they were happening in slow motion. Either that or Jannik knew what was coming and was deliberately slowing his reactions, giving Nick and the soldiers time to end it.

He thunked the attaboy, depressed the virtual button. The action instantaneously transmitted a signal to all of Jannik's mnemonic cursors. They exploded in sequence, microseconds apart. Medically, it was equivalent to a massive and fatal stroke.

"I'm sorry," Nick whispered.

Jannik's head jerked sideways. His arms and legs spasmed. He tried to say something but the words came out too slurred to comprehend.

His eyes rolled back in his head and he crumpled to the floor.

Slag and the others approached warily, thrusters still at

the ready. But Nick knew he was dead. The scarlet button was a kill switch. Its sole function was the termination of a malfunctioning unit.

"What now?" Basher asked. "Try to capture another of these crazy bastards alive?"

Nick had no answer. At the moment he was too frustrated to dwell on one. Doctor Emanuel's plan might have proved a bust, but he wasn't about to give up – yet he had a sinking feeling about the workability of his four-person team. Although validated by the sim, it just might be impossible to implement under real world operating conditions. Finding someone who not only had mastered the Cohe wand but didn't suffer from excessive swagger or outright craziness was looking more and more like an impossible task.

TWENTY-SIX

Bel tried to control her growing annoyance as she heard her assistant getting increasingly frustrated on the line to Pablo Dominguez's chief assistant.

"The director is about to leave for the day," Dominguez's assistant was saying, using the haughty tone of a man accustomed to not being contradicted. "He has an important dinner engagement. I'm sure this can wait until morning."

Bel leaned over and cut in to the conversation. "This is Director Bakana. No, it can't wait until morning. Find your boss and get him in my office *now!*"

Long before Bel's promotion to director, she'd cultivated professional relationships with individuals in most E-Tech departments. A short time ago, one of those connections had paid a major dividend. A high-ranking operative in Intelligence, a man who'd lived with Dominguez for a time and had gone through an ugly breakup with him, had sent her some surprising information.

Although the man claimed to want to do what was right, Bel was sure he was leaking the information to get back at Dominguez over the unpleasant end to their relationship. But it didn't matter if this former lover had petty reasons. All that was important was whether or not his information was correct.

Dominguez strolled into her office, friendly and confident as always. His amicable vibe departed when he saw the look on her face.

She wasted no time on pleasantries. "You deliberately held back intel from me. Director Witherstone came into possession of vital information from an unknown source. And you sat on it."

He eased his imposing frame into a chair, intertwined his fingers as if contemplating a response.

Dominguez's lover claimed not to know the nature of the intel. But given what Bel had learned from the meeting with Ektor Fang and Olinda Shining, she guessed it must have something to do with Thi Maloca and the secret Ash Ock research project.

"Well, Pablo?" she demanded. "I'm waiting for an explanation."

"Director Witherstone did inform me that he'd come into some hot intel. But he never revealed the nature of it. And this all occurred just after he arrived in the office, less than an hour before his assassination."

"But you've been keeping this knowledge to yourself ever since. Why?"

"As I stated, there was nothing specific to pass on. The only information I had was the director stating that he'd learned something that could have great impact."

"And he didn't so much as drop a hint?"

"Not a word, other than mentioning it had something to do with the assassins. But a majority of our intel these days is related to the Paratwa. He'd verbally scheduled a meeting with me for early the next morning and mentioned that he'd be asking several other department heads to attend. Presumably he intended to reveal what he'd learned at that time."

"If it was so important, why would he delay?"

"I'm guessing he wanted to do some prep work, put together

a formal presentation. Maybe outline a specific action plan."

Bel nodded. That had been Director Witherstone's working style.

"Could he have revealed the details to anyone else?"

"I checked and double-checked with every department head." Dominguez paused, aware that the statement excluded Bel. "Every *relevant* department head, those who he'd normally take into his confidence on matters involving sensitive intel. But he apparently didn't pass it on to anyone."

"Could he have made notes, jotted something down in his pad?"

"I've been over his files, both here and at his home. I couldn't find a thing."

Bel believed him. Yet if it truly was priority intel, Witherstone wouldn't have taken the chance of it being lost in the event something happened to him. He was far too careful. Somehow, somewhere, he would have taken steps to preserve the information.

"What about the source of this intel?" she asked. "Any leads there?"

"I reviewed the director's movements throughout the twenty-four hours leading up to his death. I checked on every meeting he attended and had my people interview every person he encountered."

"And?"

"And nothing. If one of those individuals fed him the information, they're not admitting to it. But frankly, none of them rise to the level of suspicion."

"I want a list of those people anyway."

Earlier, she'd debated whether to bring Dominguez into her confidence and reveal some of what they'd learned from Ektor Fang. But she'd decided to hold back, which was her prerogative as head of E-Tech. And right now, she was too upset with him for keeping her out of the loop.

Dominguez transmitted the list of people Witherstone had

come in contact with to her pad. He ran a hand through his long hair, using the motion to disguise a glance at his antique analog wristwatch.

"Maybe the director didn't meet this source in person," Bel proposed, recalling what she'd learned from Ektor Fang. "The intel could have been communicated some other way."

"I checked all his recorded messages as well. There's nothing there. Of course, he might have erased something."

"What about people in Director Witherstone's personal life?" He had an ex-wife and an adolescent daughter who lived apart from him. The divorce had been finalized only a month before the attack.

"The ex was in Hanoi, a business trip for her firm. No recent contact between them. He did speak to his daughter about fifteen minutes before the attack. But according to her, it was all family stuff, inconsequential."

Bel had met thirteen year-old Mattia Witherstone at a few E-Tech functions. It was a long shot, but maybe her father had said something to her that Dominguez and his people had overlooked. Bel would do her own interview.

Her anger cooled. Had she been in the Intelligence director's shoes, she probably would have had similar reticence about passing along such vague information. Her initial suspicion that Dominguez hadn't divulged it because he remained resentful of Bel's promotion and wanted to undermine her efforts as director now seemed petty. She'd never seen a shred of evidence suggesting he'd do something like that. Still, there was a more ominous reason why he might have held back.

She recalled Ektor Fang's words. *Be very careful about who you trust within your own headquarters. The Paratwa have spies everywhere. There are rumors that one of them is a deeply embedded sleeper agent operating at your highest levels, perhaps even one of your associate directors.*

Pablo Dominguez was a loyal twenty-five year employee.

Any suspicions she might entertain to the contrary had to be pure paranoia. He was passionately dedicated to E-Tech's cause and would never betray it.

But what if the real Dominguez was the victim of a sapient supersedure like the Codrus mole on E-Tech's board? Or what if Bull Idwicki was a sleeper and the incompetence of his Security department a deliberate ploy to better enable E-Tech to be penetrated by spies, as well as hindering the organization's defenses to make it easier for them to be attacked?

I'm getting like Nick, distrustful of everyone.

"Is there anything else?" Dominguez asked, clearly in a hurry to depart.

"Pablo, in the future, please keep me in the loop on anything of this nature. Even if the intel is vague, I'd like to know about it."

"Understood. My mistake."

He departed. Bel called Nick, told him what she'd learned. He had news of his own and revealed the latest failure regarding the team, the death of the former tway, Jannik Mutter.

She could tell by Nick's voice just how disheartened he was. It made her feel glum as well. Despite the sense of kinship she'd felt last night with Olinda Shining, the knowledge that they shared a dream of seeking a brighter path, the cruel attack on headquarters was never far from her mind. It remained important to strike back, to show humanity that it needn't be helpless against the onslaught of the assassins.

TWENTY-SEVEN

Stone Face had disposed of Jannik Mutter's body, at least from the neck down. The severed head had been preserved in a chill box and taken to the mobile surgical theater where the false memories had been implanted. The skull had been cracked open and removed, and a polycon laser used to melt away inconsequential tissue. That left Doctor Emanuel with a cerebrum he could work with.

Stone Face sat in the corner, reading some ancient hardcover book. Nick, impatient, checked the time on his attaboy. Early evening, almost 7:30. Bel would already be on her way to his apartment.

The doc had been doing his thing on Jannik's brain for over an hour. He'd inserted postmortem accumulators to access the billions of phantom brain cells that survived for a time after death and scoop up Jannik's final batch of short-term memories. He'd removed and examined the mnemonic cursors. All recorded data had been run through neuro software in an effort to determine why the personality restructuring had failed.

Nick didn't need to hang around, of course. He could get a full report in the morning. But as badly as he wanted to spend a soothing night with Bel and hopefully forget the day's troubles, his desire for answers was equally strong.

Sosoome remained at Nick's apartment. He'd attaboyed the mech a short time ago with instructions to let Bel in and explain he'd been delayed. Sosoome had promised to entertain her, which was not exactly reassuring. He could only hope the mech wouldn't say or do anything so obnoxious or gross that she'd bolt before he got there.

"Any progress?" he asked, trying to contain his urgency.

The doc was seated at a workstation. He paused to look up from his monitor. "Having you peering over my shoulder and asking that question every five minutes will not hasten the process."

"Sorry."

"The contradiction between conflicting internal forces is perhaps the oldest dialectic unique to the human spirit."

"Come again?"

"Curiosity is a byproduct of the cerebral imagination. Sex, or at least the promise of it, is a byproduct of a more primordial neurological region. Ergo, conflicting forces."

"Yeah, it's true, I want to get laid." He gestured to the brain, whose hemispheres had been split open like the halves of a peach. "But I need to know what happened to our friend here."

"I recall you once telling me that patience is a virtue."

"I must have been drunk when I said it."

He checked the time thrice more before Doctor Emanuel finally turned off his monitors. Retrieving his cane, he hobbled over to the sink to wash up. A frown warned Nick that the news wasn't good.

"Perhaps you should go make love to your girlfriend first. Increased endorphin production might better help you deal with disappointment."

"I'll survive. Hit me with it."

"The cause of Jannik Mutter's behavioral breakdown was twofold. First and foremost, the synaptic restructuring could not overcome the deepest embedded response characteristics based on his dualistic nature. I'm now convinced the problem is endemic to binaries."

"You're saying mnemonic cursors, this whole process, won't work on *any* Paratwa."

"Unfortunately, that appears to be correct. I'm surprised this one lasted as long as he did without cracking."

"What if you increase the level of control, make him into a retroslave?"

Doctor Emanuel shook his head. "Jannik Mutter's nature could not have been effectively camouflaged. Even if I'd implanted enough mnemonic cursors to make him pliable to someone else's will – a true retroslave – the fact that he was a tway could not have been overcome. It would always burst through."

Nick's worst fears about the suitability of a tway-led combat team had come to pass. They couldn't use a former assassin. And it seemed increasingly unlikely they'd be able to find a human skilled with the Cohe who possessed the right qualities for combat. He was back to square one.

The doc finished washing up and dried his hands under an antibiotic heater. "Go home. You'll feel better in the morning."

Nick grabbed his jacket but hesitated at the door. "You said the breakdown was twofold. What's the second reason?"

"Even if his true nature hadn't erupted to overwhelm the false memories, the presence of that termination program would have done him in sooner or later. The neurological reason in this instance is a bit more difficult to describe in layperson's terms. Suffice it to say, the installation of such wetware causes a reaction somewhat equivalent to the phantom limb sensation in a human patient who's suffered the loss of an appendage. In the case of a former tway, it accentuates the feeling that something is missing within him, ie his former tway."

"What about another type of kill switch? A lackluster or a consummator?"

"I'm afraid not. The concept simply isn't viable."

Nick repressed an urge to let out his frustration by hitting or kicking something. He could only hope the worst of his foul mood was gone by the time he got home. But he wasn't optimistic.

Thunking his attaboy, he turned off the com link. He didn't want to deal with any calls at the moment, particularly from Bel. Best to tell her everything in person.

"OK, screw it, doc. I'm outta here. Sure you don't need a ride?"

"Stone Face is driving me." The aged face broke into a smile as he glanced over at the soldier, still engrossed in the book. "I'm looking forward to continuing our conversation. He has some rather interesting views on the relative merits of contemporary court systems versus historic merchant networks for resolution of commercial disputes."

Nick's frustration was clouding his judgment. He couldn't tell whether the doc was joking.

TWENTY-EIGHT

"My father could be clever at times," Mattia Witherstone admitted. "But if Daddy had some kind of special information, he wouldn't have passed it on to me. He kept E-Tech business to himself. 'Kiss kiss,' he'd say."

"Pardon?" Bel asked.

"Kiss kiss. Keep it simple, stupid. And then he'd repeat for good measure. Want to know what I'd say back to him?"

"No, what?"

"Glub glub, fire in the tub!"

Mattia laughed. Bel had no idea what the phrase meant or why the thirteen year-old found it amusing. Maybe it was a mnemonic remnant of some blast ad she'd recently chewed on. In any case, teenspeak had changed radically since Bel's schooldays.

She should have been at Nick's apartment by now. But the Witherstone condo was on the way and an informal interview wouldn't take long. Besides, it would be one less task to deal with tomorrow, which was already looking to be a long day at the office.

Mattia's gangly torso still displayed the signs of budding adolescence, unusual for her demographic. By that age, most of her female contemporaries would have had breast and hip augmentation to make them appear more mature, with the boys opting for penile amping and hirsute accelerants. Perhaps Mattia's parents had been more traditional and hadn't permitted such bodmodding.

Still, they'd allowed her to tint her short hair with luminescent grayglo, suggestive of maturity yet with serious side effects, including a propensity toward female baldness and early onset senility. She'd also apparently been allowed to remain home alone with only an indifferent drudge for supervision.

Bel sat in a plush chair in the living room across from Mattia. Her host was a meter off the floor, strapped upright to a voodoo slab, the latest rage for adolescents. Bel didn't grasp the attraction of binding oneself to a vertical platform that inflicted its user with random pinches, jabs and electric shocks, all in the name of producing, according to the ads, "ecstasy through agony." Then again, she wasn't in the midst of those prime experimentation years, not to mention dealing with grief over the recent loss of a parent.

"Mattia, if you don't mind me asking, what did you and your father talk about during that last conversation?"

"Oh, the usual. He asked me how my studies were going. Our Social Survival class is doing a practicum at University of Penn. It's really exciting. We're working with La Gloria de la Ciencia to design a new kind of wall that the unsecs will never be able to breach."

Building new walls won't stop the erosion of our culture.

Bel wanted to chime in with further thoughts on the absurdity of La Gloria de la Ciencia's ideas, as well as voice her overall disdain for the goals of the proscience fanatics. But now wasn't the time.

Besides, at least Mattia hadn't surrendered hope and was trying to stay involved, unlike so many others of her generation. Young people, at least those fortunate enough to be raised in sec areas, were coming of age in a world where the zeitgeist indoctrinated them with the idea that an apocalypse was imminent.

It was no coincidence that the scholastic dropout rate was the highest ever recorded. And E-Tech surveys showed that nearly eighty percent of individuals between the ages of twelve and twenty had at least considered joining one of the numerous doomers' cults or committing suicide as a solo act.

"Did your father happen to mention anything that might have had to do with the Paratwa?"

Mattia grimaced. The voodoo slab had apparently just administered a notable pinch, jab or jolt.

The sensation passed. Her face relaxed. "I can't recall Daddy saying anything about Paras. But again, he didn't talk about that stuff very often. When Mommy was still living with him, she used to say, 'No politics at the table, kiss kiss if you're able.' But for her, it meant something a little different. Instead of 'Keep it simple, stupid' it was 'Keep it simple, *Syobew*.'"

Mattia lowered her voice to a conspiratorial whisper. "Syobew was her pet name for Daddy. It had to do with how much he really liked his vodka."

Bel shook her head, not following the teen's train of thought. Mattia gave an exaggerated sigh at her slowness.

"Syobew. It's WeBoys spelled backward. That vodka was his all-fave. He talked about it constantly." She rolled her eyes, indicating how boring it had been to listen to such talk.

"Mommy used to say Daddy liked his WeBoys better than he liked her. But he could only afford one bottle a month. Come to think of it, that was about as often as they had sex." Mattia giggled. "I used to sneak my buzzbee into their bedroom to spy on them until Mommy found out and swatted it down."

The teen convulsed. Appendages flopped and her head whipped from side to side in a rictus of agony. It looked like the voodoo slab was electrocuting her.

"Are you OK?" Bel asked, coming halfway out of her chair, ready to rush to her aid.

The convulsions stopped. Mattia shrugged and continued

as if nothing had happened.

"Daddy used to have some robot buy his WeBoys for him on the sly so the purchases wouldn't show up on his statements. Because if Mommy ever found out he was spending that kind of money on vodka, she'd go all wailpissy on him and have our drudge flush it down the toilet. That's why Daddy only kept those bottles at his office."

"I see," Bel said, trying to swing the talk back to that final conversation between father and daughter. But Mattia was on a roll.

"Daddy drank way too much. I think that's why their marriage descrambled. Actually, I think marriage is a dead institution. Even my Optimism tutor says so. She's in a menage à trois with a transwoman and an engineered hermaphrodite, and she says noncommittal multisex is the future of relationships. Glub glub, fire in the tub!"

Bel sensed there was nothing more to be learned here. She stood up to leave but couldn't resist offering a spot of adult advice.

"Relationship commitments are important, Mattia, no matter what certain people say."

"Uh huh, right. Oh, and Ms Bakana, if you ever want to try out my voodoo slab, just let me know. Come on over anytime Mommy's not here. Which, come to think of it, is pretty much anytime!"

She erupted into a fit of wild laughter, which ended an instant later when the slab administered its next affliction. As Mattia winced and squirmed, Bel made her way to the door. In her own teen years, exotic pleasure-pain activities had mostly been the province of the boys, who engaged in violent smashsports or consumed bellyache-inducing chemicals in order to emit sweet-scented farts. She hoped that whatever sort of ecstasy Mattia hoped to achieve was worth the suffering.

The Witherstone condo was on the seventy-eighth floor.

By the time the high-speed elevator reached ground level seconds later, a vague thought had morphed into an idea. Bel had a theory about where Mattia's father might have sequestered the intel that had gotten him killed.

It can't be that simple. And yet...

She called Nick but couldn't get through. He must have turned off his attaboy. As she settled into the back of the limo, she contacted Sosoome.

"Tell Nick to meet me at my office. Tell him it might be important."

"*Might* be important?" Sosoome challenged. "Yo girl, that's pretty damn vague."

She was getting used to the mech's default mode, which was giving people a hard time. "Just leave him the message, Sosoome," she sternly ordered.

"Yes, *ma'am.*"

TWENTY-NINE

It was a short ride to E-Tech headquarters from Witherstone's. Bel dismissed the bodyguards. During a frosty encounter with Bull Idwicki after she'd ditched her escort for the zoo excursion, she and the Security Chief had come to an understanding. The bodyguards would back off when she needed privacy, and if harm came to her under those conditions his department would be absolved of responsibility.

She took the express elevator to fifty-seven. Security since the attack, at least in the evenings when the building was mostly vacant, had been reduced to a few guards patrolling the upper floors, plus the battle android stationed 24/7 outside her suite. She agreed with Nick that neither the BA nor even scores of guards would be any match for a determined assassin. But she hadn't ordered them removed. Their presence did seem to make workers feel safer.

Arriving in her office, she scanned the well-stocked bar. Despite Nick's advice, she'd been planning to have it removed. The bar was a constant reminder of her predecessor and now that she was settling into the job, she felt it important that her surroundings reflect her own style. She'd been meaning to call maintenance to make the change but just hadn't gotten around to it.

If my theory's correct, thank goodness for procrastination.

The shelves behind the bar housed more than two hundred beverages: vodkas and wines, gins and brandies, imported champagnes and colorful liqueurs. All were contained in glass bottles or labeled decanters, the connoisseur's choice over temp-controlled pumps or disposables.

She scanned the labels, looking for the WeBoys. If she was right, Witherstone had in some way recorded the sensitive intel and sequestered it with that bottle. Few people outside his family and close associates knew of his passion for the expensive vodka, which made it a relatively safe place to secure an emergency copy of the information. In the event something happened to him, one of those individuals – or perhaps a devilishly clever successor – would likely know where to look.

Or my entire theory is utter nonsense, a byproduct of a runaway imagination.

She finished the search. The shelves contained no WeBoys. Witherstone might have consumed the vodka. She could still be on the right track, however. Maybe he kept the bottle elsewhere.

That idea made sense the more she thought about it. Considering that he was known to offer drinks to the many people he'd hosted in this office, it was logical he'd want to secure his expensive fave out of sight, reserving it for private indulgences or VIP occasions.

Bel searched for signs of a hidden compartment. Finding nothing obvious, she felt around the bar for a hidden switch. Ten minutes later when Nick arrived, she was still looking.

She ran her theory by him and they searched together. Another ten minutes went by without success.

"Is that the same desk Witherstone had?" Nick asked.

"Yes, but I already went through it."

"Maybe somebody swiped the bottle. Security and Intelligence people were all over this office right after the attack."

"I suppose it's possible." If that had happened, she hoped it was a matter of simple thievery and not the actions of a sleeper agent eliminating evidence.

"I'll get a scanner from the tombs," Nick said, heading for the door. "If there is a hidden compartment, we'll find it."

"Wait!"

An idea occurred as she recalled the teen's words. "Mattia's mother disapproved of her father spending a lot of money on WeBoys. He had a robot buy it for him offline so the transactions couldn't be traced. And considering how his wife felt about his drinking, he wouldn't have used their home drudge to make the purchases."

"You think that some robot here in the building has the bottle?"

"I do. And I think I know which one."

She input her director's code into the desk terminal and summoned the battle android. It lumbered into her office, its head doing a series of rapid 360-three sixty degree spins – standard threat-assessment mode.

"Stand down," she instructed.

The hulking BA stopped rotating and faced its sensor-studded head toward Bel. It had often accompanied Witherstone as part of his bodyguard detail. Programmed to respond to the director's orders – a function Bel had inherited – it easily have been dispatched to buy his exotic vodka. By using cash or one of the non-bank currencies, the purchases could have been kept off the grid.

"I'm trying to locate a missing bottle called WeBoys," she informed the android. "Do you have it in one of your storage compartments?"

"I do not." The robot's trademark menacing voice gave the impression it was offended by her question.

"Had you ever purchased such bottles for Director Witherstone?"

"Yes."

"Where is the last bottle you bought for him?"

"He threw it away."

Bel acknowledged a stab of disappointment. Witherstone had probably finished the vodka before he'd had the opportunity to dispatch the BA for a new bottle, which meant her theory was probably wrong.

Nick wasn't as quick to give up. "Were there any items associated with that bottle that Director Witherstone kept?"

The BA didn't answer. Nick wasn't on the short list of individuals it was programmed to respond to. Bel repeated his question.

"Yes," it said. "He kept the vodka."

She shook her head, confused. "I don't understand."

Again, the android didn't respond. Her comment wasn't within its purview.

Modern battle androids had a reputation for being unhelpful and obtuse, shortcomings that were deliberately instilled. They were manufactured with limited intelligence after it was found that earlier models with higher IQs could be defeated by sweet talkers – drone-mounted enemy bots capable of disabling sophisticated processing systems by entangling them in convoluted logic loops. Armaments firms now proudly advertised their androids as being big, dumb and secure.

"Elaborate," she ordered.

"The contents of the discarded bottle were transferred to another bottle."

"And where is that bottle?"

The BA aimed a steely finger at the bar. "Fifth shelf up from the floor, fifteenth container in from the left."

Nick stood on a chair to reach the designated position. He retrieved a clear decanter from the shelf. It was half full.

"Vodka, according to the label," he said. "A lower-priced brand, pretty far down the quality ladder."

He popped the cap, took a whiff. "Bingo! It's WeBoys all

right. Distinctive cinnamon smell. Nothing quite like it."

"Hidden in plain sight," Bel said. "Anything attached to the bottle? A hyperlink marble? Handwritten note?"

Nick examined the decanter. "Nothing so obvious. But he could've used a nanodat, embedded it in the glass." He extended the bottle to the android. "Tell Sergeant Rock here to check it out."

Bel gave the order. The BA positioned the bottle in front of its chest and ran a scan.

"One nanodat detected. Double quantum encryption."

"Retrieve and decode."

She handed over her pad. The android transferred the information from the nanodat.

"Dismissed," she said.

It rumbled out of the office. Bel unrolled the pad to its max dimensions and opened the program. Nick stood beside her and they read silently.

It was indeed the missing intel. Witherstone's mysterious source was a woman, a gifted molecular geneticist. She and the director had had an affair back in their college days and had kept in touch over the decades. The message explained why she hadn't contacted him in more than a year.

Fourteen months ago, the woman had answered an ad for a lucrative job in South America. She didn't realize until too late that the job offer was a front. She'd been kidnapped and forced to work on a secret genetic research project at Thi Maloca, the Paratwa secret base.

The morning of the attack on E-Tech headquarters, she'd escaped from the lab on a stolen turbocycle. She'd known her bid for freedom was doomed. The Ash Ock had arranged for her to be injected with a poison that required a complex antidote every three hours, an antidote that could only be administered by her jailers.

Against all odds, she'd made it through the dense jungle and reached a village in a secured area. Procuring a room in a dingy hostel, she'd borrowed a satellite uplink from another lodger.

A servitor patrol dispatched from the base tracked her to the village. Moments before they entered the hostel, she transmitted a message to Witherstone, who was in his limo on the way to the office. The message described what had happened to her and everything she knew about the research and the secret base. The last lines of the message revealed that the patrol was right outside her door and that she intended to make a final stand.

Vowing not to live the rest of her life as a prisoner forced to perform research for the Paratwa, she'd outlined to Witherstone her ultimate act of defiance. Having rigged herself with a makeshift bomb before escaping, she told him she planned to detonate it the moment her captors broke through the door.

Bel was moved by the woman's tale. "It's so sad."

"Yeah. I just hope she took every one of those servitor bastards with her."

An addendum contained the details of the research project. Bel's excitement built as she recognized the impact of the information. Yet as astonishing as the goal of the research was – what the Royals hoped to accomplish – it paled beside the final riveting piece of information.

The woman had pinpointed the coordinates of the base. Thi Maloca was located deep in one of the remaining sections of the Brazilian rainforest.

"The Ash Ock must have learned she'd transmitted this message to Witherstone," Bel said. "The timeline indicates that he received it right here in this office, less than an hour before the attack."

Nick shared her excitement. "This fits with what Ektor Fang told us. And I've wondered from the beginning why the Royals used such a low-end breed, an Energía, as the decoy. But now it all makes sense. The Energía was probably the only binary available for that role on such short notice. They had better luck with the primary assassin. That Shonto Prong, Yiska, must have already been in Philly-sec on another mission or nearby."

"So they retasked Yiska for the assault on headquarters, which needed to happen lightning fast."

"Yeah. No way could the Ash Ock take the chance of Witherstone distributing this intel."

Bel sighed. "Too bad we didn't learn all this sooner. The Royals certainly would have abandoned their base by now."

"Not necessarily," Nick said, his excitement palpable. "Ektor Fang said there are spies everywhere. Let's assume for a moment that one of those spies is indeed a high-level sleeper agent, maybe even an E-Tech associate director. It was pandemonium in here right after the attack, people swarming everywhere. For something as vital as this intel, the sleeper would have been activated and ordered to search Witherstone's files to see if he'd hidden the intel. Having never made the WeBoys connection, the sleeper would have told his masters that no such information had been found."

"That's a lot of assumptions," Bel said.

"Yeah. But if I'm right..."

There was no need for him to finish the thought. If Nick was right, the Ash Ock would feel secure in the knowledge that Thi Maloca's location hadn't been compromised. An attack could catch them by surprise.

"E-Tech can't be seen as having anything to do with this," she warned.

"Of course not. It'll have to be an EPF operation all the way."

"Will they go for it?"

"Are you kidding? A chance to stick a dagger in the Royal Caste's heart, maybe even kill one or more of those pricks? And if that's not incentive enough, I've got some cash lying around that at the moment has nothing better to do with itself than collect interest. I'll offer to fund the whole shebang, including bonuses for all the troops who take part in the raid."

Bel could no longer contain her curiosity. "Just how rich are you?"

"I don't like to boast."

"Oh, come on. Boast."

"Last time I checked, I'm the ninth wealthiest person."

"In Philadelphia."

"In the world."

THIRTY

Had the assault on Thi Maloca not been shrouded in the utmost secrecy, it would have been deemed one of the most important missions in the annals of the Earth Patrol Forces. But it was a mission that Nick suspected would never be fully documented in the formal history texts. Its purpose and details were likely destined to be known only by rumor.

To prevent information about the assault leaking to the Paratwa, only the EPF's top officers, each one vetted by Nick and Bel, knew the target in advance. The soldiers, numbering in the thousands, weren't told what they were attacking until their suborbital troop carriers and auxiliary assault craft were moments away from dropping out of the noonday skies into the jungle clearing.

The EPF had lobbied for a simpler plan, one that would spare their troops from harm. They'd wanted to use nukes to destroy Thi Maloca. Fortunately, the mission planners succumbed to Nick's logic, given due weight thanks to his generous underwriting, that vaporizing the site wasn't in humanity's best interests. The potential for capturing servitors or other high-level servants of the Royal Caste and retrieving valuable intel outweighed the nuke option.

It was ten in the morning in Philadelphia. Nick and Bel sat in his apartment, waiting for the attack to begin. Although

Thi Maloca and most of the surrounding region were unsec territory and riddled with jamscram, an EPF tech battalion had saturated the area's upper troposphere with special com nets just prior to zero hour. For the duration, standard communication feeds would function, albeit on a limited basis. But it would be enough for the soldiers to talk to one another and to their mobile command center circling overhead in the stratosphere, and for an orbital spy cam to allow Nick and Bel to observe the assault via a channel routed through Sosoome.

"Wake me when it's over," the mech drawled from his place on the top bookcase. Sosoome was in lounge mode, sprawled face down, content to function as a passive conduit.

Nick's monitor displayed a panoramic aerial view as the assault began. Five massive troop carriers swooped in and touched down. The landing force's robotic contingent disembarked first: battle androids, autotanks, booby-trap defusers and other specialized units.

Resistance was light: only sporadic thruster and projectile weapons fire from half a dozen low buildings that constituted the above-ground portion of the Ash Ock's secret base. The fact that anyone was shooting back at all constituted the final proof that the kidnapped researcher's intel was valid. The complex was not what its map ID and documentation with the Brazilian government signified: a peaceful musicians' commune dedicated to melodic explorations that incorporated the rhythms of the rainforest.

The battle androids and autotanks swarmed the buildings where the resistance originated, riddling them with machine gun fire and energy blasts. One of the structures must have housed munitions. It exploded into a massive fireball that engulfed the nearest troop carrier.

The aircraft tried to lift off but couldn't get free of the conflagration. Its left engine failed, sending the carrier into a violent series of spins before plowing into the thick base of a towering kapok tree at the jungle's edge.

As the carrier disintegrated, dooming its troops and crew, flaming shards sailed back into the clearing. Half a dozen robots were maimed or destroyed.

Delta-A squads and combat platoons sprinted down the gangways of the remaining carriers, resolute despite the unexpected loss. More troops swept in from the surrounding jungles, having been dropped from hovercraft or having touched down on skyboards. The soldiers converged on the buildings, blowing open doors and storming inside. Distant gunfire and the wailing of thrusters filled the air.

Witherstone's source had revealed that the majority of the complex, including the labs, was deep underground. That's where the inevitable counterattack came from.

Three massive cylindrical structures sprouted from beneath the forest just beyond the clearing's perimeter. The rising cylinders, in triangular formation, uprooted foliage and ancient trees to pierce the canopy hundreds of meters overhead. Like medieval towers defending their castle, a barrage of gunfire and anti-personnel missiles was unleashed from the pinnacles of the towers.

Dozens of soldiers were cut down in an instant. And then the streaking blue beams from multiport range lasers ignited. In seconds, the clearing was littered with the bodies of more than a hundred troops.

Heavier weaponry erupted against the carriers, a barrage of rockets. Two carriers blew up as the concentrated fire pierced their shielding, killing the crews and any soldiers on the ground within close proximity. The onslaught continued from the range lasers, one of the few weapons capable of burning through the soldiers' crescent webs.

Hundreds of additional troops fell. In less than a minute, three quarters of the assault wave and nearly the entire robot contingent had been wiped out. It appeared as if the attack was going to end in defeat.

"Launch the second wave," Nick muttered, wishing he had

authority to issue battle orders through the mobile command center. But in spite of the money he'd spent to support the operation, the EPF weren't willing to turn tactical functions over to someone they viewed as a military amateur.

The barrage from the three towers escalated. Most of the remaining soldiers were cut down. A fourth carrier was lost, imploding into a clump of orange flame as its shielding collapsed. The battle noises grew so intense that it sounded as if a raging thunderstorm had come alive inside Nick's apartment.

"This is terrible," Bel whispered, appalled by the carnage.

Nick had suspected the assault would suffer brutal losses, although not to this extreme. He'd tried to persuade Bel from witnessing it firsthand but she'd been undeterred.

The second wave of carriers appeared high in the skies, gleaming speckles of light hovering well out of range. Flying in beneath them came the EPF's mightiest airborne assault craft: a squadron of stormlacers. Thirty strong, they swooped down upon the towers from all angles like ferocious birds of prey. Swept-winged, single-piloted, each carried enough firepower to destroy an unshielded city.

The stormlacers unleashed a thousand missiles in tandem. The tower gunners directed their range lasers and geo cannons upward, managed to shoot down a few hundred of the missiles and take out nearly half the squadron. But in the end, the towers were no match for the dense bombardment.

One by one, the towers' shields were breached; one by one, their supporting foundations were incinerated by missile strikes. Like monstrous trees hewn by the axes of nineteenth century lumberjacks, the towers tipped over. They crashed down into the jungle in a trifecta of blistering roars. Swarms of birds raced for the heavens as their avian habitats were crushed.

The second wave of carriers touched down in the few areas of the clearing not littered with bodies and debris. Fifteen hundred more troops and a support contingent of sixty robots raced down the gangways.

More than a hundred enemy soldiers crawled from the wreckage of the towers. Dozens of them, likely fanatical servitors who knew their doom was at hand, opened fire on the mass of troops and machines streaming toward them. They weren't outfitted with crescent webs like the ground troops and stood no chance. In an instant, they were shredded by concentrated thruster and projectile attack.

The rest of the survivors realized fighting back was futile and raised their hands in surrender. But the men and women of the EPF, seeing more than a thousand mutilated bodies of their fellow soldiers scattered across the clearing, were in no mood to take prisoners. The remaining survivors were cut down, exterminated without mercy.

"Son of a bitch," Nick hissed. "They don't need to do that."

He didn't give a damn about the lives of servitors. They'd chosen their fates by betraying their own species. But he did care about taking some of them alive, grilling them for potentially valuable information.

It appeared as though the EPF troops had been overcome by bloodlust and would kill on sight. If not brought under control, they might end up slaying more than just enemy soldiers. In their fury, they could eliminate the scientists, lab workers and auxiliary personnel still underground, all of whom were potentially rich sources of intel. And among those individuals would be a number of true innocents, scientists who'd suffered the same fate as Director Witherstone's friend, captured and forced into servitude.

Nick, although denied tactical control of the battle, had been granted an audio channel into the mobile command center. He signaled Sosoome, who activated the link. Nick reached one of the EPF generals and expressed his concerns.

"We're a little busy at the moment," the woman said testily. Like her troops on the ground, she was no doubt trying to manage raw anger at the slaughter of almost the entire first wave.

"General, I realize you've had sizable losses. But please don't lose sight of an important mission goal here. We need intel. What we learn from prisoners could go a long way toward determining our future success against the Paratwa. Please consider what I'm saying."

The line went dead. Nick glanced at Sosoome.

"Don't look at me, I didn't hang up on you," the mech grumbled. "Call was terminated from their end."

Nick turned back to the monitor. At least above ground, the EPF troops appeared to have the situation well in hand. Overhead, three stormlacers crisscrossed the area beyond the clearing, seeking pockets of enemy resistance or hidden escape routes. The other surviving stormlacers had headed back to their airborne platforms for rearming and refueling.

In the clearing, the autotanks began attaching themselves to one another to form pairs, and extruding wide shovels from their front ends. Transformed into makeshift bulldozers, they plowed the debris from the exploded carriers and the bodies of the fallen off to one side of the clearing.

The military tradition of bringing soldiers' bodies back home for funerals had never been an EPF priority. When the battle was over, the slain would be given their due honors. Fast-growing veggie clones from prepackaged DNA samples would provide loved ones faces to mourn. But right now, the landing zones needed to be cleared for the third and final wave of carriers, which would bring more troops, supplies and field hospitals to care for the wounded. Also touching down would be the EPF's notorious inquisition modules, filled with ruthless interrogators known to employ any means necessary to extract information from prisoners.

The bulk of the troops who'd landed in the second wave and the few survivors from the first wave poured into the buildings that remained standing. Judging by the relatively small size of the structures and the large numbers of soldiers flowing into them, access shafts leading to the subterranean portions of Thi Maloca had been found.

Nick wished he'd been granted a full-view tactical feed of the battle so he could see what was happening underground. But his entreaties to the generals had been in vain. They'd been wary that even the single channel routed to his apartment could be tapped and tactical data intercepted. He would have thought that his willingness to finance the mission would have earned him more clout. Apparently there were limits to what even a quarter billion dollars could buy.

He had an idea and called out to Sosoome. "Any chance of hacking that EPF channel, getting us some additional camera views?"

"Sure. While I'm at it, why don't I cure global insanity and institute world peace."

Nick was frustrated enough by being out of the loop and in no mood for AI sass. He picked up a seat cushion and hurled it at the mech.

"Hey dude, watch it!" Sosoome snarled, dodging the cushion with a flying leap to an adjacent shelf.

"Earn your keep, huh? Give it a try."

"I'm a simple mech, not master of all cyberspace," Sosoome groused, needing to get in the last word. But the mech closed his eyes, indicating he was attempting to comply with the request.

Nick glanced over at Bel. She looked crestfallen at the battle's terrible cost in lives. He knew that she'd seen her share of real-time horrors. But even after witnessing that mass suicide of doomers, the slaughter of so many brave soldiers was hitting her hard.

He gripped her hand. "We knew there was the possibility it was going to go this way."

"I know. It's just that..."

"Yeah, I know. Not the kind of world any of us should be living in."

She stiffened her resolve and broached a new concern. "What about the assassins? Maybe I missed it, but I don't recall any of those enemy soldiers using Cohe wands. What if there's an army of Paratwa waiting underground, ready to ambush our people?"

"Best case scenario, if there are assassins, they all died inside the buildings or the towers." *Worst case, there's a lot more slaughter to come.*

Still, Nick doubted that the troops would encounter any great force of binaries. From the brief message she had sent, it appeared that Witherstone's source had seen only a few of them during her fourteen months of servitude. Other than occasional inspections, there was really no reason for Paratwa to congregate at Thi Maloca. The one exception would be Empedocles, youngest of the Ash Ock, who supposedly remained there in training.

Much of this Amazonian region, like most of the unsecured world, had succumbed to jamscram saturation decades ago. Unless landlines had been buried deep beneath the jungle to reach the smattering of sec villages or the Royals had developed some new technology capable of overcoming blacked-out areas, constant oversight of the complex by normal means was problematic.

But "normal" was different for Paratwa and a simple solution presented itself. Although there was no reason to keep binaries at the complex, it made sense to keep a single tway of one onsite at all times. With the other tway stationed in sec territory, communication was guaranteed.

No force or barrier known to science could stop the linked halves of a Paratwa from communicating. Tways separated by any known distance constituted organic examples of the quantum phenomenon of nonlocality, what Einstein had called "spooky action at a distance." Binaries, by their very nature, were one of the most perfect com systems ever envisioned.

Nick wasn't concerned about the troops encountering a contingent of assassins. His real fear, and one shared by the EPF commanders, was that the Royals had planted nukes or some other doomsday device within the complex. If so, its detonation could not only wipe out the entire attack force, it would eliminate the possibility of personnel being captured or data systems being scoured for intel.

"What's that?" Bel asked. She was pointing to a shimmering glow at the upper edge of the monitor's panoramic view.

Nick frowned, unable to identify what he was seeing. Located at the farthest edge of the clearing, the quivering blur seemed to be slowly clarifying into a solid form.

"Some sort of optical camo," he guessed. If it was cloaking technology, it was a type with which he was unfamiliar.

The blur achieved enough definition to be identifiable. It was a small structure, hexagonal in shape. Judging by comparison to the other buildings, it was maybe seven meters across and just high enough for an average person to stand upright within.

Two platoons of soldiers who'd remained in the clearing, along with battle androids and a few autotanks not tasked with cleanup, were already moving toward it. All of them slowed as they got closer, wary of its odd nature.

"More than just optical camo," Nick mused. "Whatever cloaking technology it's using must function across a wide spectrum. Otherwise, EPF radar and scanners would have picked it up earlier."

"I don't think it was there earlier," Bel said. "See those tread marks on the ground on both sides of it? One of the autotanks passed over that exact spot."

Nick frowned. She was right. Not only was the structure utilizing an unknown form of camouflage, as of a few minutes ago it hadn't been there. His first thought was that it had ascended from some underground lair like the towers.

The soldiers and the robots halted ten paces away. The

slow-dissolving optical camo finally rendered the structure fully visible.

Its walls and roof were painted white but were streaked with broken branches and clusters of leaves. Nick abruptly understood where it had come from.

"It wasn't underground. It was hiding, somewhere out there in the jungle."

"A mobile building," Bel said.

"Yeah. Either running on treads or outfitted with hover jets."

The outlines of an ovoid portal appeared on one of the structure's hexagonal sides. The portal slid open. Two figures stepped out into the noonday sun, side by side. They raised their hands over their heads, a clear posture of surrender. Nick maximized the zoom capability of the spy cam for a tighter view.

A man and a woman. They looked to be in their twenties. They were garbed identically, in long maroon robes trimmed in black. He was tall and slender with sharp gray eyes. Blond hair cascaded across his shoulders. She was a tad shorter. Wild brown hair framed an elfin face.

They strolled calmly toward the fifty-plus soldiers and ten robots whose weapons were trained on them. The EPF forces didn't open fire. Nick took their hesitancy to mean that mobile command had reminded them of a primary mission objective: taking prisoners. Perhaps his entreaties to the general hadn't been in vain after all.

Yet there was a quality about the duo that gave Nick a bad feeling. Their movement betrayed no telltales as to whether they were human or Paratwa. But what troubled him most was that they didn't appear even mildly apprehensive. Their poise suggested a strange and unnatural calm.

Bel had the same take on the duo. "Something's not right. Could they – or *it* – be a suicide bomber?"

"Maybe." Yet those expressions of fanaticism or religious

bliss often common to those about to self-destruct seemed absent here.

Nick's bad feeling escalated. He leaned toward the monitor, trying to will the soldiers to take action.

"Shoot them," he hissed. "Shoot them *now.*"

THIRTY-ONE

Even if Nick's prompting could have reached the soldiers, it would have come too late. The man and woman moved at the same instant, a preternatural blur of coordinated speed. One moment they were side by side, the next they were back to back, crescent webs igniting.

Slip-wrist holsters shot Cohe wands into their right palms. Fingers tightened on the eggs. Black beams whipped furiously, lancing through the weak side portals of the crescent webs of the nearest soldiers, killing them instantly. A dozen more died before the neuromuscular systems of the troops even caught up to the blinding acceleration of their opponent, now unveiled as a Paratwa assassin.

The soldiers finally opened fire. But the tways jerked and twisted, either dodging the thruster and machine gun blasts or allowing their front and rear crescents to absorb the impacts. Their black beams continued flashing with relentless fury and unerring aim. In seconds, they'd cut down the rest of the troops.

Bel's face hardened, as if immune to this latest example of brutal violence. But she managed to voice a good question.

"Why aren't the robots firing?"

Things had happened so fast that Nick hadn't even realized it. But she was right. None of the battle androids and autotanks were participating in the battle. Instead, they were pivoting and squirming, aiming their weapons in seemingly random directions but not shooting.

"What's wrong with them?" she wondered.

"The Paratwa must be wearing some new kind of jamscram."

Nick had never seen the technology function in such a way. A normal AV scrambler didn't prevent autotargeting robots from firing their weapons, it merely made them miss their targets. But the battle androids and autotanks weren't able to unleash any of their formidable offenses. The assassin must possess a more sophisticated means of disrupting an opponent's AI systems.

Mobile command retasked the three stormlacers that remained on patrol over the surrounding jungles. They swept in from three directions, zeroing in on the assassin.

Two hands whipped upward. Two Cohe beams intertwined into a single powerful lance of energy. The first stormlacer was hit and exploded. A piece of flaming shrapnel from it nailed the second craft. That stormlacer spun out of control, its pilot ejecting an instant before the craft slammed into the jungle half a klick away.

The battle androids and autotanks finally erupted into action. But they didn't turn their weapons on the Paratwa. Instead, they fired in unison at the third stormlacer. It was blasted from the skies before it could get off a shot.

Nick roared to his feet, raging at the screen. "Shut down the robots! The assassin has control! Goddamn it, shut them all down!"

If mobile command was trying to issue such orders, they weren't getting through. The unknown type of scrambler utilized by the tways had taken full control.

The soldiers who had disappeared into the buildings were redirected to deal with this new threat. Hundreds of them poured from the structures and sprinted toward the scene.

The first ones there died in a hail of robotic fire. The rest dove for cover, startled that their own machines were attacking them.

"Only the robots closest to the Paratwa are affected," Bel noted. "The ones farther out seem OK."

The assassin's special disrupter/controller must have limited range, Nick realized. But that made little difference to the soldiers, who were now forced to fire upon a squad of their own battle androids and autotanks.

Nick whipped his attention to Sosoome. "Get me through to command!"

The mech opened the com link. The female general came on the line.

"Shut down your com nets!" Nick barked. "It's the only way to break through their technology."

"Being done as we speak."

An instant later, every robot in the clearing froze as mobile command neutralized its air-to-ground com nets, returning the jungle floor to jamscram status. But because the battle androids and autotanks were non-autonomous, operating strictly under centralized control, they could no longer assist either side in the battle. The links enabling the soldiers to communicate with one another and mobile command were also knocked out of commission.

The fight was reduced to a simple equation: an independent force of hundreds of battle-hardened EPF troops supported by Delta-A squads against a single Paratwa. Nick had a bad feeling that the equation gave the assassin a decided advantage.

He was right. The slaughter was horrendous. For what seemed an eternity but was probably less than sixty seconds, the back-to-back assassin waded into the troops, its Cohes stabbing and slashing with homicidal fury. A hundred soldiers perished, then another hundred.

Nick had studied numerous videos of Paratwa attacks. He knew the fighting characteristics of the products of every known genetic lab. But this creature was something new and different. It moved with the relentless determination and blinding speed of a Voshkof Rabbit or Jeek Elemental, most fearsome of the breeds. Yet to Nick's trained eye, the creature was neither. It represented a breed never before seen.

The answer came to him in a flash. "It's Empedocles, the fifth Ash Ock."

No other conclusion made sense. Still, the idea went against what was known about the Royal Caste. Intel from Ektor Fang and other sources over the years had revealed that the Royals weren't created for combat. Their strengths lay in other areas. But if Nick was right, that rule had been cast aside when it came to this final Ash Ock.

The whirlwind of destruction continued unabated. More soldiers perished or suffered grave injuries.

But reinforcements streamed out of the buildings to replace the casualties. And then the third wave of carriers landed at the far side of the clearing, unleashing fifteen hundred fresh troops.

The Paratwa might well be one of the deadliest – if not *the* deadliest – set of tways ever encountered. But despite its abilities, it wasn't impervious to the law of numbers. The strength of the opposing force and the determination of the soldiers began to turn the tide. Slowly, the assassin was forced to retreat, impelled backward by concentrated thruster blasts slamming into its front crescent webs. And then a platoon of soldiers rushed out of the jungle, outflanking the creature and forcing it to repel attackers on two sides.

Nick sensed its defeat was at hand. Within seconds of him formulating the thought, the inevitable occurred.

The woman twisted her front shield to repel fire from the flanking platoon. But that turned her weak side portal into the path of a dozen thruster rifles. The combined energies slammed into her, crushing her left midsection. With that much thruster power hitting her at the same instant, bones throughout her torso would be crumbling into dust and vital organs into gelatin.

The hits lifted her off the ground. She flew backward through the air, crashlanding on bloodstained grass ten meters away.

If there was any doubt she was dead, the man's reaction eliminated it. He opened his palm and dropped his Cohe to the ground. His face twisted into a mask of horror. His scream was so intense and of such duration that a shiver coursed up Nick's spine.

"My God," Bel whispered, equally affected by that piercing cry.

Thruster blasts slammed the man's front crescent. He was no longer resisting by leaning into the hits and augmenting his crescent web with muscle power. The blasts knocked him onto his back as if he was a bowling pin.

He disappeared from camera view as soldiers converged around him. Swift jerky movements on the part of the troops indicated he was suffering an outpouring of their rage, being brutally punched, kicked and stomped.

Nick's mind raced, formulating new possibilities. A reconceptualized version of a plan that so recently had seemed doomed began to take shape.

"Don't kill him," he pleaded at the screen.

Judging by the enraged faces of the soldiers and the intensity of the beating, the percentages weren't with the tway surviving. His screams finally ended. It was entirely possible the Paratwa remnant was already dead.

"Yo!" Sosoome yelled, drawing Nick's attention. "All com links back online. And got you an early Christmas present."

"You hacked into that EPF channel?"

"Yeah, but just a miniscule data stream, audio only. Otherwise, they'll detect me and shut down the whole link."

Sosoome turned up the monitor volume. A stern male voice, obviously a high-ranking officer aboard mobile command, was arguing with a reluctant captain on the ground.

"Dammit, Captaincaptain, I don't give a Pasadena shrimpfuck what your troops want to do to the prick. He's a goddamn tway. We want him alive!"

The captain protested that his troops deserved to enact vengeance on the assassin for killing so many of their fellow soldiers. But his superior cut him off midsentence.

"Can that revenge crap! Alive and in good condition, Captain. Or else it's your ass!"

More chatter emanated from the speakers but Nick tuned it out. If the tway did manage to survive its predicament – and that was a big if, despite orders from command – there was work to be done. He activated his attaboy and called Doctor Emanuel.

"Doc, a question. You said that mnemonic cursors and the whole process of implanting a false personality wouldn't work on binaries. That their true nature, that they're half of a single mind, a single consciousness, can never really be camouflaged, right?"

"That's about the size of it."

"OK, but what if the original binary was capable of splitting into separate individuals, each with its own distinct identity? What if you could base a new personality not on the whole Paratwa, but only upon one of these independent halves?"

"Are you telling me that a tway of the Royal Caste has been captured?"

Nick returned his attention to the monitor. Calmer heads appeared to be prevailing among the soldiers. They'd backed away to allow a med team to lift the motionless tway onto a gurney.

It was impossible to tell if he was dead or merely unconscious. He'd been savagely kicked and beaten, especially around the face. His open mouth was agape in a frozen rictus of agony and his lips were soaked in blood. The soldiers had yanked out most of his teeth, an indignity that wasn't merely a byproduct of their wrath. The circuitry for the crescent web strapped to the tway's waist, and possibly that unique disrupter/controller as well, was governed by rubber pads fastened to his bicuspids and molars. Crude dental extraction was a fast method for disabling energy shields.

Nick finally responded to Doctor Emanuel's question. "Best case scenario, an Ash Ock tway has been taken alive. Right now, all I need to know is if what I'm suggesting makes sense."

There was silence while he mulled it over. Bel, who'd heard only Nick's side of the conversation, gazed at him quizzically.

The doc finally answered. "Neurologically, we're still very much in the dark when it comes to the idea of independent tways. This is brand new territory. But I'd be willing to say there's at least a fair chance that what you're suggesting is possible."

Nick thanked him and hung up.

"Well?" Bel asked.

"I think Humanity's Avenger just might be in business after all."

THIRTY-TWO

Bel wanted to see the creature up close and personal, this tway of an Ash Ock Paratwa. She felt that meeting it would somehow alleviate the distress she felt when she considered what Nick and Doctor Emanuel were intending.

Jannik Mutter, the tway of a Fifteen-Forty assassin, had enjoyed a long history of murder and mayhem. But Bel had only read about his exploits or viewed videos after the fact. There'd been a disconnect from her personal experience. She hadn't witnessed Jannik Mutter ruthlessly murdering hundreds of soldiers, brave men and women with families and loved ones.

This Ash Ock deserves to die.

She would have been pleased to see the Royal dealt with in the same way the Thai government had dispensed justice yesterday to the so-called Human Scorpion, a one of a kind genetic freak that had been terrorizing Bangkok-sec. The Human Scorpion had murdered hundreds of pedestrians with poisonous stingers sprouting from its spinal column. The vile perversion had been caught, dragged into a lead-lined razzle box set up in Lumphini Park and publicly executed via painful injections of plutonium.

Such a deserved fate wasn't going to happen here, no matter how much the more savage aspects of Bel's personality might wish it. The Ash Ock had been groomed to lead Nick's combat team. It was meant for a more useful purpose than shooting it full of radioactive material.

The conflict of those two scenarios constituted the source of Bel's distress. Her desire for justice in its bleakest form – no fair trial, no appeals – clashed with the more rational side of her that recognized the creature might serve the greater good, give humanity hope.

Emotions versus intellect, Doctor Emanuel often proclaimed. *The ancient wellspring of most of the human animal's internal conflicts.*

Complicating matters for Bel was a third scenario, one that seemed to straddle both her raw hunger for vengeance and a desire to do what was best for her species. It was a growing acknowledgment that neither of those options was preferable, that neither executing nor deploying this surviving tway was the right thing to do.

She kept returning to the dream she believed she shared with Ektor Fang's wife, of a distant horizon, a brighter path not sodden in endless violence. That path resonated ever stronger by the day, amplified by her growing desire to become a mother, to bring new life into this world and nurture it toward...

Toward what? she asked herself cynically, terminating the entire blend of enticing thoughts. Such dreams were little more than unrestrained idealism, wholly impractical. How could such a better world come to pass in the madness of 2095 Earth?

She forced concentration back to the moment as Nick steered the Destello off the deserted nighttime street and into a small gated parking lot. Bel sighed and hopped off the back of the vehicle. Being conflicted was no easy thing. She sometimes wished she possessed Nick's absolute certainty of purpose.

They walked up the ramp toward the private clinic. He'd

bought the place only last week. Located near his warehouse, it represented another aspect of his plan to prime the Ash Ock tway to seek vengeance against its own kind.

The plan had been put in motion after Nick arranged to procure the creature from the EPF, smoothing away all objections with more massive bribes and convincing the generals to report through their military hierarchy that the captured tway had died of his wounds.

Doctor Emanuel had again performed his magic with the implants, creating a new identity for the tway. Facial reconstruction to repair the severe injuries suffered in Thi Maloca and to give the tway a new appearance had been accomplished by a team of blackmarket surgeons, each paid well enough to keep their mouths shut. The creature had been brought to the clinic for recovery.

"Too many people are in on this," Bel said worriedly as they entered the building. "I still think there's a good chance of leaks."

"Not really. The surgeons were kept in the dark about the identity of their patient and I trust the EPF people I paid off. And no one connected with the clinic knows the truth."

"So it's still just you and I and Doctor Emanuel in the loop?"

"Plus Slag, Basher and Stone Face. But you could stand those guys in front of a firing squad and they wouldn't talk."

They strolled through the unmanned lobby. Nick keyed them through a pair of security doors and into a long hallway. Bel glanced into the single bedrooms they passed. Several housed older patients, all of whom appeared to be asleep. But the majority of the rooms were empty.

"Where's the staff?" she wondered.

"Just a skeleton crew of nurses running things and a trauma physician on call."

"What about the patients?"

"They're all late-stage dementia cases."

They continued down the hallway. Bel realized they were

headed for the final room, the only one whose door was closed.

Nick broached a concern. "So far, we've only allowed male nurses and the male doctor into his room. You're the first woman he'll be meeting since his alterations."

"Afraid it won't like me?"

"Considering the sex of its tway, the doc and I aren't sure how he'll react to a female presence. It's possible you'll upset him."

Bel had dressed down for the encounter, minimizing her sexuality with baggy trousers and a nondescript jacket.

"Shouldn't be a problem," she said. "I don't look anything like its tway."

"Maybe not. But if things do start to get dicey in there, back away from his bed as far as you can. Let the security system handle things."

The sec protocol, Nick had explained, consisted of stunners and anesthetizers hidden in the drop ceiling. They would activate upon detection of any threat of violence and, in theory, instantly subdue the creature.

But no kill switch, Bel reminded herself. Doctor Emanuel had rejected that option as too risky. Even though this creature was fundamentally different from Jannik Mutter because of its ability to function independently from its monarch, there was still too great a chance that the presence of an implanted fail-safe device could shatter the personality veneer put in place by the mnemonic cursors.

Which means, if it goes crazy and manages to outwit the safeguards, there's nothing to stop it from killing us.

They arrived at the room. Nick reached for the knob. Bel hesitated.

"What do I call it?" she asked.

"Oh yeah, its name. We've christened it John Jones."

Resoundingly generic."

"I would have preferred something a bit more exotic too.

But it matches our backstory. Which reminds me: make sure you stick to the outline. The doc says it's vitally important at this early stage that we don't mess up any of the details. We don't want to give him any reason to doubt we're being truthful."

Bel nodded, recalling the narrative Nick had come up with. John Jones, at age eleven, had witnessed his parents being slain by an assassin. They'd perished along with hundreds of other civilians as the Paratwa made its last stand against Marine commandos in his Michigan hometown.

The incident, as well as John Jones and his parents, were real. That should be enough to fool the tway should it get the urge to delve into its past by researching the newsphere.

In truth, the son had never been found after the battle, presumably having been vaporized in one of the explosions set off by the marines. Nick's reworked myth not only had the boy surviving, but leaving town with one of the assassin's missing Cohe wands he'd found in the debris. Throughout adolescence, the invented story went, John Jones secretly trained himself to wield the tricky weapon, imagining that someday he'd avenge his parents' deaths. ·

He was sidetracked from that goal in his early twenties when he met the love of his life. He and his bride were on their honeymoon in South America when misfortune struck again, this time in the form of another assassin and a raging street battle. His new wife, Catharine, was one of the innocent victims, in the wrong place at the wrong time.

Bel grasped the significance of implanting the memory of a beloved mate. Should John Jones's restructured personality suffer any lapses and he started to recall aspects of his dead tway, the invented memory would serve to conflate the identities of the two females. At least, that was Doctor Emanuel's theory.

John Jones had supposedly come to E-Tech's Philly headquarters a few months after losing his wife. He'd demonstrated his prowess with the Cohe wand and vowed to help the organization defeat the Paratwa. That's when he ostensibly met Nick, who convinced him to help train and lead a clandestine combat team.

A final lie had to be added to the mix, not only to account for his new personality, but to provide a reason why he'd undergone extensive facial and dental reconstruction, as well as repairs of the other extensive injuries suffered at the hands of the EPF soldiers.

According to the fabrication, before the team could begin training, John Jones had ventured unarmed into the zoo one evening to follow a lead on the whereabouts of an assassin. But he'd been jumped by a gang of mokkers, who'd proceeded to beat him nearly to death.

Bel strode cautiously into the room, a pace behind Nick. The creature was sitting up in bed, reading or viewing something on a pad. The only remaining sign of its severe injuries was its left arm, which had suffered too many shattered bones for hyperstem regrowth and was instead encased in a qwikcast. Several tubes connected its right wrist to a standard IV panel.

It looked up as they entered. Sharp gray eyes focused on Bel, making her uncomfortable.

"Hello, Nick," it said. "Who's your friend?"

"Annabel Bakana. She's the new head of E-Tech, remember?"

The creature frowned then broke into a disarming smile.

"Of course. Those mokkers really rattled my brain. I keep forgetting things I should know."

"The doctors tell me the memory lapses are entirely normal," Nick said. "You might have some recall problems for a few days. And there will likely be some longer-term lapses. But the doctors assure me that whatever losses you've suffered won't impact your normal abilities."

Bel forced a smile at Nick's string of lies and nodded in affirmation.

John Jones extended an arm toward her. Fighting a sense of revulsion, she came forward and shook its hand. The grip was strong.

"Pleased to meet you, Ms Bakana."

"Likewise."

"My apologies for the memory lapse. In some circles, forgetting a woman of such beauty might be considered a mortal sin."

She found the attempt at charm creepy. And it didn't seem to want to let go of her hand. Its fingers tightened, squeezing their palms together with such intensity that she nearly grimaced. She sensed that the furious grip wasn't based on any desire to inflict pain but on some weird longing, a hunger for connection.

And then it did something even odder. It hunched forward and sniffed at her neck. The action made her feel even more uneasy.

Please let go of my hand.

The creature stared at her. "I like your perfume. A base of modified gardenia extract layered with faint traces of cedar and orange blossom. And I'm picking up another scent mixture, something far more subtle. I can't identify it."

"I should've mentioned that he's got a truly extraordinary sense of smell," Nick said.

Like that of a wild animal.

"The gardenia extract reminds me of... togetherness." A frown came over him and he shook his head. "Isn't that a strange thing to say?"

Bel managed a nod. He gave her hand a final squeeze before letting go. She backed away, feeling disconcerted. Despite her best efforts to resist, his comments and the intense longing in his grip had served to humanize him. She was forced to think of John Jones as a "he" not an "it."

She studied his appearance, so radically different from that rampaging tway in Thi Maloca. The reconstruction had rendered him rather handsome. He reminded her of the sort of perfect male prototype she'd often been attracted to and dated in her younger years.

He was tall and slender, with well-muscled upper arms. His hair was dark brown, cropped short on the sides but long in back. The one aspect that remained unchanged was those intense gray eyes. They seemed to be scanning the room, yet in a slow and casual manner that didn't call undue attention to themselves. She had the impression he'd been trained to constantly be on the lookout for potential threats.

Nick pushed an empty food cart aside and hopped up on the edge of the bed.

"So, John, how are we feeling today?"

"I'm good. But I've decided that my name's not John."

"Pardon?"

"I won't be using that name anymore. John Jones isn't who I am. From now on, I'm just plain Gillian."

Nick glanced at Bel, hiding his unease. *Gillian*, they'd learned, was the creature's secret name, supposedly known only to the tway and its other half, the slain female, Catharine. Those facts had come to light during the neuro debriefing, performed via emotive probes as the tway lay strapped unconscious on a surgical table. It was too bad that such probes were limited to accessing only the most recent memories. Beyond that, very little actionable intel had been gleaned.

"I don't think it's a good idea to change your name," Nick said.

The gray eyes grew distant. "It came to me in a dream. When I awakened, I knew the name was perfect." A frown overtook him, as if he was struggling to remember something.

"Changing your name might lead to even more memory confusion."

"I don't believe that will happen."

"Still, why take the chance? Why don't you put off a final

decision until you've had more time to consider–"

"*GILL-ee-uhn,*" he interrupted, using the phonetic pronunciation to accentuate the syllables. "That's my name. It's non-negotiable. The quicker you get used to it, the easier it will flow off your tongue."

Nick had no choice but to acquiesce. "OK... Gillian. Anyway, your doctors tell me you should be released in a couple of days."

"And then I start training with the team?"

"Absolutely."

"I'll need to see your initial database of potential targets."

"Let's not get ahead of ourselves. You have a lot of work to do first."

"Not really. I've been studying your four-man combat simulation. All in all, it's not a bad template but it does need tweaking. Once I've made the necessary improvements and the sim is right, it won't take me long to get the team up to performance level. Given their expertise, I estimate two weeks at the most."

Nick didn't respond. Bel could tell he wasn't happy at being one-upped and having his work criticized.

"As to the target database," Gillian continued, "send it to me ASAP. Based on my appraisal of the team's progress, I'll select the order in which we go after the assassins."

"I believe that's my responsibility."

"I'm certainly willing to consider your input. But since I'm the one putting my life on the line, I'll be making any and all final decisions in that regard."

Gillian gave him a steely smile and calmly turned his attention to Bel. "I've been reviewing E-Tech's attempts to discredit and disparage the assassins, and in particular the Royal Caste. I'm afraid you're not doing a very good job on those fronts. Even though most polls reveal strong and abiding hatred of the Paratwa by the populace at large, there's a corresponding paucity of support for E-Tech. At the very least, you need to have your people institute a far more aggressive PR campaign."

"I don't believe that hatred of the Paratwa and the popularity of E-Tech are necessarily directly related," she countered.

"Trust me, they are. I'm outlining a better methodology for E-Tech to employ. I'll have Nick send it to you. After you adopt it, you should see a trend reversal toward positive outcomes within a matter of days."

"Thank you for your suggestions," Bel said, barely able to hide her outrage at his gall.

"Anything else?" Nick asked dryly.

"That's it for now. I need to study. The two of you may come back tomorrow afternoon. We'll talk further then."

"Yeah. I suspect we have a lot to talk about."

"Oh, and Ms Bakana?"

"Yes?"

"You shouldn't hide your natural beauty behind such unbecoming attire. Your perfume choice is exquisite. But those pants and that jacket... they do little to express your deeper essence. Next time we meet, wear a dress." He offered a disarming smile. "Maroon is my favorite color. Accentuate it with black trim."

He returned his attention to the pad, dismissing them without so much as a parting glance. By the time they got outside and closed the door, Bel was seething.

"What an arrogant son of a bitch!"

"Yeah. Not exactly a model of tact and diplomacy."

"Who the hell does he think he is?"

Nick shrugged. "He's a tway of the Royal Caste. Just because he's not conscious of his true self doesn't change certain personality aspects that are part of his basic makeup. Empedocles, and by extension his tways, were groomed for power. They were trained to rule over all of binarydom, and ultimately, all of us. That kind of training produces outsized egos. And considering his breed, he's no doubt a master manipulator as well."

"Maybe so. But you'd better figure out a way to control his royal highness before he gets out of hand."

THIRTY-THREE

Gillian awoke from his dream to the cool air and faint vibrations of the unheated cargo pod. The three soldiers sat across from him in the narrow space. Like him, they were garbed in black fatigues, with tactical helmets propped in their laps.

Slag had the business end of a squeeze bottle in his mouth and was heartily sucking down the contents, live maggots infused with blueberries and cocoa. He claimed that the protein-antioxidant blend was his favorite pre-battle snack. Basher was hunched over beside him, fast asleep and snoring. Stone Face, whose impressive bulk and granite lump of a head belied a quiet intelligence, was engrossed in a book, a vintage hardcover entitled *Law and Commerce in Pre-Industrial Societies*. He'd borrowed it from Doctor Emanuel.

The cargo pod was attached to the belly of an unmanned stormlacer flying at fifteen thousand meters. Nick had bought the craft on the black market and arranged for the pod to be retrofitted.

The countdown timer on the forward wall indicated they were four minutes from the drop zone.

Gillian sat up straight on the hard seat of the shadowy pod and rubbed his brow. He was nursing a mild headache. It was a common symptom on those occasions after he'd had a dream or waking flashback about his wife, Catharine. Oddly, they seemed to happen about every four hours. He had no idea what the time interval signified.

In his latest dream, the two of them had been sitting across from one another in some sort of meditation chamber, a hexagonal room bathed in warm pastel hues. A mélange of pleasing scents circulated: bright gardenia, jasmine, apple, vanilla, the vaguest hints of rosemary and sage.

Some of the scents emanated from Catharine's perfumes; others came from the chamber itself. They conflicted with one another yet produced an overall ache of familiarity, tapping into memories that weren't memories, attempting to invoke something deeper. But try as he might, those depths remained unfocused and out of reach. He couldn't resolve them into authentic recollections.

Although the scents were distinctly Catharine, particularly the gardenia, they also produced an olfactory image of another woman, Annabel Bakana. He'd experienced an immediate attraction to her that day at the clinic when they'd met, primarily because of that gardenia scent. Yet the attraction was neither sexual nor emotional. He had no desire for Bel, didn't want her as a lover or as a friend.

Then what do I want from her?

The answer eluded him.

Another phenomenon of the Catharine dreams and flashbacks was a contradictory voice in his head that seemed to be trying to steer him away from such memories. The voice didn't utter actual words but the idea came across nonetheless.

Don't dwell on what happened to your parents or to Catharine. Think about what you're going to do about it.

Whatever the voice's cryptic source, Gillian found its advice appealing. A Paratwa assassin had murdered the woman and man who'd brought him into this world and raised him. Later, another Paratwa took away his beloved wife.

And I am going to do something about it. I'm going to kill every last assassin on the planet.

He recognized the impracticality of such a goal. It didn't matter. All that counted was the sentiment, real and potent enough to drive him toward a life's mission with relentless momentum. Yet in the back of his mind hovered a vague thought that everything was not as it seemed, that he was being impelled by more subtle forces.

"Two minutes to drop zone," the stormlacer's bot announced. "Beginning final descent."

The floor tilted downward at a sharp angle in the direction of flight. Gillian returned his attention to where it belonged, in the moment.

"Are we ready?" he demanded in a booming voice.

Basher came instantly awake. Slag put away his snack tube and tongued a fat maggot that had escaped onto his lower lip. Stone Face bookmarked the hardcover and slid it under his seat.

"We're ready!" the trio snapped in unison.

"Suit up!"

They donned their helmets. Faceplates swept down into position. Transparent from the inside, the faceplates not only provided unimpeded sight lines but enhanced peripheral vision. From the outside they remained opaque. Additionally, distorters rendered their countenances into throbbing multicolored blurs in case anyone tried scanning them with see-through technology. It was vital from this very first mission that the teams' faces never be glimpsed or recorded, their identities never compromised.

One thing bothered Gillian about the helmet, however. It limited his sense of smell, blurred together the more subtle odorant molecules. Olfaction, his most acute physical input, was reduced to mundane functionality. But he realized there was nothing to be done about it.

"Crescent webs on!" he ordered.

The four of them lunged to their feet and slid tongues

across the rubber pads attached to bicuspids and molars. Four crescent webs ignited, sparkling and hissing as they touched one another in the pod's tight confines.

"Activate jamscram!"

The technology was also tongue-activated. Gillian doubted their target would be defended by autotargeting robots but, if so, any advantages would be neutralized. In fact, this latest version of jamscram even enabled him to disrupt and take control of enemy robotic systems. Nick claimed that it had only recently been developed by EPF researchers.

"Mount up!"

They activated wrist controls in tandem. A stack of skyboard drones elevated off the floor and separated. There was just enough room for the quartet of boards in the pod's tight confines.

They hopped on the boards luge-style – on their backs, feet forward. Rear crescents compressed and sizzled as they made contact with the boards' metallic surface. Belts automatically tightened around their ankles, waists and chests.

"One minute," the bot announced. "Altitude: eleven thousand five hundred meters and descending."

"Affirm target," Gillian ordered.

"Target location is grid 1-A. No defensive shielding detected. No countermeasures detected."

"Affirm drop zone."

"Drop zone is grid 1-B. No defensive shielding detected. No countermeasures detected."

Gillian panned his gaze across the team. Combat veterans one and all, they'd gone up against Paratwa before, although never like this. Then again, who had? The four of them were about to engage an assassin in a style of battle never before attempted.

But the team had trained hard these past weeks, had mastered Nick's sim and Gillian's subtle modifications of it. They'd adapted well to the somewhat counterintuitive techniques such combat demanded. Still, he figured one last reminder couldn't hurt.

"What's the word?" he asked.

"Directionalize!" they shouted as one.

"How do we directionalize? Basher?"

"Attack one tway, defend against the other," Basher recited.

"Why? Stone Face?"

"To neutralize the assassin's single greatest advantage, force it into a situation where one tway is always on offense and the other always on defense."

Gillian nodded. "We make it fight us on our terms. Slag, why?"

"To prevent the tways from randomly shifting back and forth between offensive and defensive modes, a common tactic to confuse and overcome opponents."

"How do you know when to directionalize? Basher?"

"We don't know. Your actions provide the signal. We follow your lead."

Gillian nodded. They were as ready as they were going to be.

"Twenty seconds to target," the bot said. "Altitude: four thousand eight hundred meters."

Nick had protested vociferously at Gillian's choice for the team's first assault. "Pick one that's easier to start with, like an Energía," he'd begged.

"Too easy. I could take down a handful of those squabs on my own without breaking a sweat."

"OK, then how about a Fifteen-Forty or a Granular-D. You don't have to go up against such a dangerous breed on your first mission. And particularly not this Paratwa. Christ, you saw the videos. You know what this bastard's capable of."

Gillian had been unmoved by Nick's arguments. He'd rattled off the reasons why he'd made the best choice.

"First, there's psychological value to taking down such a repulsive enemy. When word spreads, we'll be thought of as saviors. The mythmaking process – a secret band of soldier-hunters fighting the good fight in the service of humanity – couldn't be launched in a better way.

"Second, the team's initial battle needs to be against a truly formidable enemy to build up their confidence. Not some second-string assassin that most of the population has never even heard of."

Nick had grudgingly admitted the validity of his reasoning.

"Ten seconds to target. Altitude: three thousand five hundred meters."

One other factor had prompted Gillian to select the target, a reason Nick and Bel fully supported. The location. Few people lived in this mountainous wilderness some seventy klicks east of Seattle, Washington, which meant there was little chance of civilians being caught in the crossfire. If the team's first battle produced innocent casualties, support for the team's exploits could be severely compromised.

Of course, from a standpoint of sheer practicality, the Paratwa's isolated location made it susceptible to a far easier means of taking it out. In this case, a few missiles launched from stratospheric bombers or stormlacers could have done the job.

But vaporizing the site would have done nothing for the team. Besides, there probably wouldn't have been enough evidence left to confirm the assassin's death.

Bel had voiced objections based on another reason: political concerns. In addition to the citizens of this region being strong E-Tech supporters, Seattle and its environs were part of the GNR, the Greater Northwest Respirazone.

Thus far, even the Paratwa and most terrorist groups had spared such areas from harm. Respirazones had acquired a cachet similar to that of medieval churches, the notion that they were sanctuaries from the brutalities of the outside world. Dropping bombs on a GNR, no matter what the reason, was unacceptable.

"Five seconds," the bot intoned. "Bay doors opening."

Bright afternoon light and colder air swept into the pod from below. The sudden wind was turbulent enough to cause the skyboards to shake and rumble. With the pod's floor no longer in place, only thin hydraulic struts kept boards and riders from falling into space.

Gillian silently mouthed the bot's final countdown...

"Three... two... one...

"Drop!"

The struts retracted. The boards fell into the cloudless afternoon skies. Turbulence from the stormlacer sent them tumbling. Gillian felt himself somersaulting violently out of control.

The drones' stabilizers kicked in and the autopilots took over. The boards righted themselves and went into a steep descent toward the drop zone, flying in a diamond formation. Gillian led the way with Basher and Stone Face flanking one another behind him and Slag bringing up the rear.

A fierce headwind rushed up from the hilly forests below. It buffeted the boards, forcing the stabilizers to perform countless micro adjustments. Still, Gillian had been on rougher rides. Oddly, he couldn't recall any details of when and where such rides had occurred. Muscle memory constituted the only proof.

The skyboard drones boasted full sensor shielding that blocked them from being picked up by ground or air-based detectors. The boards were also equipped with state of the art Abernathy sound muters, rendering them as silent as the gentlest of breezes.

They'd had to forego optical camo, however. It was too tricky to use on fast-moving objects against a plain sky backdrop. Imperfect camo would call more attention to them than its absence.

They'd opted for a simpler means of visual disguise: blending into the crowd. They'd chosen this weekend for the assault because it happened to be one of Seattle-sec's frequent skyboard acrobatics festivals, which brought hundreds of aerial teams to the region. A significant number of the competitors were four-person units and their standard flight formation was the ever-popular diamond. Should the assassin happen to be outdoors peering up at the sky, he likely would mistake Gillian and company for festival participants.

At least that was their operating theory. As in any surprise assault, there were always a number of unknowns.

The soldiers had lobbied for a nighttime assault, Delta-A's standard operating mode. But Gillian saw no real advantage and some potential disadvantages, and had ruled it out. Maybe in later firefights he'd opt for the cover of darkness. But considering that this was their very first test, they faced enough challenges already without having to engage the enemy with night-vision gear.

Nick had found the target's base of operation – the assassin's home – via his specialized tracking programs. Technically, their target adhered to the twenty-five thousand square kilometer rule of thumb. But instead of dimensions based on a roughly circular area, this Paratwa's kill zone was linear, a relatively narrow strip along the west coast of the USA and extending into southern Canada.

Among the biggest unknowns was whether the Paratwa was at home, a modest cabin deep within these woods. Nick's tracking programs and probability grids indicated a sixty-five percent chance of that being the case, based on an analysis of the assassin's known kills and his projected movement patterns over recent months.

As for real-time intel, the entire region was within Seattle-sec's domain, which thankfully meant that orbital surveillance remained functional. Nick had bought scan time on a couple of EPF satellites that passed over the area on a regular basis. As soon as they landed, he'd update them with the latest sat intel.

Should the target be at home and alone, they'd attack immediately. Should the cabin be deserted, they'd switch to Plan B, stake it out and wait for the assassin's arrival.

The forest canopy was approaching fast. At three hundred meters, Gillian gave the order to switch to manual controls. Taking command of the skyboards, they fired retro braking and slowed to a crawl. Vertical jets ignited. The four of them dropped slowly through the trees, touching down on the forest floor within sight of one another.

Disguising the boards with foliage in case hikers happened to be wandering through the area, they activated the optical camo for good measure. As prearranged, Gillian contacted Nick on a tight-beam sat line. For added security during the stormlacer flight, which had launched from an abandoned Canadian Army base in the Yukon, they'd maintained radio silence.

"We're down," Gillian reported. "What's the word?"

Nick's voice sounded in their earpieces. "Good news and bad news. Satellite shows the target is definitely at home. Arrived about ten minutes ago."

"And the bad news?" Gillian asked.

"He has company. A family of four. Two female parents and two teens, ages eleven and fifteen. Kidnapped them in broad daylight from a Positivity Clinic they were attending in downtown Seattle. Bold son of a bitch."

The contingency option in case the assassin was found to be in the company of civilians was a temporary mission hold until the civilians were clear, and if conditions didn't change, a mission abort. Nick was adamant that from a PR standpoint, the death of innocent bystanders during this, the team's initial battle, was to be avoided. The team's actions had to be unsullied, unimpaired by any tragic incidents that could lessen the hoped-for psychological impact of destroying an assassin. People needed to experience only positive feelings as they were led into rooting for "Humanity's Avenger."

Gillian analyzed the situation. If he overrode Nick's concerns and went forward with the mission, the family might die during the battle. Then again, if they put the mission on hold, they would certainly perish. Their target, Alvis Qwee, would again act out his ritual, torturing to death three of the kidnap victims while making the fourth one watch in a state of unadulterated horror as his or her loved ones were slowly murdered in the most excruciatingly painful ways.

He acknowledged that he didn't know exactly how to feel about that. He should be experiencing revulsion, a normal human emotion, at the very idea of such cruelty. Yet he wasn't as bothered by the possibility to the degree that social mores suggested he should be. Innocents died every day. It was the way of the world.

"I know it's a tough call," Nick said. "But I think we need to go straight to an abort. There'll be a permanent blemish on the mission if you do a temporary hold until the incident with the family is resolved."

"Resolved?" Basher growled. "Don't you mean put through hell?"

"Hey, I get it. But no matter what you do, there's no guaranteed good outcome. Even if you attack immediately, that family's probably going to die, if they're not dead already. If you choose to wait, same outcome. But for our overall purposes, waiting could be even worse. Rightly or wrongly, the impression will be that the team failed, that you didn't arrive in time to save the family. As terrible as it is to say, we have to stay focused on the larger issue of building public support for your actions."

Slag, Basher and Stone Face were focused on Gillian, their faces unreadable. It was his decision. They would accept whatever choice he made.

Nick continued lobbying for an abort. "Call it off now and come on back. I'll contact EPF. With a little luck, they can dispatch a battalion and be onsite in time to rescue the victims."

Gillian knew the chances of that happening were slim to none. Even if the EPF arrived and triumphed, the family would perish in what was sure to be an all-out firefight. And if by some miracle they didn't die in the crossfire, a cornered Alvis Qwee would surely kill them out of spite.

He turned to the others. He'd come to a decision. But he wanted it to be unanimous.

"What do you think?"

"An abort is the smart move," Basher said.

"Absolutely," Slag affirmed.

Stone Face nodded.

Basher's face dissolved into a lopsided grin. "But hey, what the hell? I say fuck smart moves and all of this PR bullshit."

"That family deserves a chance," Slag said.

Stone Face nodded.

Gillian made it unanimous. He had only three words for Nick before terminating the signal.

"We're going in."

THIRTY-FOUR

They approached the assassin's lair from the southeast, guided by video from a swarm of buzzbees. The tiny drones zipped back and forth through the trees, their movements programmed to be as random as the flights of natural bees to avoid standing out. Nick had dispatched the swarm upon locating the cabin.

The buzzbees' imagery was being fed to Gillian's tac helmet. He would have preferred the feed to be less jerky but it was best to err on the side of caution rather than risk detection. Besides, providing visuals to the team wasn't the buzzbees' main purpose. They were here to locate and, at the last moment, disable any warning sensors protecting the cabin. They'd performed the first function well, discovering two dozen sensors planted underground in a ten meter perimeter.

If any sensors had been overlooked, the team's chance of catching Alvis Qwee by surprise would be lost. That would make for a messier and far more dangerous mission. Still, a buzzbee swarm operating in secure territory wasn't likely to miss much. The odds were with them.

Gillian was on point. He halted the instant he spotted the cabin through the foliage, about twenty meters away. He signaled the others with a raised hand. They froze and assumed flanking positions on his right.

Alvis Qwee's home was a midsized geodesic dome made of rebar-infused concrete block. It was painted in tans and green to blend with the surroundings. Several Douglas firs towered over it, partially hiding the cabin from overhead view. A smattering of windows dotted the single-story structure. Daylight illumination was augmented by a ring of skylights.

Parked near the only entrance was the Paratwa's ride, a Buick Kuai van. The Chinese import had reached the cabin on a winding gravel access road.

Nick had located the building plans from the original owner, who had sold the hemispheric cabin to Alvis Qwee eighteen months ago. That was just around the time that the Du Pal began his kidnap/torture rampage up and down the west coast. Although the assassin always transported and dumped the dead family and the sole survivor far from this location, Nick was convinced that all of Qwee's sadistic rituals were performed here, most likely in the basement.

"Ready?" Gillian whispered.

Three heads nodded. Three right hands drew thruster pistols that were juiced up with special batteries to enable automatic fire for short periods.

He tabbed a switch on his belt, activating the buzzbees' interference function. A light on his display went green, indicating that the drones had ignited their jamscram, suffocating the area in a blanket of electromagnetic interference. Alvis Qwee's sensors were now disabled. Any hidden cameras would be displaying only multicolored blurs.

"Go!"

The four of them sprinted toward the door. Presumably, the assassin had been alerted that his sensor net was compromised and would be racing to the nearest window. Best case scenario was that he was in the basement having his way with the family and that the team breached the cabin before he could identify the threat.

Gillian lashed out with his Cohe. Four quick slashes

formed a large rectangle of smoldering metal around the door's perimeter. He leaped to the side to allow Stone Face to serve as a battering ram.

The big man crashed through the portal with ease. The door flattened. Stone Face curled into a tight ball and rolled across it and deeper into the cabin. His crescent webs contorted with him, forming a near-perfect sphere that shrank his exposed side portals to minimal size. The first man to breach a target was always in the greatest danger of being fired upon. The compressed energy shield gave him the best chance of surviving an initial counterstrike.

It didn't come. Alvis Qwee was nowhere in sight.

Gillian, Slag and Basher rushed in. Stone Face roared to his feet.

The Du Pal hadn't altered the circular layout of the main floor. It remained a single large space, seven meters across and roughly divided into thirds: lounge area, bedroom, kitchen.

A bathroom and a pair of closets offered the only possible hiding places. Gillian X-slashed their doors with his wand before Slag and Basher whipped them open.

The bathroom had been redesigned for a binary: twin sinks and a dual-seat toilet. The closets contained attire for two men, one of them with a slightly heavier build. A number of the shirts, pants and jackets were smoldering, ruined by their encounter with Gillian's Cohe. There was no sign of their target or his victims.

The four of them approached the curving staircase to the basement, Gillian in the lead. The steps were on the wall of the bedroom area, behind two single beds aligned binary style, headboard to headboard.

The curving staircase was narrow, forcing them to descend single file. Gillian didn't like it. Their vulnerability was heightened. But there was little choice.

An unpleasant screeching noise grew louder as they approached the wooden door at the bottom. The eerie sound resembled the cries of an infant yet also bore a mechanical quality, as if produced by some sort of machine. It randomly ebbed and flowed, although never dropping to a level that could be considered tranquil. At its loudest, it was clamorous enough to suggest that it must be earsplitting on the other side of the door.

A quizzical look at the team was met with puzzled shrugs. They also had no idea what the source of the sound might be.

Could they have lucked out? Gillian wondered. Amid such a racket, could Alvis Qwee be unaware of their entry, maybe too busy to have bothered monitoring his sensors?

It didn't matter. Either way, they were going in.

Slag pressed a scanner against the door. Measurements appeared on the tiny screen. The door was mounted on simple hinges and wasn't reinforced, although it was locked from the inside. The most important dimension was its thickness, less than three centimeters. Gillian wouldn't have to use his Cohe. It was thin enough to be kicked in, ideally giving them the greatest element of surprise.

He lifted his left foot and rammed his boot heel into the area just above the knob.

The door flew open. He lunged through, followed by the others.

The circular basement had the same dimensions as the main floor. It consisted of a single open space covered in a thick carpet. There the comparisons ended. The upstairs was meant for living. The basement was outfitted for pain and death.

Alvis Qwee stood in the center of his torture chamber. His four arms were folded across his chests and his faces were twisted into expressions of amusement. Gillian knew in an instant that their entry somehow had been tracked, possibly even before they'd breached the upstairs door. The Du Pal was waiting for them.

Gillian formed an assessment of the room in an instant.

Three of the kidnapped family members – the two moms and the eleven year-old daughter – were strapped upright against the wall behind the assassin. In front of them was a bed draped with a selection of pain inflictors. The standard sadist options were present, including whips, paddles, cuffs and a bevy of surgical instruments, as well as more exotic torture devices such as finger melters and orifice sealers. A small table held a slaughterhouse deboning module. It was used to inject acids that would dissolve an animal's skeletal structure.

The three family members didn't appear to have been harmed yet, at least not physically. Their mouths were stuffed with ball gags, their eyes wide with terror.

Next to Alvis Qwee, the family's fifteen year-old boy lay naked on his back, bound to a narrow table. His face was contorted with agony and his body was convulsing. His mouth was closed, the lips having been glued together. VR lenses cloaked his eyes. EEG pads were attached to his forehead, their wires running to a small red box attached to the ceiling. The screeching sound emanated from the box's speakers.

Gillian realized what the box was, although he'd never heard one in use before. It was a *sufrimiento*, a device invented by the Paraguayan military and now employed by intelligence agencies worldwide to torture prisoners for intel.

The harsh sounds triggered synapses in the victim's limbic system, the heart of the emotions, specifically those having to do with any sort of repressed childhood or infantile pain. Everyone had such pains, even if they were minor. Even something as simple as sadness over losing a favorite toy was enough to leave a subliminal mnemonic trace that the *sufrimiento* could access and amplify. Augmented by VR imagery depicting violence and destruction, the multisensory device was said to create internal agonies worse than many forms of pure physical abuse.

Alvis Qwee hit a switch at the side of the table. The screeching noise ended; the boy's quivering body slumped into unconsciousness. The only sounds were the muffled cries and moans of the gagged family members.

"Welcome," Alvis Qwee offered in stereo.

Gillian said nothing. Better to allow an enemy to revel in its overconfidence.

The assassin continued, alternating between the tways.

"Visitors"

"so rarely"

"come here."

The tways smiled.

"At least not"

"volun-"

"tarily."

The tways were short and wiry, one with slightly wider shoulders. Similar angular chins hinted that they could be natural brothers. Their hair was trimmed short and provided the main distinguishing feature. The tway on the left had red hair, his counterpart black.

"Directionalize," Gillian whispered into his mic while taking a step to the left. Slag, Basher and Stone Face, their legs moving in tandem, eased to the right.

Alvis Qwee seemed unconcerned. His heads angled toward one another.

"What should we do?" Redhair asked, beginning a mock conversation with himself.

"It's up to you," Blackhair responded.

"Should we kill these pests?"

"I suppose that's best."

"It seems unfair, four against one."

"Screw the odds, let's have some fun."

"Now!" Gillian hissed.

Slag, Basher and Stone Face opened fire on Blackhair with their thrusters. Gillian whipped a straight Cohe beam at Redhair at the same instant.

As he'd expected, Alvis Qwee was too fast to be fooled by

such a simple attack. The tways' crescent webs came alive. The tways jerked away from one another, easily dodging the thruster blasts and Cohe strike. But the purpose of the initial assault was merely to force them apart.

Gillian lashed at the space between the tways, not trying to hit either one, trying only to keep them separated. All the while, he glanced at the team, calmly reviewing what he'd taught them during the intense training sessions.

Keep shooting, but don't aim for where your opponent is. He won't be there by the time you pull the trigger. Aim for where you think he'll be microseconds from now.

Blackhair sidestepped most of their blasts. And he was too experienced to allow the strikes that did splatter against his front crescent to drive him backward or knock him off balance. He leaned into each of the hits at just the right moment.

Stay in triangular formation, two in front, one in back. Alternate your fire – one, two, three – one, two, three. Keep up a machine gun barrage.

Blackhair thrashed at them with his Cohe but they maintained their steady assault. Guns fired in one-two-three cadence, filling the basement with a cacophony of thruster shrieks.

Keep your webs tight. Stay in constant motion, spinning as a group and easing forward. If you stop moving, you'll give him a clear shot through your side portals.

Red sparks sizzled among the soldiers' close-quarter webs. Slag, Basher and Stone Face followed Gillian's dictates, attacking only Blackhair while maintaining their primary defensive posture against Redhair. And whenever Redhair attempted to slash or stab his beam through their weak side portals, Gillian attacked that tway with renewed fury.

To the terrified family, the firefight must appear like a blur of crazed movements. All six bodies boasted enhanced neuromuscular systems. Alvis Qwee was marginally faster than the soldiers but that fact had been foreseen and accounted for.

Gillian's speed provided the advantage. He was faster than all of them although he didn't know why. Yet even now, in the cauldron of combat, he had the strangest feeling that he'd been trained by the very best, that he'd apprenticed with someone who was a remarkable fighter as well as a brilliant tactician and strategist. Words from that unknown instructor echoed in his head.

In combat, you must simultaneously balance two states of mind. Exist in the moment yet exist five steps ahead of the moment, or ten steps, or a hundred if you're able.

The words triggered muscle memories that Gillian didn't even know existed. He perceived the tways as arcs of movement, vibrant chess pieces on a board whose boundaries were defined by the basement's perimeter.

Absorb the subtle clues that reveal your opponent's multiple futures. Perceive every spatiotemporal possibility that he might conceivably occupy.

Gillian adhered to the words of that mysterious mentor. He studied the battle even as he fought it, seeing all of Alvis Qwee's futures, selecting the one that offered the best resolution.

He waited for that future to develop and, at the perfect moment, abruptly shifted his tactics to pure offense. Striding calmly toward Redhair, he flogged his beam with such frenzy that the air became streaked with overlapping bands of twisting black light.

The relentless assault drove the tway backward. Gillian took a fraction of a moment, perhaps mere nanoseconds, to perceive the other half of the battle. The soldiers and Blackhair appeared to be at a stalemate, neither able to take down their opponent. And whenever Redhair attempted to shift his attention to the soldiers and try a fresh attack them with his Cohe, Gillian escalated his attack.

Perfect. The moment was here. His attention didn't waver from Redhair's face. He was attuned to the tway's every minute expression.

In the space of seconds, Redhair betrayed a sequence of attitudinal changes. Overconfidence gave way to surprise, which in turn gave way to nascent fear. Alvis Qwee had never encountered such an opponent, had never conceived of the possibility that he could be defeated by four mere humans.

Redhair began twisting frantically, trying to avoid Gillian's wily beam. Desperation overtook him. He leaped sideways, put himself directly in front of the three family members bound to the walls.

To Gillian, the move was blatantly obvious. The assassin hoped that his opponent would hesitate for fear of harming the prisoners.

But Gillian didn't experience the reactions that Alvis Qwee hoped for. He was neither hesitant nor fearful. Besides, there was little risk to the family, at least not from his end. His control of the Cohe was too precise. Only the Du Pal could hurt the prisoners now. And he couldn't afford to do that, couldn't afford to distract himself from Gillian's assault for even a microsecond.

Gillian feinted left then lunged right. His movement, coupled with the simultaneous twist of his wrist and the perfect amount of squeeze pressure on the egg-shaped weapon sent his beam darting away from the tway. It boomeranged into a one eighty degree turn and shot straight through Redhair's weak side portal.

The black energy penetrated his left ear. From a practical standpoint, Redhair died at the instant Gillian's beam burned through his brain. But the curious state of binarydom maintained certain bodily functions active. Both halves of Alvis Qwee screamed even as Redhair's eyes closed and he crumpled to the floor.

Alvis Qwee, torn in half, found his remaining tway reduced

to a quaking squall of agony. Out of control, Blackhair spun and jerked madly across the room. His mouth opened and closed, altering the volume of those harsh noises erupting from his throat. His teeth chattered crazily. In the process, he somehow deactivated his crescent web.

He crashed against the table holding the unconscious boy, ricocheted toward the soldiers. His arms thrashed and quivered as if they were no longer his own. Fingers spasmed open. The Cohe dropped from his hand.

Stone Face lowered his thruster and took a step toward the tway. He threw a single mighty punch, shattering Blackhair's nose. The tway flew halfway across the room and landed on his back, unconscious before he hit the carpet.

The dual screaming ended. A peaceful silence descended on the room. Basher frowned and shook his head, as if surprised the team had triumphed. Then he broke into a grin and pummeled Slag's back in celebration.

"Son of a bitch! We actually did it! We killed one of these fuckers!"

Gillian gestured to the family. The soldiers freed the moms and daughter who were pinned to the wall and removed their gags. Gillian undid the bindings of the unconscious boy and checked his vital signs.

"Your son's hurt. But I believe he'll survive."

Hearing Gillian's words, the moms cried and hugged one another and their daughter, then rushed over to their son.

"You'll need to get him med care immediately," Gillian said, nodding to Stone Face. The soldier picked up the boy and carried him toward the stairs. Slag urged the family to follow.

"Take the assassin's van," Gillian instructed. "Drive to the main road at the end of the lane and make a right. There's a town with a clinic about twenty kilometers from here. Tell the doctors he was attached to a sufrimiento. They'll know what to do."

"Thank you," one of the moms whispered, the tears streaming down her face as she panned her gaze across the four faces hidden behind the visors. "Thank you for saving us."

Gillian nodded and turned his back on them. He didn't need compliments. Stone Face headed up the steps with the unconscious boy. The family followed.

"What about the one that's still breathing?" Basher asked, motioning to Blackhair.

"Let's make him comfortable," Gillian suggested.

Basher and Slag lifted the unconscious tway onto the basement's only chair, a sturdy wooden contraption with built-in organocuffs. The chair, like everything else in this horror show of a basement, was intended for torture. Electroshock clamps protruded from its headrest.

Slag touched a button at the back of the chair. The organocuffs came to life, snaked around Blackhair's wrists, ankles and midsection. The cuffs tightened.

"Think we can still get any intel out of him?" Basher wondered.

"Wake him up," Gillian ordered.

Slag withdrew a safak from his utility belt, detached the mini needle and stabbed it into the med griddle's flamer drug. He syringed the tway's neck, injected the full dose.

The flamer hit the tway's central nervous system in three seconds. His eyes sprang open, jerked madly back and forth. Gillian pivoted the chair so that Blackhair faced the dead tway who lay sprawled across the floor.

At the sight of his slain half, Blackhair dissolved into a fresh volley of screams and tried futilely to escape the cuffs. His head whipped back and forth with such fury that Gillian wondered whether he might be capable of snapping his own neck vertebrae.

Slag shook his head. "He's done. Bisectional hemiosis. Total psychotic break."

"Want to put him to sleep and haul him back with us?" Basher asked. Even within the helmet, he had to almost shout to be heard above Blackhair's shrieks. "Maybe Nick or the doc want to try using emotive probes or some other fancy shit."

Gillian shook his head. "He's not worth the trouble."

"Then bye-bye, fucker," Basher said, grabbing a clump of the tway's hair to stop the head from moving. He switched his thruster to short-range microburst and pressed the barrel against the tway's forehead. On that setting, Blackhair's skull would implode and his gray matter fracture into pulp.

Gillian grabbed Basher's wrist, yanked the gun off-target before he could fire.

"No. We let him live."

Basher shrugged and holstered his weapon. Gillian sensed Slag regarding him curiously.

"Alvis Qwee always left a survivor at the end of his nasty little games," Gillian explained. "I think it's appropriate that we show him the same consideration."

Basher grinned. "Hell yes! Works for me."

Slag shrugged and nodded.

Gillian wasn't being truthful. His decision to leave the tway alive wasn't driven by a desire for some form of raw justice. The real reason eluded him. All he could discern of his own motives was that having one tway survive the death of its complete self seemed proper. It was the right thing to do.

"Let's go," he ordered. "As soon as that family makes it to town, this place will be swarming with cops."

They headed outside. The van was gone and Stone Face was waiting. Gillian led them back onto the winding trail toward the place where they'd hidden the skyboards. Even a half kilometer away through the dense woods, the faint screams of Alvis Qwee's surviving tway could still be heard.

THIRTY-FIVE

Bel had decided that today was the day she'd finally reveal to E-Tech's Board of Regents the information she'd been sitting on for far too long. She'd spent nearly a month trying to figure out just how she was going to broach the subject of Thi Maloca and the secret Ash Ock research project disrupted by the attack.

Details of the EPF raid had been effectively quashed. The public remained in the dark, with only vague rumors having surfaced about a battle deep in the Amazon rainforest. Before the media could descend upon the area and attempt to uncover what had happened, EPF had destroyed all evidence by nuking the entire site. The official military line was to deny any knowledge of a battle and insist that the annihilation itself was the result of "an accidental detonation of a thermonuclear weapons payload by unknown terrorists."

Bel's problem, why she'd held back this long, was that once she gave her report, the regents naturally would wonder how she'd come upon such a wealth of information. The mole, the tway of Codrus, would be particularly keen to know her source.

She'd finally concluded that such questions couldn't be helped and that the majority of the board members, at least those who weren't Paratwa infiltrators, deserved to be apprised of the incident. Her response to any questions would incorporate a careful blend of truth and lies.

As it turned out, she needn't have bothered stressing over the issue. No sooner had Bel entered the conference room at headquarters and taken her seat than board president Suzanna Al-Harthi launched into a full report on the raid. It was not something listed on today's agenda.

Al-Harthi began by praising the EPF for its bold initiative and expressing remorse for the loss of so many of its soldiers.

"In any case, the Royal Caste has been dealt another severe blow. First Aristotle's death and now this, the loss of a major Ash Ock facility, along with the confirmed death of Empedocles. Although it remains critical that E-Tech continues to publicly adopt a neutral stance when it comes to the Paratwa assassins, these events may prove to have certain long-term benefits to our organization."

"Not to mention to the rest of humanity," R Jobs Headly chimed in.

Bel looked over to where Doctor Emanuel normally sat, curious about his absence. He'd attended every one of these meetings since she'd assumed the director's post.

Al-Harthi turned to her. "Director Bakana, perhaps we can use this information in a way that furthers E-Tech's goals while maintaining our neutrality in the conflict. Any ideas come to mind?"

"This is the first I've heard of the raid," Bel lied. "May I ask where your information came from?"

"A high-ranking source in the EPF. I'm not at liberty to say more than that."

"Of course. I'll need some time to analyze the full report."

"The classified EPF account of the mission and other details are being distributed to you and your appropriate departments as we speak. For now, however, I'd like us to review the nature of the Ash Ock's secret research initiative. Lois Perlman has a report."

The science adviser to the Mideast Coalition panned her gaze across the room as she spoke. "Their project was quite unprecedented. Its success could have tipped the scales steeply in favor of the Paratwa.

"In simple terms, they were attempting to transcend one of the greatest limitations of binary existence, that Paratwa cannot reproduce themselves outside of a lab. No matter how a female tway becomes pregnant, whether impregnated by a human or another binary, or even by the female's own tway in the case of a mélange, the resulting child is always human.

"A Paratwa can only come into being when the fetuses of two normal humans are injected with the McQuade Unity under strict laboratory conditions. And even then, a majority of the interlinked fetuses fail to reach full term or perish in early infancy due to severe physiological and neurological disorders.

"The project at Thi Maloca was an attempt by the best geneticists in the world, many of them kidnapped and forced to do the Ash Ock's bidding, to overcome that handicap. They sought to alter the biology of a binary female so that she might become pregnant in a natural way. She would then pass on her own genetic heritage, as well as that of the binary father, by giving birth naturally to interlinked tways."

Bel noted murmurs of surprise from the majority of the regents. Apparently Al-Harthi and Perlman hadn't yet shared this intel with most of the board.

"I thought such a thing was considered impossible?" Headly asked.

"True enough," Perlman said. "But we must never forget the sheer arrogance and audacity of the Royal Caste. There are few things they consider beyond their reach. And the prize was certainly tantalizing. Imagine a world where binaries could mate and produce Paratwa babies with the same ease that humans procreate. Their numbers would increase at an alarming rate, driven by the same geometric progression that has caused our own overpopulation."

Bel nodded. Instead of humanity having to deal with tens of thousands of binaries, many of them assassins, after a few generations their numbers would escalate into the millions. That was what had been so unsettling about the Ash Ock's secret project.

Perlman went on. "I have a source who tells me the project was initiated by Theophrastus, who by all accounts possesses a rare and dazzling intellect. This source claims that the research involved a line of inquiry previously overlooked by other geneticists."

Bel hid her excitement. That Theophrastus was behind the project was *not* part of the intel that the doomed molecular geneticist had secretly passed on to Director Witherstone. Nor was it something Bel and Nick had learned by way of Ektor Fang.

Such information had to have come directly from one of the Ash Ock or from their top lieutenant, Meridian.

Perhaps the Royals, as part of their convoluted and sinister machinations, had instructed Codrus to leak that tidbit about Theophrastus to Lois Perlman, and thus to the regents. Or maybe Codrus had leaked it on his own for some other reason. Whatever the case, Bel now had a clue to the identity of the Ash Ock mole.

She recalled Olinda Shining's words. *Track the leaks. Narrow down the potential suspects. Set a trap.*

Lois Perlman might well be the key to doing that. Either she was the mole or someone had fed her the information. If Bel could follow that leak to its source…

R Jobs Headly forced her concentration back to the meeting.

"How do we know the Ash Ock have abandoned this line of research?" the financier wondered. "Perhaps they've simply relocated it to another facility."

"Possible," Al-Harthi admitted. "But unlikely, according to the details we've unearthed. My EPF source indicates that, for once, the Royals apparently attempted to reach beyond what was feasible. The data seized during the raid shows that the research had not produced any naturally born Paratwa babies and that the entire project was on the verge of being abandoned."

Perlman nodded. "Theophrastus himself was considering terminating it. We believe the raid rendered such a decision irrelevant."

"But how can you know that for certain?" Headly asked.

How indeed? Bel wondered.

Perlman shrugged. "I trust my source. You'll just have to take my word for it."

For once, Headly didn't have a comeback. Looking thoughtful, he turned to gaze out the window wall at the far end of the room.

Is the financier equally suspicious about Lois Perlman's mysterious source? If so, does that rule him out as the mole?

Bel wasn't sure. Codrus may have decided that an excellent way to disguise himself among the regents was to assume the identity of the one board member who was most openly critical of the Paratwa.

She followed Headly's gaze. Outside, a torrent of brown and gray flakes were coming down, the first snowfall of the fast-approaching winter. Bel remembered back to her childhood, back to when Philadelphia still received pristine white snowfalls throughout the season. But like many cities today, the relentless environmental degradation often produced frozen precipitation in the most dismal of hues. And a fair portion of it was mildly radioactive because of worldwide nuclear detonations over the past several decades. *Shitsnow*, the apocalyptic environmentalists dubbed it. *The Earth's backlash against the human species for having treated their world like a toilet.*

The regents continued discussing the Thi Maloca raid and the Ash Ock's failed project. Al-Harthi finally called a halt to the conversation and brought up another subject.

"I'm being bombarded by inquiries about this team of so-called soldier-hunters, as I'm sure the rest of you are as well. I've dodged the questions thus far. But after the incident a few nights ago in Kuala Lumpur, the questions are bound to become more intense. E-Tech needs to adopt a formal and consistent position on the matter."

"Humanity's Avenger," a regent muttered. "That's what the media is calling them."

"I say we give these soldier-hunters a medal," Headly said, his smile brighter than ever.

Al-Harthi scowled. "This is a serious matter. The death of that sadist Alvis Qwee was certainly cause for celebration from all quarters. I suspect that even some of the assassins may have been pleased by his elimination. But now this team has struck again and killed another Paratwa assassin. And the witnesses weren't just a terrified family spared from a horrible fate. This time there was a street battle in the midst of a major city in Malaysia, a battle witnessed and recorded by hundreds."

Headly shrugged. "Your point?"

"My point is that the ongoing conflict between humans and Paratwa is bad enough as it is. These soldier-hunters, no matter how much the media and the public might be cheering them on, are serving to throw fuel on an already raging fire."

A strange way of looking at it, Bel thought. *The sort of perspective a tway of Codrus might have.*

"It's vital that we learn more about this team," Vok Shen said, turning to Bel. "Have your people had any luck in identifying them?"

"They're masked. No one has seen their faces."

"There are other means of identification. One of the four is apparently quite skilled with the Cohe wand. I don't believe that the number of humans with that unique ability is overly large."

"Indeed it isn't. We're making every effort to uncover the identity of this presumed team leader."

Bel found herself recalling her most recent encounter with Gillian. She'd made a clandestine visit to Nick's training facility yesterday as the team prepped to take on its next target, a Fleetwood Phaeton who'd emigrated from Pennsylvania to Japan.

Following the team's workout, as Nick discussed something with the soldiers, she'd had a brief one-on-one with Gillian. He'd displayed the same arrogance as he had at their first meeting at the clinic, praising her beauty on one hand while criticizing her choices in attire and again suggesting she start wearing dresses. Worse, he'd violated her personal space, leaning to within centimeters of her body in what seemed to be an attempt to sniff at her face.

She'd quickly pulled away and stomped out of the gym, not only creeped out by the experience but as infuriated by him as she'd been at their initial encounter. It didn't help that the aggressive PR campaign Gillian had outlined for convincing people that hatred of the Paratwa should produce a corresponding increase of support for E-Tech was actually working. She'd grudgingly adopted it after consultation with Rory Connors and the approval of her other associate directors.

Vok Shen scowled at Bel. "That's it? You don't have so much as a clue as to who this team's ringleader might be?"

Bel had practiced responses to such inquiries, knowing the discussion inevitably would arise. "Pablo Dominguez has assigned his top people to unearthing everything about the team and its leader. We think the four of them are male, although at this point even that isn't certain."

Vok Shen shook his head. "They couldn't have just come out of nowhere. Some organization must be financing and training them."

"The most obvious suspect would be the EPF," Headly

offered, grinning at Al-Harthi. "Perhaps your source could shed further light on the topic."

The two regents glared at one another. Bel jumped into the stony silence.

"E-Tech Intelligence has reached a preliminary conclusion about the origin of the soldier-hunters. Most likely they're a shadow operation, either within the EPF or one of the world's other major intelligence or military entities. Pablo Dominguez has some of his best people looking into the matter. He also has our programmers running sims to determine if the soldier-hunters' methods can be emulated."

"Emulated?" barked Vok Shen, angrier than Bel had ever seen him. "The last thing we need is to have more groups of these soldier-hunters wreaking havoc!"

Words that a Paratwa might utter. Was Vok Shen the mole?

"The sims are for internal use only," Bel answered calmly. "However, you can be sure that by this team's having killed two Paratwa assassins in a manner that was once thought to be impossible, many organizations, military and otherwise, will be keenly studying their methods."

Al-Harthi nodded grimly. "Nothing to be done about that, I suppose. But Director Bakana, please give the identification of this team your highest priority."

"Of course. And if we do ID them, what does the board believe should be E-Tech's best use of that information?"

"We use it to stop them!" Vok Shen barked. "If their exploits continue, it could drive the Royals and their legions toward open war with us!"

We're already at war, she wanted to snap back. But there was no upside to escalating the argument.

R Jobs Headly rolled his eyes at the industrialist's outburst. Lois Perlman maintained a neutral expression.

"I believe our formal position on the matter should be this," Al-Harthi proposed, reading from her pad. "'E-Tech always regrets the escalation of violence. We urge these soldier-hunters, whoever they might be, to desist from further provocative mayhem.'"

"Neutral enough not to offend anyone other than the most hardcore Paratwa haters," Lois Perlman agreed. "And that group is unlikely to be swayed by any statement we issue."

Headly looked ready to speak but apparently thought better of it. No one else commented. The financier probably realized he'd lose if he called for a formal vote of opposition to Al-Harthi's proposal.

"I'll have Rory Connors put out a statement along those lines immediately," Bel promised. As always, she would be getting together with the Media Relations head and her other associate directors at the conclusion of the regents' meeting.

"Make sure it's as widely distributed as possible," Al-Harthi said. "The world needs to be clear that our agenda is to promote peace between humans and binaries."

"Of course."

Bel panned her gaze across the fifteen faces, as always wondering which one of them served a far different agenda.

THIRTY-SIX

Bel walked swiftly along the seventh floor corridor of the University of Penn Hospital. She'd received the news moments after the board meeting and had rushed straight over here.

Nick was already in the private room, standing at the head of the bed with a look of deep worry. The unconscious patient was Doctor Emanuel. He was linked to an overhead med panel via a host of IV tubes and sensors. His skin was pale, his age lines somehow more pronounced. Even for a ninety-five year-old man, he appeared terrifyingly fragile.

Nick grimaced as Bel entered and closed the door.

"What happened?"

"Acute myocardial infarction," Nick said.

"Heart attack."

"More severe than his last one. No chance to do any selfmedding at home this time. He suffered damage to the heart muscle from ventricular fibrillation." Nick swallowed hard, struggled to continue. "There were complications. His legs are paralyzed. And the interrupted blood flow to the brain has caused... neurological deficits."

"I'm so sorry."

"Stupid son of a bitch," Nick muttered, a pained look revealing the true nature of his feelings. "He could have lived to a hundred and twenty if he'd taken better care of himself. He should have had a transplant years ago."

Stubbornly independent, Bel thought. In that, Doctor Emanuel and Nick were very much alike.

"What's the prognosis?" she asked.

Nick seemed too upset to reply. He gestured to a unisex mech nurse poised in the corner like a sentinel. It activated and recited a report that was ruthlessly clinical.

"Transplantation with an artificially grown heart is the recognized procedure. Survival rate based on the patient's age and metabolism is ten percent."

"You can't always go by that," Bel muttered, knowing it was a lie. She recalled enough of her training to become a doctor to realize that few physicians would even attempt surgical intervention with such low odds.

"Presuming survival of the transplant procedure, quality of life would be greatly deteriorated and long-term nursing care likely unavoidable. The lower limb paralysis can be partially corrected through minor surgery although exoskeletal braces would be required to restore full locomotion. The neurological deficits are irreversible.

"Under these circumstances, the patient's advance care directive is clear. In consideration of the low survival odds, his wishes are to forego all surgery. A DNR order is also in effect."

"Do not resuscitate," Bel whispered.

Nick turned away from her, in obvious pain. His voice cracked. "He's going to die."

"I'm sorry," she said again, surprised at how intensely the news was affecting him. It had been obvious from that dinner at her condo just how close Nick and Doctor Emanuel were. Still, considering that the elder man was Bel's lifelong hero, she would have thought that she'd have been the one to experience such an intense reaction. She was sad, of course. But Nick seemed nearly overwhelmed by the news.

"How long does he have?" she asked gently.

Nick could only shake his head. The nurse responded. "Per the patient's directive, life support must be withdrawn within twenty-four hours of final diagnosis."

"I'll do it tomorrow morning," Nick said.

Bel heard the iron control in his words. He was struggling to hold it together.

Her thoughts jumped ahead to practical considerations. The passing of E-Tech's spiritual patriarch would be a major story across the newsphere. She'd have to meet as soon as possible with Rory Connors to coordinate their media response, as well as with other department heads to ensure that Doctor Emanuel's death was handled with the care and respect accorded to someone of his unique stature.

She was about to ask Nick if any funeral arrangements had been made when something he'd said moments ago finally registered.

"You have the authority to... pull the plug?"

"Yeah. Full power of attorney to carry out his wishes."

Doctor Emanuel's wife of nearly three quarters of a century had died three years ago and their sole offspring, a son, had been lost in one of the Hawaiian seaquakes of the 2060s. He had no siblings. Without any close living relatives, Bel supposed it made sense that Doctor Emanuel had made such arrangements with a close friend.

Nick dismissed the mech nurse and finally turned to face her. There were tears in his eyes. It was strange seeing him so broken up, considering he was one of the toughest human beings she'd ever met.

"Would you like me to be here with you in the morning?" she asked gently.

"No. This is something I'd prefer to do alone."

"Of course. Listen, I have to go, I have a full slate of meetings today. But I'll try to come back this evening."

She laid a hand on his shoulder. "It'll be OK, Nick."

"Yeah."

She struggled to come up with words that were more supportive. "I'm sure that Doctor Emanuel would be pleased to know he has someone who cares about him so much. You've been a good friend."

"He's not my friend. I mean, that's not how I think of him."

The words contained no bitterness, only deep sorrow. Bel shook her head, confused. "What do you mean?"

"He's not my friend. He's my son."

THIRTY-SEVEN

For a moment, Bel was too astonished to respond. When she finally found her voice, the only thing she could think to utter was an inane, "I didn't know."

Outside, the bleak shitsnow continued to fall. Nick stared into it. His words were distant, his sadness palpable.

"Marta got pregnant. That's why we got hitched in the first place. Still, I was crazy in love with her even though in a lot of ways we were less than compatible. We stayed together for so many years for Weldon's sake. When we finally split up, Marta married that divinity professor. They took his last name, Emanuel."

"Why didn't you tell me any of this?"

"I tried. That first night we were together." He gave a bitter laugh. "Who am I kidding? I could have told you, *should* have told you. My only excuse was that it wasn't something I was proud of. Abandoning my own child. Not exactly the kind of admission to launch a new relationship with. And later… well, I didn't want to ruin a good thing."

"Oh, Nick. You wouldn't have ruined anything."

His tears returned. He forced control, wiped them away with a sleeve.

"When things went bad for me back then, when I couldn't deal with the world and thought about ending it all, I figured

– no, I *rationalized* – that a boy nearing his tenth birthday was old enough to handle his father dying or running off into the future. I told myself that he'd be fine, that he wouldn't be hurt by my actions." He shook his head. "I was wrong."

"But when you woke up, the first thing you did was try to reconnect with him. That says something."

"Yeah, it says I was an asshole for abandoning him in the first place."

"Maybe. But the two of you ultimately reconciled."

"It wasn't easy. Even after seventy-six years he was still plenty pissed off at what I'd done."

Bel recalled Doctor Emanuel's words from the dinner about their early attempts at getting together. *A rocky start. But we worked at it, helped it grow into a most worthwhile relationship.*

"You ended up with something good. In the end that's all that matters."

"I suppose."

She wanted to hug him. But she sensed that affection wasn't something he wanted right now.

He stiffened, swallowed back his grief. "None of what I just told you can be made public. The doc and I decided from the beginning that we'd always keep this part of our lives under wraps."

"Of course. It goes no further than this room."

Nick moved closer to the bed, gripped one of his dying son's frail hands. Bel slipped out the door without another word.

THIRTY-EIGHT

Bel returned to her condo late in the evening following the earthly half of Doctor Emanuel's funeral. It had been a long day, climaxing with a service for the great man attended by thousands at the Imperius Convention Center. The toasts and the speeches were heartfelt but they'd seemed to go on forever. It was almost two am. Bel wanted nothing more than to take her ToFo meds, slip into pajamas and have the autosheets nestle her into oblivion.

Nick hadn't attended the service. He'd said his own goodbyes on that morning last week when he'd terminated his son's life support. He'd been content to watch the eulogies online from the sanctity of his apartment.

The other half of Doctor Emanuel's funeral would happen tomorrow. His corpse would be launched into space on an E-Tech shuttle flight departing for the Colonies. The great man wouldn't be going that far, however. His final wishes called for orbital vaporization. His body would be ejected from the cargo bay as soon as the shuttle reached low-Earth orbit. As the craft ignited its main engines for its final thrust toward the cylinders, his remains would be incinerated by the burning exhausts.

Nick had wanted to be alone for the evening, which was just as well. The funeral had attracted far more global media than usual and put excessive attention on Bel, with endless demands for interviews and comments. She couldn't take the chance of being followed to Nick's apartment or him being spotted coming here. It was best that their affair take a break for a few days until the frenzy relented.

She headed for the bathroom, her mind still on the funeral and what would come next. Although she didn't like to think of it in such terms, Doctor Emanuel's death would be a PR boon to E-Tech. Just as Director Witherstone's assassination had served to increase support for the organization, the passing of such an iconic figure would also contribute to keeping E-Tech's message front and center.

But what she really couldn't stop dwelling on were the ironies of the entire situation. Over the years, Bel had read numerous biographies of Doctor Emanuel. All had pinpointed the events that had led him, in his middle years, to begin writing and speaking about the long-term negative impacts of unrestricted science and technology, a famed series of articles and speeches that had inspired E-Tech's creation.

Doctor Emanuel had revealed that his inspiration for such views had come at least partly from the struggles he'd gone through after his biological father sank into depression and left them a week before his tenth birthday. The father, a figure lost to history, had been described by Doctor Emanuel only fleetingly, and then only as "a little man." The phrase was believed to reference the son's anger at the father. As far as Bel knew, no one had ever taken it for a literal depiction.

In his college years, Weldon Emanuel had composed a series of memorable articles criticizing the excesses of technology. An early target had been the explosion of com devices blanketing the early twenty-first century, which he believed served to distance people from one another, substituting a kind of faux interaction for genuine human closeness.

Later, under the tutelage of his stepfather, the divinity professor, his views had expanded into more subtle critiques of sci-tech, including several papers where he'd attacked the notion of people using technology to evade personal responsibility – a clear reaction to Nick electing to become a corpsicle, which Weldon subsequently had learned about while secretly researching his father's fate. One midcentury speech in particular echoed in Bel's mind. In it, he'd railed against the growing number of people opting to escape the troubles of the world by going into stasis.

The future is a precious gift, an opportunity to overcome the limitations of our pasts and presents. It is not a recreational drug, a thing to be consumed in order to evade the responsibilities or problems affecting us in the here and now.

Taken together, Doctor Emanuel's writings and speeches made a strong case that E-Tech's creation had been inspired by the simple fact that a father had deserted his son at an impactful age.

Bel sighed, too tired to dig any deeper into the myriad of ironies. Changing into pajamas, she made her way to the bedroom and ordered the covers to part. Just as the autosheets folded around her and she closed her eyes, her drudge pinged an alert.

She groaned and opened her eyes. The serving mech stood frozen beside her bureau, its default position. It raised its right hand and finger-flashed a holo message.

A VISITOR IS AT THE FRONT DOOR.

"At this hour?" she muttered.

YES.

She'd left word with the lobby mech that she wasn't to be disturbed other than for an emergency. But if that were the case, the drudge's pings would have been more urgent.

Climbing from bed, she donned a robe and made her way to the main room. The hall camera turned on automatically as she approached the entrance, revealing the visitor's identity on the doorscreen.

It was Gillian.

Bel was too shocked for a moment to do anything other than stare at his image. Garbed in a maroon jacket and black pants, he leaned casually against the wall across from her door, staring straight into the lens of the hidden camera.

She overcame her surprise, tabbed the intercom.

"What do you want?"

"I need to speak with you. It's important."

"How'd you get past the lobby mechs?"

"I was persuasive."

It sounded like something Nick would say. She was tempted to call him, see if he knew why Gillian was here. But she decided against it. He was either sleeping or grieving. She could handle this on her own.

"I don't feel comfortable letting you in."

"Understood. Would you feel more comfortable coming out? One of the cafes on the third floor is still open. We could meet there."

No way did she want to be seen in public with him, even in a place that would have few patrons this time of night.

"We can speak through the door."

"Not an option."

"Then tell me what this is about?"

"I need to confirm a theory."

"What theory?"

"It will be simpler if you just let me in."

"Why?"

"I need to sniff your face."

Oh sure, no problem. I always let weirdo face-sniffers into my home at two am.

"That's the most ridiculous thing I've ever heard," she snapped.

"On the surface, yes. But if you don't allow me to do this, I guarantee you'll regret it."

Her heart raced. Alarm bells went off in her head. The panic button on her wrist fob could summon her bodyguards stationed out front. But by the time they got up here...

"Is that some sort of threat?" she asked.

"Let me rephrase. Confirming my theory will provide you with vital information critical to making informed decisions about your immediate future."

She had to admit, he had her curious. But she continued to hesitate.

"Take a moment to think about it," he said. "But consider this. If I was here to do you harm, do you really believe a door could stop me?"

It was a valid point. Tightening her robe, she opened up and let him in.

THIRTY-NINE

Bel backed up as he entered, not allowing Gillian out of her sight. She halted only when her butt bumped up against the dining table. Too late, she realized that her robe was maroon, the color he'd wanted to see her wearing.

He closed to within two meters. She raised a hand, held it there as a stop sign.

"That's far enough. You need to tell me what this is about."

"As Nick mentioned when we first met, I have the ability to bind odorant molecules to olfactory receptors at a level far beyond that of the average human."

"Uh huh, you have a great sense of smell. So?"

"On our two previous encounters, I detected within you a strange molecular signature, one that I wasn't familiar with. I did some olfactory research and narrowed down the possibilities. Earlier this evening, I believe I nailed down the signature's ID. But I need to make certain before presenting you with the information. If you'd allow me to come closer, I can quickly confirm my hunch."

"And you just want to sniff at me. This isn't some attempt to do... other things."

"It's exactly what I say it is."

"Just so you know, I'm not even mildly attracted to you."

"I can't say the same. I find you... mysterious and

intriguing. I suppose part of the reason is because your aroma bears certain similarities with that of my dead wife."

He paused and seemed to gaze off into the distance, as if puzzled or in a trance. Bel found herself growing more nervous by the second. She was relieved when he finally returned his attention to her.

"Rest assured I have no desire for any sort of emotional or sexual relationship with you. The nature of my attraction is something different, something harder to fathom. In any event, none of that has any connection with why I'm here."

Good to know.

"So, may I sniff you?"

I can't believe we're having this conversation.

She lowered her hand. "All right, let's get this weirdness over with."

"Thank you."

He eased closer, brought his nose to within centimeters of her forehead. She felt the gentle warmth of his exhalation blowing down across her cheeks. His nostrils flared as he inhaled deeply.

"Relax your body and breathe normally," he instructed. "I need to sample your respiration."

She hadn't even realized she'd been tensing her muscles and holding her breath. She forced herself to go slack and released the air from her lungs.

He sniffed some more. Finally, he backed away. She folded her arms across her chest, feeling that she'd been violated somehow.

"So, what's the verdict?" she demanded.

"I've confirmed my suspicion. You're under the influence of an exceptionally powerful version of pheromone induction tranqs."

"I've been pitstopped?"

"Yes."

She shook her head, unwilling to believe it. "How can you

possibly tell that? It requires a series of tests, multiple trips to a specialist."

"Or a good nose. There's more. The tranqs are primed to react to Nick's metabolism. Your attraction to him has been artificially enhanced, if not actually created in the first place."

She shook her head even while experiencing a sickly feeling in the pit of her stomach. "You're lying. Nick wouldn't do something like that."

Gillian stared at her. His silence was unnerving.

Bel couldn't believe what he was suggesting. If he was being truthful, her sexual desire for Nick wasn't natural but neurochemically instilled. It meant that everything that had happened between the two of them over these past months was built upon a horrible lie.

No. That can't be.

Then again, Nick was shrewdly confident and without a doubt one of the most manipulative humans she'd ever met.

But it's not like him. He wouldn't have done something like this to me. He wouldn't betray me in such a way.

And yet...

She struggled to get a handle on her confusion and look at the situation logically. Such a task was probably impossible, not with her emotions caught in a whirlpool. Still, she made the attempt.

OK, first off, who's more deserving of my trust? Nick or Gillian?

Nick had opened his heart to her. Over these past months she was well on her way to falling deeply in love with him. Gillian, by contrast, was a man unaware of his true heritage. He was also a man who'd admittedly developed some sort of bizarre attraction toward her based on the fact that she smelled like his dead wife.

Attraction wasn't the right word. She suspected that a kind of psychological transference had occurred during their initial encounter at the clinic. Nick had warned her that she'd be the first woman Gillian would meet since awakening from his personality-altering surgeries. He and Doctor Emanuel hadn't been certain of how, as a former tway, he would react.

At some deep unconscious level, Gillian was conflating her with his slain tway, Catharine. Might that confusion induce him to tell outright lies? Might he tell blatant untruths in order to push Nick out of her life and enable himself to draw closer?

She shuddered at the prospect but the scenario made sense. Yet was it the truth?

She needed time alone, time to think.

"You need to go. Right now."

"Of course."

"And please understand something. I'm not going to take what you've told me at face value."

Gillian shrugged. "I wouldn't either. May I suggest that you take the appropriate medical tests. They'll confirm my diagnosis that you've been pitstopped. If I were you, I'd make the first appointment as soon as possible."

You can be sure I'm going to do just that, and before I even think about accusing Nick of something so outrageous.

Gillian left without another word. Bel returned to bed, certain she was in for a restless night.

FORTY

Bishop Rikov strode up the wide staircase and entered the brand new Wellington Cathedral. It represented the Church of the Trust's first major incursion into this country. Some nations had been more skeptical than others to the church's doctrines; New Zealand had proved particularly resistant for a number of years. But the bishop knew that perseverance could overcome any obstacle.

Considering recent events affecting the Royal Caste, he needed such perseverance now more than ever.

"Your Eminence, we're so grateful you could come," a Kiwi in the audience gushed, her face beaming.

"Hear hear!" hollered a man beside her, who was garbed in walkshorts and the blue-green vest of a Level 3 devotee.

Respectful clapping broke out among the twelve hundred parishioners who'd crammed the chapel for his special appearance at the cathedral's consecration. The bishop paused to smile at the standing room only crowd, took a short bow and continued his march to the altar. Standing at the illuminated lectern, he gazed out over the faithful with his most solemn expression.

"You are children of the Spirit of Gaia," he began. "And those who adhere to the Trust shall know the glory of eternal life."

He continued with the rest of the speech by rote, having given variations of it on hundreds of occasions. But his mind was divorced from that which poured from his mouth, having locked onto the grimmer meaning of those last two words, "eternal life."

Eternal life indeed. Two of us are dead.

The Ash Ock were accustomed to setbacks, at least normal everyday ones. But the devastating events of the past few months went far beyond that.

First Aristotle had perished. And then young Empedocles had joined him. The sphere of the Royal Caste, their unofficial iconic logo, was missing two of its five components. A quintet had been reduced to a trio.

The bishop could sense that his tway and their monarch, Codrus, were similarly troubled. The links among their unique tripartite mentality were never fully severed, just weakened to a point where the tways could operate in an independent manner. His tway and monarch were painfully aware that the Royal Caste's exquisite and carefully constructed long-term plans had suffered a series of dire blows.

Their breed, superior in so many ways to all sentient beings, human and binary, had been bred to rule. Each Ash Ock was endowed with a special skill, and the breed as a whole possessed interlocking abilities, forming a potent hydra with five heads – or ten heads, depending on one's perspective.

In any case, Empedocles was to have been the final piece of that magnificent quintet.

Sappho had known early on that many of the breeds would fail to accord the Royals the loyalty they deserved. The reason, she'd explained, was because the Ash Ock weren't real assassins. They didn't possess the formidable combat skills of those they sought to rule over.

Empedocles was intended to remedy that. He was to have been the one Ash Ock that even the most obstinate of the breeds could not help but respect. Should any Paratwa assassin or group of them ever think to challenge the Royals' supremacy by force, Empedocles, as adept at strategy and tactics as he was at combat, would have proved a daunting opponent.

Better yet, he would have possessed greater mental stability than Reemul, the liege-killer. Sappho's errand boy was loyal but more than a bit unhinged. Reemul's inherent viciousness was exceeded only by sexual quirks, demented even by the most liberal of standards.

But all of Empedocles' training had been for naught. He was gone.

The loss of Thi Maloca itself was another major blow to the Ash Ock cause. Although Theophrastus' exotic project had been unsuccessful, the facility had remained an important asset, equipped to handle other cutting-edge research. Besides that, it was the place where their breed had come into being, a place that for each of them in distinctive ways harbored the sweet sensorium of youth, the pleasing and evocative memories of home.

And now Thi Maloca was gone, its loyal servitors wiped out, the above ground and underground structures stripped of their secrets and reduced to ashes by a nuclear warhead.

Perseverance, a part of him whispered even as he continued reciting key phrases of the religion.

"The Trust shall forever bless those within its folds. Those who maintain the Trust shall be blessed in perpetuity. They alone shall come to know the Spirit of Gaia as the true kingdom of all life."

Twelve hundred eager faces hung on his every word. But his thoughts continued to dwell on other setbacks to the Royals' cause, not the least of which was yesterday's unsettling discovery of a traitor within their midst.

A Paratwa at the highest level, likely one of the Ash Ock's most trusted lieutenants, was feeding information to humans. The traitor's identity remained unknown but enough data had been assembled to leave no doubt as to its existence.

Sappho had tasked Theophrastus to track down the leaks and unveil this vile serpent. The bishop was certain that the traitor would soon be identified, as would the humans to whom it was leaking vital information.

However, vigorous debate surrounded what should be the culprit's fate. Codrus agreed with Theophrastus that the most ruthless measures should be enacted. Once the traitor's identity was learned, the liege-killer should be tasked to torture it for information, then kill it in a public way that would prove instructive to other binaries or servitors considering such treason.

But Sappho, ever the subtle one, argued that not only should the traitor be spared, it should be allowed to continue unfettered in its role. It would then unknowingly again serve its true masters, the Ash Ock, this time in a counterintelligence capacity by feeding false intel to the humans.

Sappho's voice always carried inordinate weight but she didn't always get her way. Most likely, the Royals ultimately would approve some kind of compromise plan for dealing with the traitor.

"Perseverance and loyalty are the keys to staying within the graces of the Trust," the bishop droned on. "Such qualities will prove a magnificent reward to you and your everlasting souls."

He paused for effect, then hit the congregation with his final uplifting remark. "For we must never lose sight that a wondrous afterlife awaits those who remain faithful to the end!"

He whipped from beneath his robes a glowing vial of blue misk, blessed liquid of the church. He held the vial above his head, noted how the congregation's eyes were fixed upon it, as if it were something of great value. In truth it was plain distilled water mixed with food coloring and glittering traces of aquatic cobalt.

He smashed the vial against the side of the lectern. Luminescent droplets sprayed the first two rows.

"I consecrate this cathedral, New Zealand's first, in the name of the great Spirit of Gaia!"

Thunderous applause filled the chapter. The bishop feigned a modest smile, a part of him already calculating the income that today's speech and ceremony would produce for the Ash Ock coffers. Some of the monies would flow in before the day ended. Church of the Trust clerks were poised to contact every one of the twelve hundred parishioners to arrange for their donations and tithings.

The ceremony was over but many of the faithful weren't leaving. Instead, they surged toward the altar, seeking personal blessings or private consultations with the bishop. All were gracefully intercepted by the Wellington Cathedral staff, who'd been instructed to pass on his regrets that he couldn't stay, that the perpetual demands of the church required his presence elsewhere. In fact, he was due aboard a suborbital flight leaving in an hour for Turgay, Kazakhstan, where he was to make a speech at the church's major cathedral there.

He exited through a back door into a private chamber. His personal travel staff, who should have been gathered at the back door ready to accompany him to the Wellington Spaceport, instead were huddled around a monitor.

The bishop sighed. Senior acolytes or not, they too often became enamored of worldly events, mainly anything to do with sports contests, rather than strictly attending to his needs. But he tried never to chastise them for such minor failings. One had to accept their limited attention spans the same way one accepted how small children were easily distracted. They were, after all, only human.

"Another exciting game of football?" he speculated, offering a weary but accepting smile. "Are the final seconds ticking down and the outcome for the home team in great peril?"

"Apologies, your eminence," offered Valahen, the white-bearded man who coordinated his travel arrangements. "It's Humanity's Avenger. It's struck down another Paratwa assassin. The battle concluded only minutes ago."

The bishop joined them in front of the monitor, listened to the frantic jabbering of a female witness at the scene. As in that previous incident in Kuala Lumpur, the combat had occurred in plain view of hundreds, this time on a crowded street on the outskirts of Kyoto, Japan. Dozens of eyewitness videos were already online.

"I've never seen anything like it!" the witness exclaimed through a translation bot. "The assassin never had a chance! Our team attacked it with such fury that the Paratwa was practically overwhelmed!"

Our team, the bishop mused, more disturbed by the public's growing hero worship of this band of soldier-hunters than by the deeds themselves.

"Have they said what breed of assassin was involved?" he asked.

"No one's certain as of yet," Valahen said. "But some of the expert commentators are suggesting it could have been a Fleetwood Phaeton."

The Phaetons, bred by a large American vehicle manufacturer, were no pushovers, if that indeed was the Paratwa who had been slain. Still, this so-called Humanity's Avenger thus far had been going after mid-level assassins, exceedingly dangerous in human terms, yet not among the most lethal. Certainly this team would be no match should it ever dare face a truly formidable foe from one of the premier breeds, such as the Jeek Elementals. Going up against a Reemul or a Meridian surely would lead to a different outcome.

The bishop gently urged his staff away from the monitor and back to the business at hand, namely, getting him to Kazakhstan, and then later to Moscow for an important church conference. Yet as he and the entourage prepared to depart, he sensed a faint tinge of worry echoing from the consciousnesses of both his tway and his monarch. Codrus in particular had deep concerns.

A full linkage was necessary. As soon as the bishop was airborne and alone in his private compartment, he would stare into a mirror. Thousands of kilometers away, his regent tway would do the same. As they gazed at their own reflections they would see one another, and bring about the peculiar interlace that was solely the province of those who could exist either as one or as two.

There were other means for enabling the interlace. But the mirror was one of the simplest and most reliable. In any event, although physically separated, the mind of Codrus would awaken. Their monarch would then be free to apply his full, undivided intellect to this upstart band of soldier-hunters, and consider what needed to be done about them.

FORTY-ONE

Nick could tell Bel was mad at him but couldn't figure out why. The two of them were alone in her condo, which her drudge had decorated for the holidays. A multifaith glow tree hung from the ceiling, its branches representing the world's major religions, including Christianity, Islam, Hinduism, Judaism, Buddhism and Church of the Trust.

This evening was the first time they'd been together since she'd visited him at the hospital as his son lay dying. They'd shared a quiet dinner, discussing the latest success of Gillian and the team in the battle four days ago against the Phaeton in Japan. The overall plan was working. Humanity's Avenger was becoming what they'd hoped, an inspirational success. Having taken down three Paratwa assassins to date, the team had achieved one of the highest global Q-pop scores on record. People all over the world were throwing celebrations in the soldier-hunters' honor. The human race had itself an authentic hero.

"Dessert with your coffee?" Bel asked, motioning her drudge to the table.

"Depends what's on the menu?"

"Anything your precious heart desires."

Is that sarcasm? Nick wondered. Whatever it was, the words lacked genuine warmth, continuing the chill that seemed to have descended upon her since his arrival.

"I'll have vanilla ice cream over apple cake," he said.

"Too gluttonous for me. Coffee only."

The drudge nodded and retreated to the kitchen. Bel stayed quiet and stared at a spot somewhere above the glow tree until the mech returned a minute later with his dessert and a portable starbuckian.

As the drudge transfused their coffee into waiting mugs, Nick dug into the dessert. He smiled appreciatively.

"Scrumptious! They say instant cake isn't as good as fresh-baked but I'll take it anytime."

"You should help yourself to more," Bel suggested with a cold smile. "After all, you're accustomed to having whatever you like."

Just what the hell is that supposed to mean? Was it some sort of snide comment on his wealth?

He ought to confront her, force her to upchuck whatever bone she had stuck in her craw. But he held back, sensing that it was better for her to unleash in her own good time. Besides, he felt as if he needed more information first, or at least a clue as to what was behind her behavior.

As long as their conversation dwelt on Gillian and the team, E-Tech matters or other businesslike concerns, Bel seemed fine. But every time he ventured into something of a more personal nature, especially having to do with their relationship, she grimaced and found a way to change the subject. And her attitude wasn't limited to verbal frostiness. Earlier, on his way back from the bathroom, he'd passed behind her chair and playfully run his fingers through her hair. She'd flinched and yanked her head away.

Could her anger be some sort of delayed reaction for his having kept the truth from her about his son? Or could it have to do with his grief over Weldon's death, his raw emotional display at the hospital? Was she so accustomed to seeing him acting strong and on top of every situation that those few moments of weakness had unnerved her?

He reviewed the questions and quickly dismissed them. Something else was bothering her.

What about the unkind remarks he'd made about Ektor Fang's wife? Bel had made it clear that she admired Olinda Shining, whereas he'd made no attempt to hide his hostility toward the woman.

That couldn't be it. She might not like the fact that Nick despised servitors on general principle but she wouldn't get this bent out of shape over it. No, whatever was pissing her off correlated with something of a more intimate nature.

He wondered if the fact they hadn't slept together for a while could be the cause. But again, the explanation didn't hold up to scrutiny. He couldn't imagine that lack of sex would make her *this* hostile. And the turbulence of recent events had been responsible for them not sharing a bed of late. It had nothing to do with lack of desire on his part.

He imagined that a night snuggled together under the autosheets just might thaw her icy demeanor. But considering her mood, there was a better chance of the world's smog magically disappearing than there was of him getting past her bedroom door.

He shifted the conversation back to impersonal matters. They discussed what the official response should be to the Brazilian government, which had lodged formal protests with E-Tech and a host of other international organizations over the Thi Maloca raid and the subsequent nuking of the site. The country was understandably upset at the violation of its sovereignty and wanted everybody to condemn the EPF's actions.

Have I violated your sovereignty somehow? Is that why you're mad? But Nick couldn't think of an incident that fit such a scenario.

"The regents are still considering the Brazilian matter," Bel said. "They haven't reached a consensus yet."

"E-Tech should stay as neutral as possible. You don't want to piss off Brasilia but you also don't want to come down hard on the EPF."

"My thoughts as well."

Nick no longer had unfettered access to what was discussed by the Board of Regents. Weldon had been his confidential informant among them, had kept him apprised of all notable happenings.

He hoped Bel would continue passing along relevant information. But even if she did, it likely wouldn't be as comprehensive as what he'd gotten from his son over the years. And as E-Tech director, she might feel obligated to keep certain information sequestered.

He couldn't fault her for that. After all, he'd kept a number of secrets from her over the time they'd been together. It would be hypocritical to deny her the same right.

His attaboy signaled – a priority call. He thunked a switch and Sosoome's words sounded in his earpiece.

"Yo dude, there's something you need to see. Might want to stop groping your babe for a few minutes."

If only, Nick mused.

"Looks like Humanity's Avenger is at it again. The firefight's happening as we speak, inside the Nairobi Securities Exchange. No news yet on the breed of assassin."

That can't be right. The team wasn't scheduled to hunt another Paratwa until after the start of the new year. And Nick's target database had no listings for an assassin whose home base was the Kenyan capital.

"Is something wrong?" Bel asked, noticing his distraction.

"Yeah. We need to take a look at the newsphere."

Bel signaled the drudge, who activated the largest wall screen. The monitor tuned to the hottest story, which not surprisingly was the Nairobi battle. Shaky video from a drone whizzing around inside the Securities Exchange building displayed the tumultuous combat.

The assassin was in motion, striding boldly across the main floor side by side, its Cohe wands flashing in tandem. Nick was shocked to recognize the tways.

Ponytail and Albino.

"Yiska," Bel murmured.

The assassin who'd attacked E-Tech headquarters was coming toward the team, which was attempting to flank it. The foursome was in their familiar one-by-three attack formation, Gillian to the left and the soldiers to the right.

Gillian's Cohe whipped madly through the air, trying for a kill shot through the side portal of the closest tway, Ponytail. But his beams kept going astray, or were neutralized as they intersected or ricocheted off the tway's crescent webs.

The three soldiers were barely holding their ground. Armed with thruster rifles instead of their usual pistols, they were concentrating their fire on Albino. All around the battle, dozens of civilians were huddled on the floor, trying not to move, trying not to become a target. For some of them it was obviously too late. Smoldering wounds indicated they'd been hit by the deadly beams, likely collateral damage from the firefight.

Nick watched with escalating dread. Not only did the team seem outmatched but there'd been no civilian casualties in its previous three outings. That was an important consideration for maintaining "Humanity's Avenger" at peak popularity.

"Why are you doing this?" Nick whispered at the monitor.

Following Gillian's initial insistence that he be solely responsible for selecting targets from Nick's database, they'd come to a more equitable understanding. The two of them would study the list together and only finalize a target through mutual agreement. They'd talked about going after Yiska if Nick could pin down a location, which so far had proved to be an elusive task. Nick was secretly glad that he wasn't able to locate the Shonto Prong. He didn't think the team was ready to take on such a formidable assassin.

But what was happening right now, nearly halfway around the world? Had Gillian and the team gone rogue?

"Why did you send them out without telling me?" Bel demanded.

"I didn't. I have no idea what's happening."

Her look said she didn't believe him. But her skepticism was the least of his concerns at the moment.

He returned his attention to the battle. The assassin was starting to drive the team backward, putting them on the defensive. This wasn't how his sim was supposed to work in real time.

"I think there's something wrong with Gillian," Bel said worriedly. "See how his left arm is pinned against his side?"

She was right. He appeared to have been wounded.

The situation worsened. One of the assassin's beams penetrated the side portal of the biggest soldier's crescent web. It went through his chest and out the other side. He dropped like a rock, heart and lungs fatally baked by the searing beam.

"Stone Face," Nick whispered, hoping against hope that the battle wasn't lost even while knowing it was.

Another soldier fell and then the third. The Paratwa was now free to turn its full wrath on the wounded Gillian. The tways slashed and stabbed with their Cohes, looking for the kill shot. Gillian was no longer even attempting to fight back. It was all he could do just to stay alive. He twisted and jerked his body as the writhing beams seemed to come at him from all angles.

The inevitable happened. A beam got through his web's left side portal. Gillian crumpled to his knees then fell onto his back.

"Oh my God," Bel whispered, throwing a hand over her mouth.

Nick was too shocked for words. He could only stare at the screen as the triumphant assassin approached the body.

Albino plunged a hand through Gillian's side portal. He

rammed his fingers into Gillian's mouth and deactivated the crescent web. Ponytail yanked off the tac helmet, revealing the soldier-hunter's identity.

"All right!" Nick shouted with glee.

The dead man wasn't Gillian. He was a stranger. That had to mean that the others weren't Slag, Basher and Stone Face.

"Success breeds imitators," Nick said. "But not as skilled as the genuine article."

"Thank goodness it wasn't them," Bel murmured, smiling with relief.

He decided to take advantage of the break in her foul mood. Moving toward her, he opened his arms, seeking a hug. But her face instantly defaulted to frost mode, stopping him in his tracks.

"I'd better get out of here," he said, backing away. "I need to touch base with Gillian."

"That's probably the right thing to do," she said coolly.

The words reverberated with hidden meaning. But whatever the cause of her anger, right now he had more important issues to deal with. He headed for the door.

"Nick, wait."

He stopped and turned, hopeful that she was finally going to get off her chest whatever was bothering her.

She hesitated, then seemed to change her mind. She shook her head and folded her arms protectively across her chest. "Forget it. It's nothing."

"I'll call you later," he said.

Maybe he was misreading her bad mood and it wasn't connected to their relationship. Maybe by tomorrow she'd be OK and willing to discuss things.

In any event, right now he needed to concentrate on more pressing matters. There'd been serious PR damage done by the imposters, whoever they were. The news of their defeat would be spreading fast. The backlash could wreck the careful public relations campaign he and Bel had put together.

The timeline for the next strike by Gillian and the team would have to be advanced. Humanity's Avenger required a fresh triumph as soon as possible.

FORTY-TWO

Bel dismissed the drudge and started clearing the dinner dishes. She needed to keep busy in order to stop churning things over in her head. Physical labor might wrench her away from a turbulent amalgam of emotions.

There was anger at Nick for pitstopping her. There was pain and bitterness at his betrayal. And there was a strong measure of confusion directed at her own cowardice in being unable to confront him about it.

She'd gotten confirmation earlier today after her third visit to a pharma specialist. There was no doubt Gillian was right. She'd been pitstopped. The specialist had also run the DNA sample of Nick that Bel had submitted, which she'd lifted from his personnel file. It had proved beyond a doubt that the pheromone induction tranqs were primed to Nick's metabolism. Their sole purpose was to cause her to be subliminally attracted to him.

Their entire relationship had been the product of the most callous and ruthless manipulation.

Her anger flared. Trying to corral it, she picked up a stack of dirty plates and carried them toward the kitchen.

The specialist hadn't been able to determine the exact date Bel had been drugged, only narrow it down to a two week window. But her first encounter with Nick had occurred during that period. Most likely, the tranq had been slipped into a drink. She recalled the very first time they'd met, the morning of the attack. She'd ushered him into her office ahead of her so she could have Maria Jose check on his background. She recalled that her coffee mug had been in plain sight atop her desk.

Devious son of a bitch!

Her hands shook with rage. One of the dishes slipped off the top of the pile, cracked into pieces as it shattered on the kitchen floor. It was authentic china, a platter that had been in her family for five generations. She didn't know why she'd even used it tonight. Nick deserved nothing better than disposables.

"Goddamn it!" she hollered, dropping to her knees. Frustration bubbled over and she burst into tears. The drudge came running.

"It's OK," she snapped, waving off the mech. "I've got this."

Forcing control, she wiped away her tears. She picked up the dish and cleaned up the worst of the mess. The drudge would deal with any remaining stains during its next housecleaning session.

She should have confronted Nick this evening, got everything out in the open. The reason she hadn't suddenly became clear to her.

It's up to him to come clean.

Nick must have known from the way Bel had acted tonight that she was on to him. But instead of admitting what he'd done, he'd pretended to have no idea why she was so angry.

If he wants to play it like that, so be it.

Her final visit to the specialist was slated for the day after Christmas. By then, the unique pitstop antidote would be synthesized for her metabolism and the first of seven daily doses ready to be ingested. After that week-long drug regimen, Nick, quite literally, would be out of her system.

FORTY-THREE

"They never had a chance," Gillian said as he watched the multicam videos on the cargo pod's ceiling monitor. Split screens showed the killing of the imitators at the Nairobi Securities Exchange from various angles. The assassin had also murdered a score of people unlucky to have been conducting business in the exchange.

"Strictly amateurs," Basher said, commenting on their fallen doppelgangers. "They had no business going up against a Paratwa."

"Not complete amateurs," Gillian argued. "They had some skills."

"Maybe, but they were in over their heads," Slag said. "They didn't know their own weaknesses and limitations."

Gillian nodded. It was a fair appraisal, especially for someone believing they could handle an assassin as deadly as Yiska.

Slag and Basher traded more disparaging comments about the slain team. Stone Face ignored the discussion, his attention buried in a book.

The Kenyan battle had occurred less than fifteen hours ago and the team was already airborne. Once more they were in the pod hanging from the stormlacer drone, flying toward Mexico's Pacific coast and the hastily chosen target Nick had located. It was an El Sigiloso, a breed originally created by CISEN, the Mexican intelligence agency.

They didn't know the target's name, only its domicile, a spacious hacienda on the outskirts of Puerto Vallarta. The assassin had recently murdered a judge known for dispensing harsh sentences to binaries of the non-assassin variety who appeared in his courtroom for minor crimes.

Nick's best intel revealed that the assassin had parted ways with CISEN and was serving the Ash Ock. Nothing out of the ordinary about that: an estimated ninety percent of the assassins were now believed under the sway of the Royals. What was unusual about this El Sigiloso was its sex: female-female. Not quite as rare as a mélange but not mainstream either.

Nick had set things up fast. Gillian agreed that it was important for the real Humanity's Avenger to make a public splash with all due haste. Bel and Nick had already flooded the net with stories claiming that the Kenyan firefight had been carried out by a brave but foolhardy imitator. A quick public kill of the El Sigiloso by the genuine article would confirm those stories.

Gillian returned his attention to the video and replayed the battle. He wasn't seeking further insight into the slain team. His interest was on the assassin that had defeated them, Yiska.

He'd reviewed the Kenyan incident several times already, as well as videos of the assassin's earlier attack on E-Tech headquarters. What had troubled him about the first assault was apparent in the Nairobi incident as well. The Shonto Prong betrayed none of the usual weaknesses common to its breed. There hadn't been so much as an infinitesimal moment's hesitation or the slightest misstep. Yiska was a perfectionist of the highest order.

The assassin had managed to escape from the Securities Exchange without a trace. That indicated full-blown physical alteration, probably via facial wipes and morphing attire.

Although not impressive in and of itself, it was notable because the tways had managed to disappear without being spotted on any of the numerous surveillance cams inside and outside the building. That took careful planning and impeccable timing. Yiska had displayed similar timing during the E-Tech killings when he'd crashed through Bel's office windows and landed on that skyboard.

Gillian had studied the characteristics of all the breeds. He couldn't remember just when or where he'd studied them, which was odd. Then again, that seemed to be true of many of his long-term recollections since he'd suffered those grave injuries, being beaten by the mokkers. Nick had warned that some of his memories were probably gone for good.

Whatever. The bottom line was that Yiska somehow had transcended the limitations that kept his breed from reaching the very pinnacle of the assassins. He seemed to have become his own unique category. Shonto Prong, version 2.0.

Nick and Bel very badly wanted to locate Yiska. Their reasons weren't wholly rational, were driven in part by a mutual desire for vengeance upon the assassin responsible for the death of E-Tech's former director and many others. But as much as Gillian hated to admit it, he was glad that Nick's efforts to find the Shonto Prong had so far been thwarted. The team needed more experience and additional training before attempting to go up against such a masterful foe. But someday...

"Five minutes to drop zone," the stormlacer's bot warned. "Three minutes to final descent."

"Ready?" Gillian asked.

"Hell yes," Basher said with a grin. "Ready to stomp some twofer."

"Don't get cocky," Gillian warned. "An El Sigiloso is no pushover."

"Maybe not. But at the end of the day, just another asshole with two assholes."

"Female assholes," Gillian pointed out, making sure the soldiers kept that in mind. There was a well-documented phenomenon of male hesitation when the enemy combatant was a woman, something psychologists believed spoke to the very essence of maleness, a predisposition to protect the childbearing members of the species from harm. He'd stressed the issue to the trio throughout the team's compacted training schedule even though they'd assured him they'd faced female fighters before without incident. Still, it was best to keep them aware of the phenomenon lest they fall prey to it.

He would have preferred more prep time, at least another day or two for the team to study the El Sigiloso's strengths and weaknesses. Nevertheless, they were ready. He would have scrubbed the mission if he'd felt otherwise.

And Gillian found himself hungering for a new battle. They'd taken down three assassins thus far, and for hours or sometimes days after each triumph, he found himself replaying the fight in his head, relishing every detail from beginning to end. There was something about pursuing and killing assassins that made him feel more alive, that tuned his psyche to some indefinable frequency at the very core of his being. The feeling went beyond notions of vengeance against Paratwa for the death of his parents when he was a boy and his wife Catharine years later. It was something more fundamental than that, a simple truth.

I was born to hunt them.

FORTY-FOUR

Sosoome had headed out earlier in the evening in search of coitus. It was more than a bit depressing that Nick's mech was probably going to get laid tonight while he spent New Year's Eve alone in his apartment. That hadn't mattered so much to him in previous years. But since Bel had come into his life – and then ruthlessly exited it – he'd become more attuned to feelings of longing, of loneliness.

She'd refused to tell him what he'd done wrong. She'd simply called the day after the faux soldier-hunters had been slain in Nairobi and announced that their intimate relationship was over, and that from here on out things between them would be "one hundred percent professional."

"Care to tell me why?" he'd asked.

"I think you know why."

"Believe me, I don't."

"That's not my problem," she'd snapped, hanging up.

Nick's attention was drawn through the open bedroom door to the back window. Outside, the vivid colors of a holo show erupted above the rooftops of a row of houses a block away. Someone had begun their celebrating a few hours early.

The laselumed image was vibrant enough to pierce the smog cover. It was an accurate depiction of a Roman chariot and four horses cavorting across the polluted heavens. He had a momentary irrational desire to board that chariot, be carried away from his personal troubles.

He sighed and returned his attention to the latest box of his son's belongings. He hadn't realized the man had been such a pack rat until he'd finally had the chance to go through Weldon's apartment the other day. He'd hauled away a plethora of vintage oddities, including a selection of early century videogames made for entertainment platforms long consigned to technology's dustbin.

More germane to the brilliance of Doctor Emanuel's life was the massive number of printed papers, a lifetime's worth. Some were articles he'd written, including dozens that as far as Nick knew had never been published. Others were torn from magazines or newspapers, items that at one time or another over the decades had snared his attention.

Nick supposed it was only proper that a man dedicated to placing limits on science and technology wouldn't have granted his full allegiance to digital storage. Still, the amount of physical paper he'd saved was downright fetishistic. Nick had thrown all of it into cartons, two dozen of which were now stacked against his bookcase.

He'd just finished going through the seventh box, which included such irrelevancies as the yellowing receipt for a computer Weldon had purchased in 2016, when Sosoome crept in through the cat door. The mech barrel-rolled back and forth across the living room floor, ejecting purple sparks from its battery packs. That was Sosoome's unique way of signifying he'd just had an outstanding copulatory experience.

"Do I know her?" Nick asked absently as he sliced open the eighth carton with his safak.

"Not her, him," Sosoome corrected. "And no, I don't believe you've ever met Whammo. He's a drudge for the Elbersons who live in that pseudo-Victorian mansion over on Bill Gates Boulevard. Ran into him a few times at the park when he had the Elbersons' cheetah out for its daily exercising. Oh man, is he ever hot!"

"Interesting," Nick offered, not at all interested in the details of Sosoome's sex life. "Anything noteworthy in the newsphere this evening?"

"The usual human bullshit, wars and plagues."

"Anything out of the ordinary?"

"Somebody set off a micronuke in Antarctica, blew away a Swedish-Norwegian research station and put a big-ass hole in the ice. Oh, and a new biotoxin was released in Los Angeles that apparently drives its victims insane. Given the city's reputation, some newsphere wags are speculating that the biotoxin's effects will go largely unnoticed."

Sosoome paused to allow Nick to react to the humorous aside. When he didn't, the mech continued.

"There are rumors of another major doomers' conflagration. It's set for New Year's Day, location unknown."

Nick frowned. Mass suicides, and the culture's unhealthy fascination with them, had dramatically increased in size and number over recent months. Another sign of a coming apocalypse?

"Oh, and here's one for the 'ya gotta be shittin' me' column. That El Sigiloso the boys wasted a couple weeks back? Well, it turns out that our female twofer was hitched. She had a pair of human husbands. And the two hubbies have launched a civil suit against Humanity's Avenger in the World Court, in absentia of course. They're looking for two billion pesos for pain and suffering."

"Good luck with that."

"Maybe I oughta go that route, try suing you for all the crap I have to put up with."

"C'mon, you know you love it."

Sosoome's remarks about the El Sigiloso brought Nick's thoughts back to the team's fourth triumph. The battle had gone smoothly; there'd been no hesitation on the part of Gillian and the soldiers because of the tways being female.

More importantly, the victory had returned the soldier-hunters to the status of heroes in the public eye.

As a bonus, a glitch in Gillian's personality, a subliminal holdover from his true identity as a Royal, apparently had been corrected. Gillian's penchant for wanting the second tway left alive after killing the first one had been a problem since the first mission against Alvis Qwee. True, the remnant of that sadist hadn't survived long. Left bound to a chair, the crazed tway had bitten off its own tongue and chewed through its cheeks to drown in its own blood.

During the team's second battle in Kuala Lumpur, the tways had perished simultaneously. But half of the Phaeton they'd terminated in Kyoto had been left alive, writhing in the street until an angry Japanese mob put it out of its misery.

Nick had warned Gillian that his habit could create sympathy for the assassins and lead to the perception that the team itself was sadistic for not killing the second tway. Fortunately, his advice finally had been heeded. Observing the battle through the team's helmet cams, Nick had watched with satisfaction as Gillian immediately executed the El Sigiloso's remaining half.

For better or worse, the team's successes had started a trend. Since Nairobi, three additional four-person combat units had surfaced across the globe, all attempting to mimic the original. Unfortunately, all had lacked the requisite skills and been quickly terminated in battles with assassins.

Nick wondered if some of those teams were actually hardcore servitors, dispatched by the Ash Ock on suicide missions against Paratwa for the specific purpose of failing, thereby stealing some of the publicity from Humanity's Avenger. In this type of warfare, the PR battle was as important as the physical one.

Still, as long as the team continued to be successful, no amount of imitators would tarnish its reputation. The soldier-hunters would fulfill their promise of offering hope and optimism to the species, helping to counter the massive weight of zeitgeist-fueled negativity.

He turned his attention to the eighth carton of Weldon's papers. The first few sheaves he removed were more of the same, inconsequential items. But underneath them he came across a small sealed envelope. He recognized his son's handwriting.

TO NICHOLAS GUERRA, FOR HIS EYES ONLY. TO BE OPENED AFTER THE DEATH OF WELDON EMANUEL.

Nick tore open the envelope. Inside was a hyperlink marble. He pitched it to Sosoome, who snared it with a paw and stuffed it in an orifice.

A life-sized holo of Weldon took shape above the mech. He was standing and leaning on his cane, a typical pose. Judging by the background, the holo had been recorded in his apartment.

"Hello, Dad. By now, I'm assuming I've been reduced to orbital dust and that you've gotten past whatever degree of mourning you deemed an old man to be worth."

The ancient face broke into a smile. Nick felt a fresh stab of grief.

"I'm afraid I've been keeping a few secrets from you of late. But now that I'm gone you deserve to know the truth. I realize these deceptions may make you angry, especially the second one. But know that in both instances, what I did was with the best of intentions.

"First, regarding Gillian. When I was performing the surgery to cloak his true identity, make him believe he was human, I quite by accident made a remarkable discovery. This tway of Empedocles – and most likely, all of the Ash Ock – possesses a synaptic structure unlike that of any human or binary ever autopsied.

"Your intel from Ektor Fang revealed that the Ash Ock have extended lifespans. I can confirm that such a conclusion is an understatement. No one could have guessed the true extent of what the Royals have achieved. Gillian's neurological makeup reveals that barring accidental death, he's capable of living for some six hundred years."

"That's some scary shit," Sosoome muttered. "Hell, I'm only rated for one-fifty."

"Given such a remarkable capacity, I felt that Gillian deserved the chance to someday know the truth about himself, perhaps reconcile with his real identity. Unlike a regular Paratwa, an Ash Ock's ability to exist as an independent tway may enable him, in some distant future, to survive such knowledge without going insane. Therefore, I took it upon myself to implant an additional set of mnemonic cursors in the deepest recesses of Gillian's mind. I created a program that can be used to trigger these cursors and awaken his true self."

"That was a dumb and dangerous thing to do," Nick muttered.

"I knew you wouldn't approve, which is why I kept this from you. Nevertheless, it's a decision I stand by. The program file is located on this marble. What you do with it is up to you.

"But I hope you'll come to reflect on the uniqueness of a creation like Gillian, who may well outlive you by half a millennium. Buried deep in his mind could be knowledge of the actual techniques used by his creators to give him such a radically extended lifespan. They've apparently come closer than anyone in history to discovering the mythical fountain of youth. His authentic self could hold the key to passing on such a gift to the rest of humanity."

Nick grudgingly admitted that his son's reasoning for implanting the additional mnemonic cursors was sound. *But you should have told me.*

Weldon hobbled across the room and eased himself into a chair. A grim expression came over him.

"And now to my second deception. There's no nice way to

reveal this one, so I'll just come out with it."

Nick listened intently, his anger growing. What his son had done to Gillian was one thing. But this second disclosure was unforgiveable. When Weldon reached the end of his revelations and the holo dissolved, Nick could barely contain his fury.

"You goddamn manipulative son of a bitch!"

Sosoome raised a quizzical eyebrow. "Runs in the family, does it?"

"Shut your face or I'll shut you down!"

The mech ran a paw across its mouth, the universal symbol for *my lips are sealed.*

Nick clenched his fists, trying to control his rage. It was vital that he show Weldon's holo to Bel immediately. He activated his attaboy and thunked her number. Not surprisingly, she didn't answer. Since she'd dumped him, she'd been refusing to take his calls, requiring him to leave messages.

"Bel, it's an emergency," he began, straining to hold back his anger. "You need to come over here right away. This is more important than you can imagine. Please!"

He paused and added a final sentence. "And just in case you're suspicious, the reason I'm asking is one hundred percent professional."

That wasn't true, of course. He glanced into the bedroom. As mad as he was at Weldon's second deceit, it also provided Nick with a shot at redemption.

FORTY-FIVE

"She's here," Sosoome announced, letting Bel through the downstairs entryway without comment.

Nick's anger had been reduced from a boil to a simmer in the forty-five minutes since he'd made the call. The fact was, his son's blatant manipulation had a silver lining. Still, he wasn't sure if he could ever forgive Weldon for what he'd done.

He opened the door as Bel reached the top of the stairs. She froze when she saw him. For a moment he had the sense that she was going to change her mind and dash back down the steps.

"This had better be good," she warned, brushing past him and entering the apartment.

She had on a winter coat he'd never seen before, black and gold and expensive looking. His offer to hang it up was met with an annoyed grimace.

"Want to sit down?"

"Get to the point, Nick. I'm supposed to be at a charity auction when the new year strikes."

"This won't take long," he said, nodding to Sosoome.

The mech replayed Weldon's beyond the grave message, starting at the point where he'd come clean about his second deception.

"You've been as good a father as any son could expect. There were plenty of years when I didn't realize that. Obviously, in my younger days, such a viewpoint was greatly distorted by anger at your having abandoned me and my mother. But during the decade that we came to know one another as adults, your true nature became as clear to me as one of those rare days when the smog pulls back and the sun shines through.

"I've had a good life, Nick. I have no major regrets with one exception. That exception, unfortunately, involves you.

"I know that you never really got over the divorce with Mom, and that it's the main reason you left us. It's also the reason you've avoided any close relationships in this era. But honestly, Nick, you deserve the special happiness that I enjoyed with my own wife for nearly three quarters of a century.

"And so, admittedly with a few qualms, I decided to try my hand at matchmaking. I took steps to push you toward a woman with whom you were clearly enamored, a woman who you believed could develop deep feelings for you."

Nick glanced at Bel. Her expression remained cold.

"There was a chance that you and Bel would have gotten together naturally. However, my gut told me that such a thing was unlikely. Too many barriers to overcome, both social and personal. You both would have rationalized, for different reasons, that it wasn't a smart idea to develop a personal relationship. That probably would have been the end of it."

Weldon paused and leaned forward in his chair. "And so, just in case you haven't figured out what I've been leading up to, here it is.

"Three days after the attack on E-Tech headquarters, I listened to you talk about what a wonderful and engaging woman you'd found Bel to be, and that you sensed she was attracted to you as well. And so I took action. I pitstopped you, Nick. I spiked your wine when we were dining together that evening. The next morning, at the regents' meeting where Bel learned she would be E-Tech's new director, I did the same to her, adding the tranqs to her coffee. Naturally, beforehand, I'd surreptitiously obtained DNA samples from both of you in order to prime the tranqs and create a mutual attraction."

"My God," Bel whispered, shaking her head in disbelief.

Weldon stopped talking, as if aware that at this point a few moments were needed to absorb the revelation. When he spoke again, his voice was more subdued.

"I realize it's cowardly of me to tell you all this after I'm gone. I don't have to face your anger. But even if I was still around, I wouldn't apologize for my manipulations. I believe they were in the service of a good cause. You deserve to be happy, as does Bel. Both of you deserve a shot at the kind of satisfying and fulfilling existence that I enjoyed for more than my fair share of years. I hope that when you get past your initial reactions you'll be able to look at this from the perspective that it was done out of love."

A faint smile touched the ancient face. "As you know, I don't believe in an afterlife. But just in case I've figured wrong, please remember to look me up when you get there."

The holo dissolved. Nick turned to Bel, waiting for her to speak. When she didn't he jumped into the void.

"My son was on the money about one thing. I was honestly attracted to you from the first time we met."

He wasn't sure if Bel actually heard him. Her cheeks had reddened and her jaws were clenched with barely contained rage.

"The bastard! He had no right!"

"No argument."

"It borders on criminal!"

Actually, it doesn't. Considering the greater acceptance of emotional manipulation throughout this culture, Nick figured it could be grounds for a civil suit but little else. He kept his mouth shut, however. It wasn't the right moment to slam Bel with such rational ideas. She was too mad. No doubt some of her anger arose from the realization that Doctor Weldon Emanuel, her personal hero and the man who'd inspired her toward a career, could be capable of such a betrayal.

She finally seemed to calm down. She drew a deep breath, as if trying to gather her thoughts.

"I had no right to be angry at you, Nick. I made a terrible mistake. I'm sorry."

"Completely understandable. I'm just glad I finally get why you were so pissed at me. I gather you did the test regimen for pitstopping?"

"And took the cure. Medically, you're out of my system."

They both hesitated, unsure of what the next step should be for repairing the fracture.

"Look, it's OK," he said finally. "I'm not upset that you came to believe that I was the one who'd tranqed you. Hell, knowing what a manipulative person I am, I'd have come to the same conclusion."

"Amen," Sosoome whispered.

Nick glared down at him. The mech took the hint, trotted toward the cat door.

"I think I'll go out for a stroll. I expect the fireworks will be starting soon."

Bel waited until Sosoome was gone before explaining.

"I wasn't suspicious of you, Nick. That's not how things happened."

She told him about Gillian, about the face sniffing. Nick frowned. He and Gillian had been in close proximity far more often than Gillian and Bel had. There was an obvious conclusion to be drawn from that.

Gillian picked up on my pitstop scent too but decided not to tell me.

Was his reason for holding back related to his weird attraction to Bel, part of some subliminal plot churning in the depths of that unique tway-mind? A way for Gillian to push

Nick out of Bel's life so that he could worm his way in?

They were questions without answers.

"I should go," Bel said.

"I really wish you wouldn't. Look, we both have the right to be mad at Weldon. But there's no sense in continuing to be that way with each other."

"Honestly, Nick, I'm not mad at you. Not anymore. It's just... this is all a lot to absorb."

"Then stay and we'll absorb it together."

"It's this charity auction. I really have to show my face."

"You've got a couple hours to midnight. Stay for a little while."

She hesitated. He pressed on.

"Despite what my son did to us, he was only building on what was already a mutual attraction. What we had was real between us from the beginning. The best parts of what made us *us* were not neurochemically induced."

That last statement wasn't exactly true. And at this moment, Nick felt the need to be completely and utterly honest with her.

"Actually, all forms of attraction are chemical at a certain level. If you really think about it, animals are drawn to one another because of an interlocking set of complex responses. When you get right down to it, human sexual desire and love are really nothing more than–"

"Nick?"

"Yeah?"

"Stop talking."

Bel took off her coat and eased closer. She whispered in his ear. He liked what he heard and followed her toward the bedroom.

Sosoome darted back into the apartment before they got there. Nick angrily snatched an ancient hardcover from an end table and drew back his arm, preparing to throw *The New Dictionary of Thoughts* at the mech for interrupting at an inopportune moment.

"Wait!" Sosoome urged, raising a protective paw to his face. "We've got company. Somebody just tripped the backyard sensors. They're on the fire escape, on their way up here."

"Got an ID?"

"Can't lock on. They're wearing a facial wipe, forensics filters and some kind of AV scrambler. Whoever it is, I got a hunch they're not here to party."

"Armed?"

"Can't be sure."

Nick turned to Bel. "Did you come alone?"

"Just my bodyguards in the limo. But I told them I was here on business, a quick stop before we go to the auction. Even if it was some emergency, they certainly wouldn't try to sneak in." She hesitated. "Should I call them?"

"No."

Nick slipped his compact Glock from the holster attached to the underside of the coffee table. Sosoome wasn't authorized to bear firearms but Nick had crafted a mini thruster for him. The mech retrieved it from under the sofa and snapped it onto his right foreleg.

"Stay here," Nick instructed Bel.

He and Sosoome slipped into the bedroom and took up flanking positions around the bed. Sosoome activated his optical camo and blended into the woodwork at the foot of the bureau. They aimed their weapons at the back window, the only possible entry point for someone sneaking up the fire escape. Outside, the Roman chariot holo had trotted away, leaving in its wake only smogged darkness.

"The intruder is attempting to remote scan the apartment," Sosoome silently reported over Nick's attaboy link. "They're using a Z-Rex 8000."

That was serious high tech military gear, not readily available to the average person. *Whoever it is, they're a pro.*

"I can't block the scan," the mech said.

The intruder would know they were lying in wait. They

might even be tapping into Nick's attaboy, monitoring his conversation with Sosoome. If so, there was nothing to be done about it. Nick knelt beside the bed, steadied the Glock in a two-handed shooter's stance.

"Don't fire until I signal," he whispered.

"Got it."

A silhouette appeared as the intruder reached the fire escape landing outside the window. The figure stopped, leaned forward and tapped gently on the glass.

"Nice of them to knock," Sosoome said.

"Don't drop your guard," Nick hissed, easing toward the edge of the window.

He hit the lift control. The window hummed as it slid open.

The intruder appeared to be a woman. She was dressed in black and wore a jacket with the hoodie up. He didn't recognize her. But with access to such tech toys, she might well be disguising her identity, even her birth sex.

"Sorry for my entrance," the woman said. "I didn't mean to alarm you."

Nick recognized the voice, which made him come even more alert. He kept his gun trained on her as he motioned her to come inside.

She climbed through the window and swept back her hoodie, revealing brown curly hair and a heavy jowled face. She rubbed a silver ring on her little finger against her forehead. The ring deactivated her facial wipe. Skin paled and cheeks lost their baby fat. Her hair straightened into bangs the color of ripening peaches.

It was Olinda Shining.

FORTY-SIX

Bel was disappointed at the interruption yet pleasantly surprised at seeing Olinda again. She'd thought about Ektor Fang's wife often since their initial meeting, especially on those occasions when her mind was inescapably drawn to that distant horizon free of violence and war.

Olinda walked slowly out of the bedroom followed by Nick and Sosoome. Their weapons remained trained on her back.

"Put down your guns," Bel said, making eye contact with Olinda. "She's not here to harm us."

"And we know this how?" Nick asked.

"Call it a hunch."

Nick looked reluctant, but he laid his Glock on the coffee table and motioned Sosoome to stand down.

"What's wrong with using the front door?" Nick demanded.

Olinda directed her words at Bel. "My husband is in trouble and needs help. There wasn't time for him to go through the usual complexities to set up a meeting. I couldn't find Nick's address so I picked up your trail at E-Tech and followed you here. If I'd come in by the main entrance, your bodyguards in the limo out front would have spotted me. I couldn't take the chance of being seen. The fire escape seemed more prudent."

"How'd you know she'd come to my place?" Nick asked, his face brimming with suspicion.

"I figured the two of you would be getting together on New Year's Eve." She paused. "It is, after all, often a celebratory night for lovers."

It was Bel's turn to be suspicious. They'd kept their affair under wraps. As far as she knew, only Doctor Emanuel had known. And neither she nor Nick had mentioned their status on the night they'd met Olinda and Ektor Fang.

"How'd you know about us?" she asked.

"There are signs if you know how to read them."

"You've had training in covert activities," Nick concluded. "Your little tech toys alone prove it."

Olinda nodded. "I'm a special investigator with the Department of Defense. Domestic counterintelligence unit."

"You're DOD?" Bel uttered in surprise.

"Yes. When I'm working, it's Major Shining."

Nick scowled. "And do your superiors happen to know you're a servitor?"

Bel laid a hand on his arm. Now wasn't the time.

"Exactly how is your husband in trouble?" she asked.

"He contacted me a few hours ago on a private channel we'd set up for emergencies. He's certain that his CI status has been compromised and that the Ash Ock know he's betrayed them." Worry flashed across her face. "If they catch him, he's dead."

She turned to Nick. "To answer your question, no, my superiors certainly don't know I'm married to a Paratwa assassin. Which means I can't bring him in. I can't offer him sanctuary or even protection. The DOD would blacksite a Paratwa assassin, suck him dry of intel by any and all means. And they'd do the same to me when they found out about our relationship, which they no doubt would in due time."

"Where is he?" Bel asked.

"On his way to a safe house, one the Royals supposedly don't know about. It's just across the border. I can get us there without going through a transit station."

Nick remained skeptical. "Why don't you just call him and ask him to meet us over on this side of the wall?"

"I don't dare. That emergency channel is one-way, meant for him to reach out to me. If I tried using it to contact him, the call could be traced. And by now the Ash Ock certainly will have put Reemul on his tail."

"Who's Reemul?" Bel asked.

"Sappho's errand boy, the one they call the liege-killer." A faint shiver seemed to pass through Olinda. "My husband has had a few encounters with him over the years. Reemul is crazy dangerous. A sick twisted freak of a binary, as awful as they come."

"All the more reason for us not to risk a clandestine get-together," Nick said.

Bel agreed. "The liege-killer could be closing in on your husband as we speak."

Olinda regarded her with pleading eyes. "Help bring Ektor Fang in. Give him asylum and a new identity. In turn, I promise you that he'll provide detailed profiles on every assassin he's ever met. Plus tactical info, locations of secret bases, much more. He has a wealth of knowledge about them. He's been one of their most trusted lieutenants. You could learn more in one session than he's revealed in all your previous meetings."

Bel was intrigued. She caught Nick's eye. She could tell he was tempted as well. They might never again have such an opportunity. It could be worth the risk.

Olinda continued pitching. Her tone sounded increasingly desperate.

"Bel, I swear to you. If you save my husband, I will make sure he gives you everything, every last bit of intel he has on the Paratwa."

Nick gave Bel a subtle nod.

"All right," Bel said. "We'll do it."

"Thank you."

"I'll go to this safe house with you," Nick said. "Bel can stay here."

"No, Nick," Bel countered. "I'm coming with you."

"It's too dangerous. Think about it for a sec and you'll realize it makes no sense putting both of us at risk."

"That's a good point. So if you want, you remain behind and I'll accompany Olinda."

Nick sighed.

"I'll go downstairs first and get rid of my bodyguards. I'll tell them I've gotten another ride to the charity auction."

Bel terminated further objections by donning her coat and heading for the door. Nick wasn't pleased but she clearly wasn't going to allow him to dissuade her.

Bel reached the street, explained to the bodyguards. As the limo disappeared around the corner, Olinda and Nick emerged from the apartment house.

"I'm parked just down the street," Olinda said.

"Shit!" Nick muttered. "I forgot my gun."

"You won't need it."

"Yeah, right. We're going into the zoo after dark to meet a renegade assassin who's being hunted by the liege-killer. What could go wrong?"

He dashed back into the house.

It was a cold night, free of snow but with icy patches from an earlier storm. Olinda tightened her hoodie and stared worriedly into the distance.

Bel laid a hand on her arm. "I'm sure your husband will be OK. Between Nick and me, we'll figure out a way to keep both of you safe."

Olinda forced a smile. "I know your reasons for doing this aren't altogether altruistic. But thank you anyway."

Bel nodded. She could only hope that the promise she'd just made was, for all their sakes, achievable.

FORTY-SEVEN

Olinda took control of her four-door Buick and drove it across Philly at a breakneck pace. The main avenues had been de-iced from the last storm but many side streets lacked thermal strips and remained slippery. That didn't slow Olinda down. She gunned the vehicle through intersections and skated it around icy corners. Bel, accustomed to slow and steady limo rides, found herself gripping the sides of the passenger seat cocoon and hanging on for dear life.

She glanced at Nick in the back seat but he didn't look worried. Then again, he'd been born in an era where everyone drove their own vehicles and violent crashes were the norm.

They made it safely to their destination, a narrow street about two kilometers from the wall. Olinda led them into a brick row home that looked to have been built in the same era as Nick's apartment house.

They descended into the basement. Olinda pulled back a false wall to reveal a locked metal door. She keyed an entry code and paused for optic and DNA scanners to authenticate her identity. The door opened. They stepped into a multidirectional freight elevator that dropped several stories before stopping and changing to horizontal travel mode. The compartment whisked sideways at a gradually accelerating rate.

"Nice way to make a crossing," Nick offered.

"The DOD doesn't mess around with half-ass tunnels and sewers," Olinda said.

"What's it used for?" Bel wondered.

"There's a lot more back-and-forth trade between sec and unsec regions than most people are aware of. We import a fair supply of our military recruits from unsec regions. They tend to make good soldiers, tough and resilient. Some we train and send back over to the other side as assets."

"Spies."

"We prefer to think of them as eyes on the ground. As for exports, we send over a lot of food and clothing as well as some tech, mostly low-end stuff. The DOD isn't only about using troops and weapons to defend our country."

Bel understood. E-Tech and many other international organizations and businesses also donated necessities to help the unfortunates living in the world's unsec regions. She wished she could say it was all done strictly for humanitarian reasons but most donors had an agenda. Providing aid packages was a tried and true method for keeping a large and impoverished people stable and under control. The greatest fear among those living in secured areas was the ever-expanding population of unsecs fanning the fires of revolution and storming the walls.

The elevator slowed to a stop. They exited into another basement and headed upstairs. The house they were in appeared to be abandoned. But from outside came the whoops and shouts of a street party going full blast.

Olinda peeled back a torn curtain and peered through the cruddy window. The street was crammed with New Year's Eve revelers.

"Must be a couple hundred of them," Nick said. "How far away is this safe house?"

"Right around the corner," Olinda said. "But…"

"You're worried they'll bother us," Bel concluded.

"I can't spot any gang IDs," Nick said. "At least not from any of the really lethal bangers."

"That doesn't mean we won't run into trouble," Olinda said.

Nick shrugged. "We've come this far."

Bel nodded in agreement.

Olinda opened the front door. "Follow me and stay close. And Nick, no matter what happens, don't draw your gun. That's a sure-fire invite for a shootout."

"Duh. This ain't my first rodeo."

Bel followed Olinda, with Nick bringing up the rear. They slipped easily into the crowd, most of whom appeared well-inebriated or sky-high on various pharma. They passed a trio of mokkers vaping from belt pouches. One of them glared at Bel. She avoided eye contact but sensed him watching her for a long moment. Finally, he turned away and ambled off into the crowd.

They'd just about reached the party's outer perimeter when an obese man garbed only in dirty underwear stepped in front of Olinda. He wore a morph mask of a grinning frog-faced cartoon character.

"You and me, babe," he grunted.

"I don't think so."

Olinda took a step to get around him but Frogface moved to block her. The morph mask reacted to his new emotional state, transformed from a grin into a pulsating scowl. He grabbed hold of her arms.

"I said, you and me, bitch!"

Olinda opened her mouth wide...

...and projectile vomited in his face.

"What the fuck!" he screeched, shoving her away and wiping puke from his mask.

"I am so sorry. I have a highly contagious disease."

She threw up again, this time aiming for the ground in front of him. Vomit ricocheted off the macadam, splashed across his bare thighs.

That was enough for Frogface. He scurried away, disappeared back into the masses.

"Cool trick," Nick said. "TSU?"

Olinda nodded. Bel frowned, perplexed.

"Tactical spasm unit," Olinda explained. "The trigger is a tongue-activated molar implant and you swallow the paroxysm pill ahead of time. You just have to eat a decent meal before activating it."

"Lucky for him you weren't using the militarized version," Nick added. "That one sprays sulfuric acid."

They made it around the corner without further incident. There were more vintage row homes. A few people were scattered along the pavements but none appeared likely to give them trouble. Olinda led the way to a decrepit house in the middle of the block.

"We're just going to walk right in?" Nick challenged.

"It's OK," Olinda said, breathing a sigh of relief. "The upstairs shades are down."

"And no one would *ever* guess that's the all-clear signal," Nick muttered.

Olinda didn't hear him. She was already rushing through the door, anticipating a reunion with her husband. Nick drew his gun. He and Bel scurried after her.

The front room was devoid of furniture but reasonably clean. There was no sign of Olinda. A moment later, her joyous shout emanated from the next room.

Nick holstered the Glock but kept his hand near the butt as they entered a dilapidated kitchen. Bel couldn't help but smile. Olinda and one of Ektor Fang's tways were warmly embracing. The other tway had his back to them, was peering out into the backyard through a crack in the shade.

"I'm so glad you're safe," Olinda said, still beaming as she pulled away. She motioned to Nick and Bel. "They've agreed to help us."

Both tways turned to face them. "Thanks."

"You"

"were"

"our strongest"

"hope."

"First order of business," Bel began, "is getting you safely into Philly-sec. After that we can make arrangements for a new identity for you and Olinda. A fresh start."

"Not so fast," Nick said. "What about the liege-killer? Could he have followed you here?"

"No. I was"

"very careful. But what about"

"the three of you?"

"Could you"

"have been"

"followed?"

Nick shook his head. "I've been checking. No tails."

"But we'd better get back across the border quick," Olinda said. "I've arranged with my people for their other Paratwa source to meet us." She turned to Bel and Nick and explained, "Not everyone in the DOD is onboard with this. Having Mister X there will help smooth the way."

Ektor Fang seemed to consider the idea for a moment then nodded in unison.

Bel was confused. *Who was Mister X?* Olinda hadn't said anything about the DOD having another Paratwa informant. She glanced at Nick, knew he was hiding similar confusion. She decided it was best to go with the flow and reserve any questions for later.

The four of them headed outside. One of Ektor Fang's tways walked in front and his other half brought up the rear. Olinda nestled up to the tway in the lead and held his hand.

"I've missed you," Olinda whispered to her husband.

"I know. But we're together again. That's all that's important."

They passed back through the street party with no trouble

and entered the house with the DOD's secret elevator. Nick paused to peer through the edge of the torn curtain. Bel joined him at the window.

"You see something?" she asked.

"No. I think we're good."

He moved away, allowing Bel to glance out. But an instant before she was about to release the curtain, she saw two men in hoodies slip around the corner from the same direction as the safe house. The pair reached the far edge of the crowd and stopped.

The distance and the dim glow of the streetlamps served to keep their faces mainly in shadow. All she could ascertain for sure was that one was taller. Yet she had the strangest impression, no more than a fleeting gestalt, that the shorter one had a melancholy expression while his companion wore a faint smile.

They stood side by side and scanned the crowd. The taller one looked in her direction. Even though Bel doubted he could see into the darkened room, a chill went through her. Intuition warned that they weren't two men at all, but a Paratwa assassin that had been following Ektor Fang.

"C'mon," Nick urged from the top of the stairs. "We need to get out of here."

She rushed down the steps after him. Olinda and Ektor Fang were already in the basement. Olinda accessed the elevator. Bel breathed a sigh of relief when the door closed and the compartment took off horizontally for the first stage of the return trip.

No one spoke for a time. Olinda nestled up against one of the tways and finally broke the silence.

"I hope you don't mind, dear, but I told them about our big plans. About us deciding that in the new year we're going to try for a baby."

Both tways smiled. "I'm glad"

"you told them."

"It isn't something"

"we'd be able"

"to keep secret"

"for long."

"I know. Skinny me. I'll be showing pretty quickly."

Bel's confusion escalated. Olinda hadn't said a word about wanting to get pregnant. But whatever was going on, she realized she needed to play along.

Olinda smiled warmly and held onto the tway's arm. Bel had a sudden urge to do the same with Nick, to snuggle against him, to feel his physical touch. The evening's turn of events had interrupted what she'd intended to be some seriously apologetic makeup sex for believing that he'd pitstopped her. But now wasn't the appropriate time to display her affection.

"Before we meet Mister X," Olinda said to the tway, "there's something important you need to know about him."

"What's that?"

"He doesn't exist."

Olinda whipped a slate-colored knife from beneath her jacket, stabbed it through the tway's heart. The short blade erupted out his back, its edges strangely blurred.

He screeched and fell to the floor, writhing in agony. Even through Bel's shock she realized the tway had been pierced by a flash dagger, an energy weapon with an extendable reach by means of a hot particle stream flowing down the length of the physical blade.

The next few seconds became a blur of raging movements.

Nick whipping out his Glock, taking aim at Olinda...

The surviving tway launching a Cohe wand from a slip-wrist holster and igniting a crescent web...

The din of Nick's gunfire in the enclosed space pounding Bel's eardrums...

Olinda lunging left...

...causing Nick's three rapid-fire shots to miss her and deflect off the far wall.

One of the shots ricocheted, ripping into Bel's flesh.

Whether it was the sudden pain from the bullet hitting her shoulder or some form of hyperawareness taking control, Bel realized what Nick didn't.

He was aiming at the wrong target.

"Nick, no!" she shouted at him as he jerked the Glock's barrel toward Olinda's new position.

The surviving tway remained fully functional. It displayed no signs of bisectional hemiosis from the mortal stabbing of its other half.

"Look at him!" Bel hollered. *"He's not a tway!"*

The survivor stabbed at Olinda with his Cohe. She ducked low. The black beam flashed over her head. She sliced the dagger toward the survivor's weak side portal.

The survivor jerked sideways. The tip of Olinda's dagger crackled against his front crescent in a burst of crimson flame.

"It's not a Paratwa!" Bel screamed.

Her words finally registered. Nick switched targets, plunged his gun arm through the survivor's right side portal. He fired once, into the ear. A spray of chunky scarlet exploded out the far side of the survivor's head, tattooing the back wall of the elevator.

The tway that wasn't a tway crumpled to the floor.

It was over. Olinda and Nick knelt beside the two bodies, checked to make sure they were dead. Bel sat down in the corner, clutching her shoulder.

Nick realized she was injured. He rushed to her side.

"It's OK," she assured him. "The bullet just grazed me."

It was painful but not unbearably so. That likely would change shortly when her adrenalin-pumped system returned to normal levels.

Nick shook his head, angry at himself. "I misread things. I thought Olinda was showing her true colors."

"I know." Nick's hatred of servitors created a huge blind spot for him. In the pulse of the moment, that blind spot had almost led him to make a bad call.

He dabbed at her wound with a hankie. "I'm really sorry. I could have–"

"But you didn't. Anyway, it's not me you should be apologizing to."

Olinda was running her fingers across the dead men's necks, feeling for something.

"They've got attaboy implants as I suspected," she said. "This compartment is com-shielded but as soon as we'd have reached the surface, they'd have been able to contact their masters. I had to stop them."

The elevator eased to a halt and switched to ascent mode for the final part of the journey.

Olinda used her silver ring and a marble-sized unikey to deactivate their facial wipes. They weren't even twins like the real Ektor Fang. The two faces bore no obvious relation to one another.

"Recognize them?" she asked.

Bel and Nick shook their heads.

"Servitors?" Bel wondered.

"Even more extreme, I'm guessing," Nick said. "Biwannabes. Fanatics willing to do anything the Royals asked…"

He trailed off, exchanged a knowing look with Olinda. He lunged to his feet.

"Stop the elevator!"

Bel was closest to the controls. She jumped up and slammed the emergency button. The compartment jerked to a stop.

Olinda withdrew a scanner from her pocket, ran it across the bodies.

"What's going on?" Bel demanded.

"If they're biwannabes, they could be on a suicide mission," Nick said.

"Not could be, *are*," Olinda said, grimacing at the scanner's readout. "Their midsections are packed with K-90. Must have been surgically implanted."

"Phony tways turned into human bombs," Nick muttered. "Ready and willing to die for the cause."

"How'd you know they weren't a binary?" Bel asked Olinda.

"I suspected the moment I set eyes on them. Something didn't feel right. And then when I hugged him..."

Pain flared across her face. Bel knew she was struggling not to dwell on the fate of the real Ektor Fang.

"Anyway, I was pretty sure they were fakes at that point. I thought they might try to kill us in the safe house. That's why I made up the story about the other Paratwa source."

Bel understood. "Give them incentive not to take action until we reached Philly-sec by tempting them with a high-value target. Then they could kill us and take out this unknown CI as well."

"Can the bombs be disarmed?" Nick asked.

Olinda shook her head. "Not with any gear I have on me."

"Then we've got a serious problem. When we get to the surface and open the elevator door, our com links will start functioning again. Whoever is running these two will know in an instant that they're dead. They'll immediately trigger the bombs."

"Why don't we cut out their attaboys and smash them to pieces?" Bel suggested.

"Wouldn't work," Olinda said. "The attas will have been linked directly to the bombs, just in case these two came to their senses and decided against suicide."

Nick agreed. "If we mess with those coms, they'll blow for sure."

Bel had another idea. "We might have at least a few seconds before the controller is able to pull the trigger. Maybe enough time for us to get out of the elevator and shut the doors?"

"You don't understand," Olinda said. "We're talking about military-grade K-90. When the bombs go off they'll take out a city block. We'd never get clear in time, not to mention a lot of innocent people dying along with us."

"We have to do something. Obviously we can't stay here."

"No, we can't," Nick said. "But there might be another way. Messing around with the bodies won't stop the bombs from going off. But we may be able to create enough electromagnetic interference in this elevator so that when we reach the surface, their com links won't function."

Olinda followed the direction of his thoughts. "I have an attagirl, you have an attaboy. If we connect them together…"

"Yeah. The two of them physically mated ought to generate enough EMI to do the trick. Which means we need to do a little amateur surgery."

"I'll cut yours out first," Olinda said.

Nick shook his head. "No, I'll go first."

"Have you done this before?"

"Hell no. Have you?"

"No. But is this really worth arguing–"

"It's *not* worth arguing about," Bel interrupted. "I'm the one who once studied to be a doctor. I'll do you both."

FORTY-EIGHT

Olinda had a tiny medkit with a single dose of anesthetic, the same as Nick's safak. That meant the two of them would have at least some relief from the pain of having the subcutaneous com links cut out of their necks. But it also meant there was no painkiller left for Bel. She'd have to endure the increasing agony of her shoulder wound while performing two delicate surgeries.

Olinda taped gauze around her bullet wound to stem the bleeding. Bel forced herself to ignore the pain.

Nick went under the knife first. Using the safak's smallest blade, Bel carefully made three intersecting incisions and peeled back the flap of skin to expose the attaboy. Nick grimaced but gave her a thumbs-up.

She sliced through the thin band of neural connectors and yanked out the com link. There was a lot more blood than she'd anticipated. She put a clump of gauze in Nick's hand and told him to press it over the wound.

Five minutes later, Olinda's attagirl was out too. By this time, the pain in Bel's shoulder was getting bad. Clenching her fists, she leaned against the back of the elevator and watched Nick and Olinda wire their com links together.

Nick placed the joined attaboy and attagirl between the bodies. "It won't have much range but it should be enough to knock out their com links."

Olinda went to the control panel to restart the elevator.

"Shouldn't we test it first?" Bel asked.

"No way to do that," Nick said. "It either works or..."

Olinda pressed the button. The elevator continued its ascent. In seconds they reached the terminus in Philly-sec.

The door opened. They exited into the basement. Bel was pleasantly surprised to find herself still among the living. Olinda quickly closed the door, sealing the explosive bodies in the com-shielded compartment.

She accessed an emergency pad inset into the wall, made contact with a DOD official and related their situation. Nick and Bel sat on the bottom step, nursing their respective injuries.

"How's your shoulder?" he asked.

"It hurts. Your neck?"

"Not bad. I feel kind of naked without an attaboy, though. Guess I may as well get a new one wired in while the wound is still fresh."

Olinda completed the call and perched on the edge of a rickety wooden chair. "We need to wait here. A DOD scram unit is en route to evac us. A bomb squad won't be far behind."

Bel gripped Nick's hand. She didn't like waiting, not with the explosives this close. Nick sensed her concern.

"If they didn't blow by now they probably won't go up," he said.

Probably didn't sound very reassuring. But she trusted his judgment.

"I made it clear to the scram unit that this is a high-level counterintelligence matter," Olinda said. "They'll be discreet and won't reveal your identities. And I'll make sure your involvement with what happened tonight doesn't leak."

"What exactly did happen?" Bel asked. "I mean... your real husband?"

Olinda stiffened, fought to keep her voice free of emotion.

"Obviously, Ektor Fang was caught, probably right after he called me. While he was being interrogated, those two biwannabes would have been prepped to assume his identity. There wouldn't have been enough time for them to undergo a full-blown sapient supersedure. All that was required was for them to have similar builds. The rest was done with facial wipes and some minor flesh sculpting. It was never meant to be a long-term deception."

"He sounded like a real binary," Bel said. "His speech, his movements."

"The most fanatical of the biwannabes train to be passable," Nick said.

"We have to assume that the three of us have been compromised," Bel added. "The Royals will know our identities."

"Certainly that's true for me," Olinda said. "But I think you two are still safe. Ektor Fang had a plan in case he was exposed. He wouldn't willingly give up any information. Of course they'd have attempted torture. But it never would have gotten to that point. He had a suicide implant. It was thunk-triggered, instantaneous."

She stared blankly into the distance and clenched her fists before continuing.

"They would have used postmortem accumulators on him, of course. But the implant would have wiped out everything but his most recent short-term memories, and then only those with a strong emotional component. They certainly would have learned that I existed and garnered a good physical image of me, as well as enough intel to know where we were supposed to meet."

Nick nodded. "Their plan would have been flexible. I assume that option one was to capture us right then and there. But when you made up that story about a Paratwa source, this Mister X waiting for us across the border, they elected to go with option two. Accompany us back to Philly-sec and then trigger the bombs. Take out us and the source, along with any other of Ektor Fang's human contacts."

Bel mentioned the two figures she'd glimpsed through the window. She voiced her suspicion that they were a Paratwa.

"I don't think they – or it – saw us. The pair seemed to be following us, though."

"Did one of them look kind of sad and the other amused?" Olinda asked.

"Yes. How'd you know that?"

"We may have been luckier than we thought. I'm pretty sure you saw Reemul."

Bel shivered at the idea of how narrowly they might have escaped. Being blown up in a blinding instant was one thing. But being captured and tortured by the liege-killer...

She shook her head, pushed such dark thoughts from her mind. The night had been turbulent enough without imagining more dire events.

Nick had further questions. "You said you suspected immediately that those men weren't your husband. But you must not have been absolutely sure until you ran that flash dagger through his chest."

"If it had been the real Ektor Fang, I wouldn't have been fast enough. The blade never would have touched him. But by that time I knew for certain anyway."

Bel understood. "That comment you made to him about the two of you planning to get pregnant. It was a lie."

Olinda nodded. "We never discussed such a thing. There was no need. The truth is, I'm *already* pregnant. Seven and a half months from now, Ektor Fang would have been the father of a baby girl."

The admission shattered Olinda's carefully maintained veneer. Her face contorted with pain. She slithered to her knees. Her words emerged as a whisper.

"I c-can't believe he's gone."

The dam burst. Tears streamed down her face. Bel rushed

over to comfort her. There were no words to be uttered that could lessen her agonies. Bel simply hugged Olinda and let her cry.

She glanced at Nick. Even her tears and tonight's events hadn't softened his antagonism toward the woman he viewed as a traitorous servitor.

Olinda brought her emotions under control. Wiping the moisture from her cheeks, she got to her feet.

"I'm all right now," she said.

Bel caught Nick's eye. He read her silent message and grudgingly offered Olinda his condolences.

"I'm sorry about your husband."

They turned toward the stairs as voices sounded from above. The scram unit was entering the house. As the soldiers rushed down the steps, Bel heard the distant sounds of fireworks.

The new year was upon them.

PART 3

STORM

FORTY-NINE

Bel waited in the end booth of the Hollywood Hurrah, one of the so-called epoch cafés springing up like wild grass in Philly-sec and elsewhere. Her lunch date was running late. To say that she'd been shocked to get that morning's cryptic message from Olinda Shining was an understatement.

It was early December, 2096, nearly a year after that terrifying night of the Ektor Fang imposter. That was the last time she'd seen Olinda, who within hours had resigned her officer's commission as a major in the DOD and disappeared.

It had been a vanishing act based on necessity. By noon of New Year's Day, Nick had been picking up chatter from his CIs that the Royal Caste had put out a contract on Olinda's life. Open to all Paratwa, it offered a large bounty for her capture or a lesser amount for confirmation of her death. Going off the grid had been her only chance of surviving the myriad of assassins likely to have been hunting her.

Bel always figured that Olinda would have had a decent chance of evading them, that her counterintelligence skills would give her the edge needed to stay hidden. And because the Royals had made no open moves against Bel or Nick, presumably Olinda hadn't been captured and forced to divulge information about her human contacts. Still, until she'd messaged late yesterday about wanting to meet, such assumptions had remained hypothetical.

Bel glanced around the crowded downtown restaurant. The Hollywood Hurrah was populated mainly by a trendy and youthful business crowd. Each epoch café featured a different twenty-first century time period and theme. This one's claim to fame was a staff of lifelike mech servers crafted into imitations of actors and actresses who'd been popular in Nick's original era.

Glowing nametags flashed holo streams of biographical data for each star and highlights from their entertainment appearances played on flexible belly screens. Bel wasn't a history buff, at least not when it came to entertainers. Jennifer Lawrence, Samuel L Jackson and Meryl Streep meant nothing to her.

Outside, Philly-sec was again decorated for the holidays and shoppers were out in force. Shitsnow was falling, dusting the pedestrian-only street and sidewalks with a layer of glistening brown. The flakes were darker and somehow even more sinister than last winter.

By almost every environmental and social indicator, 2096 had been the worst year on record. Increased pollution had produced insanely high ToFo levels. Biodiversity was plunging, with nearly a million additional species having been wiped out. Severe escalation of global warming had occurred and, along with it, further losses of coastal communities as oceans rose, as well as the increased destruction of vital natural resources. Every one of the major geoengineering projects aimed at halting atmospheric degradation that had come online in the past few months had been deemed a failure.

The list of things going wrong with the world seemed endless. There was increasing religious fervor and a spiking murder rate. Virtual reality escapism had reached an all-time high, with millions suffering from the addiction. A significant percentage of them were dying of starvation, dehydration or VR stroke after attempting 24/7 immersion in artificial environments.

And it wasn't just the ecosphere and the social order under siege. Many institutions were failing as well, both governmental and corporate. Nuclear and biological terrorism were on the upswing. Last month alone fourteen urban areas had suffered nukings or deliberately released plagues. In the less stable nations, ruthless dictatorships were coming to power and overwhelming democratic institutions.

The year had begun with the largest mass suicide ever by doomers. It had occurred on New Year's Day in the UK, engulfing an estimated three thousand five hundred souls and torching an entire British town. Even more ominously, a number of secured cities, including massive Mumbai-sec, had been overrun by unsec hordes. In India alone, there'd been more than a million casualties from the still-raging civil war between the haves and have-nots.

The secret efforts of the Royal Caste to render the planet unlivable were almost certainly responsible for much of the mayhem. Yet Bel realized that they couldn't be blamed for every calamity, nor for the overall mess humans had made of their home.

There'd been too many centuries of the profit-progress cycle, too many technologies created not to bring about a better world but simply to satisfy greed and thus maximize economic disparity. The ideal of striving to improve the human condition had been smothered beneath technolust and avarice.

The world is disintegrating. That zeitgeist now dominated the culture at nearly every level. It explained the rise of these epoch cafés. Intense fascination with past eras was a byproduct of the widespread belief that the world had no future. Even E-Tech's most optimistic projections indicated that Earth had reached a tipping point, that its cataclysmic failure as a sustainable habitat was inevitable.

In Bel's role as director, she was forced to keep up appearances. She maintained a positive attitude, gave optimistic speeches about E-Tech's principles and promoted the idea of the planet's ultimate salvation. But privately, she suspected the end was near.

Her most important efforts increasingly focused on the Colonies. In the past year alone, hundreds of thousands of settlers had passed the rigorous immigration tests and had begun a new way of life far from Earth and its woes. The massive space cylinders now represented humanity's most viable future.

She sighed. Dwelling on the state of the world was depressing, and such thoughts coursed through her all too often these days. Trying to distract herself, she gazed out the window. She spotted one of her bodyguards huddled under the café's portico. Bel hadn't told her security detail that today's lunch was anything out of the ordinary, listing it simply as a meeting with an old friend. But she really didn't know what to expect. Could the Olinda Shining who'd contacted her to set up the lunch meeting be an imposter, their encounter some sort of trap set by the Royals?

"She's already fifteen minutes late," Sosoome grumbled from under the table. "How long are we going to wait?"

"Be patient."

Bel had called Nick immediately after getting Olinda's lunch invite. He'd insisted she borrow his mech for the public encounter as an added precaution in the event of a worse-case scenario. And if things were on the level, Sosoome's AV scrambler would counter any attempts to eavesdrop on what could be a highly sensitive conversation.

"I'm bored," Sosoome said. "None of these servers are exactly my type."

"You're not here for sex."

"In the larger context, everyone is *always* here for sex. Anyway, if I had my pick of doing it with any of them, it would be Christian Bale over at table seven. But that Shailene Woodley is pretty hot too."

"Just behave yourself," Bel warned, not for the first time since their arrival. "I don't want any interruptions with Olinda."

"Me? Interrupt?"

"That goes for snide comments as well. Remember, Nick gave me the override code to mute your vocal function."

Sosoome rolled onto his back and glared up at her.

Bel's attention shifted to a stranger entering the café, a fortyish blond woman in a bulky trench coat. The woman scanned the crowd, spotted Bel and strode toward her.

"I think she's here," Bel whispered.

The woman sat down across from her and opened the coat. Bel was surprised to see a slumbering baby girl harnessed to her chest in a sealed carrier, which provided a steady stream of clean air. Pollution-free breathing was especially vital for infants.

Bel glanced down at Sosoome. The mech flashed a message. REMOTE DNA ANALYIS MATCHES PREVIOUS SAMPLING FOR OLINDA SHINING. ACTIVE FACIAL WIPE. NO DETECTABLE WEAPONS.

The woman checked a ToFo wristband. Apparently satisfied the café's air was pure enough, she peeled open the carrier and lifted out the baby. The little girl yawned and started to awaken.

"She's beautiful," Bel said. "What's her name?"

"Ektora. We use other names in public, of course. But my sensors picked up your mech and its AV scrambler. So today we can keep it real." She smiled faintly. "Of course, I have to keep this facial wipe active pretty much all the time."

Olinda sat the baby on the table facing forward and gripped her midsection for support. Ektora Shining gazed around curiously at her surroundings before settling her attention on Bel.

"About four months old, right?" Bel said, extending a hand to allow Ektora to grasp her finger.

"Just about. Sometimes I don't know what I would have done after losing Ektor if this little princess hadn't been on the way."

Olinda's words touched a nerve. Gradually over the past year, Bel's biological clock had kicked into overdrive. She managed to repress the desire during the day by keeping busy. But often at night she dreamed of babies, dreamed of cradling an infant in her arms.

"Are you and Nick still together?" Olinda asked.

"We are."

"Still clandestine?"

"Uh huh. I've offered to change the status quo, even proposed marriage a couple of times. But Nick... he has some issues with that level of commitment. Probably best that we keep things private anyway. We already have a complicated professional relationship."

"Marrying the boss. That's usually problematic."

"Among other things."

Bel had raised the subject of having a baby with Nick on more than a few occasions. Sensitive to his reluctance, she'd even offered to take full legal and ethical responsibility for raising the child. But he remained dead set against the idea of getting her pregnant. Lately, even just broaching the subject had led to arguments between them.

His stated reason for refusing wasn't entirely irrational. "With Armageddon right around the corner," he'd say, "it's crazy to bring a child into this world."

Not long ago, Bel had held a similar view. But whatever hormonal changes were pushing her toward motherhood refused to succumb to such a rational interpretation. She'd also countered Nick's argument by pointing out that throughout history, the species had created new life under even the most adverse and horrendous conditions. It was the nature of humans to reproduce, no matter how dire their existences.

Nick wouldn't discuss his real reasons for not wanting to make a baby. It was obvious to Bel that they were based on his early relationship with his son and the tremendous guilt that still gnawed at him for having abandoned Weldon at a critical juncture of boyhood. Nick refused to risk enduring such pains again by fathering another child.

Bel could get pregnant without him, of course. She'd toyed with the idea of various other forms of insemination. But having a baby that wasn't his could become an obstacle between them somewhere down the line. Besides, she was still crazy about Nick. She wanted the baby to be his biological offspring.

Ektora made a cute bubbling sound with her lips and drew Bel's attention back to the table.

"So, is motherhood treating you well?"

"It most certainly is," Olinda said, breaking into a wide smile. "Pretty amazing, actually."

"What else have you been doing with yourself?"

"You mean besides trying to avoid being assassinated, or captured and tortured?"

"Uh huh, besides those things."

"Keeping busy. Trying to maintain a fairly low profile, of course."

"Nick says you're still a top target for the Royals."

"I've sort of lost track of the black market for assassinations. What's the reward on me up to these days?"

"Twenty million if you're taken alive, one fifth of that if you're..."

Bel trailed off. There was no need to finish the sentence.

In both scenarios, the numbers on Olinda represented one of the most substantial of the illicit bounties. Still, it was nothing compared to the amounts being offered for Gillian and the team, which now had more than twenty Paratwa kills to its credit.

"The Ash Ock still don't know exactly what I learned about

them through Ektor," Olinda said. "That's why they want me so badly, particularly alive. An interrogation to determine what sort of damage my intel might have caused, or could cause in the future if I haven't yet passed along everything I know. There's also the more mundane reason, of course: old-fashioned vengeance. Make an example of me to other Paratwa and servitors, a warning of what will happen to anyone who crosses them.

"Anyway, as to what else I've been doing, it mostly boils down to using my counterintelligence skills as a freelance consultant. I help various civilian clients protect themselves from corporate espionage, internal criminal activities, those sorts of things. I shy away from businesses that have strong military connections, anything that might put Ektora and me at risk."

"Sounds lucrative?"

"It is. But that brings up the reason I wanted to meet. Actually, there are two reasons. But I'll start with the selfish one."

Ektora frowned and suddenly looked on the verge of tears. Olinda sensed the mood change. She picked up the baby, gently rocked her.

"I'm well-paid but the hours have been getting crazy and I'm travelling way too much. I want to spend more time with this little wonder."

Bel was surprised. "You're looking for a new job? With E-Tech?"

"If the hours are reasonably decent."

"There are always opportunities. In fact, right now there happens to be an opening on my staff. But it wouldn't pay anything like what you're accustomed to."

"I have a pretty solid financial cushion. It's not about that. What's the job?"

"I need a new chief assistant."

Maria Jose was moving her family to a Respirazone in

the Australian Outback. She'd told Bel that she wanted to be in a better place when God ended the world at midnight, December thirty-first, 2099. Even though the date wasn't technically the changeover to the new century, it was being popularized by many religious and secular groups as the time of Armageddon.

"I need someone for the position with more experience than anyone on my staff has," Bel said. "I've interviewed a number of candidates but I haven't found one with the right skill set. I'd have to set up a formal interview for you, of course. But I'm sure you're overqualified."

"I'm interested," Olinda said. "Let's do it."

A tall red-haired server named Nicole Kidman arrived and asked if they were ready to order. She had an Australian accent.

They opted for salads and spiced veggie sandwiches. Bel waited until the mech departed before asking about the other reason for the meeting. Olinda countered the question with one of her own.

"Any progress on identifying the mole on your Board of Regents?"

Bel hesitated. Although Sosoome's scan proved she was speaking to the real Olinda Shining, there was still a possibility that Olinda had been turned by the Ash Ock and was a double agent sent here to elicit information.

But her suspicion quickly dissolved. Bel had trusted her instincts about this woman from their first encounter in that locker room beneath the streets of the zoo. She wasn't about to forsake those instincts now.

"We've made no progress, at least nothing substantial. A few leads but none that have led anywhere. Nick and I believe we've eliminated a couple of the regents as possible Codrus tways. But even in those cases we're not a hundred percent certain.

"We've tried nailing down when and where a substitution

might have been made. We've discreetly monitored regents' friends and relatives to see if any of them noticed unusual behavioral changes, something that might suggest a sapient supersedure had taken place. We've studied newsphere data and surreptitiously accessed medical records in the hopes of finding any discrepancies."

"I dealt with a few supersedures during my time at DOD," Olinda said. "Med files, unfortunately, are relatively easy to fake."

"As we've learned. We've tried a host of other means and methods historically proven to unearth spies."

"What about canary traps?"

"Uh huh, three of them as a matter of fact. In each instance, we provided slightly different versions of the same fabricated story to all fifteen regents, then scanned for any intel blowback from among known Paratwa or servitors that E-Tech Intelligence has been tracking."

Bel shook her head. "Nothing's worked. We're no closer to flushing out the mole than we were a year ago."

"Codrus is smart. He might not be the guiding light among the Royals but that doesn't mean he isn't formidable. He'd have been very careful at hiding his tracks." Olinda smiled. "But even an Ash Ock can make mistakes."

Bel felt a touch of excitement. "You've found something."

"For the record, what I'm about to tell you has nothing to do with whether or not you hire me. I just received this intel yesterday and I'd already been thinking about coming to you about the job change. A fortuitous coincidence.

"Anyway, one of my clients is the World Bank."

Bel knew of them. Their headquarters were in Philly-sec, less than a kilometer away from Bel's office. E-Tech and the bank coordinated the occasional funding initiative. The bank, founded in the twentieth century, adhered to its original mission of reducing poverty by providing development funds, these days mostly to unsec regions across the globe.

Olinda continued. "The World Bank maintains a for-profit arm that brings in heaps of cash, all of which is supposed to flow into the bank's general fund. But a few months ago there was an incident of serious fraud on the profit side. I won't go into all the details. Suffice it to say, the perpetrator was caught. He was a mid-level manager. I was brought in as part of the interrogation team to see if we could track down the extent of his damage.

"I knew right away the perp was binary, a tway. He'd been well trained to hide it but I'd spent enough years with my husband to be able to spot the signs. I didn't tell the rest of the team. But after we finished with him and he was turned over to the authorities, I launched my own private investigation.

"This manager insisted he'd acted alone but I knew he couldn't have pulled off fraud of this magnitude without help from someone much higher up the food chain. The bank has a large board of directors, more than twice the size of E-Tech's. One of those people had to have been in on the scam.

"I wasn't able to ID this person. And they're too well insulated for me to probe any deeper, not without alerting all the directors that they're being investigated. But yesterday, the financial manipulations I'd uncovered crystalized into something solid. I have incontrovertible evidence of Codrus's hand in all this. Bottom line, I've confirmed that one of his tways is a World Bank director.

"Last year, not long before my husband was found out, he overhead Sappho and Theophrastus talking about Codrus, about the fact that one of his tways was in charge of a large international organization with satellite locations in nearly every country."

"But not the World Bank."

"No, he's only a director there. Codrus apparently had been complaining about the duties of running this massive organization, that it kept him too busy traveling, and that he missed being able to be in the same physical location as his other tway. Unfortunately, the organization's name wasn't mentioned."

"That leaves a pretty big list of suspects," Bel said. There were thousands of businesses, institutions and agencies with such global reach.

"True enough. But the conversation led Ektor to conclude that this organization was so time-consuming that he had no hours left for being a bank director or an E-Tech regent."

Bel's excitement grew as she grasped the impact of that statement. "Then Codrus's other tway, our mole, must also be the same tway who's the bank director."

"Exactly."

Olinda withdrew a folded piece of paper from an inner pocket, passed it across the table as the faux-Nicole Kidman arrived with their lunch. Ektora had drifted to sleep while they were talking. Olinda placed the baby back inside the strap-on carrier and dug into her meal.

Bel opened the folded paper. It was a short list, just three names.

Olinda forked a clump of lettuce from her salad, froze the utensil at the edge of her lips.

"These are the only three regents who also serve as directors of the World Bank. One of them is your mole."

FIFTY

Nick sat in the control room of the training warehouse, mulling over Bel's latest news, that she'd hired Olinda Shining as her new chief assistant.

He had mixed feelings about the surprise reappearance of Ektor Fang's wife. On one hand, presuming Olinda was correct and her list of three suspects valid, she'd paved the way for a plan that could finally expose the Codrus tway among the regents. On the other hand, he just couldn't bring himself to completely trust a servitor.

Sosoome had calculated that there was a three percent chance that Olinda Shining was actually a Paratwa double agent dispatched to infiltrate the office of the E-Tech director.

"Still, ninety-seven percent trustworthy ain't bad," the mech had added. "Hell, dude, that's a higher rating than I give you."

Nick had to admit the odds were with them moving forward with his plan. Still, even presuming Olinda was on the level, he'd never liked the effect she had on Bel. From their very first meeting more than a year ago, Bel seemed to regard the wife of a Paratwa assassin as some kind of long-lost soul mate. He didn't understand how the two of them could be so simpatico.

He'd toyed with the idea of an intervention, confronting

Bel with a stack of evidence on the devious nature of servitors in general, on how they all too frequently betrayed humanity. He knew what she'd say, that Olinda was different from those others. In any case, he'd held off. A confrontation might push her even farther into Olinda's corner. Besides, there was already enough tension between them with Bel's desire for a baby.

She'd been increasingly bringing up the idea of her getting pregnant, which he'd been resisting. He didn't think she'd trick him into a pregnancy. Just to be on the safe side, he'd switched over to an even more potent spermicide. Bottom line, he had no intention of being a biodad, not with the whole goddamn world unable to pull out of its crash dive. Not today, not tomorrow.

Not ever again.

Then why don't I have an irreversible vasectomy, permanently put the issue to bed, so to speak?

He wasn't sure. He supposed that deep down, avoiding that option had something to do with the fundamental notion of his masculinity, the idea that his seed should remain vibrant even though he had no intention of ever planting it anywhere.

His attention was snared by an exterior surveillance cam. A driverless van pulled off the dark evening street and slid into the warehouse garage. Interior cams revealed Gillian and the team disembarking from the back of the vehicle.

Moments later, the four of them entered the control room. Nick hopped up on a stool and opened a two-liter bottle of cabernet sauvignon imported from the fledgling space Colonies. Wine was one of the few products being exported to Earth and oenophiles were claiming that grapes raised in the agricultural cylinder of Lamalan, where the wine was bottled, boasted a flavor unrivaled by any earthly vineyard. Nick wasn't enough of a connoisseur to make such distinctions but at nine thousand dollars a bottle, his hopes were running high.

"Congratulations!" he exclaimed, pouring the wine into a line of goblets and handing them out. "You four are the men of the moment!"

His upbeat reaction was more than a bit forced, as it had been following the team's other recent triumphs. But after twenty-three straight Paratwa kills, it was hard to match the genuine excitement he'd felt after their earliest victories.

Still, number twenty-three was unique and worth a special celebration. For the first time, the team had faced one of the premier breeds, a Voshkof Rabbit, combat-trained by Russia's reincarnated KGB. Nick had been more nervous than usual observing the battle through the live feeds from the team's helmet cams.

In an alley behind the Push 'n' Shove speedball arena in Calgary, Alberta, Canada, Slag, Basher and Stone Face had performed to perfection. Their fluid yet precise mix of lunges and feints – attacking one tway, defending against the other – had kept the assassin off balance. But as always, it was Gillian and his incredible skill with the Cohe that made the difference.

Basher grinned at Nick's praise and downed five hundred dollars worth of cabernet in a single gulp. Slag sipped the wine slowly while Stone Face gently swirled his goblet to aerate the beverage. Gillian took an infinitesimal sip and set the glass aside.

"A fantastic accomplishment," Nick went on. "I mean, wow, think about it! You guys took down a Voshkof Rabbit!"

"Fuck yeah, we did," Basher said with a mad grin, swallowing the rest of his wine and extending the glass. Nick gave him a refill.

"So, any problems or issues we need to review?" Nick asked. He'd do a formal debriefing in the morning but always liked to ask the question with the battle only hours old and their memories still fresh.

"It was a clean kill," Gillian said, staring intensely at some spot in the distance.

"All good, mate," Slag added. "No worries."

Basher agreed. "So much for one of those kickass Voshkofs. Just another twofer. Sucker went down like a bowl of rabbit-fucking-stew!"

Nick repressed an urge to warn Basher against getting too cocky. But he kept his mouth shut. This was, after all, a victory celebration. There'd be time enough tomorrow for reviewing his notes, mostly a series of minor criticisms he'd noted during the battle. He dished out a similar list after every victory.

"You see me put the screamer out of its misery?" Basher asked.

"I did," Nick said.

"Did you see his fuckin' head implode?"

"It was hard to miss."

Gillian had killed the Rabbit's first tway, which was the inevitable way the team's battles ended. The crazed survivor, aka the screamer, was then finished off by one of the soldiers. Lately, Basher had been doing the honors, silencing the Paratwa's horrendous racket by setting his thruster to microburst and pressing the barrel against the tway's forehead.

"Want to know something I figured out about screamers?" Basher asked, motioning with his goblet for another refill. "Want to know why they carry on like that?"

"Bisectional hemiosis," Nick said.

"Nah, that's not it at all. It's because they're *angry*. They can't deal with the fact that they're dead. It pisses 'em off."

Basher laughed heartily, inordinately pleased by his observation. No one joined in.

Nick offered a few more choice words of praise but he could tell the four of them were losing interest. That wasn't surprising. Their string of triumphs had produced a jaded cynicism, a sense of boredom with the routine of it all.

Of course, there was nothing routine about going up

against a Paratwa assassin, something he endlessly reminded them. Still, a growing monotony had become apparent of late, particularly among the soldiers.

They continued to perform at peak levels. The problem came at these down times, between kills. As soon as Nick's computer programs identified the location of a new potential target and Gillian approved the selection, they'd be all business again and train rigorously for the next mission. Under Gillian's tutelage, the practice sessions would be tailored for the breed they were going up against.

Nick tried to offset the monotony with extravagant bonuses and other perks. After their last victory against an assassin from the Loshito breed in the south of France, he'd given the four of them an unlimited weekend pass to Marseille-sec's famed Palais des Prostituées, said to employ the most exquisitely trained sex workers in all of Europe.

But such offerings were losing their effectiveness. Slag, once the most talkative member of the team, of late offered only the most cursory remarks, keeping his thoughts tightly leashed. Basher, besides taking an unhealthy delight in the blood-and-guts aspects of the battles, was drinking way too much. Stone Face, who had developed an odd relationship with Nick's son, had never seemed quite the same since Weldon's passing. The big man spoke even less these days and withdrew more deeply into his vintage books.

Nick had tried other appeals to keep them motivated. He frequently pointed out that the continuing success of Humanity's Avenger remained a bright spot and a source of hope in a world growing ever more dismal and pessimistic. Still, even those reminders seemed to be having less of an impact of late.

One of the problems was a backlash from the public. Its earlier pride in the team's accomplishments was morphing into less savory emotions. On the black market for assassinations, the Ash Ock had upped the price on the team to a hundred million dollars if taken alive, ten percent of that amount upon proof of death via intact bodies.

The net was exploding with discussions on how best to collect such prizes. A large portion of the citizenry who earlier had cheered the team's successes was now making underground wagers about when and how a Paratwa would finally take them down. VAHA lotteries – Victory against Humanity's Avenger – were springing up all over the world.

Basher polished off the rest of his goblet. He snatched the bottle from Nick's hand, upended it and took a long guzzle.

"I'm outta here," he said. "Anybody in the mood for some serious partying?"

Slag and Stone Face took him up on the offer, leaving Gillian and Nick alone in the control room.

"They're getting jaded," Gillian said. "Overconfident."

"I'm glad you noticed. What can we do about it?"

"Up the ante. We need to go after even bigger fish. The team wasn't ready a year ago but now I believe we are. I want us to take on Yiska."

Nick was abruptly reminded of that famous old business theory, the Peter Principle, whereby managers were promoted until they reached the level of their incompetence. Applied to the current situation, it meant that Gillian and the team would seek to fight ever more dangerous assassins until they reached the level of their incompetence.

At which point, the assassin would win and they would die.

He shook off such dismal thoughts. "I see what you're saying. Escalate the challenge, keep the team focused. But there's just one little problem. I can't locate Yiska." *A good thing, since I still don't think you're ready.*

"Not enough data?" Gillian asked.

"Just the opposite."

When it came to Yiska, there was more than enough information about his movements. Since the slaughter at

E-Tech headquarters, the Shonto Prong had been among the most active of the assassins.

Nick's tracking programs were based on ferreting out subtle patterns in the deeds and movements of the assassins. However, certain Paratwa like Yiska and the deadliest of the Jeeks, including Reemul and Meridian, didn't fit neatly into any of his probability matrixes. Such Paratwa remained ciphers, their actions unpredictable.

"Yiska's like a piece on a chessboard that doesn't move in accordance with logical rules," he said.

Gillian gave a thoughtful nod. "I've been thinking the same thing. But it's more than just unpredictability. There are things about Yiska that don't make sense."

"What do you mean?"

"For one thing, the fact he's shifted from Pa to Ma killings. Why would he do that?"

Nick shrugged. Since the attack on E-Tech, it was certainly true. Prior to that, all of Yiska's known killings had targeted a single person or a small group. But over the past year, he'd been leaving a trail of destruction that encompassed more than a dozen mass annihilations. The pinpoint assassinations typical of his breed, and his own earlier exploits, had been abandoned.

Last month he'd attacked a science lecture hall at the University of Oxford in England. The target had been a professor who'd published a paper suggesting that binaries, despite their great prowess, were fundamentally inferior to humans on a genetic level.

Yiska had killed the professor and then, for no apparent good reason, slaughtered everyone in the hall as well as a number of citizens outside. Equally confusing, Cohe wands and thrusters remained his primary weapons of choice rather than the bombs, poisons or micronukes more characteristic of Ma-type killings.

"It's a mystery," Nick concluded. "I can't get a handle on

it either. At any rate, our only hope of locating an assassin like that would probably be to have a deep throat within the Royal Caste."

He could have added, *someone as highly placed as Ektor Fang.* But Gillian had been kept in the dark about the Du Pal, who'd been dead almost a year now. Nick saw no reason to loop him into the matter at this juncture.

"Anyway," he continued, "it's all moot. Certain assassins we're just not going to be able to take on."

But Gillian wasn't deterred. "If we defeated Yiska, it would be a big morale boost for the team. And a real shot in the arm to everyone associated with E-Tech. They're losing the high ground, you know. More people are favoring unlimited technology as the world's ultimate salvation."

"I know," Nick said, taking his first sip of wine. It wasn't dreadful but he'd tasted better. Even with the high transportation charges to bring it down from the Colonies, the bottle was overpriced.

"We need to think outside the box," Gillian said.

Nick shrugged. In truth, he'd fantasized about the team killing Yiska as a kind of weird gift to Bel. That was about as far outside the box as one could get. But the devil was in the details.

He knew why Gillian kept pushing the issue. It wasn't like he really cared about such abstract notions as the good of the team or E-Tech morale. The tway of Empedocles was driven by an almost fanatical hunger to hunt the assassins. It was a hunger that, unlike the motivations of the soldiers, seemed to grow more intense with each new kill, driving him to seek ever more dangerous game.

"We're talking in circles here," Nick said. "Bottom line, we're limited to going after assassins we can find."

"What if there was another way?"

He sighed. Gillian had a bone and wouldn't let go. "I'm listening."

"I know how to make Yiska come to us. We just need to offer the right kind of incentive."

Gillian unleashed his idea, which he'd obviously been considering well before this evening. Nick extended him the courtesy of hearing him out before responding in the strongest possible terms.

"Absolutely not! That is crazy dangerous."

"Life is dangerous. And it's *my* life we're talking about, not yours."

"Let's not forget the team. They've got a say in this."

"I never said they didn't."

Gillian seemed ready to push the argument further but apparently changed his mind. "I was just floating ideas. I guess that one does sound impractical."

Nick was instantly suspicious. Gillian backing off and admitting he might be wrong about something was as unnatural as Sosoome being modest.

Gillian left. Nick stared after him for a long moment, pondering his behavior. Then he turned his attention to a more vital matter, assembling the final pieces of the plan to expose an Ash Ock Paratwa.

FIFTY-ONE

It had been less than three weeks since Bel had hired Olinda Shining and she was already proving her worth. The former DOD major was efficient in the extreme. She'd reorganized the duties of Bel's staff to improve their productivity and had done so in such a way that no tempers were inflamed.

Bel had become used to Olinda as an older blond although she'd dropped her facial wipe a few times in private. Ektora seemed accustomed to both of her mother's faces and unconcerned as long as the same woman was breastfeeding her.

Part of Olinda's success in the new job had to do with her baby, which she kept with her throughout most of the workday. The young staffers in the outer office, especially the women, enjoyed the presence of an infant. Bel knew that several of them desired offspring but had decided to put off getting pregnant. Their rationale was that E-Tech's message needed to spread more deeply throughout the culture, thus creating the conditions for a better tomorrow in which to raise children. Bel found it remarkable that their optimism remained strong in the face of such increasing evidence to the contrary. Then again, it wasn't too long ago that she'd shared such beliefs.

Olinda sat in Bel's office going over some minor scheduling

issues. Bel listened half-heartedly, her attention drawn to Ektora. The baby was nestled in her carrier, which was strapped to a wall hook near the main windows. She seemed intrigued by the view, not that there was anything much to see outside. It was another high ToFo day, nearing the record for the end of December. The wind-whipped smog had reduced visibility to a few meters.

Ektora's frequent presence had pushed Bel's desire for a baby even further to the forefront. She vowed to have another talk soon with Nick. She'd planned a new strategy, one that would shower him with compliments and proclaim that he was the most logical choice to become her baby's genetic father because of his brilliant mind and exceptional abilities. With any luck, the heavy ego-stroking would break down his resistance.

Bel's pad chimed. It was one of her staffers.

"Ma'am, Board President Al-Harthi has arrived."

"I'll be right out," she said, turning to Olinda. "We can still call this off. If things should backfire–"

"They won't."

But even now, at the last minute, Bel wanted Olinda afforded the opportunity to veto the plan she and Nick had concocted.

"No matter what the outcome, you'll likely be putting yourself and Ektora in even greater danger. Are you absolutely sure about this?"

"Codrus is one of the Ash Ock bastards ultimately responsible for my husband's death. This is the best chance we have to bring him down. I wouldn't have brought the intel to you in the first place if I wasn't all in on this."

There was nothing more to say. Olinda picked up the baby carrier and they headed for the outer office. Bel greeted Suzanna Al-Harthi with a handshake. She introduced her new chief assistant, using the pseudonym Olinda had chosen.

"Down to business then," Al-Harthi said, greeting Olinda

with a scant nod and paying no attention whatsoever to Ektora's curious stare.

Olinda went to busy herself with other tasks. Bel led the regent back into her private office and closed the door.

"So, Annabel," Al-Harthi began, taking a seat. "What was so urgent that it required a private face-to-face?"

Bel laid it all out for her about the Codrus mole, about how she'd known for some time that the board had been infiltrated by a tway of the Royal Caste, about how she'd recently received information that reduced fifteen suspects to three. She admitted only that the intel about the mole originated from a deep source whose identity needed to be safeguarded.

Al-Harthi reacted as expected. First came astonishment, then disbelief, then a string of interjections to the effect that such a thing wasn't possible. But Bel had constructed a convincing case.

"What do Pablo Dominguez and Bull Idwicki think of this?" Al-Harthi asked.

Bel admitted she hadn't told the heads of Intelligence and Security. "We're pretty sure the Royals have other spies planted throughout E-Tech, perhaps even at the associate director's level. Keeping this knowledge tightly sequestered is the only way to avoid leaks."

Al-Harthi remained skeptical. "You can't seriously believe that those two are also serving our enemies."

"I hope not. But we can't take the chance of alerting Codrus that we're on to him."

"For the sake of argument, what if you're mistaken about a tway of Codrus on our board? What if this is all part of some sophisticated disinformation campaign by the Royals, meant to create rifts and trust issues among the regents?"

"It's not."

"But Annabel, please realize that if you are wrong, you'll be finished at E-Tech. The regents would have no choice but to call for your dismissal with prejudice. You're willing to risk your career?"

"I am."

Al-Harthi again glanced down at the list Bel had handed her, shaking her head as she uttered the three names.

"Vok Shen. Lois Perlman. R Jobs Headly. I know there've been supersedures of such magnitude before. But still, I can't believe it could be one of these three. Especially not Lois. My God, we've known one another since grad school. Our families had dinner together last month."

"We can't rule any of them out."

Al-Harthi gave a grudging nod of acceptance. "All right. So what's our next step?"

"We'll expose the mole at Monday's board meeting. I need you to do two things. First, cancel that security service you normally use to do those last-minute sweeps for bugs."

Bel explained why and went on to the second request, handing a paper across the desk.

"I need you to make this announcement at the start of the meeting."

Al-Harthi read the few short paragraphs, frowned. "This is factual?"

"Parts of it. The stuff about the impending deal with Olinda Shining is a mix of truth and lies."

"But you do have this servitor in custody?"

"We do, in a secure location." *Actually, she's sitting less than ten meters from you, probably nursing her baby.*

"You want me to read this verbatim?" Al-Harthi asked.

"Feel free to ad lib as long as the gist of the information comes across. I'll jump in at some point."

"Why not make these revelations yourself?"

"Codrus's tway might be more suspicious if the information is coming only from one person. But from the two of us, he'll be hard pressed to doubt that it's genuine. And bouncing things back and forth between us will give the revelations a higher degree of urgency. Remember, we have to convince him that what we're saying is true and force him into an immediate reaction. If he doesn't buy in right away, the plan will be dead on arrival."

They discussed a few more aspects. After Al-Harthi departed, Bel called Olinda back in.

"Everything's set. If things go according to plan, in less than forty-eight hours we'll have the tway of an Ash Ock Paratwa in custody."

The second one we've captured, Bel mused. She hadn't told Olinda anything about her connection to Gillian and the team.

Olinda looked somber. Bel hoped she wasn't having second thoughts.

"This is going to work," Bel insisted. "The plan is solid."

"I know. It's just that when I was with DOD, we had a little saying about the notion of things going according to plan."

"Which is?"

"Expect the unexpected."

FIFTY-TWO

Tomorrow would be the one year anniversary of that violent day, December thirty-first, 2095, when Nick had killed his first and only human being.

It wasn't like he was troubled by guilt or second thoughts. In fact, the opposite was true. When he thought back to pulling the Glock's trigger and putting a bullet through the skull of the fake Ektor Fang tway in that elevator, he was filled with a weird pleasure. It was pride in his aggression coupled with the satisfaction of extinguishing an enemy before that enemy did the same to him. The feeling must be similar to what Gillian and the team experienced when they took down an assassin.

Nick sensed Bel stir beside him and slither from his bed. He thunked the time. 10:37 pm. He guessed she wouldn't be staying at his apartment overnight. Tomorrow morning was the board meeting and she probably wanted to get a good night's sleep at home. The meeting was already slated to be a memorable one as it was to include year-end financial reports and the annual review of the status of E-Tech's major initiatives. For the fifteen regents, particularly one of them, it would be remembered for a far more notable event.

Nick got up and donned a robe. He found Bel in the kitchen. Wearing only panties, she was leaning against the fridge and nibbling from a bag of Planetary Certitudes. The sweet-sour crackers were her favorite post-coital snack.

He lowered his gaze to her breasts, bare and inviting.

"I'm taking off," she said, killing Nick's fantasy of one more romp in the sack. "Any last minute details we need to go over?"

"I think we're good."

"Did you get into the conference room OK?"

"Snuck in late this afternoon after Security did their last bug sweep." With only a small staff working on a Sunday, it had been relatively easy for him to fake a pass to the executive floors.

"You're sure no one saw you?"

"Don't worry, I was careful. Now it's up to Al-Harthi to do her part."

"She'll come through for us." But Bel's words sounded less than confident.

"Everything's going to work out," he assured her.

She forced a smile. "If it doesn't, we're in for a hell of a day."

"Yeah."

"Nick?"

"Yeah?"

"Whatever happens tomorrow, I want you to know that... I love you."

"Likewise."

She seemed to want say something else but hesitated. He had a strong hunch about what was on her mind and decided to short-circuit it.

"Listen, can we not talk about the B word tonight?"

It was the wrong thing to say. Bel's mood changed in an instant. Hackles went up and her tone became frosty.

"The B word? Is that what you're calling it now? You can't even *say* the word 'baby'?"

He tugged the Planetary Certitudes from her hand, set the

bag on the counter and gripped her palms.

"I apologize. Bad choice of phrasing. All I'm asking is that we not do this now. I swear to you that after the meeting's out of the way, the two of us will sit down and have a long and rational talk about it."

"Tomorrow night, my place?"

"Deal. I'll bring the champagne."

He wasn't looking forward to such a talk. It might start rationally but possibly wouldn't end that way. He knew neither of them was about to yield from their inflexible positions. She wanted a baby by his seed and he didn't want to give her one. Period. Until recently, they'd kept the dispute on a fairly even keel. But lately, tempers had been starting to fray.

The truth was, they were arguing about a lot of things these days, matters having nothing to do with "the B word." They'd come to terms with his son's pitstopping, the original glue that had brought them together. Both of them had moved on. Still, he sensed that something else was stirring inside Bel besides her urge to be a mother. Some restless and powerful force seemed to have taken hold of her. And whatever that force was, it was serving to slowly pull them apart.

In all fairness, the changes within Bel weren't the only threats to their relationship. He knew that he loved her, maybe not as much as he'd loved Marta but close. Yet ever since he'd done his own series of visits to a pharma specialist and had Weldon's pitstopping reversed, something had changed in him as well. It wasn't as if he'd lost interest. But certainly the intensity of his earlier passion for her had diminished. Maybe those pheromone induction tranqs primed to Bel's metabolism had indeed been a key element of his desire. Or maybe he'd just arrived at a point where the thrill of discovery was gone and it was necessary to push their relationship to the next level.

Or end it.

He forced a smile. She relaxed and leaned down to kiss him. Sosoome padded into the kitchen, interrupting their moment of intimacy as he was in the habit of doing.

"We've got company," the mech announced. "It's Gillian."

Bel frowned. "Did you...?"

"Invite him?" Nick shook his head. "No way. We weren't supposed to get together until tomorrow."

Nick went to the front door. Bel returned to the bedroom to dress or hide, probably both.

Gillian strolled in. He threw his coat on the coffee table and sniffed the air. "Good. Bel is here."

"We were just doing some last minute planning for tomorrow."

"You were having sex."

Nick didn't bother denying it, not with that sensitive nose of his.

"And why are you here?" he demanded.

Gillian didn't answer. Instead, he settled into the sofa. Bel reappeared a minute later, garbed and ready to depart.

"Stay," Gillian said. "Nick and I are going to have a drink."

"I'm not really thirsty. And I've got to run."

"No, you don't have to run."

The words didn't sound overtly threatening. Yet Nick sensed menace hovering beneath them. He could tell that Bel had heard it too. She folded her arms across her chest in a defensive posture and backed up against the bookcase.

"Pretend you're thirsty," Gillian suggested, his face breaking into a humorless smile. "Think of it as practice for the lies you'll be telling tomorrow when you expose your Ash Ock mole."

She gave a wary nod. Gillian turned to Sosoome.

"Vodka and tonic for me and your master. And for the lady of the evening?"

"Pinot noir."

Sosoome paused for confirmation from Nick, who gestured

toward the kitchen. The mech scampered to the liquor cabinet.

"Why don't you have a seat?" Gillian said, motioning to Bel and patting the cushion beside him.

She sat down opposite him on a chair. Nick hopped onto the sofa's armrest at the farthest point from Gillian. The three of them gazed at one another from the triangular seating arrangement, no one speaking. Nick's annoyance grew.

"So again, why are you here?"

Gillian didn't answer. Sosoome returned and distributed the drinks. The mech positioned himself at the edge of the sofa and glared up at Gillian, making it clear what he thought of their uninvited visitor.

Gillian glared back. "Go away."

"I don't take orders from you," Sosoome snapped.

"Maybe not. But did you ever see a Cohe wand declaw a cat?"

His tone convinced Sosoome not to push the issue. The mech glanced at Nick for a counter order. Grateful to see none, he scampered under the sofa.

Gillian stared into his drink. Suddenly, a chuckle escaped him, followed by a hearty peal of laughter. Nick had never seen him in such a strange mood.

"What's going on?" Nick asked.

"Just finding a little humor in the situation."

"What situation?"

"You have a mech servant and a human girlfriend and nearly unlimited financial resources. Yet you still don't feel complete, do you?"

"I don't know, I feel pretty complete."

"You're not."

"OK, I'm not. I'm only ninety-five percent complete."

Gillian raised his highball glass. "To incompleteness."

Nick and Bel traded wary looks. They both suspected that the incompleteness Gillian was referring to was his own, a subconscious recognition that a part of his true self was missing.

They raised their glasses and toasted. Gillian eased his drink toward his mouth but hesitated with the glass centimeters from his lips.

"Did Nick mention my idea to you?" he asked Bel. "About how to draw our nasty little friend Yiska into the open?"

"He said something about it."

"What do you think?"

"Sounds risky."

"It is. But worth the risk to take down the assassin that murdered so many of your coworkers."

Bel frowned. "I'm not too sure about that. To be honest, it almost strikes me as a bit…"

"Suicidal?"

"I was going to say desperate."

"I don't believe it's either of those things." Another weird look came over Gillian, a kind of perplexed amusement. "Then again, can any of us truly know our own minds?"

Gillian lowered the glass from his mouth without sampling the drink. He seemed to change the subject.

"Did you hear about the megalion that got loose at that Turkish animal preserve last month?"

Nick recalled the incident. The engineered beast, six meters long, had eaten some Chilean tourists before being downed by thruster fire from an emergency response team.

"Do you know why it got loose?"

"Something about a faulty lock in its compound?" Nick said.

"That's the official explanation. The real reason it escaped was a failure of imagination. The preserve didn't consider the possibility that the lock *could* be faulty."

"Uh huh. And your point?"

"Same one I made earlier. We need to think outside the box."

Nick sighed. He had to dissuade Gillian from his crazy idea once and for all.

"Has it occurred to you that by issuing a personal challenge to Yiska to confront the team at a specific place and time, you'd be inviting disaster? If Yiska knows your location, why would he even go to the trouble of facing you? Why not just vaporize the site?"

"Or show up with a small army of assassins?" Bel added. "You'd be outnumbered and wouldn't stand a chance."

Gillian shook his head. "Two reasons why those things wouldn't happen. First, the Ash Ock want to take me alive, or if not me then at least one of the team. Why do you think the bounty's ten times higher for that scenario? The Royals and every other assassin out there want to know why we're so effective against them. They want intel as much as they want vengeance or cash. There won't be any bombs or biotoxins or anything of that sort. It'll be a straight-up firefight."

"And you're willing to stake your life on that?" Nick asked.

Gillian ignored the question, plowed on. "The second reason is that the very deadliest of the assassins, the ones like Yiska, take a certain pride in going up against an enemy formidable enough to be considered their equal. The rules of honorable conflict will apply."

"Honorable conflict? What the hell have you been smoking? You're crazy if you think this is going to go down like some romanticized Wild West gunfight."

"Yiska will accept the challenge. He'll face the team head on without any backup or attempts at subterfuge."

"How could you possibly know that?"

Nick regretted the question the instant he asked it. He glanced at Bel, saw her trying to hide a grimace. She'd realized his mistake too. In his haste to derail Gillian's idea, he'd asked the sort of open-ended question that could push Gillian into dredging up memories that Weldon's mnemonic surgeries had effectively buried.

Gillian went quiet and lowered his gaze to his feet. It was obvious to Nick that he was attempting to access some distant and elusive recollection. Nick took solace in the idea, according to his son, that such efforts would likely be unsuccessful. Still, Weldon had made it clear that fate shouldn't be tempted by asking such questions.

Nick tried to cover his mistake by blurting out a series of less inflammatory queries.

"For the sake of argument, how exactly would you go about challenging Yiska? How would you know if he accepted? Where would this big confrontation take place?"

Gillian didn't answer. He kept his gaze pinned to the floor. He seemed to be withdrawing deeper into himself.

"Did you hear what I said?" Nick prodded.

Gillian mumbled something under his breath.

"I didn't catch that."

"I move – I am. I want – I take."

Nick tried to cloak his increasing anxiety. Had his screwup indeed awakened some aspect of Gillian's true self?

"I think it's the beginning of a nursery rhyme," Gillian said, finally looking up at them. "Those exact words come to me every so often. There's more to the rhyme but I can never recall how the rest of it goes. The thing is, why does something like that pop into my head? Why does it seem important?"

Nick's concerns grew. Jannik Mutter had behaved in a similar odd manner just prior to Weldon's mnemonic cursors experiencing catastrophic failure. Nick wished he had his gun on him. The Glock remained in its holster on the underside of the coffee table.

Not that it would do me any good. Trying to outdraw an assassin wasn't even close to making his bucket list.

"Every four hours, I find myself thinking about... certain things," Gillian said. "I used to get a headache from it. But now I get this weird flash of golden light inside my skull. Do you have any idea why?"

"Not a clue," Nick answered.

Gillian stood up so swiftly that Nick and Bel were startled and nearly jumped out of their seats.

"I should leave," he said, placing his untouched drink on the coffee table.

Without another word, he walked swiftly out the door. Nick and Bel waited with bated breath until they heard his footsteps retreating down the stairs.

Sosoome slithered out from under the sofa. "Well, that was creepy."

"I'll say," Bel said. "And not just because of what happened when you asked that direct question. He's usually weird but tonight it seemed worse. Do you think his real memories are starting to surface?"

"Maybe."

"Could his behavior be related to what's going to happen tomorrow at the regents' meeting?"

"What do you mean?"

"We're going to expose a tway of the Royal Caste. Maybe that's affecting him subconsciously. After all, he and Codrus are of the same breed. Deep down, he might be experiencing a sense of guilt at the idea of doing harm to a binary that he may have once considered a brother."

"I doubt a member of the Royal Caste is that sentimental."

"I wouldn't be too sure."

Nick had to admit her theory made sense. It could explain Gillian's behavior. Still, he had a hunch that the problem was rooted in a more ominous place.

"Maybe it's time to put an end to all of this," Bel suggested. "Send Humanity's Avenger off into retirement."

Nick had been considering the idea. He was certain he could convince the soldiers, who were close to burnout stage. But Gillian...?

He won't stop until someone stops him.

FIFTY-THREE

Bel arrived a few minutes early for the board meeting. Most of the regents had beaten her to the fifty-sixth floor conference room. The last two popped in as holos as she ambled to the snack table and selected a negative-calories lemon roll made of certified inorganic ingredients.

She gazed longingly at the starbuckian, wanting coffee. But she knew she had to resist, having already consumed her daily quota of caffeine this morning. She was nervous enough. It wouldn't be good to be sitting here with shaking hands as the plan unfolded.

From the corner of her eye she watched the man in the uniform of Al-Harthi's private security service finish panning the room with his scanner. The man didn't recognize her but she knew him, although they'd never met. He was part of Humanity's Avenger. His op name was Slag.

The three soldiers had been kept in the dark about Bel, about the fact their efforts came with the covert blessing and support of E-Tech's director. Conversely, the soldiers knew what Gillian didn't, that he was an invented persona, his real self artificially repressed by Doctor Emanuel's surgeries. And Nick kept things from all of them, Bel likely included.

Secrets piled upon secrets, spies and traitors everywhere. Their entire crumbling society seemed constructed on layer upon layer of deceit. Yet even as the notion coursed through her, a fleeting gestalt of that distant horizon once again beckoned, an ideal of a better world.

But that ideal is pure fantasy, she reminded herself. *Reality is what is happening at this moment, in this room.*

"You're looking well, Annabel."

Startled, Bel jerked around and took a step backward at the sight of Vok Shen, who was waiting to transfuse coffee from the starbuckian. She silently cursed herself for behaving as if he was a leper. The last thing she needed was to be putting one of their suspects on the alert.

"You seem jittery," he said.

"I guess I am. Last minute busyness combined with one cup of coffee too many."

Across the room, Slag finished his sweep and nodded to Suzanna Al-Harthi that the room was free of bugs. It wasn't, of course. The phony check was strictly to keep up appearances, make today's meeting seem no different from any other. Slag's scanner had been preset to ignore the presence of the special nanocams that Nick had planted throughout the room yesterday.

Slag headed for the door. He would exit the building but would station himself out front in case the tway of Codrus had some escape plan they'd overlooked. Originally, Gillian was to perform those duties. But after last night's weird behavior, Nick had reconsidered and assigned the task to Slag. Gillian hadn't seemed upset about the last minute change. Then again, his real feelings were hard to gauge.

R Jobs Headly ambled over to the snack table. Bel suddenly found herself sandwiched between the financier and Vok Shen. Maybe the third suspect, Lois Perlman, would like to join them as well?

Her sarcasm was a defense mechanism to hide anxiety. A quick glance revealed that the science adviser remained ensconced in her chair, chatting with another regent.

Thankfully, all three suspects were here today in person, which was one of the reasons the plan had been set for this annual meeting that wrapped up E-Tech's fiscal year. It was the one gathering where tradition encouraged physical attendance. Only those last two arrivals, both relentless globetrotters who rarely came to Philadelphia, had elected holopresence.

"I hope today's agenda has no hidden surprises," Headly said.

Bel froze. It sounded like the financier knew something. She stuffed the rest of the lemon roll in her mouth, chewed furiously to disguise a sudden bout of paranoia.

"I have another meeting to scurry to after this one," Headly explained. "Why does every organization feel it's appropriate to cram their meetings into the last few days of the year?"

"Tradition," Vok Shen offered.

"Or perhaps a devious plot by the pastry industry," Headly said, smiling as he made obvious reference to Bel's frantic chewing. "They know that Executive Directors are nervous about presenting annual fiscal reports and thus tend to consume more snacks."

The two men, who normally were at each other's throats, broke into bright smiles. Bel didn't think the remark was at all funny. Worse, she had the impression that their expressions of mirth were strangely synchronous. Her fears went into overdrive.

What if Olinda got it wrong? What if both *tways of Codrus are regents?*

Al-Harthi called the meeting to order, relieving Bel of having to respond to Vok Shen and Headly with anything more than a lame grin. She turned her back on the two men and walked toward her seat. Her muscles felt so tense that she had the impression she was lumbering along like one of those old cinematic Frankenstein monsters.

Nick's soothing voice filled her head through the micro

earpiece he'd provided, helped rein in her paranoia.

"All set for the big show?"

Her silence meant yes. If there had been a problem, she would utter one of the code phrases they'd worked out, disguising her meaning by putting it in the form of a question or comment to one of the regents.

As was now customary for a board meeting here at headquarters, Bull Idwicki had stationed a trio of Security personnel in the entry hallway just outside the door. One of Bel's code phrases would prompt Nick to notify the Security Chief that there was trouble and that he should summon the guards. But if the threat was more immediate, Bel could simply hit the panic button on her wrist fob.

Everything had been planned down to the tiniest detail. Still, she wished Nick was here with her in the flesh rather than just a voice in her head.

"Before we get to the agenda," Al-Harthi began, "I have a priority announcement. Some extraordinary information has just come into E-Tech's possession."

"Let the games begin," Nick said in Bel's ear.

Bel suddenly wished she'd opted for coffee. Clutching a mug would have given her something to do with her nervous hands.

Stay calm, she urged herself. *It will all be over soon.*

FIFTY-FOUR

Nick had taken a sick day so he could monitor the board meeting without any work-related interruptions. He sat on the floor in his apartment, his back against the bookcase, watching the faces of the three suspects. Their projections emanated from the trio of virtual amplifiers Sosoome had rigged in a line in the center of the living room. The holos were real-time transmissions from the special nanocams Nick had hidden in the conference room.

Gillian was sprawled across the sofa, looking far too relaxed for such an occasion. Fortunately, last night's weird attitude seemed to have passed. But Sosoome still kept a wary eye on him from his perch atop an end table.

The holos were important, enabling Nick and Gillian to observe facial reactions as the cameras autotracked the countenances of Lois Perlman, Vok Shen and R Jobs Headly. Still, they represented only a minor part of Nick's surveillance grid. The more important data, transmitted to the pad in his lap, would come from the extra instrumentation installed in the cameras. It was that data which hopefully would unveil the mole.

The cams were set up to read unconscious physio-emotional reactions of the three suspects. Micro expressions would be analyzed. Thermal imagers would reveal slight skin temperature changes and microwave Doppler radar would read subtle heartbeat variations. Audio detectors would measure decibel, pitch and other vocal factors. All of those quantities would be instantaneously cross-referenced and compared with known baselines. The overall goal was the detection of escalating anxiety.

But that alone wouldn't constitute proof that one of the suspects was a tway of Codrus. The mole needed to be tricked into taking a specific action that he or she normally would avoid when in public.

As the data streamed into Nick's pad and was formulated into animated graphs and charts, the words of Al-Harthi's opening gambit filled the room.

FIFTY-FIVE

"Less than an hour ago," Al-Harthi announced, "E-Tech took into protective custody a servitor. Her name is Olinda Shining and she is known to have a large bounty on her head, one of many such rewards the Royal Caste is offering for various individuals whom they consider their enemies. In Olinda Shining's case, the bounty is for her alive or dead."

Bel swept her gaze across the room. She fought an urge to focus on the three suspects.

"Olinda Shining came to us of her own volition," Al-Harthi continued. "She is being kept in a secure location until she can be provided with a new identity. She has promised to pass on valuable intel to E-Tech in exchange for that new identity and additional considerations."

The range of the expressions around the table was notable. Several of the regents expressed surprise or excitement. Others appeared doubtful.

Lois Perlman was one of the skeptics. "Additional considerations? May we presume that this servitor also seeks a financial reward for her information?"

"That is the case, yes. The amount is being negotiated as we speak."

"How do we know she isn't some kind of scammer?" Vok Shen quizzed. "Are you certain you're dealing with the real Olinda Shining?"

"More facts need to be verified," Al-Harthi admitted, "but we don't believe this is a deception. Preliminary analysis, based on verifiable data from Ms Shining's years as a major in the DOD, indicates she's genuine. And besides asking for money, she wants a guarantee that she will not be subject to any future prosecution for her involvement with the assassins. It wouldn't seem likely that a con artist seeking a quick payout, and no doubt planning an equally fast disappearance, would be interested in such a consideration."

"Can E-Tech even make such a guarantee?" one of the holopresent regents asked.

Al-Harthi hesitated. That was Bel's cue to jump in.

"We believe we can. It would have to be a joint effort with the DOD and civilian legal authorities, but a strong case could be made that she be granted a full pardon."

Fourteen faces that had been focused on Al-Harthi turned in unison to Bel's end of the table. Surprisingly, she was no longer nervous. Now that the plan was unspooling, she felt confident, on top of the situation. She pushed on.

"Naturally, we'll require complete verification before promising Ms Shining anything. However, as a sign of her good faith, she has already passed on a sampling of her intel. If verified, it has the most extraordinary ramifications."

Bel paused, waiting to see if any of the suspects demanded further details about the nature of that intel, but no one spoke. She wasn't surprised. The tway of Codrus was likely too shrewd to be the one to ask such a question. He'd wait for Bel or Al-Harthi to get to the revelation in their own good time.

Nick whispered an update in Bel's ear.

"All three suspects are displaying elevated readings. But that's probably true for everyone in the room. Nothing yet to pinpoint a suspect."

Al-Harthi took up the ball again, teased the gathering with

further claims about the profound importance of Olinda Shining's intel. She followed the script, though, and provided no fresh details.

We need to stretch things out, maximize the tension, Nick had explained earlier. *That way when Codrus finally makes his move, his telltales will be rendered even more noticeable.*

Al-Harthi spoke for a time until Bel jumped in again. Forcing the regents to pivot between opposite ends of the long table was another aspect of the plan.

A simple psychological ploy. It'll keep them slightly off balance, ultimately produce stronger emotional reactions.

Bel expanded on what they'd already revealed about the servitor without offering anything new.

Tantalize and repeat. Escalate the anxiety. Give the mole more time to worry.

Bel babbled on, speaking in the authoritative tones of a long-entrenched bureaucrat while offering no fresh information. It wasn't a native skill. She'd always prided herself on clear communication. But she'd spent a good deal of time over the past few days practicing this indirect approach.

She'd been concerned that by acting so out of character, the mole would become suspicious. But Nick had reminded her that at this juncture, the prompting of unconscious reactions was the only thing that was important. Turbulent emotions flowing beneath the strata of intellectual awareness would push Codrus into giving himself, or herself, away.

A regent finally interrupted Bel's repetitive discourse, urged her to get to the point. Lois Perlman seconded the request.

"Please be more specific," Perlman said. "What precisely is the nature of this intel that Ms Shining has promised?"

"Now," Nick whispered in her ear. "Hit them with the bombshell."

"Olinda Shining has promised to reveal the identity of a tway of the Royal Caste," Bel said. "She's been holding back on giving us the details until we can guarantee in writing her new identity, as well as the money and freedom from prosecution. I was told only moments before entering the room that the deal should be finalized shortly.

"I can tell you that what she's provided to us so far is remarkable. She claims that this Ash Ock tway is highly placed in human society, that he or she is in charge of a vast international organization with satellite locations in nearly every country."

Bel paused again and glanced around the table, trying to look at everyone in turn and not concentrate only on Vok Shen, R Jobs Headly and Lois Perlman. As far as she could ascertain, expressions throughout the room were genuine. The regents were reacting with a mix of astonishment and disbelief, chattering amongst themselves, debating the impact of the revelations. No one displayed any obvious hints that they had stopped being an individual tway and had come together to form Codrus, their Ash Ock monarch.

Vok Shen faced Bel. Maybe she was imagining it but she had a sense that the industrialist was more disturbed than the others.

Is he the one?

"Has Ms Shining offered any particulars about this organization?" Vok Shen asked.

"Not yet. However, she did say that in the past, this tway of Codrus has complained to the other Royals about the duties inherent in running the organization, that he or she is kept too busy traveling. Apparently for the Ash Ock, there is some added stress in the tways being physically separated for lengthy periods."

"Excellent," Nick said. "That's more than enough details to force Codrus's hand."

It better be, Bel thought. *That's just about all the relevant information we have.*

But if Nick was right, it should do the trick. The mole would be persuaded to bring on the interlace. A Paratwa of the Royal Caste would appear among them.

FIFTY-SIX

As Director Bakana and Al-Harthi spouted out their incredible revelations, the regent tway of Codrus sensed the meandering ripplets of concern emanating from his other half, Bishop Rikov, thousands of kilometers from Philadelphia.

Without a doubt, E-Tech indeed had in custody the wife of that accursed traitor, Ektor Fang. Such privileged information, that a tway of Codrus was in charge of a large international organization and that his duties too often kept the tways apart, was too accurate to have been gleaned through any other source.

Which meant that as soon as the deal with the traitor's wife was completed, she would give up the bishop's identity.

Codrus made it a point to avoid interlacing in public. The sudden ascent of the monarch and the corresponding diminishment of the tways could induce spontaneous physical changes, anything from mild facial contortions to muscle spasms. The reaction period was brief, the intensity marginal, the risks minimal. Yet it was best not to take chances.

But this situation cried out for unity, demanded the presence of Codrus's superior intellect. And even if the tways resisted coming together, it could happen in spite of them through *the whelm*, the forced union of tways into monarch. Such an event didn't require a mirror or other means for interlacing. It could be brought on by an immediate and dire threat.

Waiting for the whelm to occur wasn't an option. The regent tway allowed his strongest emotion – worry for the bishop tway's safety – free rein. The fear encapsulated within that feeling fostered the connection. He could feel his own disparate consciousness receding as the interlace began to form.

If his tway here in the E-Tech conference room displayed a noticeable physical reaction, it surely would be mistaken for an idiosyncratic phenomenon, merely one regent's reaction to the startling news about Olinda Shining.

The transition was complete in a matter of seconds. Codrus, monarch of the Royal Caste, panned his gaze across the faces of E-Tech's Board of Regents.

Simultaneously, he sprang his bishop half into action, enacting an emergency plan prepared for just such a contingency. Bishop Rikov excused himself from the midst of a parishioner council and walked swiftly out the back door of the London cathedral of the Church of the Trust. A limo awaited him. He would take a short ride to an Ash Ock safe house and remain there until the situation clarified.

FIFTY-SEVEN

"Yes!" Nick exclaimed, bolting to his feet.

Sosoome reacted to Nick's excitement by hopping off the end table and scampering around the living room. Gillian showed no such enthusiasm. He remained sprawled across the sofa, merely angled his head in Nick's direction.

Although the holos provided no obvious indicators, there could be no doubt. The charts and graphs on Nick's pad had revealed an abrupt series of spikes. One of the three suspects had literally transformed into a different personality. The tells for the transformation were clear and unambiguous.

"Got ya, you Ash Ock son of a bitch!"

FIFTY-EIGHT

Bel endured an agonizing moment of silence waiting for Nick to deliver the news.

Who is it? she wanted to shout. *Who, dammit!*

"Codrus has arrived," Nick said triumphantly. "R Jobs Headly is the tway."

Bel whipped her attention to the youngest regent before she could think not to. Whether intentionally or by accident, he happened to be turning toward her at the same instant.

Their eyes met. Mutual comprehension passed between them. Bel knew that *he* knew that his secret had been revealed.

FIFTY-NINE

Quite clever of you, Codrus admitted, giving Annabel Bakana a faint nod, silent praise for her ingenuity. Even now, under such dire circumstances, he couldn't help but admire their plan.

There was no proof that the plan had originated with the director but Codrus was certain she'd had a hand in it. Annabel Bakana had turned out to be far craftier and more formidable than the Ash Ock had anticipated when they'd arranged for her ascendance to E-Tech's top job following Witherstone's death. It was a rare mistake on the part of the Royals in having underestimated a person's abilities.

Yet the plan also smacked of the Czar, the name Sappho and Theophrastus had given to the mysterious and shrewd human – or perhaps a consortium of humans – who operated behind the scenes to thwart the Royals. Some believed that the Czar might be an E-Tech programmer, or group of programmers. Whoever he, she or it was, and whether they had been involved in setting up this trap, would have to await analysis at a more opportune time.

The basic outline of the humans' plan was obvious. The conspirators had learned just enough from the traitor's wife to impel his tways to bring on the interlace. No doubt, some trusted associate had arranged for the conference room to be secretly outfitted with the appropriate detection gear to register the physiologic changes inherent in his transformation from singletons to binary.

Looking back on the meeting from its start, there'd been hints of trouble brewing. Director Bakana's nervous anxiety was a clue that something out of the ordinary was happening. And Al-Harthi's last minute bug sweep of the room, although a routine event, had been performed by an individual the regent tway had never seen before. The fact that the board president's independent security contractor had tasked the job to a different employee was not in and of itself enough to arouse suspicion. But in retrospect...

Codrus deduced in that instant of eye contact with Director Bakana the flow of upcoming events. Guards would be summoned. The regent they knew as R Jobs Headly would be ordered into custody. With the board president and the director backing the order, it would be followed without question. Afterward, those two would come clean to the rest of the regents and offer a full explanation.

His captured tway would be whisked offsite as quickly as possible. In all likelihood he would be handed over to security forces less inclined to abide by E-Tech niceties. The tway would be rendered unconscious to prevent his other half from acquiring the location of the ultimate destination, no doubt some well-prepared black site.

His tways possessed a rudimentary bilocating system, an organic version of GPS. But it would only enable a potential rescue party to track him to within an area of roughly two thousand square kilometers. Unless his rescuers got lucky or the humans were sloppy – both scenarios highly unlikely – once in custody his fate would be sealed.

The real R Jobs Headly had been captured just prior to his appointment to the Board of Regents more than a year ago, and the sapient supersedure process initiated. After being persuaded to divulge every possible detail of his life, the Headly prototype had been terminated and his body incinerated to prevent any recovery of physical evidence.

For Codrus's regent tway, the interrogation would be conducted by coldly intelligent beings similarly at ease with the more primitive methods of intel extraction. As had occurred with the regent prototype, his tway would be kept alive only as long as it served the humans' purposes.

But Codrus wasn't about to allow the situation to get that far out of hand. He'd prepared his tways for the possibility of exposure. Even now, as his London half enacted the escape plan, Bishop Rikov was contacting the Ash Ock's most loyal servitor within E-Tech, the sleeper agent who over the space of many years had risen through the ranks to become an associate director. All Codrus needed to do was buy the sleeper a little time to get down here from his office on the executive floor above.

He rose from his seat at the conference table. Simultaneously, behind the church, his bishop tway sat down in the back of the limo. In a less critical situation, Codrus might have enjoyed a certain intellectual relish from examining the dialectic of standing and sitting at the same instant.

"My fellow regents, I have something to say to all of you," he announced via his Philadelphia mouth. "A profound admission."

Fifteen pairs of eyes locked onto him. Codrus stretched out the moment by favoring each of the regents and Director Bakana with a slow piercing gaze.

"It is something that may well shock many of you," he continued. "Yet it will not necessarily be a surprise to some, who clearly have been harboring a degree of suspicion for quite some time."

Half a world away, his tway made the call. The sleeper was informed that one of his masters, a lord of the Royal Caste, was in jeopardy. The man would be racing to arm himself and then rushing down to the conference room. In short order, a solution to Codrus's predicament would be at hand.

SIHTY

Bel listened intently as Codrus talked. Yet he seemed to be doing what Bel and Al-Harthi had done moments ago, dancing around the topic while refraining from admitting who he really was. He spoke at length about his time among the regents, offering up a series of platitudes that expressed his admiration for E-Tech's objectives.

Every pair of eyes was locked onto R Jobs Headly, waiting for him to get to the point. Vok Shen ran out of patience.

"Enough of this," he snapped. "What is this profound admission?"

"I apologize for keeping you in suspense. However, I'm afraid there has been a change of plans. I find that my presence is urgently required elsewhere."

Bel realized he'd been stalling at the same moment Nick did.

"Call the guards!" he hissed in her earpiece. "We need to take him right now."

Bel touched her wrist fob, preset for the panic button. The tway of Codrus took notice of her faint movement. The face of R Jobs Headly broke into an expansive smile.

You won't be smiling soon, Bel thought, no longer bothering to maintain a neutral expression. She glared back at him with open hostility, knowing that in the next few seconds, Bull

Idwicki's trio of security people stationed outside would barge in.

She glanced at the door, waiting. It remained closed.

"What's keeping them?" Nick demanded.

A chill swept through Bel. *Something's wrong.*

From the hallway outside came a series of mechanical shrieks. Bel's heart pounded as she recognized the sound.

Thruster fire.

Codrus's tway walked calmly toward the door, leaving behind surprised looks and confused muttering. Bel lunged from her chair, grabbed hold of Headly by the collar.

"You're not going anywhere!"

"Unfortunately, Ms Bakana, you are mistaken."

She heard the door open behind her. She whirled. Rory Connors stepped calmly into the room, thruster in hand. He pointed the weapon at Bel.

"Let him go," Rory ordered.

For a moment, Bel thought Rory was misreading events, that he believed *she* was the threat for the way she was gripping Headly's collar. But then she caught a glimpse into the hallway behind Rory. The three guards were sprawled across the floor, face down, unmoving. They appeared to have been shot in the back, probably while rushing toward the door to respond to Bel's summons.

"You," she whispered, stunned that the man who'd replaced her as head of Media Relations was a murderous traitor.

"Don't panic," Nick urged in her ear. "More Security people are on their way."

Rory withdrew a second thruster from under his jacket and handed it to the tway. Codrus turned to Bel and stuck the barrel in her face. She froze, too frightened to move a muscle.

Regents erupted from their seats shouting, flabbergasted by what was happening. The tway ignored them, kept his attention on Bel.

"Good plan, Ms Bakana. Executed with precision. It's sad for you that it must end this way."

"We need to go," Rory urged. He was waving his weapon at the other regents, warning them not to try anything.

The tway pressed the barrel against the bridge of her nose. Bel sensed his finger tightening on the trigger. In that instant she thought back to Director Witherstone's final seconds, confronted by Yiska yet defiant in the face of certain death. Her own terror reached a tipping point, morphed into newfound courage.

"Humanity won't be defeated, Codrus. Your end will come."

"Let's go!" Rory hissed.

The tway stared at her. Then his face brightened into a smile and he lowered his weapon.

With Rory in the lead, the two of them raced out the door. They leaped over the bodies of the Security people and ran toward the elevator bank at the far end of the hall.

Bel, ignoring the shouted warnings from Nick and the other regents, bolted through the door after them.

"You won't get away!" she yelled.

The tway ignored her and stepped into the Exec express elevator. The door closed, leaving Rory in the hallway. He turned and raised the thruster, his eyes burning with malice. The last traces of the mild-mannered politico were gone.

Bel leaped back into the conference room as Rory fired. Multiple rounds of thruster fire pounded the edge of the doorframe, splintering the veneer and warping the underlying metal.

A booming male voice shouted, "Drop your weapon!"

Bel recognized the voice. Bull Idwicki. She peeked into the hallway.

Idwicki was leading a contingent of Security people out of the emergency stairwell beyond the elevators. They were marching slowly down the hallway with guns raised, forcing

Rory Connors to retreat back toward Bel.

"Seal the building!" she yelled to the Security Chief. "Arrest R Jobs Headly! He's in the Exec elevator!"

Nick's voice boomed in her head. "Dammit, get back! You're going to get yourself shot!"

"We have to stop Codrus!"

"I've already notified Security. The elevators are in lockdown."

Rory turned and made a run for the conference room. Idwicki and the Security people rushed after him but held their fire. They were obviously unclear about the nature of the situation and were being understandably cautious. Even Bull Idwicki was savvy enough to realize that shooting an associate director in the back, with the Board of Regents as witnesses, might not be a smart career move.

Bel ducked back into the room. She positioned herself behind the door and steeled herself. As Rory dashed through the portal, she lunged forward and thrust out her leg.

Rory tripped over it and went down hard. His chin slammed into the carpet. The gun flew out of his hand, skidded across the floor.

Bel dove for the weapon. But Rory was closer. Recovering from his fall, he scampered toward the gun on all fours. He snatched the thruster just as Idwicki and his people rushed into the room.

"Last chance!" Idwicki hollered. "Drop your weapon now!"

Half a dozen thrusters were trained on Rory. His features dissolved into a mad grin.

"My lords, I am forever your servant-son!"

He reset his gun to microburst and pressed the barrel against his forehead.

"Don't do it!" Bel shouted.

"Rebirth comes, two not one!"

Rory pulled the trigger. His skull imploded, breaking into dozens of shards. The remnants of the head collapsed in upon itself. Liquefied gray matter oozed out from between the fragments, flowing like melting candlewax down across his shoulders. In a moment, there was nothing left above the neck but a dangling clump of spinal column.

The regents erupted into horrified gasps. Idwicki and his Security people lowered their weapons. Bel turned away, urgently whispering to Nick.

"Did they get him? Did they get Codrus?"

"No. He must have had a QKI on him. Bastard overrode the lockdown and switched elevators. They believe he's somewhere above the lobby floor."

"We can't let him get away."

"Don't you think I goddamn know that?"

Bel forced herself to stay calm, not get caught up in mutual frustration. "He may try making for one of the stairwells, get out through a side or back exit."

"Yeah. Slag is watching the front of the building and I have Security heading for the other exits. Oh, and sorry about the yelling."

"Forget it."

Nick was silent but had left his mic on. She could hear him arguing with Gillian about something.

"What's he saying?" she demanded.

"Nothing. Just Gillian being Gillian. He says that if I'd gone with the original plan and snuck him into the building instead of Slag, Codrus wouldn't have outwitted us and escaped."

Bel had to raise her voice above the increasing din. Regents were barking orders and demanding answers from Bull Idwicki. Fresh waves of Security people were pouring into the room. Someone threw a jacket across the grisly upper half of Rory Connor's body.

"We can't be sure he escaped," Bel said, speaking as much to reassure Nick as convince herself. But even as the words left her mouth, she acknowledged a sickening feeling that Gillian was right, that they'd been outwitted.

SIXTY-ONE

"Cheers," Bel said, refilling their glasses with the expensive champagne Nick had bought weeks ago in preparation for tonight. He was sitting beside her on the sofa in her condo. The lights were dimmed, which seemed a better way to listen to the raucous celebration outside.

The street party was going full blast. Shouting and whooping filtered up from below. The noise was oddly muffled by the pollution, making it seem as if it was originating from kilometers away. Fireworks occasionally streamed past the windows as did vibrant laselumed holos. One 3D display showed a band of unarmed proto-humans being attacked by other proto-humans with clubs. Bel recalled that the scene was from some famous historic movie she'd learned about in elementary school. But she couldn't place the film's title.

The new year was in its infancy, 2097 literally minutes old. Bel had downed her first glass of champagne at the stroke of midnight. From here on out she'd slow things down, take delicate sips, make it last until she and Nick finally had *the discussion*.

"Cheers," he muttered, clinking his flute against hers, his usual enthusiasm absent. He'd been glum since arriving and the champagne didn't appear to be alleviating his mood. But she wasn't about to let him wiggle out of his promise to have a serious, solution-oriented talk about her desire for a baby. First, however, she needed to put him in a better frame of mind.

"Now listen to me," she said, aware that her tone sounded eerily like the one used by her mother when she was a child in need of guidance. "Today was a big win for us. We exposed the mole and forced an E-Tech sleeper to reveal himself."

"But Codrus got away."

"Yes, but it's still a victory. E-Tech will have the opportunity to become a better organization without an Ash Ock Paratwa and a highly placed servitor poisoning the waters."

"Biwannabe," Nick corrected. "You heard Rory's final words. One of those dyed-in-the-wool nutbags if ever there was one."

Bel nodded. *And one whose potential existence we should have taken more seriously.*

The rumors about a highly placed sleeper agent embedded in E-Tech had never been confirmed. That such an individual might interfere with their plan to expose Codrus had been discussed. Still, they hadn't seriously considered that he might be a biwannabe ready to do anything, even sacrifice his own life, for the Paratwa cause.

Bel accepted her own negligence, a lack of imagination in considering such a possibility. But Nick wasn't letting himself off the hook so easily. He insisted on bearing the full burden of responsibility over the failure.

"I should have known," he said with a scowl, beating himself up with the same phrase he'd been uttering since the Ash Ock tway had eluded them a mere fifteen hours ago.

"We did our best," she countered.

"I not only missed the sleeper but I didn't anticipate that Codrus would be carrying toys."

The toys he referred to were the QKI used to override the elevator lockdown and some unknown type of jammer that had scrambled all surveillance monitoring within half a kilometer. The devices had enabled the tway to slip out a back door and vanish into Philly-sec's dense morning crowds.

"It happened," Bel said firmly. "We need to accept that reality and move on."

But thinking back to the event and realizing how close she'd come to dying prompted the question that had been troubling her all day.

"I wonder why Codrus didn't kill me?"

"I don't know. A triumph of intellect over emotions, I suppose. The Royals don't do things in haste, as least when it can be avoided. He probably realized that he needed to confer with Sappho and Theophrastus before taking such drastic action."

Bel nodded. The explanation made sense. Still, and despite her brave stance, she suspected that the image of the smiling Ash Ock pressing the barrel of a gun between her eyes would haunt her for a long time.

Nick swallowed the rest of his second glass of champagne. She waited until he was halfway through another refill before shifting the discussion. But she didn't plunge headlong into the dreaded B word. Instead, she eased toward it by first mentioning the fate of Olinda and her infant.

"Three weeks must be the shortest tenure on record for a director's chief assistant," she said nonchalantly.

"Yeah. Can't say I'm disappointed the woman's gone."

"I know. Not the biggest fan of servitors and all that."

"After today, even less so. Still, I guess I should appreciate what you did for her. I suppose she does deserve a fresh start for helping us."

And that she would get. Bel had used her clout as E-Tech director to arrange for Olinda and Ektora to be granted Colonial citizenship. Earlier this morning, well before the start of the board meeting, mother and baby had left Earth on a shuttle bound for the cylinders.

There was no guarantee they'd be safe from retribution

up there. Still, the Colonies were the one place where they'd have a real shot at living free, far from the easy reach of assassins and their followers, far from the ubiquitous shadow of the Ash Ock.

"Off into the wild blue yonder," Nick said, raising his flute. "To Olinda Shining. May she find peace and happiness and... oh hell, whatever she's looking for."

He gulped the rest of his champagne. Bel figured it was time to trot out the B word.

"I'm glad she and her baby are safe. Which reminds me of something. Is there a baby in *our* future?"

"Nice segue," he said with a grin.

"I've been practicing."

"OK. Pour me another one and let's do it."

Bel filled his flute only halfway this time. She didn't want him totally soused for the discussion.

She began by telling Nick how much she cared for him and the deep pleasure she would get out of knowing that he was the father. She offered a cascading series of compliments revolving around his genetic suitability for parenthood because of his brilliance. She'd just gotten to the part where she'd reiterated her willingness to take full responsibility for the child when Nick interrupted by raising his hand.

"Sorry," he said. "I have a call."

He went quiet as he listened to the voice in his head through his attaboy. Bel inwardly seethed at the interruption but forced patience.

"It's Gillian," Nick explained. "He claims it's important. He wants to talk to both of us. Turn on your monitor."

Bel had shut down her drudge for the night, oddly feeling that discussing a baby was too intimate for the ears of a mech. She waved at the remote on the sofa arm and the largest wall screen brightened.

Gillian appeared to be in a tavern. The wide-angled cam view was from a slightly elevated angle and showed him perched casually on a stool in the foreground. The long bar behind him, as well as tables off to the side, were occupied by people in outlandish outfits. Many of them wore morph masks.

At the bar, two women in blond Marilyn Monroe wigs and skintight white dresses flanked a smaller man in the ruffled shirt, dress coat and top hat of a Victorian dandy. An Albert Einstein lookalike sat nearby, hunched over and slurping phosphorescent pink liquid through a straw.

A foreground table featured four individuals of indeterminate sex masquerading as contemporary political figures in business suits. The foreheads of their morph masks were riddled with fake bullet holes. Chunky brown fluids leaked from the faux wounds and flowed down their cheeks to be recaptured by other holes on the edges of their mouths. The fluids were perpetually recycled.

They were protesters with the hugely popular "Shit for Brains" movement. SfBers believed that all governments and corporations were corrupt and incapable of solving the world's problems. But Bel saw the protesters as just another cynical contributor to apocalyptic despair.

Music was playing in the background, a popular destructorap melody for scream synthesizer. The overlapping chatter of multiple conversations could be heard above the song, as well as some muffled "Cheers!" for the new year. A chorus of voices shouted "Happy fuckin' tomorrow!" and followed it with a round of crazed laughter.

Gillian gazed up at the lens. Either he'd planted the camera or had tapped into the tavern's surveillance system.

"Where are you?" Nick demanded.

"Murphy's Enigma Club."

Bel had heard of the place. It was an infamous tavern in the heart of Boston-sec. For reasons that eluded her, the club required its patrons to don Halloween outfits year-round. Gillian seemed to be an exception to the rule. He was garbed in regular attire, a maroon jacket and black pants.

"What are you doing there?" Nick asked.

"Monitoring the ambiance."

A young man uniformed in the gray-blue trousers, jacket and mailbag of a vintage American postal worker suddenly lurched in front of the camera, momentarily blocking their view of Gillian. Clearly inebriated, the man raised his glass and shouted to no one in particular, "Send priority mail and you won't fail!"

Chuckling, he staggered out of camera range to continue on his drunken route. Gillian, with a cryptic smile, returned his attention to Bel and Nick.

"Do you know why people really celebrate the new year?" he asked.

"They want to look forward to a brighter tomorrow," Bel suggested.

"Half true. But they just as badly want to escape a bleak yesterday. It's always the dialectic that's important, the interpretation of opposites. The coalescence of past and future, the blending of what was with what is yet to be."

"Yeah, that's deep," Nick said, injecting a note of boredom at Gillian's philosophical ramblings. "Now, again, what the hell are you doing there and what's so urgent you need to call us tonight?"

"Serving the spirit of the dialectic."

Gillian almost had to shout the words to be heard above a sudden eruption of hooting and hollering from a table of women garbed like medieval peasants. One of them had pulled her dress down to her waist, revealing herself to be a quadtitty, a genejob with two vertically aligned nipples on each breast.

"The team has a training session scheduled tomorrow morning," Nick reminded Gillian. "If I were you, I'd make it an early night."

"We cancelled the session."

"We?"

"The vote was four-zip. The team came up with a better idea."

Bel was getting a bad feeling. "I thought people had to wear a costume to be let into Murphy's?"

"I have a costume. I came as part of Humanity's Avenger."

Gillian reached down between his feet and retrieved his tac helmet.

"What are you doing?" Nick muttered.

He answered with a grin and donned the helmet. Only his eyes remained visible through the open faceplate.

Nick stood up, agitated.

"I extended an invitation," Gillian said. "Our guest should arrive shortly."

Bel grimaced. "You challenged Yiska."

"Enjoy the show. The surveillance system has been reconfigured to follow the action. Not as intimate as seeing it through our helmet cams. But I figured it's always good to expand your worldview, perceive things from a new perspective."

Gillian's faceplate snapped into position, hiding his eyes.

"No!" Nick shouted. "Don't do this! Get out of there now!"

Gillian didn't answer. He must have cut his mic feed.

Behind him, one of the caricatured politicians removed his SfB mask. It was Slag. Bel glimpsed his face for only a moment before he too donned a tac helmet.

"Goddammit!" Nick growled.

Bel wondered why Gillian would choose such a public venue for the confrontation, put so many innocent bystanders at risk. She grasped the reason even as she framed the question.

He doesn't care if anyone gets hurt.

Gillian and Slag got off their barstools and ambled across the crowded tavern. The view switched to another cam, a wider overhead angle. The two of them jostled amid the tightly spaced tables, past celebrants representing a dazzling potpourri of cultures.

Two men in Aztec warrior regalia seductively fondled one another's colorful feathered headpieces. A big-boned man in the uniform and helmet of a vintage American football team sat alone, nursing a beer pump. A woman in sunglasses, sequined blouse and cowgirl miniskirt chattered away, her words directed at the lanky cowboy on the other side of the table who was studiously ignoring her.

A helmeted motorcyclist garbed head-to-toe in black leather stood up. The footballer rose at the same moment and fell in step with him. The two men followed Slag. Bel realized the footballer was Stone Face and the man in leather, Basher.

The four of them reached the end of the tables, a wide vacant area fronting a stage set up with antique pianos and a drum set. The stage was empty. Murphy's New Year's Eve crowd apparently had no interest in live music and dancing.

Gillian separated himself from the three soldiers, who clustered together into an outward-facing triangular configuration. The team stood rock still, as if waiting for someone.

Seconds later, two men appeared from the left. They had short hair and were garbed in early twenty-first century army combat fatigues. Bel didn't recognize their faces but her attention flashed to their hands. The men were tapping the index and middle fingers of their left hands against the legs of their camo pants.

"Yiska," she whispered.

She felt her body tensing. It was as if she was there in the tavern, experiencing what was about to happen.

In unison, the two men deactivated their facial wipes. The taller tway grew a side ponytail. His companion's hair withered away until he was bald. A layer of fake skin decoalesced, revealing his albino essence. None of the other patrons seemed to take notice of the transformation brewing in front of the stage.

Over the past year, Bel had continued experiencing vengeful dreams and fantasies directed at the murderous Shonto Prong that had decimated E-Tech headquarters. Now that Gillian and the team were actually face to face with the assassin, those feelings intensified. She not only looked forward to Yiska's death but hoped that the assassin would suffer terribly.

Yet even as those base urges stormed up from the depths, her other fantasy took shape. Equally potent but draped in positivity, it sprouted from a more mature place, from that distant horizon of peace and comradeship where humanity transcended its worst qualities, where people united with one another to showcase their finer virtues. As Yiska and Humanity's Avenger approached one another, those two contradictory forces struggled within Bel, fighting for her allegiance, perhaps fighting for her very soul.

The spirit of the dialectic.

In that moment, she felt she understood something fundamental about Gillian, about what motivated him to seek out and challenge ever more lethal opponents. It wasn't simply the idea of wanting to hunt bigger game. Deep down, in some twisted, repressed part of his subconscious, he'd come to believe that by going up against the most extreme assassins, someday he would confront one with the power to restore what he'd lost.

A binary that would make him whole again...

...or kill him in the process.

SIHTY-TWO

Gillian studied Yiska's tways, Ponytail and Albino. As always at this pivotal moment before the firefight's explosive energies were unleashed, before his entire world compressed into a purified state of speed and violence, he was gripped by a strange calmness totally at odds with what was about to erupt. He knew that experiencing such serenity was one of the qualities that made him a formidable opponent. That and his skill with the Cohe wand.

The tways didn't speak. Ponytail focused on Gillian and Albino on the soldiers. Yiska would be experiencing a similar feeling of tranquility, a similar confidence.

The assassin not only enjoyed a superior level of abilities among its own breed, it had the advantage of having been able to study the numerous videos of the team's triumphs that saturated the net. The Shonto Prong would be aware of the most subtle intricacies of Humanity's Avenger's combat technique: attack postures, calculated feints, a thousand other micro-elements that constituted the profile of an adversary. Yiska would also know that the three soldiers were the lesser part of the equation, that they existed mainly to reinforce Gillian's unique skill set.

Gillian and Nick had perpetually modified Nick's original sim for a combat quartet in preparation for each breed they'd fought. Still, it was important not to lose sight of the fact that they'd never faced an assassin like Yiska. Here was a Paratwa who not only possessed superior abilities but remained immune to Nick's tracking program.

And beyond that, there were those ethereal and indefinable qualities about the assassin, those things that simply didn't make sense, that defied Gillian's every effort to comprehend. Somehow, Yiska had transcended the inherent limitations of his breed.

Compounding the confusion was the fact that over the past several years, the assassin had radically shifted from exquisitely stylized pinpoint assassinations to deranged mass annihilations. Yet neither Yiska's transcendence into Shonto Prong 2.0 nor his Pa-to-Ma transition had impacted a perfectionist's discipline and control.

Gillian didn't like that their opponent was shrouded in such mystery. Still, it had little impact on his motivation for instigating this battle. Yiska would be the most challenging foe the team had ever faced.

The notion excited him in a way that remained unfathomable.

Other than the team's first firefight in Alvis Qwee's torture basement, Gillian had adopted the policy of allowing their opponent to attack first. Such a strategic feint gave the assassin the erroneous impression that it was determining the structure of the fight. It enabled Gillian to make a series of subtle moves, surprising the enemy and thus gaining a tactical edge. Surprise was a weakness, inducing it an advantage.

But Yiska didn't attack. The tways just stood there, motionless and calm. The Shonto Prong was equally aware of the advantage of allowing an enemy to strike first. Gillian decided to provoke a reaction.

"Thank you for meeting us, Yiska." he offered, his tac helmet distorting his voice in case the Paratwa was using vocal ID scanners.

The tways remained silent. Gillian continued.

"Should things end with bisectional hemiosis, you have my word that your surviving tway will be dispatched quickly."

Ponytail reacted with a faint nod. Albino spoke.

"Yiska thanks you for such consideration. Yiska is pleased."

Gillian had no time to dwell on why the assassin was speaking in the third person. Albino fell into a crouch, pulled out a thruster and propelled a Cohe wand into his other hand from a slip-wrist holster. Ponytail pivoted so that the tways were back to back and made the same series of moves to draw weapons. The assassin's crescent webs ignited.

Gillian and the team reacted within microseconds. Guns and Cohe were drawn. Webs came alive.

Directionalize. Attack one tway, defend against the other.

Slag, Basher and Stone Face had fought enough battles with Gillian and knew the drill. They required no prompting to carry out the unspoken order. Moving as one, they defended themselves against Albino's furious attack while opening fire on Ponytail.

Gillian ducked low, dodged a horizontal slash of Ponytail's beam. The streak of black light continued across the room, sparked and splattered against Slag's crescent web.

Patrons stampeded toward the far exits to escape, morph masks and real faces grimacing in terror, screams filling the air. Even through Gillian's helmet, his olfactory sense remained potent enough to smell their fear.

Don't allow the assassin to shift between offensive and defensive modes.

The soldiers kept up their barrage against Ponytail, ignoring Albino's ruthless assault upon them. Gillian charged toward Albino, stabbing and slashing his Cohe, forcing the tway to divert some of its energies toward protecting itself from his beam.

"Switch!" Gillian barked.

The soldiers instantly shifted their assault to Albino,

continuing to spin as a trio to repel Ponytail's assault with Cohe and thruster. The tways reacted with seamless precision to the change, not deceived in the slightest.

Ponytail slammed his beam down upon the dance floor. It formed a curving destructive arc behind and to the right of the soldiers, gouging out chunks of plastic tile and subflooring. The debris, hurled into the air and superheated by the wand's energy, rained down upon the panicked patrons. The cowgirl screamed as a clump of burning material landed on her bare leg.

For an instant, Gillian thought the floor hit was the result of a misdirected beam. Then Albino's Cohe emulated what his tway had done. It ripped through the floor in front of and to the left of the soldiers.

The three soldiers now stood in the middle of a smoldering circle three meters wide. Yiska, like Gillian, would have dug up the building plans and construction history, would have learned all he could about the combat environment. The assassin would know that the dance floor rested atop the main basement of this nineteenth century building, which had minimal crossbeams and a paucity of supporting columns.

"Jump!" Gillian hollered as the circular portion started to give way.

The soldiers perceived the danger. Slag and Basher leaped forward, made it outside the circle just as the floor shuddered and collapsed beneath them. But Stone Face was positioned behind them at that moment, farther from safety.

He jumped but didn't make it. He landed on his feet a scant thirty centimeters from the edge. The floor dropped. Stone Face went down with it. A loud boom shook the air as the cut-out section crashed into the basement. Plumes of smoke erupted from the hole.

The tways went back-to-back, galloped toward the jagged edge. They took a mighty leap. As they soared across the chasm, a small dark object shot out the bottom of Albino's pants leg and vanished into the basement abyss.

"Thermic bomb!" Gillian yelled.

The warning came too late. A savage explosion rocked the building. A shaft of blue-white flame as hot as burning metal erupted from the hole, hissing as it splattered and danced across the fireproof ceiling. In the basement debris below, the detonation and heat flash would have reduced Stone Face to clumps of charcoal.

Gillian had trained the team to fight with a missing man. Slag and Basher reacted fast, went into back-to-back mode. They kept spinning in tandem, limiting the exposure of their weak side portals as best as possible.

But Stone Face was gone and with him, the team's delicate balance. Yiska came at Slag and Basher from both flanks. Cohe wands slashed and stabbed. Thrusters fired alternately in a machine gun rhythm. Gillian was forced to modify his own assault, strike at both tways in an attempt to keep the soldiers from being overwhelmed. But the tways moved with terrifying precision, dodging his beams with ease.

Slag was hit first. Ponytail's beam penetrated his left portal. It lanced into Slag's arm, went through part of his torso and exited through his lower back.

The gun fell from the soldier's hand. He staggered three steps, stumbled and collapsed onto his back.

Basher, whooping with maniacal fury, made a suicide charge at Ponytail. Albino's Cohe caught him low. The slicing beam gutted his right leg from knee to ankle. He stumbled forward, fell toward the gaping hole. An instant before he went over the edge, Ponytail finished him off with a Cohe stab up under the neck and into the brain.

The battle was over.

Gillian eased hand pressure on the Cohe, assumed a neutral posture. Not surprisingly, the tways did the same and lowered their weapons. As he'd anticipated, they would make an effort to take him alive.

He felt no fear, only a sense of remorse at the team's first – and last – failure. Another emotion hovered beneath the surface, however, one he couldn't shape into words. The closest he could come to defining the feeling was to perceive it as a kind of disappointment, yet one not directly related to the team's defeat. Instead, it seemed to revolve around an ethereal desire for some momentous event to have occurred during the battle. Whatever the nature of that event, it clearly hadn't happened. Hence the disappointment.

Movement caught his eye. Slag was still alive. Mortally wounded after being pierced by one of Yiska's beams, he was struggling to crawl across the floor and reach his fallen thruster.

There would be no last minute heroics. Gillian knew that Slag couldn't be saved.

Two Cohes ignited, one microseconds ahead of the other. Ponytail's leading beam stabbed into Slag's skull just above the right ear. An instant later, Albino, with a series of strange wrist contortions, coiled his beam around Slag's neck.

The second beam squeezed inward like a crushing noose, decapitating the soldier. Even as Slag's head rolled away from his body, insight flooded Gillian.

The head hadn't been sliced off, it had been *garroted*. No Shonto Prong had ever developed such precision with the wand. The technique was called the lariat and the delicate skills necessary to employ it required special training, beginning at an age when most Paratwa were barely toddlers.

Only one breed had ever been taught to master the lariat. In a moment of utter clarity, the mysteries of Yiska's behavior unraveled.

Transcending the limitations of his breed. A piece on a chessboard that doesn't move in accordance with logical rules. A shift from elegant assassinations to savage massacres.

Yiska wasn't Shonto Prong 2.0, merely an exceptional assassin. He was a different breed altogether.

A Jeek Elemental.

Gillian didn't try to hide his surprise. He stared at the tways, who'd assumed side-by-side formation. The Paratwa, gazing back, realized Gillian had grasped the truth. No longer needing to hide its true identity, the Jeek allowed its faces to default into their natural expressions.

Ponytail adopted a smile, Albino a sad, melancholy look.

SIXTY-THREE

"Reemul," Bel whispered.

Nick was too stunned by the team's defeat to say anything. The revelation that Yiska and the liege-killer were one and the same only served to amplify the tragedy. Detailed analysis of just how and why such a substitution had taken place would have to wait. Yet even with Gillian at the precipice of death or worse, a theory streamed into consciousness.

The attack on E-Tech headquarters may have been the beginning of the substitution, of the liege-killer pretending to be Yiska. The Ash Ock urgently needed to have Director Witherstone silenced before he could pass on the Thi Maloca intel, and Reemul must have been in Philadelphia that morning or close by. He'd been tasked with the murder.

Yet the Royals, likely guided by Sappho's shrewd perception, may have realized that using the notorious liege-killer would focus even more attention on the director's killing, perhaps inspire investigators to delve deeper and seek the real reason behind the attack. Rather than risk the possibility, they'd ordered Reemul to disguise his identity.

Then again, Nick's entire theory could be wrong. Perhaps a simpler motivation was behind the substitution. *A sick twisted freak of a binary*, Olinda Shining had called Reemul. The liege-killer might simply derive some kind of bizarre pleasure from